"Lie still and let me teach you, my lovely Penny," he whispered, and his mouth on hers silenced any protest.

His tender kisses made her lips burn for more. His touch caused her to arch reflexively and his hand was there to catch her movement, caressing her breast.

Penny's breathing grew ragged as he explored her nakedness, lingering at the soft roundness of her hips. She drew her breath even deeper when he pulled her into the curve of his body, teaching her the first of many lessons the night had in store. . . .

LOVE
FOREVER
AFTER

LOVE FOREVER AFTER

by

Patricia Rice

AN ONYX BOOK

ONYX
Published by the Penguin Group
Penguin Books USA Inc., 375 Hudson Street, New York, New York 10014, U.S.A.
Penguin Books Ltd, 27 Wrights Lane, London W8 5TZ, England
Penguin Books Australia Ltd, Ringwood, Victoria, Australia
Penguin Books Canada, 2801 John Street, Markham, Ontario, Canada L3R 1B4
Penguin Books (N.Z.) Ltd., 182-190 Wairau Road, Auckland 10, New Zealand

Penguin Books Ltd, Registered Offices:
Harmondsworth, Middlesex, England

First published by Onyx, an imprint of Penguin Books USA Inc.

First Printing, May, 1990

10 9 8 7 6 5 4 3 2 1

Copyright © 1990 by Patricia Rice

All rights reserved

 REGISTERED TRADEMARK—MARCA REGISTRADA

Printed in the United States of America

PUBLISHER'S NOTE
This is a work of fiction. Names, characters, places, and incidents either are
the product of the author's imagination or are used fictitiously, and any resemblance to actual persons, living or dead, events, or locales is entirely coinci-
dental.

BOOKS ARE AVAILABLE AT QUANTITY DISCOUNTS WHEN USED TO PROMOTE PROD-
UCTS OR SERVICES. FOR INFORMATION PLEASE WRITE TO PREMIUM MARKETING
DIVISION, PENGUIN BOOKS USA INC., 375 HUDSON STREET, NEW YORK, NEW
YORK 10014

Chapter 1

THE gilt-framed looking glass reflected a white face and shoulders above an even whiter lace-edged night shift, and Penelope wondered distraughtly if this day had finally made a ghost of her. She pinched her thin cheeks and a small spot of red appeared, but in the light of two tapers, the effect did not enhance her translucent complexion.

Occasional strands of gold glinted through her light brown hair, but she did not possess the vanity to notice. Instead, she wondered nervously if she ought to let down her heavy chignon or plait it as she usually did before retiring. Her mind desperately turned to the few romances she had ever read, but she had no memory of one covering the topic of what happened to the heroine's hair on her wedding night.

Hesitantly she began removing the pins while covertly watching the ominously closed door leading to the next chamber, fearful of the moment when that door should move. Every imagined noise made her jump, and the thick strands were soon knotted and unmanageable, with pins buried in unreachable places.

She murmured curses a vicar's daughter shouldn't know as her shaking hands untangled the knots and reached for the homely familiarity of her ivory-backed brush. Some unseen maid must have unpacked her few small things while her new husband had been introducing her to the household below.

A sudden pang of homesickness struck so painfully that Penelope bit her lip to prevent crying out. At home now Augusta would be brushing her hair, and they would be discussing the Smiths' new baby or the time to plant the spring onions. She would be with friends in the comfortable familiarity of her shabby room, instead of this elegant but unknown chamber. Augusta would be able to untangle this wicked mane and soothe her fears—some of them, at least. But Augusta had chosen to stay behind, not wanting to leave her home nor intrude upon the newlyweds.

Remembering the fearsome bridegroom preparing himself somewhere beyond that other door, Penelope hastened to make order of her hair. As she brushed, she saw in the mirror her night shift's low neckline trimmed in delicate embroidery and wondered nervously if she should not have chosen another gown. Would such lack of modesty entice or enrage the strange man she had married but scarcely knew?

But Augusta had made this gown for her wedding night, and it was the most beautiful thing Penelope owned. She had no better. Perhaps it was not silk or satin, but the gossamer weave clung delicately to her slender figure, and she knew if only for this one night, she looked almost pretty.

It did not seem to matter to her new husband that she had been an old maid at twenty-two, she knew, but it mattered to Penelope. Men preferred young girls. She felt certain his first wife must have been young. How would she compare? With a shudder, Penelope halted that train of thought, not wishing to dwell on the ordeal to come. It would have been easier if she were some young ingenue head-over-heels in love. There ought to be something, some tingling of anticipation, some small hope of love to brighten this moment, but nothing came to mind other than apprehension as she thought of the maimed man waiting behind that door.

Light hair falling in soft curls across her shoulders and down her back, Penelope again threw the connecting door a nervous look. What was taking him so long? If he would only come, perhaps she would remember what madness had possessed her to agree to this marriage.

Glancing around the shadow-enshrouded grandeur

of the room he had brought her to, Penelope knew deep within her what she had done, but her heart had not yet accepted it. In a few minutes she would give her body to a man she scarcely knew, whom she could not and never would love, and her heart and mind and body all screamed denial.

Not that she knew much of what happened between man and wife. Her mother had died before she reached an age when such explanations would normally come, and her father would never have thought of making such explanations even had he lived. And poor Augusta—well, she had tried, dear thing, but Penelope had learned more from barn animals than Augusta could teach her. That little bit of knowledge only multiplied her fears, not just of the act, but of the man himself.

Not knowing if she should wait in that huge, curtain-hung bed or sip the wine left thoughtfully on the table, Penelope wandered to the hearth and stirred the glowing embers into small flames. She shivered even so, and her eyes filled with tears. She had only herself to blame, but the tension and the terror building inside her did not ease by placing blame.

Not wanting to think of the minutes to come, she turned her thoughts backward to the weeks before. Weeks, mere weeks, when she had been single and unanswerable to anyone. It did not matter that she had been near enough to penniless, she had lived like that most of her life. Could she honestly say she had been happy? Perhaps not, but she had been content and not terrified.

Penelope lowered herself into the hearth-side chair and stared into the dancing flames, remembering the day it had all started—the first of April, a misty, cool day, but with signs of spring bursting out all over.

What had she gone into the orchard for? She couldn't remember, but she had been carrying a basket. More than likely she had been just wandering, wanting out of the house after being confined all winter. The large shadowy form stepping out of the mist had startled her, but not until he had drawn closer had she felt anything akin to fear.

Walking beside a very respectable thoroughbred, the cloaked and cowled figure emerging from the mist resembled the specter of death in her father's old books, except there was nothing gaunt or ephemeral about this creature. The horse was no dainty mare, but this man used the huge beast as a crutch, limping beside the animal with his arm thrown over the saddle. His size and the fact that she could not see his face had seized Penelope with foreboding, but secure in her surroundings, she refused to acknowledge fear.

As he limped toward her, she said nothing, and the stranger spoke first.

"How far is it into the village?"

His voice was deep and seemed to growl from the depths of a barrel, but Penelope found nothing terrible in it or his words. She gave the answer as accurately as she was able.

"The village is a good half-hour walk from the gates of the vicarage, and we are some ten minutes from there. Has there been an accident? Are you injured?"

Small droplets fell from the bare, gnarled branches above them, and a gust of cool wind flapped the stranger's long cloak as he stopped in front of her. Penelope wished she could see his eyes, and self-consciously, she tugged her old woolen pelisse tighter at the throat. The brown had faded in places, but it still kept her warm, and she had seen no reason to replace it until now. She must look a fright with her hair all damp and blowing about her face, wearing garments that no longer even reached her ankles. She tried not to think about that.

"Thor lost a shoe about a mile back, and the leg is one that has only recently mended. I did not wish to strain it with my weight. If you could direct me to the vicarage gate, I shall find my way from there."

That did not explain his limp, but Penelope refused to pry. "It is time I returned. I will show you the way if you do not mind getting your boots wet. I failed to mention the walk to the vicarage is through the field and not by road.''

Penelope thought she heard him chuckle as she led him down the path through the orchard. She had not meant the remark to be funny. Some gentlemen were very particular about the polished leather of their expensive boots. Admittedly this man did not wear fashionable Hessians, but good, solid knee boots, yet they looked expensive to her eye. She knew quality when she saw it, and even oddly garbed as he was, she could see the quality of the fabric in his cloak and knew the cost of the high-strung thoroughbred.

"My boots have seen worse than good, clean Hampshire mud. Lead on, my lady.''

My lady! Surely he did not know her. No one around here used her title. It was a quite ridiculous title in any account. It must be his manner of speaking. She would certainly remember if she had met anyone the size of this man. The breadth of his shoulders beneath that concealing cloak made him a giant in her eyes.

"We do not see many strangers in these parts, sir. I meant no insult.''Penelope lifted her skirts slightly as she reached the grassy field, though there was no real need of it. She had already soaked her hem in the longer grasses of the far field, and these scarcely touched her skirts.

"And none was taken. Forgive me for not introducing myself. I am Graham Trevelyan. I am a guest of the Stanhopes at the manor, should I ever reach there. Would you know how much farther on it would be?''

"I am called Penelope Carlisle, and Stanhope Manor is not so very far if you could ride. I would not recommend walking the distance.''

By this time, she had become very aware of the stranger's pronounced limp and wondered if it would not be better to lame the horse than himself. She could not imagine him walking even the half hour to the village. His obvious injury relieved her from some of the fear of his size.

"I trust there is some sort of blacksmith who can shoe the horse in this village?''

"Yes, of course, but the village is the opposite direction of the manor. You will be out of your way."

On the spur of the moment, perhaps because she was bored and was eager for company, perhaps because she could not allow someone obviously in pain to walk such a distance, perhaps just out of simple curiosity, Penelope offered her hospitality.

"Why don't you come in and have some tea with us while one of the boys walks your horse to the smithy? I promise they are very reliable and will be thrilled to death to be put in charge of such an animal."

"Your brothers, Miss Carlisle?" His tone showed interest as he glanced down at her.

The small freckles on her nose accentuated the fairness of her slender face as she turned laughing eyes upward. "One would think so, but no, Mr. Trevelyan, they are just neighbor lads who help me out from time to time, though sometimes I am persuaded their appetites cost me more than wages."

The vicarage came into view, and Penelope gazed upon its ivy-covered brick walls with fond pride. She had been born and reared here, and though there had been many a time she had railed against the fates for making her poor, she had always loved her home. The neatly tended lawn and shrubbery welcomed them now.

Her guest hesitated at the gate, seemingly reluctant to enter. "Your offer is a tempting one, Miss Carlisle, but perhaps it would be better if I were to go on."

Misunderstanding his hesitation, Penelope pushed the gate open and held it for him. "Fustian. Augusta will be delighted to have company to serve for a change, and I assure you, she makes an excellent chaperon."

Unable to refuse this generosity, the cowled stranger reluctantly proceeded forward, his head turning slightly as he observed the tiny cottage, the neatly mended picket fence, and the empty stable at the end of the drive. The vicarage spoke of genteel poverty, but in a pleasant way.

"Is your father at home? Perhaps I should speak with him?"

Penelope smiled. "Only if you wish to continue on to the churchyard. My father has been dead this year or more."

Before she could say more than she should, two lads of about eleven and twelve raced each other around the corner from the kitchen garden.

"Penny! Penny! Can we walk him, can we, please?" They ground to a screeching halt before the magnificent thoroughbred, their reverent gazes scarcely noticing the cloaked figure beside it for awe of the expensive beast.

"George, Thomas, behave yourselves, please. This is Mr. Trevelyan. Make your bows properly."

The two urchins immediately scrambled to attention, made short, formal bows, and offered their hands. "How do you do, sir?" came from both suspiciously chocolate-covered mouths.

If there was anything of amazement in the newcomer's greeting, it couldn't be heard in his voice as he shook both grubby hands, then glanced cautiously at the young lady who had brought about their sudden transformation.

"Do all children always mind you so well, Miss Carlisle?"

Penelope glanced up in surprise at this remark. "Oh, George and Thomas are good lads. They just need to be reminded occasionally of their manners. Do you think you could trust them to walk your horse into the village and back? I will vouch for them."

The stranger's gruff growl as he turned it on the boys brought solemnity to two anxious faces. "You must promise to walk him both there and back. He is much too strong for you to ride, and you will hurt both Thor and yourself should you try."

"Yes, sir." "We'll be careful, sir," piped both boys, who now directed their awe to the massive figure beside the horse.

"Then I will trust you with him. He is as well-behaved as whoever leads him." The stranger slipped a long walking stick from a sheath on the saddle and releasing the horse, handed the reins to the boys.

Leaning on the heavy stick, he watched as they disappeared down the lane, then limping slowly, he followed Penelope down the walk to the cottage.

Inside, Penelope flung her cloak on a rack in the entry, then turned to similarly dispose of the stranger's. Perplexed that he had made no attempt to remove it, she wondered if his injury was such that he could not.

She held out her hand in a gesture to help. "We have no servants, unless you wish to call Augusta one. If you would permit me—"

A gloved hand hesitated over the clasp, and Penelope sensed his searching gaze upon her.

"This is perhaps not a good idea. I do not wish to frighten you. If you will just guide me to the kitchen, I will make myself comfortable there until the boys return."

Gradually, Penelope began to understand his hesitation, but she did not know how to ease his fears. Remembering a young man in the village who had been severely maimed on the battlefield, she tried to gauge the stranger's feelings by this example.

"I am the daughter of a vicar, Mr. Trevelyan. My mother died when I was but twelve and I have carried out her parish duties ever since, including tending the sick. A vicar and his family come to know all the evil and good, beauty and ugliness of human life. You do not strike me as an evil man, Mr. Trevelyan, and only evil can frighten me."

"That is a very pretty speech, Miss Carlisle, but I daresay you have never been faced with a visage as beastly as mine is said to be. Very few women care to be in the same room with it. None offer to take tea with it. Your kindness momentarily distracted me. Do not let me take advantage of it. Show me the kitchen."

"Upon my word, you do make it difficult! And what would you do there, terrify Augusta into a witling instead of me? Take off the cloak, sir. I can certainly deal with any beast that the ladies at the manor can."

At this scolding the stranger obediently unclasped his cloak and shook off his cowl. Defiantly he watched her reaction to the sight revealed before removing the garment entirely.

Penelope met his maimed stare without flinching. The one golden eye she could see appeared arrogant and rebellious, but not terrifying. She imagined it could be, if he wanted. With a black patch covering the other eye, all his intensity centered in this one, and she would not wish to see it angry.

Her gaze studiously surveyed the remains of what once might have been a handsome face. Prematurely silver hair surrounded a high brow that pulled into a pucker above the patched eye. A long scar drew the skin of half his face together from his temple down over his eye and through his high-boned cheek. The whole side of his face disappeared beneath the mangled tissue of scars, and vaguely Penelope wondered how he could open his mouth to speak. His mouth on that side had been savaged and sagged downward.

"You should thank God each day that you are alive," she stated simply, then held her hand out for the cloak.

"For years, I cursed God each day that I did not die. Do not ask me to make any larger steps just yet." He surrendered the cloak and watched intently as she hung it up and turned to face him again. When she did, without flinching, he relaxed and slowly followed her to the parlor.

"I am not my father. I will not preach. Am I permitted to ask in which battle you took your wound?" She showed him a chair at the fireside where he could warm himself. The sound of footsteps down the stone passageway indicated Augusta had heard them and was hurrying this way.

"No battle. I could have accepted a war wound. No, this was a casualty of too much carousing and being in the wrong company at the wrong time. It is rather difficult to accept that one has wasted one's youth and ruined his future. You are too young and too good to understand that."

"I am neither very young nor very good, but that is not the topic, is it? Here comes Augusta. I believe she may have scones today."

Trevelyan turned his face to the fire as the elderly woman pattered into the room. As Penelope explained the situation, he did no more than make a slight nod in the woman's direction, keeping the less damaged side of his face turned toward the room so as not to frighten her.

"I shall get out the jam from last summer's berries," Augusta replied excitedly, seeing nothing amiss in the morose gentleman's staring into the fire. Quality were peculiar, and this one had the smell of quality all about him. "And there is still some of that honey left from Mr. Stillwell's hives . . ." She drifted out again, leaving the chilly parlor in sudden silence.

"Is she a relative?" The growl came from the fireside.

Penelope ignored his gruffness, understanding the source. She pulled up a tea table and curled up in the chair opposite his. She saw no reason for formality now after they had already dispensed with so much.

"Better than a relative. Most of my relations are cold, unfeeling people. Augusta is the warmest, cheeriest person I know. I rather think she came with the house. She was here when I was born and has been much a mother to me as my own. I cannot imagine this place without her, though I know she is much older than my father was when he died. Perhaps it is not the good who die young, after all."

"I'll argue that," Trevelyan grumbled, finally turning from the fire to admire the charming sparrow perched on the chair across from him. He took no note of the room. One parlor was the same as another. But he had always had an eye for women. "I and a lot of others like me would have been long dead did it work your way. You must come around to it and admit your Augusta is a wicked woman and your father a saint."

Penelope looked momentarily startled, then realizing he jested, she laughed. "If that be the case, I should prefer to go to hell with the sinners and Augusta. Preserve me from the saints!"

His crooked mouth turned upward in a faint imitation of a smile. "Surely, you cannot hint the late vicar was less than a saint?"

Penelope lifted her hand to make a gesture, then primly returned it to her lap. "I will not speak ill of the dead, but he was a man with all the faults of a man. No one would decry him as a saint."

Augusta bustled into the room carrying a tray and the best china. Penelope held her breath as the contents clattered and clanked under the old woman's uncertain grip, but she knew better than to offer assistance. In the presence of company, she would have been insulted to have anyone else wait on guests.

"There you are, my lady, the scones are still warm. Will there be anything else?"

Penelope caught the stranger's one visible eyebrow arching at the title addressed to her, but she made no explanations in front of Augusta. Although they often shared tea in the kitchen, she knew the older woman would refuse to join them now. She exclaimed in delight at the repast dredged up from nearly bare larders and gave Augusta a warm smile.

"I do not know what I would do without you, Gusta. It looks delicious. If you don't mind, I'll serve Mr. Trevelyan." Her broad wink hinted of the nice coze they would have later to discuss the afternoon's occurrences.

Augusta returned the wink with a grin and a quick curtsy and hurried off again, her fragile frame looking as if a wind could lift her from her feet.

When Penelope turned to face her guest again, he gave her a quizzical look. "My lady?"

This time, Penelope did gesture eloquently. "Baroness. Baroness Penelope Carlisle of Wyndgate, if you please."

Chapter 2

VISCOUNT Graham Trevelyan stared at the over-slender figure in her outdated, girlishly modest white gown and felt the first stirring of an idea. He dismissed the thought summarily, but nonetheless, his interest had been firmly engaged. An impoverished vicar's daughter did not arouse curiosity, but one who was a baroness in her own right presented certain possibilities. It had been a long time since any woman had captured his jaded interest, but charming as she was, it was more Lady Penelope's background than her person that interested him.

"A title and good looks will give you entrée to most of London's fashionable houses. Why are you not whirling about the city, setting your cap for a wealthy young man?"

Penelope sent him an amused look as she poured the tea. "Putting aside your flattery, wouldn't I make quite a sight whirling about the city in this gown? Provincial that I am, even I am aware the fashions have changed. And I am much too old to be setting my cap for a young man. Any day now I expect to retire to one."

"Too old?" He raised his unscarred eyebrow. "Then I had best make my funeral arrangements whilst I can still toddle about. You are funning me."

Before Penelope could refute his argument, a hurried knock at the door interrupted, and before she could rise to answer it, the door exploded open with a force from without. Two golden-haired children tumbled laughingly into the passage, followed by their harried mother who peeped around the corner into the parlor. Spying Penelope first, she breathed a sigh of relief while the two youngsters raced down the hall to the kitchen.

"Penny! I am so glad you are here. I must go into the village . . ." She stopped abruptly at the sight of the silver hair on the other side of the high-backed chair facing the fire. "Oh, I am sorry, you have company. Excuse me, the twins begged so, but I'll gather them up . . ."

"Fustian! The twins will be fine here. Mr. Trevelyan has injured his horse and himself and is resting before traveling on to the manor. If you would, when you are in the village, tell one of the Widow Baker's boys to carry a message out to the manor telling them where he is and that he will arrive as soon as his horse is shod. Is there any other message you need send, sir?" She turned to her guest.

"No, that is much more than is necessary. They will not worry about me." Trevelyan made some small attempt at acknowledging the other woman's presence without revealing himself. "I will thank you in advance should you stop by the smithy and be certain two small boys are warned again not to try riding Thor."

"Of course, sir. I will be more than happy to. I will go tell the twins to remain in the kitchen and not trouble you." The woman sent Penelope an anxious, puzzled look. Gentlemen of any sort seldom frequented the vicarage parlor. One who did not rise or turn to greet her seemed oddly out of place in this polite house.

Before Penelope could protest, the twins erupted into the room again, each holding a sugary biscuit in one hand. "Penny! Play games with us!"

Penny rose and grasping the empty hands of both shinily scrubbed six-year olds, steered them toward the door with their mother. "Kiss Mama good-bye first, then sit yourselves properly on the settee where you belong."

Obediently the twins did as told, and their mother was persuaded to take her leave. When Penelope returned to the parlor, the twins were whispering between themselves, and Trevelyan had retreated entirely behind the chair back, not easy for a man his size to do.

"John, Janie, I have company for tea today so I cannot play. Do you wish to sit with Gusta and play with the kittens or stay and have tea like a proper lady and gentleman?"

The little girl's eyes widened to blue saucers. "We can have tea and scones and sit in the front parlor? May I pour tea?"

Her brother gave her a look of irritation. "Who wants to sit in an old parlor? I want to play with the kittens."

"Very well, John, go on back to the kitchen and tell Augusta we will need another setting in here."

When the boy ran off, Penelope took a deep breath and muttered a silent prayer before introducing the terrifying gentleman to the little girl. He would not like it, she already knew, but she would not turn away old friends for new. "Janie, I would like you to meet Mr. Trevelyan, my friend. He has been in an accident and hurt his face. You may pour tea when Augusta brings the cup and saucer."

Speaking in firm, no-nonsense tones, she answered Janie's questions before they could be asked and diverted her attention before she could stare. The little girl bobbed a curtsy before the silver-haired gentleman, gave his crumpled face a look of curiosity, then climbed up in the chair Penelope pulled up for her. She crossed her hands politely in her lap and waited for Penelope to sit.

"May I have a scone now or must I wait for Gusta?"

Trevelyan's irritation at being thus displayed turned quickly to guarded interest at the look of relief and affection in the baroness's pert features, and he watched in fascination as the golden-haired hoyden turned to model child beneath the lady's direction. Even the child's surreptitious glances toward him did not divert the viscount's captivation from the phenomenon. When the requested china arrived, the small girl carefully poured her own tea and politely requested three cubes of sugar.

"You are very quiet, Mr. Trevelyan. Have I offended you by inviting another guest? We are a most informal household, if you have not already surmised."

"No, I am not offended, merely amazed. How do you do it? It is as if you wave a magic wand and turn little monsters into fairy creatures. I have never seen the like."

Janie took umbrage at what she perceived to be a slur to her best behavior. "I am not no little monster. Aunt Penny says I am a fallen angel."

Penelope covered her laughing gasp with one hand and sent a look of amusement to her guest, who received it in the same spirit. A slow grin twisted his mouth awkwardly. It had been a long time since he had shared this kind of understanding with another, man or woman, and the comfort of this tiny cottage wrapped around him.

"You most certainly are, Miss Jane. I have a daughter just about your age, so I know all about angels."

"You do? Can she come play with me sometime?"

Even as he chatted nonsense with the little girl, he felt the lady's questioning gaze watching him. He did not attempt to explain then. There was plenty of time to do it in the future.

When the viscount finally arrived at the manor in time for a late dinner in the seclusion of the study, he set about finding the answers to some of his own questions first. The Stanhopes were both family and friends, and he had no fear of their sympathy or horror. He watched as his sister politely spoke to every guest in the far room before entering the study to perch on the arm of his chair and kiss his hair fondly.

"The city must be truly dreadful this year to bring you all the way out here. You never visit, you know. How is Alexandra?"

"Well, as usual, and you are blooming, Adelaide. Married life suits you, though how you can isolate yourself out here I cannot know."

"Fie! I know you too well, Trev. You adore the Hall and if it were not for your evil pursuits in the city, you would bury yourself alive. If you wished to escape London, what brings you here instead of home?"

"That is a cruel taunt, Adelaide, and you know it. The Hall is yours anytime you want it. I cannot go back there. Let us change the subject. I notice you have invited any number of your illustrious neighbors for the evening. Why do you not invite the baroness?"

"The baroness?" Adelaide looked momentarily bewildered. Younger than her brother by some years, she still had a child's blond fairness, though her small, pointed face spoke of mature intelligence. "Oh, you mean the vicar's daughter! Whatever made you ask of her?"

"I will tell the story later. I did not mistake, she is a baroness is she not?"

"Oh, you did not mistake. She comes of very good family, very few of them left now, I understand. The father was a younger son of a younger son or some such when he became vicar. He unexpectedly inherited the title and a small sum a few years back. Hied himself off to London where he drank and gambled to excess and was scarcely seen again until they carried him back in a coffin. I don't know why Lord Chase never turned him out. I suppose the elder Chase never was much of one for religion and was just as happy not having a vicar preaching about his evil ways. The new Lord Chase is a different story, I hear. Now that you bring the thought to mind, I heard some mention young Samuel was asking around about a man suitable for the position. He's rebuilding that little church over the hill, you know. Oh, dear, I wonder where that will leave the little baroness?"

Years of his sister's company had taught Trevelyan to sift through the maze of her thoughts and follow their direction. He did not like to think of that cheerful cottage in the hands of some stiff-necked parson, but that seemed to be the message Adelaide tried to convey.

"I daresay she has relations to go to if worse comes

to worst, but you have not answered my question. Why did you not invite the baroness this evening?"

Adelaide ruffled his hair and rose. "I sometimes think the accident muddled your brains more than your face, big brother. I may invite her as much as I like, but she will not come because she has no clothes. Now make yourself at home and quit scowling like some ferocious beast. Lady Chatham just glanced in here and she looks ready to faint."

Penelope expressed no surprise when Graham Trevelyan appeared on her doorstep the next morning. Over a spirited game of chess, he gave her the latest gossip of Princess Charlotte and the Prince of Orange, and she advised him of the best place in the village to send mending and to obtain medicinal herbs. If she conveyed a little more of herself than she intended, she blamed it on a lack of new faces. Everyone else knew all there was to know about her.

When he appeared a second and third day, gossip began to flow, and Penelope's curiosity almost overcame her good breeding. She knew this oddly reclusive man disliked meeting strangers and hated to be an object of pity or rude attention, but the steady stream of visitors through the cottage did not seem to deter him. She sensed his need for companionship, but surely the manor folk could give him that. Whatever his reason, she rather enjoyed the diversion, and she welcomed him honestly, until the day she refused the invitation to Stanhope Manor.

She heard the furious gallop of his horse and knew the visitor before he was announced. She did not expect the angry gleam of his golden eye when she answered his knock.

Stalking into the passageway without invitation and slamming the door behind him, Trevelyan waved the letter with her refusal beneath Penelope's nose. "Why? Is this an example of country manners? I may visit here but you may not visit me? I thought to offer you some recompense for the hospitality you have bestowed upon me, and this is what I receive in reply?"

"Do come in, *Lord* Trevelyan." Penelope expressed her anger with irony, emphasizing the title she had learned not from him but from gossip. "Or will you no longer darken my doorstep because I cannot cross yours?"

"Cannot? Or will not? Has my family caused some offense that you cannot accept an honest invitation? I offered to send around a carriage so you need not walk the distance. I even asked that you bring Augusta so you could be certain I had no evil intent. Why can you not cross my doorstep?"

His rage had carried him into the small parlor where the combination of his massive size, swirling cloak, and heavy walking stick threatened the row of figurines on the bric-a-brac and overwhelmed the delicate settee and ancient side chairs. He wore his hair much too short for the current style and it escaped about his forehead in wild dishevelment, emphasizing more than ever his resemblance to a maimed lion or untamed beast.

"Upon my word, my lord, you will make yourself ill before you terrify me. Roaring may work very well with frightened servants or empty-headed henwits, but do not try it here. I have excused you much, but I will not excuse your rudeness in my own home. There is no law anywhere that compels me to accept your invitation as if it were a royal summons. You have received all the answer I intend to give and more than you deserve. Good day, sir."

To Trevelyan's astonishment, she stalked out of the room, leaving him to dismiss himself. He couldn't remember the last time anyone had walked out on him or did it so well. She had held her head as proudly as any queen, and her old-fashioned skirts had rustled with just the right amount of injured pride. He would wager his fortune that she even wore a stiff-laced corset beneath those petticoats. A low chuckle threatened to erupt into full-fledged laughter as he headed for the door.

Penelope buried her face in her hands as the front door slammed. Pride goeth before a fall, they say, and her fall would be a mighty one if the height of her pride served as any measure. But she could not bear the titters of the manor's inhabitants as the Baroness Wyndgate was introduced as a country mouse wearing threadbare skirts. She did not mind her looks so much on her own ground, but to be laughed at by people who were supposed to be her equals was more than pride could allow.

She hoped she had not wounded the viscount's feelings too badly. He meant well, she was certain, and obviously he had been hurt many times before to act with such rage, but she simply could not countenance such behavior. He had been less than honest with her by not giving his full title, as if she would have taken advantage if she had known. He had been given what he deserved, but she could not help feeling unhappy about it.

The fact that the viscount did not return that day or the next was lost in the overwhelming sense of disaster that overtook Penelope when she heard the next piece of gossip that came her way. Whispers reached her ears first, well-meaning friends coming to her for verification. She could scarcely believe their truth, and before she worked herself into a panic over nothing, she promptly put on her best gown and strode across the fields to confront Lord Samuel Chase, himself.

After spending an hour in the company of the new Lord Chase, Penelope reeled from the mansion in shock. Afterward she did not know how she found herself wandering through the orchard once again. This time, the mist was more of a drizzle, but she scarcely felt the damp as she stared over the vista beyond the orchard's edge. From here she could see all of the countryside spread out around her, the village like little toy houses in the distance, the vicarage just beyond that grove of trees. A welcoming swirl of smoke drifted from the chimney, and she nearly cried at the thought of never seeing that cheery kitchen again.

Lead lay where her heart belonged as Penelope contemplated the alternatives open to her, but her mind refused to function reasonably. The vicarage was her home. Augusta was her family. How could she part from both of them? How would she tell Augusta she no longer had a home?

That hurt the worst, and Penelope strived desperately not to think of it. There had to be a way. No one could be so cruel as to tear an old lady from the only home she had ever known. But his lordship had not sounded particularly concerned for the fate of one doddering old woman in the face of all his grandiose plans of restoring church and faith to these benighted denizens.

The twig she held between her fingers snapped, but Penelope neither knew she held it nor that she broke it. Her life had been one series of blows after another: her mother's death, the ever-present poverty, her father's desertion, and now this. She had always had the cottage to comfort her, Augusta's shoulder to cry on. It was as if some cruel fate had decided to strip her of what little she had left.

Fate stepped in now, in the form of a shadowy hulk materializing out of the mist as before. This time, however, Penelope knew his name, and she did not bother to approach him. She did not need one more humiliation this day.

The viscount refused to ignore her turned back. Placing his weight on the walking stick that resembled a club more than a fashionable ornament, he dragged his stiff leg until he reached Penelope's side.

"You have heard," he stated without preamble, staring down at her fair head and not the view.

"Was I the last to know?" she asked bitterly. "Did you stay to watch me fall or help to bring me down?"

"That's unfair, Penelope." It was the first time he had called her by her given name, but neither noticed. "I heard rumors that first night. It is not easy for me to make acquaintance with strangers, but I have spent these last few days trying to talk him out of it. Lord Chase is quite a determined young man."

Eyes of delicate violet filled with tears as they turned up to gaze upon the scarred and horrible face of this man fate had sent to intervene. "The cottage is his, though I have managed to faithfully pay the rent on it all these years. I cannot say he is wrong in asking us to leave, but how can I tell Augusta? She came there when she was but a child. She knows no other place. I can go to one of my cousins, I suppose, but how can I ask them to take in a second mouth to feed? They might resent my presence, but I can make myself useful. What promise can I make of that for Augusta? She is old and frail. To uproot her would be cruel enough. To force her to work in a stranger's home and be treated as a servant would break her heart." She choked back a sob and swiftly turned away.

"His noble lordship has agreed that to sell the cottage would enable him to build a new and better one closer to the church." Trevelyan offered these words tentatively, feeling his way over precarious ground.

Penelope uttered a hopeless laugh. "Fine, and would he sell it for what I pay in rent each year? Would that buy him a nice, new vicarage for his pious parson? Do you know how many dozens of eggs, how many pints of jam it takes to make that rent? If it were not for the small sum my mother left for me, we would starve. And even that small sum cannot buy a house."

Trevelyan steeled himself for her reaction to his next words. "I could buy it for you."

Penelope threw him an incredulous look that mixed hope with outrage and diminished into anguish at the look in Trevelyan's one handsome eye. She shook her head dully and turned to follow the path back to the cottage. "I thank you for the thought, but you know I cannot allow that."

He did not try to keep up with her hasty steps as she hurried away. Instead, he hoped his words would reach her before she could make good her escape, before he had time to change his mind. "You could if you were my wife."

Penelope's steps slowed as the viscount's reply sank in. She did not know whether to run, or turn and embrace him. Unable to do both, she sank to a fallen log and wrapped her arms around her knees. How could she answer?

Understanding her dilemma, Trevelyan eased himself into a position against the tree in front of her. She wore no hood or bonnet as usual, and water streamed down a loosened curl at her cheek. She had lost what sparkle of life she had left, and he knew what he had to offer gave little hope of its return, but it was a choice, of sorts.

"You do not need to answer immediately. I have had all week to think of it and you have not. I understand Lord Chase has not yet promised the position to anyone. There is time."

"All week?" Curiosity propelled Penelope's gaze upward, seeking the reason for this madness. He had courted her all week, knowing this day might come. Why? She could not read that enigmatic face, nor could she even know the man behind it.

Keeping his scarred face in shadow, Trevelyan tried to explain. "I told you I have a daughter. She has never known a mother, only a succession of housekeepers and nannies and governesses. Because I was so long in recovering from my injuries, she scarcely knows me, and I terrify her. She is a very quiet, sensitive child, and she quails at the sight of me. She needs a mother. She needs someone permanent in her life, as you have Augusta. Should anything happen to me, she would have no one. You offer the perfect solution, Penelope. You were meant to be a mother. Can you not consider my daughter a little when you decide our fate?"

She heard the plea in his voice, read the future in his eye. For herself, it did not matter, she had long since accepted her place as impoverished old maid. But for Augusta and for her home and for a frightened little girl— He had no right to force her to make such choices.

But force her, he did.

Chapter 3

GRAHAM lingered in the shadowy doorway, watching the despondency on his bride's pale features as she stared into the fire. Exhausted, she had slept in his arms for almost the entire carriage ride to London, and the memory lingered with him. The warmth of her slight weight had stirred a protectiveness within him he had not expected, a protectiveness he had not felt for many years. He had chosen this woman because of her maturity and independence, but he had forgotten how fragile and innocent a young woman could be. She had never been from her home before. He should not have made her leave on their wedding day. But she had refused to go to the manor without a trousseau, and he could not impose on the limited resources of the vicarage. The choice had been Penelope's, but he knew she only chose the lesser of two evils with each decision that had led to this moment.

With a sigh of resignation, Graham rapped his walking stick against the hardwood floor and proceeded into the room.

Penelope leapt, startled, from her seat. She had not heard the door open, or noticed his approach until he was nearly upon her. He had a way of moving silently that did not match his size or lameness. Hair tumbling loosely over her barely concealed breasts, she felt suddenly naked beneath her husband's appraising stare. She had never worn anything so revealing in her life, and certainly had she never stood before a man in such disarray. She could not raise her eyes to meet his.

"All women should look as you do when they come to their husbands on their wedding night."

Did she hear a note of regret in that gruff voice? Penelope raised her gaze slowly, prepared to flee at any untoward movement, but Trevelyan merely rested his weight against his stick and stared down on her. He had doffed his formal frock coat and cravat and replaced them with a deep green satin robe, but he had apparently not disrobed more than that. Her gaze returned to his powerful stockinged legs, then fell upon the glove he still wore on his left hand. She had never seen him remove the glove. One more thing she did not understand about this man.

"I am trying . . . very hard, to be a proper wife, but my instructions have been few, I fear." She gulped out this message less smoothly than she had hoped.

Graham raised his hand to touch a shining strand of honey-brown hair, thought better of it, and gestured toward the chair she had just vacated. "Sit. There are a few things we should have discussed before now, but they did not seem proper topics for an unmarried maiden. You may still be maiden, but you are most certainly married now, for better or worse."

Trying to conceal her nervousness as he reminded her of what she had tried to forget, Penelope slipped into the chair indicated, and out of habit, curled her feet up under her. She did not understand the slight upturn of her husband's lips as he watched her, but it gave her strength enough to return his gaze. She wished he were not of such a formidable size. He would terrify her even had he two eyes and a normal face under these circumstances. She did not wish to think of sharing a bed with such a creature, or of what would happen there.

"Penelope, stop looking at me as if I had suddenly grown two horns and a tail. I do not intend to touch you this night or any other night. Does that satisfy some of your fears?"

Violet eyes widened and a hint of color rose to her cheeks as Trevelyan loomed over her, waiting for an answer. Groping for words for a topic that had always been forbidden, she tried to clarify his amazing declaration.

"I am not sure I understand you, my lord." She hesitated, hoping he would help her, but he only waited patiently for her to continue. "I . . . We are man and wife. I agreed to that. You need not . . ." She stammered to a halt, unable to finish.

Wearily Graham poured a glass of wine and handed it to her. "You could at least learn my name now that we are married. Most people call me Gray, a rather apt appellation, you must agree."

Penelope took the glass and almost managed a smile. "I prefer Graham. It sounds very distinguished. I think I can manage that command. Are there any others?"

"Are you a genie who will obey my every whim? My wishes are few, but rather impossible, of course." He leaned against the bed's edge, keeping a safe distance.

"If I am a genie, I am not very good at answering my own wishes, but I shall try my best to answer yours." This half-jesting manner of speaking they had fallen into from the first relaxed Penelope's nervousness to a degree. Talking was something she knew how to do. If she did not look at him, she could almost forget where she was and what was expected of her. She could pretend they sat over the tea tray in the cottage.

"Then we will test your strengths on very small commands, at first. Call me Graham, do not interrupt me until I finish, then say, 'your wish is my command,' and hop off to bed and sleep." Trevelyan spoke firmly, as much for himself as for Penelope. It would be very tempting to forget good intentions, otherwise.

Pressing her lips tight to keep from smiling, Penelope did as told. She waited without interrupting.

"You could have at least said, 'Yes, Graham,' " he complained with a hint of self-mockery. "Well, then, let me try to say this as politely as I am able. This is London. You will be moving in circles a little different from the one you are accustomed to. Their customs may seem a trifle odd to you, but they're all for the best, under the circumstances. You have heard of marriages of convenience?''

The smile slipped away, but Penelope nodded. ''Yes, Graham.''

This bit of spirit reassured him, and he continued. ''That is what we have. I wanted a mother for Alexandra and you wanted a home for Augusta. We have accomplished that. You are very young and inexperienced, and I have no intention of taking advantage of that fact. I want you to learn about London, have the coming out you should rightfully have had, feel the freedom to fall in love as you will. All I ask in return is that you be discreet, that you do nothing to impair your relationship as mother to Alexandra, and that you not interfere with my manner of living. I think I know you well enough to trust you in that.''

The astonishment in Penelope's eyes grew as she comprehended his meaning and a dozen questions danced in her head, but she remembered his commands quite clearly. If she obeyed his commands, then he would be happy, and she would be . . . It did not matter. She nodded her head. ''Yes, Graham.''

''Thank you, my dear.'' With those whispered words, the bridegroom dragged himself from the room.

Closing the door behind him, Trevelyan leaned against it heavily, the look of weariness all but extinguishing the usual life in his face. With difficulty he pushed himself upright again, and with a quick glance around his half-lit chamber he rang for his manservant. Without waiting for a reply, he peeled off his glove and reached for the gargoyle guarding the heavy wardrobe by the window. A grating noise sounded from within, and leaning his walking stick against the wall, Graham threw open the wardrobe door and disappeared inside.

The portly servant who appeared shortly afterward did not seem surprised to find the chamber empty. Gently closing the wardrobe doors and securing the chamber locks, he settled himself in a long settee and waited.

* * *

Whether from wine or exhaustion, Penelope slept soundly in her grand bed that night but woke to the distinct impression that she was no longer alone. Judging by the light behind her eyelids, it was daylight, but she feared to open her eyes. She held still, trying to find the source of the sensation. She sensed the bed was empty of anyone but herself, and she gave a mental sigh of relief. There could not be anything more frightening in a London town house than her husband. She would have to wake and see.

Her first full sight of her new home left her awestruck. Pale blue satin draperies looped about her bed and a matching comforter kept her snug. A veil of fine gauze hid the room from clear view, but she could see high windows and a pillow-filled window seat. It would be easy enough to lie here and pretend she was a princess, but it wasn't in her nature to be idle.

Carefully Penelope drew aside the veil of gauze and looked out. Her gaze immediately encountered the dark one of an elfin child perched in a blue and gold brocade chair in the corner. She did not speak as they studied each other.

The girl could be no more than five or six, but her thin features held an unexpected maturity. Black hair tumbled loosely about a heart-shaped white face, but Penelope noted a resemblance to the father in the strong line of her jaw and the set of her thin lips. Quiet and sensitive she might be, but Penelope was willing to wager an obstinacy and temper to match her father's lurked behind that innocent exterior.

The child broke the silence first. "Are you my new mama?"

Word traveled as quickly in London as in the village, Penelope surmised, searching for the proper phrases to reply. The girl's expression gave no clue as to how to go on. "I have always wanted a daughter. Do you think we'd suit?"

Alexandra's face broke into an enchanting and unexpected wreath of smiles. "Will you take me to the park?"

"I should think so, as soon as I find out how. I've never been to London before."

"I've been to the park before," she declared proudly. "I saw a little girl there riding a pony. Can I ride a pony, too?"

"I don't know why not. Do you know how to ride?" Penelope wondered in which of the massive wardrobes her dressing gown had been stored, but it seemed more important to learn about Alexandra than to look for it.

The child shook her head negatively. "But I know I can if I just have a pony," she added defiantly.

"I can't promise you a pony. That's for your papa to say," Penelope said.

Alexandra grew paler. "He won't give me one. I've been a bad girl."

At just that moment the connecting door between the bedchambers opened, and without a look back Alexandra leapt from her chair and dashed for the door to the hall. In one swift movement Penelope threw aside the covers and set her feet to the Turkish carpet at the bedside. It was only a matter of steps to come between the girl and the door, and she caught her up in her arms just as Graham reached the room's center.

His gaze quickly noted his daughter's struggling figure in Penelope's bare arms, then wandered momentarily to admire tousled hair and feminine dishabille. His distraction didn't last long, however, as he remarked dryly, "I see you have met Alexandra."

Penelope regretted her instinctive reaction to the girl's flight, but now that it was done, she intended to make the best of it. Not noting her husband's fascination with her state of undress, she sat back down on the bed and held the child firmly in her lap.

"We were having an interesting conversation before you came in." Penelope pushed Alexandra's hair back from her eyes, but the child buried her face against her shoulder and wouldn't look up. "Alexandra, why don't you ask your papa about the pony? If you want something badly enough, you have to be willing to fight for it."

"I can't" came the whisper from her shoulder.

Penelope glanced from the child's head to the father's expressionless face. Her heart went out to both of them, and she prayed she had the ability to bring them together again. Life held too many hurts and too little love as it was. If Trevelyan could save her home and Augusta, surely she could show this terrified child the love behind that wounded face.

"Alexandra would like to be able to ride in the park, but it seems she has no pony and cannot ride. I know nothing of London, Graham. Is it possible for little girls to go riding in the park?"

The answer rumbled from deep within his chest. "I see no reason why not. She will need to learn to ride, first."

Alexandra's head jerked upward, and she peered suspiciously over her shoulder, but she could not see her father's face from that angle. Saying nothing, she clung tighter to Penelope.

"I can, I know I can," she whispered defiantly.

"I could teach her, Graham. I'm not a great equestrienne, but I can certainly teach her to ride a pony. Could it be arranged?"

Graham studied the small dark head buried against Penelope's shoulder that now turned with a wary look of hope in his direction. A similar look appeared on his own face as he met his bride's eyes. "I will have my groom look for a suitable mount for both of you today. There shouldn't be any difficulty."

The tension left the child's small frame and abruptly she scrambled down from her seat. With a quick, bobbing curtsy halfway between her father and Penelope, she darted them both a shy glance and said formally, "Thank you very much. Mrs. Henwood will be looking for me."

This time, when she ran for the door, Penelope let her go. When she turned back to face Graham, she found him studying her, and she remembered her attire. Blushing, she hastily pulled the covers around her, to find her efforts rewarded with his half smile.

"You will do very well, Lady Trevelyan. Shall I have your maid come up now that my daughter has introduced herself in her own inimitable manner?"

Penelope frowned slightly at her own thoughts. "I think I must talk with this Mrs. Henwood. Is she the governess?"

Graham looked vaguely startled but replied easily. "Yes, a very respectable widowed lady. She has done very well given Alexandra's propensity for disappearing at any hour of the night or day. Shall I send for Mrs. Henwood?"

"Not yet. It might be better if I talked to her first." Penelope wriggled uncomfortably under his gaze, not certain if she should reveal her suspicions. "Alexandra said you would not give her a pony because she was a bad girl. Have you told her that?"

This time Graham definitely did look startled as he stared at his own personal genie wrapped in flowing robes of blue satin. "Me? The child runs every time I come in sight. I would have no idea if she were good, bad, or indifferent, no less the opportunity to tell her so."

"That's what I thought. Well, I will talk to Mrs. Henwood and will take care of that shortly."

"Devil take it, Penelope, what are you trying to tell me? That the prim, upright Mrs. Henwood has been calling my daughter a bad girl? From all reports, the child is incorrigible, but bad will suffice. I admit, calling her bad does not sound like a healthy practice, but what else can you say?" He sounded exasperated.

Penelope returned his irritation. "The child is neither bad nor a model of good behavior, as any child that age would be. What concerns me is that she connects you with her bad behavior. I very much suspect Mrs. Henwood has threatened to hand her over to you every time she misbehaves, rather like the mothers in the village threaten their children with hobgoblins if they don't behave."

Graham uttered a curse that was new to Penelope's repertoire, but her curiosity as to the origin of the word did not prevent her leaping from the bed once again to keep him from storming off after the governess. She spread her arms over the door and met his glare bravely.

"If she is a good governess, you do not want to lose her. Let me take care of this, Graham."

The fire in that one golden eye warned he was severely tempted to bring his stick down over her head, but taking a deep breath and calling on an inner strength, he refrained. "Only with the exception that if you find she is the one who has made my daughter fear me, you will allow me the pleasure of tearing her limb from limb."

"Thank goodness I never met you before you learned to curb your temper. We would most certainly not have got on at all." Penelope stalked from her position before the door and threw open the wardrobe. Somewhere she had to find her dressing gown. "And I won't tell you anything if you're going to lose your temper with some poor old woman who doesn't know any better and is probably repeating what others have told her works best. People can be very stupid sometimes, but that is no reason to tear them limb from limb."

Torn between laughter at her effrontery or turning her over his knee to teach her a lesson, Graham did neither. Instead he admired his bride's very pretty posterior as she continued rummaging in the wardrobe.

"What happened to my wish is your command?"

"I'm still working on it" came the muffled reply.

"Work harder," he whispered gruffly from right behind her.

Before Penelope could leap in surprise, a strong arm caught her by the waist and lifted her into the wardrobe. She heard him call out as the door closed, "I'll send your maid to rub the magic lantern in a while," and then it went dark.

Once released from her embarrassing imprisonment, Penelope did not see her husband again that day. He had apparently made it known to the staff that they were to defer to her wishes on all household matters, for she spent the remainder of the day answering questions on matters that had long been neglected by the master of the house.

She also had a long talk with the prim Mrs. Henwood who objected coldly to any interference in her realm. When Penelope made it quite clear that certain dismissal would result if she threatened the child again in any manner, the governess made a hasty reassessment of her position. They parted amicably with the decision that Penelope would be the one to deal with misbehavior.

Even as she firmly took the reins of the household in hand, Penelope's mind did not let go of the embarrassment of being locked in a wardrobe on her wedding morning. That the maid came hastening in shortly after did not excuse Graham's behavior, though by the end of the day Penelope was better able to look at it with humor. Still, if he thought she would silently accept such treatment, he might as well learn otherwise right now.

When she learned that the cook routinely sent up a cold supper platter in the evenings, since his lordship seldom did any entertaining or appeared for meals, Penelope sweetly offered to carry the tray herself. The kitchen staff approved of this gesture heartily and with knowing smirks, but when she also removed an exceedingly large measure of pepper from the condiments cabinet, they stared after her with amazement.

Since he had so blatantly ignored her all day and made it clear that this was a marriage in name only, Penelope felt confident that Graham had made no change in his routine on her account. She knocked on his chamber door daringly, but only John, his manservant appeared.

"I have brought Graham his supper. Is he not feeling well?" she asked solicitously, suddenly a good deal less confident than a second ago. She knew the household spoke of her husband as an invalid, but other than his handicap, she had seen little evidence of ill health.

"His lordship has taken to his bed for the evening, my lady." The portly servant gazed upon her with a look much like sympathy. "The traveling has caused him much pain. He always takes to his bed after a journey."

Penelope's eyes widened and she had second thoughts about the pepper-laden meal in her hands. "Perhaps I should fetch some liniment and compresses. I know how to nurse the sick."

John remained adamant. "His lordship would not want it. He will be fine by morning. I will take the tray and place it by his bed in case he wakes during the night."

She had no choice but to hand over the meal and return downstairs. Sometimes she was too hasty in her judgments. Just because Graham had a terrible temper did not mean that he felt well. She would really have to be more careful in the future. Despite these charitable thoughts, the picture of his reaction to the sabotaged meal made her smile. He deserved that.

In the empty bedchamber John helped himself heartily to the supper his lordship seldom ate. Within minutes his eyes began to water. His throat and tongue turned to fire, and even an entire glass of wine did not quench the flames. Wondering if he had been poisoned, he sniffed the food and instantly sneezed half of it off the plate.

Alternately sneezing and gulping wine, the tormented man had reverted to a limp rag with a red nose slumped in his usual chair by the time the viscount crept back into the chamber later that evening. Graham took one look at his miserable manservant and lifted the cold remains of his supper to his nose. He sneezed and heaved the dish into the hearth, but the smile on his lips grew broader as he realized the deviousness of the vicar's daughter's revenge.

At the sight of John's miserable look he began to chuckle, and as the man threw him a malevolent gaze, his roar of laughter woke the occupant of the adjoining room.

Penelope opened one eye and wondered if her husband were quite sane, but the pleasant sound of his laughter eased her fears and she soon drifted back to sleep again. She did not think to wonder how he would even the score.

Chapter 4

THE next day Penelope decided Graham's revenge was more fiendish than she could possibly have imagined. Shortly after breakfast she was inundated by a parade of tradesmen, milliners, glove-makers, jewelers, seamstresses, cobblers, and modistes he had ordered to attend to her wardrobe, and she had nary a minute's quiet for the remainder of the day. Not only must she try everything on and be measured and pinned and stuck and turned about like a cloth doll, but she had to endure the audience of half the staff at one time or another as they continued to besiege her with questions about menus and linens and minor household emergencies. Whether Graham intended revenge or generosity, she did not care by mid-afternoon. If he had put in an appearance, she would have scarred the other half of his face.

Instead Alexandra materialized like a magic fairy. Perched on a dresser out of the chaos, she soon bedecked herself with stray feathers, over-large kid gloves, and a scrap of pink satin that had been thrown aside. She watched with solemnity as Penelope ordered simple muslin gowns for day wear, selected a pair of gloves and a pert hat and pelisse for wearing outdoors, then protested vehemently as the modiste insisted that wardrobe to be suitable for a servant, but a viscountess must have much, much more.

"I cannot possibly need any more than this! Perhaps a gown for dinner, that gold crepe is very fine, but I cannot justify more than that. Lord Trevelyan does not entertain, there is no need. . ."

Over her protests a basted gown of lilac silk trimmed

at the hem and the sleeve with ruffles and embroidery and scooped low with no more than a sheer chemise to cover the rise of her breasts and throat was pinned in place. The mirror revealed a scandalously fashionable lady, but Penelope could no more imagine herself appearing in public like that than she could imagine doing somersaults before the Regent.

"I can't wear it, " she insisted, picking at the pins in an attempt to free herself.

"Oh, no, my lady, it is perfect for you!" the modiste exclaimed, gesturing hurriedly for a jeweler waiting nearby. The clerk rushed forward with a display of his wares and the modiste chose a splendid display of amethysts and diamonds, placing it around Penelope's throat to demonstrate the effect. "See? A gown like this is made for royalty. His lordship will be proud of you."

"His lordship will think me a very expensive investment should I indulge myself so," Penelope scoffed. "I would have to have his permission before I could possibly agree."

Figuring that would sabotage the saleswoman's plans, Penelope waved away the necklace. The chances of these people daring to face her husband seemed small. She had already learned enough from the staff to know Trevelyan seldom ventured from the house, that he used his secretary and footmen to carry out his business by letter. Should he walk in here now, in all likelihood these tradespeople would flee in terror. She felt safe in putting them off in this manner.

She had not reckoned on Alexandra. From her corner the child piped, "Papa is downstairs in the study. Why don't you ask him? If he gives me a pony, he ought to give you something pretty. Can I have a frock just like that when I grow up?"

The modiste stepped back triumphantly as Penelope turned to answer the child's question. "Of course, but we need to find you a riding habit right now. I don't think we should disturb Papa."

"Oh, he won't mind," Alexandra announced cheerfully. "He sent me up here to see how you were doing. I'll go get him if you like."

Penelope contemplated the satisfaction of allowing the child to do just that, but it would be unfair to Graham to expose him to these crass people. There was nothing for it. She would have to ask him just what he intended for her to buy.

With a sigh of resignation she lifted up the lilac skirt, and in stocking feet traipsed off to Graham's study on the floor below.

He looked up when she entered and rose slowly to his feet, his gaze sweeping boldly from her head to her toe. "I see Madame has had time to whip something up for you already. She is a clever lady. Come closer and turn around. Let me see."

Penelope hadn't expected this sort of interest in her wardrobe from a man who seldom kept his coat on if he could take it off and who wore only the plainest of cravats and waistcoats. She advanced at his command, spinning around to show the elegant frills in the back, then curtsying wryly before him.

"I think it a trifle indecent even for a genie, my lord, but I promised I would ask your opinion. I did not mean to disturb you on so trivial a matter, but your daughter seemed to think you had some interest."

As she realized Graham's gaze lingered overlong on her daring décolletage, she hastily stood up again and retreated toward the shadows. She cursed herself for not thinking to bring a shawl.

"Most definitely. I like to see where my money goes. It certainly seems well spent in this case. It's a decided improvement over those drab high-necked muslins of yours. Have Madame make up as many as she likes. It might behoove me to come down to dinner occasionally to see what Madame creates, if not just to keep an eye on the seasonings."

Penelope had the grace to blush, but before she could reply, a knock on the door interrupted. A footman waited in the half-open entrance, card tray in hand. Graham glanced at him with impatience.

"What is it?" His growl was so curt, the servant

literally shook in his boots, but his reply caused an even greater roar. "Guy Hamilton? That's impossible! Have him in. No, wait," he glanced toward Penelope in her scanty gown and stocking feet. "Tell him to—"

But it was already too late. A tall, slender gentleman in his early thirties swept eagerly through the door, his dark blue eyes instantly seeking and finding his friend. Penelope noted his blond hair did not have the latest fashion of dishevelment, but it gleamed smooth and golden above a high, wide brow, intelligent eyes, and well-formed features. His blue superfine fit perfectly, revealing wide shoulders and narrow hips concealed in tight, buff pantaloons. He seemed the epitome of all a London gentleman should be, and he greeted Graham without pity or condescension. She liked him at once.

"Gray, you damned devil, I had been told you were all but on your death bed, and look at you! I knew it had to be lies. Now tell me—"

Graham cut him off, gesturing toward Penelope in the shadows. "Penelope, I would like you to meet an ancient friend of mine, Sir Percival Hamilton."

Hamilton's gaze instantly swiveled in Penelope's direction as Graham concluded, "Guy, I would like you to meet my wife."

Penelope read the amazement on those fine features, but a look of approval soon replaced surprise as his gaze took in her apparel. "Sir Percival, so pleased to meet you." She held out her hand as steadily as she could under the circumstances. She was unaccustomed to greeting strangers in her stocking feet.

"Lady Trevelyan, this is a delight." He took her hand and bowed deeply over it. When he returned upright, his gaze swept admiringly over her attire. "If you had warned me this would be a formal affair, I would have dressed accordingly."

"We were discussing fashion, Hamilton. My wife is something of a prude and objects to my taste in gowns. I need not ask your opinion of it." This last had a wry note as Graham settled back into his desk chair, observing the reaction of his friend to his provincial wife, and vice versa.

"If you do not mind my saying so, the color compliments your lovely eyes, my lady. For what occasion is it to be worn? I must be certain to obtain an invitation to see the full effect on the male populace of London."

Penelope hesitated, glancing to Graham for aid. She had no occasion for such a dress, but surely this man ought to know that? Graham came to her rescue, but not in the manner expected.

"Penelope has never had a proper coming out. I thought perhaps I ought to invite a few friends over so she might be introduced." There was a wariness to his voice as he watched Hamilton, noting the other man's slowness in releasing Penelope's hand.

"A few friends will not suit for a gown like that. You will need to have a crush of some sort to do it justice. No one even knows you've married. You could make it a formal announcement party." Hamilton remained standing, since Penelope made no effort to sit. His gaze had turned to Graham, however, and Penelope noted a degree of puzzlement in it.

"You have been away too long, Guy, and the battlefields have obviously addled your brains. I have no intention of setting myself up as an object of curiosity for half of London. The gown can be saved for another occasion."

"I do not need the gown at all, Graham." Penelope stepped closer to her husband, touching his hand gently. "It is thoughtful of you to consider it, but I am quite content here. I do not need a come out or fancy gowns. Let me return upstairs and tell them no."

"By Jupiter, if you think I will selfishly keep you from your proper society as your father did, you think wrong, my lady. You will have that gown and every other and there will be no further debate!"

Hamilton instantly stepped in to intervene, certain such a roar would send a delicate female flying from the room in tears, but he did not reckon on Penelope.

She withdrew her hand and without rancor inquired, "That is your wish, my lord?"

To Hamilton's amazement, Graham's ravaged face hinted at a smile. "Consider it your command."

Penelope wrinkled her nose and stuck out her tongue. "So be it. You shall be bankrupt by the morning."

She sailed out of the room, head held high, stockinged feet gliding silently across the polished floors. Both men watched with admiration until the door closed firmly behind her. Then Hamilton put an end to his friend's chuckles by throwing himself into a nearby chair and demanding, "What the hell is going on here?"

Graham met his gaze coldly. "I don't know what you mean."

Guy leaned forward, studying his friend's scarred and damaged face closely. "I still do not believe it. When I joined that bloody war, I thought you were as good as dead. The physicians said you didn't have a chance. When I got back a few days ago and made inquiries, everyone agreed you still lingered at the gates to hell. No one has seen you. You haven't been anywhere. They gave up visiting when you turned them all away. Then I heard about Exbury, and Deauville, and Rochester, and a few others, and I knew, by God, it had to be you. Now tell me you don't know what I mean."

Graham grabbed his stick and lifted himself painfully from the chair, dragging his lame leg as he walked to the grate. Balancing the stick in his gloved hand, he reached for a piece of kindling with the other. The effort almost unbalanced him, but he regained his composure and idly stirred the fire. The sound of soft applause behind him brought a scowl to that part of his face mobile enough to frown.

"I heard about one or two of our old club mates. What of the others?" Graham asked casually, turning around with all trace of the scowl gone.

"They're dead or gone, you sapskull, and don't tell me you don't know it! Exbury, that weak little snot-nosed bantam joined the cavalry and went off to war and never returned. Deauville hurriedly discovered a plantation in the Caribbean none even knew he had and hasn't been heard of since. Rochester had his throat cut in a rather unsavory gambling hell. Smythe dueled with a phantom and lost. Why in hell am I telling you all this when I know good and well you have savored every detail of their demises?''

"Hamilton, you always had more imagination than sense. If it eases your mind to believe I am what I once was, I will spare your delusions. Just do not mention them to Penelope. She knows nothing of the past and I prefer to keep it that way."

"Damn it all, Trev, it does not ease my mind! I should have been there with you. It was just as much my fight as yours—"

Graham held up his hand. "No more of it!"

Dark blue eyes held a rebellious expression as the two men glared at each other, but without Graham's cooperation, no more could be said. In resignation Hamilton threw himself into a nearby chair and regarded his friend's patched eye with interest.

"I remember the time you played Bluebeard at that theater in—where was it? Salisbury? Damn good performance, Trev. If you had not been born with buckets to spend, you would have made a damned fine actor. Pity you grew so much bigger than the rest of us. Hard to disguise someone head and shoulders taller than the rest of the populace," he mused.

"Hard to disguise a face as handsome as this one, too," Graham snorted, unconcerned by his friend's insinuations. "At least you've kept yourself in one piece. What do you intend to do now that Boney has hied himself off to his deserted island?''

"Settle down. Get married, I fancy." Guy stretched his long legs out and contemplated the polished toes of his boots with boredom. " 'Tis the season, is it not? Think there's any more out there like your Penelope? I've never had a lady greet me before in bare toes and then stick out her tongue at me when I curse her. Where can I find another such rare gem?''

Graham made an impolite noise. "Take a fancy to someone else's wife this time, Hamilton. Make it easier for both of us."

Guy lifted his taut face to meet Graham's harsh gaze. "I can never tell you how sorry I am. I should not even be here, but I could not stay away. Even Boney couldn't kill me, though, I daresay I walked in front of enough of his bullets. That must mean I have some other purpose in this world than to send up Spanish flowers, don't you agree?"

The harshness fled his face and a note of regret tinged Graham's reply. "You're a damned fool, I agree, but you are not the only one. Brandy?" He reached for his decanter.

Later that evening, Graham startled Penelope by appearing in her doorway while she stared in dismay at the profusion of drawings and fabrics the modiste had left behind for her to decide between. She had never seen such extravagance in her life, and Graham's appearance provided distraction, if not relief.

"This is sinful. I cannot possibly wear all these, Graham. What does one do with these things?" She picked up a useless frill of a hat that balanced precariously between her chignon and her forehead, a sweeping feather sprouting from its brim to tickle her eye.

Graham limped into the room to inspect the object of her disdain more closely. "I think you are supposed to wear some of those silly curls along here." He drew a line along her temple. "Then do something horrible like chopping all that lovely hair so you can wear it like so." He moved the hat back to perch even more precariously at the back of her head. He surveyed the result. "But I recommend throwing it away altogether."

With great rapidity Penelope flung the offending article across the room, "Thank you. Now if we could equally dispose of the remainder of this extravagance, I'm certain there is some poor soul out there who could better use the money than your Madame Whatever-her-name-is."

Graham leaned against the bed and regarded his amazing wife with amusement. "Madame is so well-known that she need only be called Madame for anyone to know of whom you speak. Other women would give their firstborn sons in exchange for just one of those gowns you so casually scorn. Do not let your opinion get about or you shall be stared at as the same sort of freak as I."

"They shall do that in any case. You saw Mr. Hamilton's reaction to my provincial ways. I trust you did not have your heart set on a wife who set the standards for the *haut ton.*" Penelope swept aside a mountain of delicate lingerie and curled up on the brocade chair much as Alexandra had done the day before.

"For Alexandra's sake, you must have some acquaintance with society, and it wasn't your provincial ways that attracted Guy's notice. You have made your first conquest, my dear, although I recommend you do not take it too seriously. He tends to fall in love with any woman who bears his company for more than two minutes." He watched Penelope with curiosity for her reaction.

"He did not strike me as being quite that foolish." Penelope returned her husband's gaze with equanimity, wondering where this conversation led. She had already learned her husband was not given to idle talk.

"Then you will not object if he acts as host in my place for the dinner I intend to give in your honor? Admittedly it is an awkward situation, but I cannot think of a better one offhand. If my sister would ever come to town, that would be more appropriate, but she seems content where she is."

Penelope looked dismayed. "You would have me attend my first social occasion on the arm of a man I barely know? Oh, surely Graham, if I must be launched, it could be in the company of just a few of your close friends. I would be much more comfortable with you at my side."

His brow went up in genuine surprise. "Would you? What an odd sort of person you are, Lady Trevelyan. I should terrify the company and leave them with no

.stomach for their dinners. No, it will be better my way. If we have the dinner here, I will not be far away. There should be no trouble over it. Hamilton is a good man. He can be trusted.''

"Is this another of your commands? I thought we were to begin with simple ones.'' Penelope hid the sinking feeling his words engendered. She had not quite understood what Graham meant by a marriage of convenience. It was convenient not to have to sleep together, but to pretend she had no husband at all was not within the bounds of propriety that she knew. Wives simply did not let other men escort them to social occasions, but he seemed to think otherwise. It was all very puzzling, but if no harm was done, perhaps it could be managed.

"It will be quite simple, you will see.'' Graham gave his assurances as he retrieved his walking stick and prepared to leave. "By this time next month you will be a part of the social whirl and will forget you have a husband.''

Penelope stared in growing dismay as the door closed behind him. He might wish to forget he had a wife, but how could she ever forget a husband such as hers?

Chapter 5

PENELOPE gave the glittering dinner table one last critical look, adjusted a crystal wine glass, removed a wilted marguerite from the flower arrangement on the sideboard, and sighed. She had never given a formal dinner party, and it was growing increasingly obvious that Graham's domestics were either very new or long out of practice. If she lived through every minor disaster looming on the horizon, she could walk on water.

Dashing back up the stairs, she took a hurried look at the coiffure her lady's maid had arranged. Wisps of honey-brown hair already escaped their imprisoning pins. She had not quite intended an artfully disheveled look, but there was no time left to remove all the pins and try to catch all those stray pieces that had been the bane of her life. Twirling the loose ends around her fingers, she succeeded in creating a halo of light curls about her face. That would have to suffice.

She had refused to wear the low-cut lilac gown, but finally succumbed to Graham's urging that she need not wear high necks and long sleeves for evening. She had finally decided on a simple Italian crepe of fine gold with a ruffle of creamy Valenciennes lace at the throat and cuff. Though her throat and much of her shoulders were shockingly bare, the lace made her feel a trifle more modest.

She spun around at the sound of a knock on the door, then watched anxiously for Graham's reaction as he entered. Dressed casually in a gray frock coat and pantaloons against an immaculately white cravat and waistcoat, he presented an extraordinary figure of masculine virility and grace while standing still if one did not have to look above his neck cloth. Then he leaned on his cane and dragged himself into the room and the image dissipated. Even in this position his eyes were on a higher level than Penelope's, and she had to look up to try to read his expression.

It was useless trying to interpret the meaning of the glow in one golden eye, and she smiled wryly at his stare. "You must have your tailor construct eye patches to match your coats, my lord. The black is quite distracting."

She almost raised a grin with this quip. Graham rested both hands on the massive head of his cane and looked her over thoroughly. "That fashion suits you. If I can persuade you from your high-necked frocks, I might consider your suggestion for eye wear. I'll cast it up before the Beau the next time I see him."

"Guy tells me Mr. Brummell is no longer in favor, and that you are quite free to dress as you please. I do wish you would come down with me tonight."

"Mr. Brummell did us all a favor when he encouraged daily bathing. I'll not desert him for that flock of perfumed peacocks who surround the Regent now. Beau might be idle and sharp-tongued, but he is a gentleman after my own taste. He would not appear in public looking as I do just to see how many stomachs he can turn. Nothing should detract from your introduction to society, my dear. I'm more than content to watch from the sidelines."

Penelope grimaced. "You are throwing me to the wolves, Graham. Will you at least be within screaming distance and come to my rescue when the flambé sets the draperies on fire and the gentlemen use the champagne fountain to douse them?"

This time, he did chuckle, and he caressed her cheek gently with his gloved hand. "I'm not certain of how much use I will be, but I'll come stand and scream beside you should that be the case."

"Very gentlemanly of you, I'm sure." The whisper of his glove along her cheek made her nerves jump, and she was almost relieved when the maid arrived to tell her Sir Percival was here. She did not look back at Graham as she dismissed the maid and checked her image in the looking glass one more time.

"Before you go down, I thought you might want to wear these. They should go well with the lace." Graham's hands slid around her throat and hooked a collar of pearls at her nape.

Startled, Penelope touched the translucent glow of ivory about her neck and looked up to meet her husband's gaze in the mirror. "I have never seen anything quite so lovely before. Is it a family heirloom?"

Graham did not answer, but appeared fascinated with her reflection in the mirror. He touched one bare earlobe and frowned. "I did not think. You should have earbobs, too. I am quite out of practice, I fear."

His gaze didn't dwell long on her ear, and Penelope felt a strange sensation in her stomach as her eyes met his in the glass. He did no more than touch her shoulder, however.

"Guy will think you have grown hen-hearted, my dear. Your guests will be arriving soon. You'd best go down."

Penelope gathered her courage and turned to press a kiss against his good cheek. "Thank you, Graham. I shall try my best not to shame your family tonight. Wish me luck."

Trevelyan shook his head in amazement as she disappeared out the door in a small flurry of dancing curls, rustling skirts, and lavender scent. Penelope seemed to have no idea of her enchantingly feminine charms, which only made her that much more attractive. He would have to peel her suitors off the walls before the week was out.

Grunting in disgust at that depressing thought, Graham set out for the upstairs library. A good book and a good brandy should see him through this ordeal.

Guy had only just presented her with a posy of gardenias when the first guests began to arrive. In the hectic rush to follow, Penelope clung to the posy as she greeted the elderly Earl of Larchmont and his dashing countess, several lordlings of varying ranks but all seemingly well acquainted with Guy and Graham, and a requisite number of young ladies and their doting parents. All greeted Guy with the ease of long acquaintance, made polite words of welcome and concealed curiosity to Penelope, then glanced around the gracious drawing room as if searching for some lost object. Hiding their disappointment at not finding what they sought, they immediately joined the growing throng of guests with small cries of greeting.

In a lull between arrivals Penelope whispered to Guy, "They are looking for Trevelyan. Are they all old friends of his?"

Guy sent a cynical gaze over the crowd. "Oh, yes, of one sort or another. After all these years I suspect they mostly come out of curiosity, however. Producing Trev would provide their entertainment for the evening and raise their popularity as the possessors of the latest *on-dit* for many nights to come. He was right not to come down. This way you will be the subject of conversation for the next day or two. Speculation has already begun, I'm certain. Prepare yourself."

Penelope saw what he meant when she began to circulate among the guests. This gathering was not so very different from a village with a stranger introduced in their midst. She had thought London would be much more cosmopolitan in its interests, but the small circle of the *haut ton* had the same limited access as her home, and the inhabitants grew just as bored with each other. Any new face offered the opportunity for excitement. The story of how the provincial baroness nabbed the reclusive viscount in his lair promised much divertissement.

Penelope proved equally elusive, however. All questions concerning how she met Trevelyan were answered with "through his sister," and anything hinting at his health was answered "well enough." Since society had thought the viscount at death's door, "well enough" took on several meanings, but none dared question "well enough for what?"

Dinner did not prove quite the disaster Penelope had anticipated. Trev had chosen his guests well and animated conversation covered the few flaws in the service. Penelope winced as a carafe of wine nearly missed landing in the countess's lap as the confused footman approached her glass from the wrong side, and she sent up a silent prayer that no one noticed the new serving maid picking up a fallen potato and replacing it in the serving dish as she returned to the kitchen. It could have been worse; she could have done it on the way to the table. One should always be grateful for small favors.

The countess patted her hand after the last remove. "You are very brave, girl. I had hysterics at my first dinner party when the maid nearly took off the prime minister's wig with a serving fork. They had to carry me out and give me smelling salts. Let's leave the men to their vile habits and withdraw to that charming salon of yours."

With a grateful smile for her kindness, Penelope did as suggested. She had been relying on Guy all evening to supply names to faces, and she threw him an imploring look as she rose to lead the ladies out. Whether or not he understood, she could not tell. His appreciative look followed her out but did not provide the support she needed to endure the interrogation ahead.

Within minutes of seeing that all her female guests were comfortably situated, Penelope found herself caught in a polite circle with the older ladies of the group. The younger ones talked and entertained themselves, but Penelope sensed half their attention remained on the conversation of their elders. She listened nervously to the stories of Trevelyan's first wife, of her beauty, wealth, and charm and of what a handsome, romantic couple they had been. A love match, they said. They shook their heads sadly over the tragic ending to the glittering fairy tale, the fateful carriage ride that had killed one, and maimed the other for life.

Penelope sensed they waited for more, eager to embellish their tales with hitherto unknown information, but she had nothing to offer them. She knew even less of her husband than they, and she would not offer the news that theirs was a marriage of convenience. Pride kept her from admitting that she was any less than the first viscountess.

Caught up in her own fears and worries, Penelope lost track of her younger guests. She was vaguely aware that they had apparently fallen into an intriguing conversation that involved much whispering, and she rather wished she could join them, but as a married woman she felt excluded. She must have turned her back when one of the more intrepid girls slipped from the room. She did not notice her absence until some minutes later, when hysterical shrieks began to echo from above stairs.

The men had just begun to join them when the first shriek split through the growing murmurs of conversation. Wildly, Penelope glanced up in search of Guy. He caught her frozen look and the same thought passed between them. Graham!

The crowd surged toward the entrance hall and the stairs, but Guy was swifter and Penelope right on his heels. An explicit gesture sent the butler and Graham's manservant to blocking the stairway and turning the guests about while their host and hostess raced to the source of the screams. Several of the younger men broke through and followed while the others bent to the task of supporting the anxious females fluttering and fainting behind.

The screams had stopped by the time they reached the library, but Penelope unhesitatingly pushed open the half-closed door. With the velvet draperies drawn, the library was a dim chamber at best. Tonight, only a candelabra and the fire lit the Chippendale wing chair at the hearth where Graham usually sat to read. The chair was empty, but Penelope quickly found her husband's towering form leaning over the sofa.

Ignoring the whispered comments and hesitation of the young men behind her, Penelope rushed to Graham's side. The stricken look on his poor, maimed face cut her to the quick, and she hastily looked down to see what foolish chit had caused his pain.

She vaguely remembered being introduced to the strawberry blonde miss with the irrepressible dimple and dancing gray eyes, but she could remember nothing else of her. With dismay she noted the bacon-brain was already coming around and would probably begin screaming all over again when she found Trev's piratical features hovering over her.

Touching a hand to his coat sleeve to get his attention, she nodded toward the door leading to their suite. "I'll take care of her, Graham."

Looking up to note Guy and her curious escorts approaching, he nodded quickly and made his escape. Guy blocked the way to keep their company from following him.

"She's coming around. Will someone pour a glass of sherry? There should be some glasses in the case over there." Calmly Penelope diverted their attention.

Guy knelt beside the sofa and made a pillow of his arm while the two would-be knights-errant brought the requested refreshment.

"I say, was that Trevelyan? Rude of him not to stay. Not at all like, considering." The younger gentleman with the high shirt points turned to stare at the place where his massive host had disappeared.

Penelope bit back a caustic comment as Guy lifted the lovely redhead to allow her to sip from the goblet. "She must have seen one of our legendary ghosts. Graham is going to inspect the old stairwell to see if someone is playing tricks."

They seemed to accept that explanation eagerly. After ascertaining that the fainting beauty would recover, unharmed, they began prowling the paneled walls, looking for hidden passages.

Puzzled gray eyes opened to find Guy's brilliant blue ones and Penelope's anxious ones hovering over her. A shudder went through the distressed maiden as she glanced hastily to the hearth over their shoulder, and she sipped gratefully at the sherry.

Realizing she leaned familiarly against the broad shoulder of a man she did not know, she gently disentangled herself in an attempt to sit up. "I am so sorry. I do not know what came over me."

Guy appeared reluctant to release his lovely patient,

but Penelope removed the glass from his hand and gently inserted herself between the two as the other gentlemen hurried over and a commotion on the stairs indicated one or more of the girl's parents had broken through the barrier.

"I was just telling Sir Percival that you must have seen one of our family ghosts. We're quite acquainted with them, ourselves, and often forget to warn others." The warning note in Penelope's voice caught the girl's ear and she looked quickly at her hostess. Not unintelligent, she lowered her eyes at the stern look she met there.

"How very Gothic," she murmured faintly.

"Tell us, Miss Reardon, what did it look like? All white and whispery? Did it say anything?" The younger gallant leaned eagerly over the sofa while with a trace of scorn, his companion lit a candle.

"I cannot say. I vaguely remember, the shock . . ." She allowed her words to drift off as her undaunted mother swept into the room.

Lady Reardon had a fiery eye for the gentlemen leaning improperly close to her lovely daughter, and only Penelope's presence prevented a tongue-lashing from casting the swains aside. She sent the proper-looking Lady Trevelyan a questioning look as she cleared a path to her daughter's side.

"Miss Reardon seems to have taken a fright. We seldom entertain in these rooms because they are so very dark." Penelope allowed just the barest hint of reproval to enter her voice. She would not have Trevelyan hunted down in his own rooms.

"I don't know what's come over her. Dolly, are you all right? Whatever possessed you to wander up here?"

As the abject Dolly made murmured apologies beneath the admiring gazes of the gentlemen, Penelope slipped away through the adjoining door. She found Trevelyan in front of the fire in the small salon that led to their rooms.

He looked up at her approach, but his features were an impenetrable mask. "How is she?"

"She'll live," Penelope said dryly, coming to stand

beside him. "I don't know what possessed her to come up here and disturb you. Did she give you a dreadful fright?"

Graham's mouth pulled up in what might be a wry smile as he mimicked her phrasing. "I'll live. I'm sorry to have broken up your dinner party in such a manner. Since it wasn't the flambé and you weren't doing the screaming, I thought perhaps you would not need my voice in accompaniment. Was I wrong?"

Penelope smiled at his gentle reassurances. He hid his pain to assuage hers, and she understood why she had consented to marry him. Fearsome as his features might be, and terrible as his temper could be, she knew they both hid a gentle nature, and she felt secure in his company.

"I think a singular roar to match Miss Reardon's shrieks would have given all London something to talk about for weeks to come. You have disappointed me, but I'll forgive you this time. I'm certain tonight will provide enough meat for gossip-broth until we come up with something better."

"Lady Trevelyan, I suspect that innocent exterior hides a wicked tongue and a cynical mind. I believe we shall suit."

Graham's chuckle gave her a curious pleasure, and Penelope returned his smile bravely. "You may be right, though what that says for either of us I'm not prepared to dwell on."

She left him to return to their guests downstairs. Guy hurried forward as the others began to crowd around, but she merely smiled pleasantly and asked after Miss Reardon.

"The silly chit has gone home moaning of ghosts and spirits," the countess announced disdainfully. "Has Trevelyan come up with a better explanation? Where is the boy?"

"Higdon says he's up and about and searching for Dolly's ghosts. Why ain't he down here?" another voice demanded.

Ignoring this rude question, Penelope answered the countess. "There's something of a draft in the upper hall. Graham believes Miss Reardon may be a reader of too many Gothics and too much imagination. He apologizes for not joining us tonight, but he's not well enough yet to be comfortable for long in public. I did not know him before the accident, of course, but I understand he has changed considerably. You must be patient with him.''

''Of course, you are perfectly right, my dear. Give the dear boy my regards, will you? And you must certainly make every effort to attend my ball next fortnight. Hamilton, you will see to that, won't you?'' The countess's dark eyes settled shrewdly on the young baronet hovering behind Penelope.

The remainder of the guests followed the countess's lead. Issuing invitations, assurances, and messages for Graham, they took their leave. The evening had been every bit as entertaining and enlightening as they had hoped.

When the last of the guests had been handed into their carriages and the front door finally closed, Guy and Penelope took a well-deserved rest in the intimacy of Graham's study where the bustle of maids cleaning up would not disturb them. Penelope gestured toward the decanter of brandy.

''Help yourself, sir. I am too weary to stir.''

Continuing to stand, Guy shook his head and leaned against the desk, crossing his arms over his formal blue frock coat as he stared at her reclining figure in the chair. ''I'll be off, too. You need your rest after this ordeal. You need become accustomed to city hours.''

''I need become accustomed to many things. I am quite grateful for your services, Guy. I may call you Guy after tonight, mayn't I?''

''Of a certainty, though I fear to call you any less than Lady Trevelyan. You are quite formidable, you know. I don't know where Gray was lucky enough to find you, but he has chosen well. Your performance tonight exceeded all expectations.''

Penelope gave a weary smile and rose to see him out. ''You see only the result of many years of experience in shepherding my father's parishioners through public occasions. Luckily tonight the most intimidating guest was the kindest. I feel I ought to send the countess a bouquet in appreciation.''

''Bring Trev to her ball and you will have acquitted yourself of all obligation.'' Guy's blue gaze was almost caressing as he looked down on Penelope's flushed features. With a polite bow he took her hand, and impulsively he lifted it to his lips for a quick kiss.

When he departed, Penelope turned back into the room to bank the fire. To her surprise Graham stood in the shadows of the far door. A shiver slid over her at his menacing size silhouetted there in the gloom, but she spoke calmly.

''I did not mean to disturb you, Graham. Why did you not make yourself known?''

In the light of one lamp she gleamed like a golden flame against the night, and Trevelyan experienced an unexpected jolt of pain at the sight. He had seen the way Guy looked at her, witnessed the intimate manner in which his friend had kissed her hand, and felt the old familiar jealousy gnawing at his insides. It had become habit, he supposed. It would not do to give in to such feelings.

He bestirred himself and answered gruffly, ''Guy is a fickle fellow. You would do better to look elsewhere. I will not keep you from your bed. Goodnight.''

All her earlier feelings of warmth and security dissipated with these cold words, and Penelope hurried to do as told. She would never understand this strange man she had married. Why had she thought so briefly that she could turn to him for the affection she had so long been denied? She must be as mad as he.

She fled to the safety of her room.

Chapter 6

THE next day a footman carried up the card of Lady Reardon, and Penelope was obliged to greet the first of her morning callers.

Garbed in what Graham termed one of her "high-necked muslins," her hair smoothed into a simple chignon, she was not prepared for a fashionable parade of callers, but she greeted the visitors with a polite smile as she entered the small salon.

"Lady Reardon, Miss Reardon, this is a pleasant surprise. I hope you have quite recovered from last night's unpleasantness."

The strawberry blonde dropped her head in embarrassment, and her mother glared at her with stiff-necked ferociousness.

"Delphinia has something she wishes to say to you, Lady Trevelyan."

Penelope felt an immediate sympathy for the girl. She looked no more than eighteen or nineteen and judging by the simple white frock she wore, this was most likely her first Season. It must be tremendously difficult to rein in high spirits and imagination and a penchant for intelligence and behave as a mature adult at all hours of the day, particularly if the adult to be imitated was the imposing dowager.

"Oh, it is my place to apologize, Lady Reardon. I should never have neglected my guests so that one was allowed to become lost in this gloomy house. It is quite old-fashioned; Trevelyan was saying just the other night that we must do something with it or level it and build another."

This blatant nonsense raised the girl's head, and she

replied spiritedly, "I beg of you, do not do so! Modern architecture is so uniformly boring, but this place has been constructed in a grand style! I much prefer the Gothic details. The gargoyles are superb. Please, I am so sorry I made a fool of myself last night. I wish wholeheartedly to give my apologies to Lord Trevelyan."

This headlong speech set Penelope momentarily aback, but she warmed to the topic instantly. With a mischievous smile she answered, "I am rather fond of the gargoyles myself, Miss Reardon. They really can be the friendliest of creatures, though they frighten the unwary intruder dreadfully."

Lady Reardon appeared nonplussed, but Dolly gave a giggle as she recognized the hidden meaning.

"Dreadfully I admit, but I will not be caught by surprise again. His lordship must think me a proper wigeon. I could not blame him if he never wished to see my face again, but I really must apologize for disturbing him so and offer my gratitude for his solicitude. Do you think he would permit it?"

"He receives few visitors, as you must understand, Miss Reardon. I will convey your messages to him, however." Turning to the dowager who appeared somewhat relieved that the conversation had taken a more sensible turn, Penelope added the mollifying touch. "Lady Reardon, you are to be commended for having such an understanding daughter. I do hope we can become better acquainted. I have met few people in London, and it would be lovely to have someone to converse with."

As they made arrangements to ride in the park, Guy appeared and insisted on being included in the party. Penelope reminded him that the outing must necessarily include Alexandra, but he did not seem deterred. Only when the butler announced the arrival of Lord Higdon and Mr. DeVere did his smiling countenance lose some of its brilliance.

He looked up sharply to Penelope. "DeVere? Is he usually a visitor here?"

Penelope gave a helpless shrug. "The name means nothing to me."

Lady Reardon finished buttoning her glove and gestured for her daughter to follow. Shaking Penelope's hand, she offered, "Mr. DeVere is the younger son of a baron. He has been abroad in the military, I believe. A well setup young man. You need not fear his acquaintance. Good day."

The gentlemen doffed their high-crowned hats as the ladies departed, then turned to enter the salon where Guy and Penelope remained standing. She remembered Lord Higdon as the gentleman of the high shirt collars from the night before, and she repressed a smile as she noted today's haberdashery included points that would make suitable blinders if they did not poke his eyes out first.

The unknown gentleman hesitated in the doorway, and her gaze was drawn to his refined air of intelligence and quietly elegant attire. While he was not handsome, his looks were striking in their darkness, and she felt the warmth of his regard with a certain amount of pleasure.

The stiffness of Guy's greeting was matched by the stranger's, however, and she reserved her welcome to a polite nod. Since Higdon seemed eager to further his acquaintance, Penelope took her seat and the newcomers did likewise. Guy remained hovering behind Penelope, resting his arm against her chair back, and she suspected, glowering at DeVere.

"Lady Reardon seems to believe you've been in the military, DeVere. Which regiment?" Guy did not believe in mincing words.

"Lady Reardon is mistaken." DeVere calmly accepted the cup of tea Penelope poured for him. "I am in the diplomatic corps. Now that negotiations for peace are under way, I have been given leave to visit my family briefly. I understand you made it through the war quite safely?"

If there were a sneer behind these words, Penelope could not detect it, but the tension between the two men was palpable and made her uneasy. Guy had seemed such an amiable gentleman; she did not understand his change in character.

Blessedly they only remained long enough for Higdon to offer his felicitations on the dinner and to determine whether Penelope intended to visit Almack's. They rose as another flurry of visitors arrived, and she had no chance to question Guy before he, too, was compelled to leave.

In all events, by that afternoon she found it a great relief to be in the company of a child again. With relish she informed Guy he would have to ride with Miss Reardon in the phaeton, since she intended to lead Alexandra's new pony. Guy seemed momentarily chagrined at being relegated to the position of entertaining a schoolroom miss while Penelope frolicked about the park lawns with Alexandra, but he overcame his dismay with great aplomb.

In fact, by the time he accompanied the Trevelyan ladies to their door, he seemed in a positive hurry to return to the waiting carriage and Miss Reardon.

Penelope laughed as he impatiently stepped inside, and she caught his hand as he reached to doff his hat. "No, sir, that is not necessary. We require no further attendance. You may return to Miss Reardon."

Guy grinned. "You are supposed to sulk that I would part from your company so easily, my lady. Someone needs to teach you the rules of the game. I shall be by this evening to commence your lessons."

"That will be amusing." Penelope laughed before sending him on his way. She turned back to the hall to dispose of her hat and gloves.

Trevelyan waited in the doorway of the salon. His expression revealed nothing of his opinion of this scene, but Penelope felt a sudden weakness in her knees as his gaze rested forbiddingly on her before he turned to greet his daughter. She could feel his disapproval, but since he said nothing, she could make no reply. She turned her attention to Alexandra who regarded her father warily.

"Give Harley your bonnet, Alexandra. I think Mrs. Henwood will excuse you this once if you don't change for tea. Why don't you go in and tell your papa how well we did in the park today?''

Graham's eyes briefly met hers over the child's head, but he could not ignore the sudden brightening of his daughter's small face, and he held out his ungloved left hand to escort Alexandra into the room. "We will let Penelope change out of her riding clothes while you tell me how many times she fell off her horse. I wager both of you spent more time picking daisies than on horseback.''

Penelope took a deep breath of relief at the sound of Alexandra's giggle and hastened to make herself presentable. Graham did not make a habit of sharing tea with them, but she hoped to make a change in that and many other things. He could not spend the rest of his life hiding in his rooms. For his own sake and Alexandra's, she would have to draw him out in public, gradually, of course.

By the time Penelope reappeared in a sprigged muslin with a scooped neckline to please her husband's tastes, father and daughter were conversing warily over tea and cakes. Alexandra was much too young to be in the drawing room, but Penelope had no intention of reprimanding either of them.

"I categorically deny everything she tells on me," she announced, sweeping into the room and taking her place beside the tea table. "And I see someone has already stolen my eclair."

Alexandra rolled off in a fit of giggles as her father hurriedly popped the last bite of the missing sweet into his mouth. Penelope sent him a severe look before brandishing the plate of finger sandwiches.

"You should be ashamed of yourself. How is Alexandra going to learn to eat properly if her father makes a glutton of himself?''

Graham meekly accepted one of the minuscule concoctions while Penelope set an assortment on his daughter's plate. He eyed the sandwich with misgiving before bringing it to his lips. When the entire treat disappeared in one bite, Alexandra went into gales of laughter again.

Penelope had to bite her lip to keep from joining in. "How long has it been since you've eaten, my lord?"

He drank his entire cup of tea while thinking about it. "Well, luncheon had already been cleared away when I came down, and I don't remember anybody carrying up dinner during the excitement last night, so I suppose—"

Penelope's cry of dismay produced a satisfied smirk on that corner of his mouth able to display such feelings.

"Oh, Graham, I never . . . ! Surely John brought something up. He cannot have been so forgetful as I."

Trevelyan gleefully helped himself to the next largest cake on the platter. "I assure you, my lady, the excitement quite drove the wits out of his head. Had I not been terrified of Cook, I would have ravaged the larder, but instead, I have endured quietly, unprotesting, until now."

Alexandra held her hands over her mouth to stifle the giggles threatening to erupt at her father's enormous bouncer. Terrified of Cook! That lofty personage quaked at so much as a sight of his formidable employer. Triumphantly she conquered her laughter to point out the obvious.

"There were plates and saucers and bread crumbs all over Papa's desk this morning. I heard the maids scolding John for it. Cook says Papa could eat a cow whole if he cooked it for him."

That sent both Penelope and Graham into whoops, and the impolite number of crumbs left after this particular tea brought no scolding from anyone. The sound of laughter poured like sunshine through the mansion's rambling rooms.

Graham entered Penelope's chamber that evening just as her maid was going out. Nervously she noted he had once more returned to the enigmatic stranger, but she gestured for her maid to close the door as she departed.

She clasped her hands in front of her as he glanced appraisingly at the pale green satin immersed tantalizingly beneath the fine white gauze of her sheathed skirt. Green ribbon accented the high waistline and puffed sleeves, but his gaze lingered longest on the expanse of fair skin revealed by the fashionable neckline. A dusting of freckles could barely be discerned above the ribboned drawstring, and Penelope flushed as he regarded them speculatively.

Sweeping up her elaborately fringed shawl, she wrapped it protectively around her shoulders. "Is the gown not to your liking?"

"On the contrary, I had not expected to like it so much. You had better pin the shawl securely or Guy will find it difficult to follow the performance on stage."

"I will stay home if you prefer. You were the one who suggested I become part of London society. I did not think I could refuse the countess's offer of her box this evening, and I know no one else to ask to accompany me. Should I cry off?"

She desperately wanted to see a professional theater performance, but not for a moment would she allow Graham to see her desire or disappointment. Her obligation to him was tremendous, and she felt as if she had returned very little of it. His wish, literally, was her command.

With a few more years of experience to draw on than she, Graham easily read the emotions Penelope meant to disguise. She was eager for this outing, and he had dashed her excitement with his disapproval. He had no right whatsoever to ask her to stay home, particularly since he had no intention of being home himself.

With a grimace he acceded to her plans. "You are free to do as you please, Penelope. I will not go back on my word. I just do not want to see you hurt. There are bound to be men of more stable character than Guy out there. The fault lies with me, I suppose. Had I kept in touch with my acquaintances, I might be in a better position to introduce you to suitable ones, though at the moment I can't think of who they would have been."

Penelope heard the wry twist of his words with interest. She knew so little of him. He had apparently moved in the upper echelons of society before his accident, and society seemed to remember him with kindness. Why had he deliberately turned his back on his friends at a time when he most needed them? His cynicism now made it seem as if he did not approve of his former acquaintances. Surely that did not apply to society as a whole?

"Graham, I would be perfectly content accompanying you to the theater. I do not need suitors. Indeed, I am quite content without them and have been so for many years. Perhaps I am not romantic. I have never once even developed a schoolgirl crush on anyone of my acquaintances. You have married a proper old maid."

"I have married an innocent country miss who knows nothing about love and romance." Graham leaned on his cane and his one golden eye sparkled as he observed his wife's embarrassed expression. "I'll taint your innocence with my opinions of love. You are entitled to try it for yourself before we compare notes."

"There are many kinds of love, my lord, I know that. So don't think me completely innocent. I just don't believe in the romantic kind. That's for fairy tales."

"And you think Shakespeare wrote fairy tales? You pretend you have a hard heart, my lady, but I think you have had no occasion for it to be touched. You are ripe for the plucking, my dear. Don't say I didn't warn you."

She laughed at him and went her way, but if she did not heed his words, Graham did. If he knew anything of the female persuasion at all—and he certainly was no stranger to the ladies—Penelope was vulnerable to the first eager suitor to whisper sweet words in her ear. Why should he stand by and let someone else break her heart? There must be ways he could do it much more gently himself. The idea had merit. He needed only time to reflect on it.

* * *

Gentlemen were not unusual in this particular gambling hell on the decidedly unfashionable East End, but the one sitting in the dimly lit corner with his petticoat choice of the evening did not appear at home here. Admittedly the piratical shock of disheveled black hair, narrowed eyes, and the fencing scar lining one cheek gave the impression of one well acquainted with these denizens. However, his obvious boredom with the buxom miss at his side and the manner in which he threw his cards down upon the table without interest showed a decided lack in the usual decadent behavior between these walls. One simply did not play solitaire when all the world's vices beckoned.

As another gentleman worked his way through the smoky maze of crowded tables and drunken occupants, the first man's interest seemed to heighten. With a flick of his wrist he sent the female at his side to capture the newcomer's attention. Within minutes the two men warily faced each other.

"Should I know you?" The newcomer haughtily flicked his gaze over the solitaire player with no attempt to conceal his dislike for the situation. Contrasted with the first man's piratical good looks, this one possessed the polished handsomeness of a courtier. Both men were dressed in the height of fashion—skin-tight pantaloons, cutaway coats, and neatly starched white linen—but the solitaire player carried off his attire with a casualness bordering on contempt, whereas the dark-complected man appeared stiff and formal.

"Not likely, but my cousin assures me you're the man to see. DeVere, is it not?"

Without admitting the correctness of the appellation, the other man asked, "And you?"

"Chadwell. You'll not have heard of me. I am Trevelyan's American cousin, on his mother's side, naturally." For a brief moment, narrowed eyes widened to a golden gleam and a particularly charming smile danced across his face. The lady at his side cooed and leaned over to kiss his aristocratically lean jaw, but

Chadwell merely brushed her aside and began flipping cards on the table with abrupt disinterest again.

DeVere didn't appear appreciative of this knowledge. "You don't sound like a savage. Why are you here?"

Chadwell shrugged. "My parents are English. Why should I talk like a savage? You want to hear my Yankee accent? I can do one very well if the occasion suits."

DeVere snorted. "So could Gray. And French, and Spanish, and Hindustani, I suppose, if he put his mind to it. The two of you are very alike, now that I notice it."

"Were very alike. Since a certain accident, he's no more than a helpless cripple, a maimed one at that. But, of course, you know nothing of that." His tone implied that DeVere knew a good deal more about that than either wished to admit, but he did not emphasize the point. "That's why I'm here. Gray tells me you are acquainted with a certain party referred to in my note." Chadwell did not look up from his card game.

"If I am correct in assuming your reference to a charioteer is the same one with whom I am acquainted," DeVere agreed coldly. "There are not many of us left. Is that your doing?"

"You flatter me. But the charioteer remains, as far as one can tell. So do you and a few others Gray does not hold responsible. From what I am told, you are far from an innocent man, but my interest is not in your particular vices. I want the charioteer. In turn I will give you the name of various parties who have an interest in seeing the peace treaty come to naught. They have hired an assassin, and I am compelled to report it as soon as I have proof, but you may do so in my stead in exchange for the information I want. Your superiors will be unable to deny your promotion again after that, will they?"

For the first time DeVere appeared interested. He studied his companion thoughtfully. In his day Graham Trevelyan had been a Corinthian of the first water. His American cousin lacked the requisite polish and manner. The coloring and scar were different, too. Height and size were difficult to determine, but he fancied Graham had been broader and more muscular. No man had been able to defeat the young viscount at fisticuffs at Gentleman Jackson's, and Gray's build had not limited his ability with the rapier and had certainly enhanced his reputation as a notorious whip. It seemed doubtful if Graham's American cousin could live up to these claims, but the cousin certainly had an aptitude of his own. Graham would never have been caught in such subterfuge as this one offered, and bargaining the lives of powerful political figures would have been beyond the viscount's pristine conscience. DeVere decided Chadwell might very well be a man after his own tastes.

"Am I allowed to inquire after your interest in the charioteer?"

"No." The one word, spoken sharply, ended that avenue of speculation. Chadwell looked up at DeVere with a challenge in his eyes.

"Very well." DeVere shrugged. "You have the right to get killed dabbling in other people's lives. The information you seek isn't at my fingertips, but I can locate him. Will you send me a note when you have your proof?"

"Of a certainty."

The two men did not shake hands in parting. DeVere worked his way back the way he had come, while Chadwell remained behind, shuffling his cards.

The blonde at his side clutched the width of his upper arm and whispered with concern, "I don't like 'im. Is it true what he said about yer gettin' killed?"

"We all have to die sometime, Nellie. Now show me where you saw those children. I might as well accomplish something constructive with this evening."

Not understanding his reply but knowing to whom he referred, Nellie hastened to oblige. She knew of no life beyond these streets for herself, but she had a soft spot in her heart for the children. Given half a chance, they might make out better than she had.

Occupied with his own thoughts, Chadwell missed the seductive smile she bestowed upon him.

Chapter 7

THE pounding at the door did not resemble Graham's abrupt knock, and Penelope wearily dragged herself from the depths of sleep to contemplate the gray dawn and the source of the noise. After the theater she had joined Guy and several other couples in a late supper, and she had arrived home shockingly late. She was not ready to wake.

The pounding continued, howbeit discreetly, and an anxious voice added to the commotion. "Oh, my lady, please wake up. Mrs. Henwood says you must come quick."

There was a whispered conference in which someone recommended going up to the attic and fetching my lady's personal maid and sending her into the viscountess's chamber, while the first voice expressed as much fear of doing that as disturbing the lady.

This foolish debate roused Penelope sufficiently from her slumber to realize some household emergency had taken place. Not wanting the noise to disturb Graham, she sat up and reached for her robe, then called for the maids to enter.

Alexandra's nursemaid bobbed a hasty curtsy and immediately launched into her woes. "It's Miss Alexandra, my lady. Mrs. Henwood says you must come. I told her I could not wake you and you being up and about all night, but she won't hear of nothing else but I come to fetch you."

Penelope hastily found her slippers and tightened the belt of her robe. "What is it, Peggy? What's wrong with Alexandra?"

"It's the fever she's got. Burning up, poor little

thing, and nothing will bring it down. She's crying for you, but she can't hardly talk, her throat's that swollen up.''

This speech had scarcely escaped the maid's tongue when her ladyship was racing down the hallway to the nursery.

By the time Graham had wakened and was apprised of the situation, a physician had come and gone leaving various instructions, liquids, and unguents that were being religiously administered by maids, governess, and her ladyship. Alexandra continued to moan and suffer the effects of fever, and a decided rash was breaking out all over her tiny pale face and chest.

At Graham's entrance Penelope glanced up with relief from where she sat beside the bed applying cold compresses.

''Oh, Graham, I didn't want them to waken and worry you, but I'm so glad you're here. Is there no other physician we can call upon? I know Dr. Broadbent is a very respected man, but his medicine does not seem to bring the fever down, and I'm at my wit's end to know what else to do. I was always taught to keep the room very warm and the patient covered until the fever broke and sweated out, but Dr. Broadbent says we must lay no fire and that she needs no other blanket. He says the rash is caused by the heat and will go away if we follow his instructions, but it seems peculiarly like the measles the children suffered last spring in the village, and no amount of unguent will make *them* go away until they're ready to. What should we do, Graham?''

The viscount ran his hand through silvered hair and stared in despair at the wan features of his usually lively daughter. He knew what it was to suffer illness and pain, and while he could stoically withstand it himself, he could not bear to watch it in his child.

Gripping Penelope's shoulder tightly, he gazed upon the face on the pillow and felt his insides twisting with helplessness. ''There is Dr. Headly back in Surrey. He is the one who tended me after the accident. He saved

with an inexplicable longing. This was the way it should have been from the very first. This was the way he had imagined it when he had first married. Alexandra's birth had rekindled his hopes. But the accident and the tragic events before and after had demolished any further pretense that he could have a normal life. And now it was too late.

He touched Penelope's shoulder, and she instantly came awake. She turned to check on Alexandra, then looked up to Graham's dimly illumined features. If only she could use magic to slide her fingers over his scarred face and restore it to health, he would be almost handsome, and she smiled at the thought of being married to the handsome prince transformed from a frog.

Her smile nearly devastated his reserve, but Graham calmly held out his hand. "Come, my sleeping beauty, you will do no one any good if you don't get your own rest. I will sit with her awhile."

"Oh, no, Graham, I could not keep you from your sleep. I am fine right here."

Her eyelids sagged sleepily as she spoke, and her voice had an unconsciously provocative note to it. Graham smiled at the seductive picture she created. "If you do not remove yourself at once, I will carry you out. You don't want that, do you?"

Penelope's eyelids flew wide open. "You wouldn't!" If she had been quite awake, she would have realized it would be impossible with his limp and injured hand, but in the dark he seemed fully capable of his command.

"I would," he replied sternly. "Now give me your hand and be off with you."

Reluctantly she released Alexandra and reached to wrap her fingers around his healthy left hand. His fingers were warm and strong around hers as he helped her rise, and she was surprised by his sudden proximity when she landed on her feet. She was not of small stature, but standing straight, Graham towered over her. The breadth of his shoulders filled her vision and she would have stepped back, but the chair pressed against her legs.

"Do you wish me to escort you back to your room?" he inquired softly.

Looking up into that one patched eye and one good eye, Penelope shook her head. "I can find my way. You will send for me if anything changes?"

"Be certain of it. I would panic without you to tell me what to do."

His smile was genuine, and Penelope resisted the urge to lean against his strong chest and seek the comfort of his protective arms. He offered friendship. She did not dare ask for more, no matter how close circumstances brought them.

Nodding, she took the candle and slipped away.

Within a few days the fever had broken and Alexandra was fretfully complaining of her confinement. But for Graham nothing was quite the same as before. Penelope had spent those days selflessly nursing his daughter from what he was certain could have been a fatal illness, and now he felt the tables had turned on him.

He had brought the little baroness to his home to act as a kind of superior governess for Alexandra and a companion and buffer against the world for himself. He had showered her generously with his wealth, offered her carte blanche for all else, and assumed he had fulfilled his obligations. These last days proved he owed her much, much more.

He knew Penelope thought no such thing. Her relief at Alexandra's convalescence was as great as his own, but that multiplied his obligation in Graham's eyes. He had offered her nothing but material things while she had given his daughter life and love. And not just Alexandra had benefited from her generous affection.

The viscount ruminated over these matters as he stared at the host of invitations that had accumulated over these last few days. The invitations were addressed primarily to both of them as a couple. That was what Penelope wanted and that was what she deserved, to be part of a loving couple. Graham wasn't certain how to go about that. He had dug himself into a proper hole from which there seemed no way out, and he was quite likely to be buried there if he continued as he had been. Besides that, it had been years since he had courted anyone in any guise. How in blazes would one go about courting one's own wife? Particularly if she was quite likely to be repulsed, if not out and out terrified by his attentions?

He could have the marriage annulled and let her go free to find her own partner in life, but he had no intention of doing so. She might be made a widow soon enough; there was little he could do in that case, but Alexandra had grown much too attached to free Penelope in any other way. No, somehow he would have to supply her with at least the attentions she deserved. Lasting affection was a dream that could only be hoped for in some hazy future of old age.

With only these vague ideas in mind, Graham sought out his wife in her chamber the next morning.

Much rested now that Alexandra seemed to be recovering nicely in the hands of her nurse, Penelope smiled up at her silent husband. "Have you some more wishes you would like to command of me my lord?" With a wave of her hand she dismissed her maid and rose from the dresser to greet Graham.

His countenance was so solemn as to be terrifying, but she was much less afraid of him now than she had been that first night. She had learned he was just as human as any man, more so, perhaps, because of his infirmity. She wished there were someway she could initiate the touching that was so much a part of her nature, but she had been schooled too well on the proprieties to break that taboo. They were no more man and wife than when first they met. They had never practiced the formality of polite conversation, but in all else they had observed the proprieties. She clasped her hands in front of her.

That missish gesture brought a grim half smile to Graham's face. "It is your wishes I wish to consult, my lady. You have not spent a minute out of this house in days. Is there anywhere in particular you would like to go?''

Penelope's eyes widened to violet saucers. "If I tell you, would you take me?''

"That is a presumptuous question. I'm sure Aesop had a fable that had something to do with looking gift horses in the mouth.''

Penelope attempted a demure expression. "Of course, my lord. I shall never look my mare in the mouth again. Would you take me to Drury Lane? I am sure Guy is quite bored with the performance, but there is an actor there who is so magnificent I feel as if I'm living in Shakespeare's time.''

Graham regarded her with a hint of amusement. "You have seen little or nothing of London since you came. Wouldn't you prefer to shop in St. James or visit Westminster Abbey or attend the opera or Vauxhall? Kean is said to be good, but how many times can you watch Macbeth?''

"A dozen, at the very least. Please, I have never seen the plays acted before. They take on so much more consequence in the flesh.'' She flushed as his eyebrow lifted slightly. "You know what I mean, so do not pretend otherwise. Or have you grown so cynical that you no longer marvel at the transformation of words into action?''

"It has been a long time since I've been to the theater and I am curious about this actor whose praises everybody sings. Drury Lane, it is. What night are you free, my lady?''

"Any night you choose.'' Face alive with expectation, she turned a steady gaze on him.

"Then we will make it tonight. I see no reason for delaying. Will that suit?''

"Yes, of course.'' Penelope continued to stare at him with hope and disbelief. "Are you certain? I do not want to ask more than you meant to give.''

With a very gentle touch Graham caressed her cheek with his gloved hand. "That is a very small fraction of what I would like to give you, my pretty Penny.''

At her shocked look he drew back and laughed. "Be ready on time or I shall leave without you."

He dragged himself out, leaving Penelope to stare at the closed door in his stead. Whatever had come over her charming ogre? To risk meeting the public eye to please her was a step she had not dared to pray for so soon, but to call her pet names and look at her as if she could possibly be . . . She almost thought "wife," but that was coming it too strong. Good friend? That did not seem right, either, but "lover" or "mistress" were out of the question.

She was placing entirely too much consequence on the gesture. She would just have to be careful to please her husband so he wouldn't regret his offer.

Chapter 8

DISDAINING ladylike grace, Penelope raced down the stairway to meet her husband at the assigned time that evening. For this special occasion she had actually consented to wearing the lilac silk, and Graham watched her approach with open admiration. He had never thought about the transformation of the vicar's prim country daughter into a butterfly of fashion, but she had succeeded beyond the realms of his imagination. Perhaps her open, honest features did not have the frail delicacy of the acclaimed beauties of the day, and the nondescript coloring of her brownish gold curls would not give poets something to write about, but she carried herself with a pride and grace that would do a duchess proud, and anything she wore would make men's heads turn.

Graham grinned at this thought. If the vicar's daughter had any notion of how very seductive she appeared in that clinging silk with only a bit of frippery to call a bodice, she would bury herself in shawls and cloaks. As it was, she seemed totally unconscious of her effect upon him, and violet eyes turned up to peruse him with merriment.

"Am I on time, my lord? You look very distinguished this evening." For an evening at the theater he had not bothered to deck himself out in silk breeches and stockings, but he had donned a formal velvet coat of midnight blue over silver-gray pantaloons that emphasized the well-formed muscularity of long legs.

Penelope blushed at the path of her thoughts, and she hastily reached to brush away an imaginary speck on his snow white cravat. To see him neatly garbed in waistcoat and frock coat with all buttons fastened and all ties tied did seem a trifle strange, and she sent him a nervous glance.

"How do I look? Do I pass inspection?" She gazed doubtfully at her simple silk and long gloves, then held out one satin shoe to be certain the ribbons were tied.

"You will hear enough flattery before this evening is over without hearing it from me. If you are not ashamed to be seen with me, I am certainly not going to complain of you. You are certain this is what you want?" Graham asked her quizzically.

"Of course." Without a hint of doubt Penelope gestured for the butler to bring her pelisse. The nights were chilly yet and the dress, very thin. By all rights she should have worn a tiny, form-fitting spencer to be fashionable, but she preferred the luxury of the pelisse Graham had bought for her. She snuggled into the fur-lined wrap and sent Graham a mischievous look as he donned a hooded cloak.

"You will look like a highwayman in that, you know. Have you sword and pistol?"

Graham gripped his walking stick with both hands and gazed at his irreverent young wife grimly. "Highwaymen are much admired by the inhabitants of Drury Lane, cripples are not. I have no desire to start a riot this night. I will thank you for a little respect."

Well accustomed to the evil appearance of his scarred face, Penelope had quite forgotten its effect on others. She knew he was adverse to showing it, but she had not realized how very painful it would be for him to make a spectacle of himself. She bowed her head in sober agreement.

"I forget others do not know you as I do. I am sorry, Graham. Are you certain you are willing to endure this?"

"Don't be a goose. If you do not mind, I can accept a few stares. Let us be off before we are caught in the crush of latecomers."

They arrived at the theater and the safety of Trevelyan's box without incident shortly before the curtain

went up. At the appearance of someone in those long
empty seats, a small murmur began to ripple through
the crowd, but Graham seated himself in the shadows
of the interior and no one could be certain of his identity before the lamps were dimmed.

Penelope threw herself into the spectacle of the play
and was totally oblivious to the opera glasses frequently trained in their direction. She turned to catch
excitedly at Graham's hand as Kean made his entrance, and she failed to relinquish it through the scene
that followed. Her husband watched her with more
amusement than the play, and he, too, paid little heed
to the stares from other seats.

Their idyll ended shortly after the curtain went down
to signal intermission. While Graham admitted Kean
had a certain presence but lacked the experience of a
performer such as Mrs. Siddons, their first visitor arrived.

The Earl of Larchmont appeared with his young
countess at his side, and while the lady threw a good-
humored wink in Penelope's direction, Graham
dragged himself to his feet to greet them.

"It is an honor, sir." He bowed politely if a trifle
cynically as the older man stared at his disfigurement.

"By gad, so you're not a ghost, after all! Thought
there might be some flummery going on what with you
being at death's door all these years and then suddenly
up and marrying a young chit, but you've got some
juice left in you yet. Welcome back, boy! I congratu-
late you on your wise choice of females." The lanky
earl turned to Penelope. "You look ravishing, my dear.
I collect it is your doing to bring the rapscallion out
of hiding."

While Penelope attempted to reply to the earl's blunt
remarks, Dolly and the dowager Lady Reardon appeared on the arm of Lord Reardon, the eldest son.
The viscount's one visible eyebrow rose distinctly, but
he made a polished bow and greeted them with cour-
tesy.

"Lord Trevelyan, I know Penelope promised to
make my apologies for me, but I did not feel that was

sufficient. Can you ever forgive my unspeakable rudeness?''

Penelope caught Graham's flinch as Lady Reardon gazed at him in horror, and the countess seemed to watch his immobilized features with horrified fascination. She came to stand beside him, slipping her hand through the circle of his arm as he leaned on his stick. "Dolly, I told you that you needn't worry. I only marry friendly gargoyles."

Graham bent his wife a skeptical look but amusement laced his reply. "On the other hand, I tend to marry horribly insolent creatures. We are well met, it seems."

By this time Guy had outraced the bevy of young gentlemen hastening toward this box. His warm gaze lingered appreciatively on Penelope before turning to salute the other ladies attendant, but his usual nonchalant air seemed to be slipping as he waited for an opportunity to intrude upon the conversation.

He glanced at Graham nervously as he spoke. "You could have found a less public place for your coming out. Half the *ton* are on their way up here. Did you have to introduce Penelope to all of society at once?"

This was all the warning they received as a stream of visitors began inundating the box, forcing out the first ones and forming a constantly moving line of staring strangers. Penelope clenched Graham's arm tightly as she began to realize most of these elegants had come to see a show as if Graham were one of the caged lions in the Tower. They stared at his mutilated face with horror, then turned to her with a solicitous sympathy that made her think of a barn cat sitting beside a mousehole. The gentlemen all but licked their lips as they bent over her hand, and she was grateful she wore gloves to keep them from slobbering.

By the time the curtains went up again, she was too exhausted from this performance to appreciate the professional one on the stage. She felt Graham's rigid tension at her side and knew his temper had kindled. She had been a fool to think this could be done with ease.

"I know how it ends, Graham," she whispered, touching his arm. "Let us go before the crush."

"We will sit here until the last bloody line," he retorted furiously.

Remembering the time he had tore into her home in a terrible rage, Penelope gulped back any further words and sat silently beside him until the play ended. Perhaps his temper would recede before they left.

She should have known he would not be so easily placated. She knew he had a wicked temper and a cynical wit and a penchant for getting his own way, but Graham had seldom been any less than kind and gentle to her. The man who left Drury Lane that evening had no resemblance to the man she knew.

He made no attempt to disguise his deformity as he left the box. In fact, Penelope could swear he went out of his way to emphasize it, scowling horribly at anyone who looked his way and pounding his walking stick obnoxiously through the hall. His leg seemed to drag worse than she had ever noticed it, and his entire right side sagged in a ludicrous transformation from his usual arrogantly athletic physique. With a viciousness she had not thought herself capable of, Penelope wanted to jerk the cane from his hand and send him toppling to the floor.

The few people to whom she had been introduced wisely changed their course at Trevelyan's scowl when they approached. Those she did not know but who apparently recognized Graham stopped in their tracks and stared when he cut them without a word. In all fairness they probably would have stared without his deliberate cut, but Penelope was in no humor to appreciate fairness.

In a far corner a saturnine countenance watched Graham's performance with inner delight. This was ideal! The invalid had come out of hiding, at last. For a while it had been enough to know the wealthy bastard had been struck down and nearly destroyed, but that was no longer enough. His vengeance had been better than expected that first time, but he knew of ways to make it complete now, ways that would have the dual purpose of destroying the viscount while advancing himself, not to mention giving him opportunity to indulge his own vices. For too many years he had lived in constant fear of being exposed, but with Graham so obviously maimed, he now knew he was safe. It would be delightful to let loose the reins again. With a smile on his face he watched the couple disappear out the door.

Unaware of this cynical observation, Penelope and Graham reached the street. There, Graham turned his terrible frown on an urchin begging for a penny, scaring the child into fleeing across the street between the prancing legs of horses and massive wheels of carriages. Furiously Penelope jerked her arm from his.

"You did that on purpose! You're beginning to enjoy the role of beast! There was no call whatsoever for your behaving like that. People cannot help being startled at the change in your appearance. What is it you expect of them?"

Graham continued walking down the street at a pace that would have left a well man breathless. Their carriage driver broke from the ranks of waiting vehicles to follow.

"I expect nothing of them. They all performed just as I knew they would. Anything less than perfection shocks their feeble wits. Why is it that you do not turn from me in horror, I wonder? Were you so desperate to be rescued from your stifling village that you would have married any monster that came along?"

Penelope gasped at the cruelty of this retort, but her better sense overcame her anger. He was hurt and striking out at the only target available. That gave him no excuse for cruelty, but understanding made it easier to take.

"I expect an apology for those words when you return to your senses. I was not brought up in the company of people who spend all their time and money on making themselves beautiful. The people I know are marred or made beautiful by their characters and actions. I am accustomed to seeing them as they are, not as they would like to be. It is not your scars I see, but your kindness. Until tonight, leastways.''

Her words reached through his rage to trigger shame at his ill-treatment of one who had never caused him harm, but his temper in no manner abated. With a signal to his carriage driver to stop, he gave Penelope his hand to help her in.

''You need not endure my evil temper, my dear. I will walk it off. Albert will take you home.''

Penelope balked at being sent away like an unwanted child. She turned and glared up at him.

''I'll not have you stalking the streets, scaring the populace while I ride home in comfort. Let us walk the streets together.''

Since she wore a skirt much too small for the kind of country walking she had grown up with, and her satin slippers would be torn to shreds on the bricks and cobblestones, Graham surmised she would not last ten minutes. Instead of arguing, he shrugged, muttered, ''Very well,'' and strode off.

Ten minutes later she was still beside him, matching him stride for angry stride. Or two strides to his one. The limitations of her clothing hobbled her as much as his affected limp, and they made a rare sight pattering beneath the gas lamps in a breathless attempt to outwalk each other.

His temper could not withstand the humor, and Graham finally called a halt to the foolish charade when his cane caught in a hole and Penelope stubbed her toe on a raised brick. Forcing back a grin, he signaled for the patient coachman once again.

''There is no point in both of us being crippled. Let us call it a night, my lady.''

''You will not growl and take my head off before we reach home?'' she asked warily, taking his hand and gratefully stepping into the carriage.

He swung up beside her, his great size filling the remaining seat cushion and enforcing their proximity. He leaned against his cane and looked down at her as the footman closed the door. ''No, your head is exactly where it should be, my pretty one. Don't ever lose it.''

Penelope smiled up at him in relief. ''I shall take great care not to misplace it then.'' Her expression turned serious as she regarded the tired lines of his face in the lamplight. ''I'll not ask you to take me out again. I did not mean to cause you pain.''

''On the contrary, we will accept the Larchmonts invitation to their ball next week. Your acquaintances are sadly lacking and I mean to rectify the situation, at once. Send for Madame and have the proper gown made up.''

He seemed so restored to humor she did not have the heart to argue. She had a wardrobe full of gowns she had yet to wear. She would hold her own on that point. This reckless extravagance on clothes had to end somewhere.

Penelope tried to concentrate on these thoughts instead of the awareness of her husband's closeness in the dark carriage. She seldom had the occasion to be this near to a man, and the event shook her a little. Graham had been in all things proper, and as her husband, he had every right to occupy this seat with her. She should not reflect so on his almost frightening masculinity as he relaxed beside her. Perhaps she was overtired and overwrought. Graham had held her hand many times before. She should place no significance in it.

But she could not help but feel the shiver up her spine when for the first time he kissed her hand before retiring. It did not signify. She had seen other men do it out of gallantry. But when the chamber door closed, she touched the place where his lips had rested with wistfulness, and she slept with that hand beneath her cheek.

my life, but he is very old and does not get out much anymore. Perhaps if I send a carriage . . .''

Penelope felt his fingers tremble and she covered them with her own, glancing up to his ruined face. She could not help but feel his pain, and she tried to draw it from him. "Let us wait until tomorrow. I would not risk the doctor's health because of my own uncertainties. The children I have nursed have never been my own. The responsibility frightens me. I'm sure she will be fine in a day or so.''

Trevelyan wanted to take her in his arms and reassure her and be reassured in return, but she might find such an action more fearsome than comforting, and he refrained. That she thought of Alexandra as her own daughter provided all the reassurance he was entitled to, and gratefully he squeezed her hand.

"I will trust your judgment, Penelope. Dr. Broadbent treats mostly the elderly. It may have been years since he's seen a case of measles. Are measles serious?''

"They can be, but at least I know how to treat them. Do you really think he could be wrong?'' Penelope scanned his face hopefully.

"I should think he is very likely wrong,'' Graham announced firmly, praying he was right. In relying on Penelope's judgment, he was relying on his own instincts. They could both very likely be wrong.

His response seemed to return Penelope's confidence, however, and when he left, she was ordering up a fire and calling for blankets.

Graham wandered in and out like a lost soul for the remainder of the day. At times Alexandra looked up at him and smiled and his heart did cartwheels in his chest. Other times she slept, and her ragged breathing tore at his insides. Whenever he appeared, Penelope was there, and her assurances relieved his mind more than anything or anyone else could do.

Toward midnight he returned to find Penelope curled up and asleep in the chair beside Alexandra's bed. The little girl's hand was wrapped trustingly in his wife's palm upon the covers, and Graham gazed upon them

Chapter 9

GUY danced Dolly over to the draped grand entrance of the Reardon ballroom and raised a quizzical eyebrow at Penelope waiting there. "Have you grown tired of dancing so soon? Shall I introduce you to the cardplayers in the salon?"

Dolly appeared breathtakingly lovely this night, and Penelope smiled at the picture these two made, the petite strawberry blonde and the slightly rakish, handsome soldier. Neither of them appeared as yet aware that they naturally gravitated toward each other in any room they entered. With over a decade's difference in their ages and experiences, that was natural, but given time—She chose not to speculate further.

"I am sorry, Guy, but I cannot help worrying about Alexandra. I know she in all probability is sound asleep, but I am so fearful she will wake and be fretful that I cannot enjoy myself. I have a driver and a footman to look after me. You needn't leave on my account."

"Oh, Penelope, you cannot leave alone! Remember that poor girl last night! Let me call one of my brothers to go with you. I would be afraid to go out at night without an armed escort."

Penelope laughed at this foolishness. "That poor girl, as you style her, was out wandering the street where she had no right to be. I cannot imagine why anyone would be so foolish as to be out in the street alone in jewels and silk. I have no intention of being bludgeoned to death. I will be quite safe with John and Albert and the carriage."

"No matter. I will go with you," Guy said firmly.

"Miss Reardon, if you will excuse me, I'll send for this foolish lady's carriage." He bowed and walked off despite Penelope's protests.

"He is quite right, so don't argue." Dolly caught her friend's arm with a rush of excitement. "Did I tell you? We received a letter from my brother Arthur today. We have thought him dead all these months, but he writes he has been injured and in a hospital. His handwriting is still very poor and the letter, brief, but I am sure we will hear the whole story when he returns. Isn't it the most wondrous thing?"

"Lady Reardon mentioned it when we arrived. I am so happy for you. Did the letter say when he would return?"

Dolly frowned. "No. I expect it depends on his injuries. But Henry is making inquiries now that we know where he is. It has been years since we've seen him. You must tell Lord Trevelyan. They were great friends once."

"Then you should be the one to pass on the happy news. Come tomorrow for tea. He should be there then."

"Not tomorrow. We will be shopping for the Larchmont ball. The next day?" Dolly inquired eagerly.

They set the date, and Penelope dutifully went off with her escort for the evening. Guy made an attentive companion, and she enjoyed his easy conversation as the carriage rolled through silent streets, but her mind was elsewhere. She had not seen Graham since the debacle at the theater the night before, and she was just as worried about him as she was about Alexandra.

Her silence did not go unnoticed, and Guy made a wry smile as she failed to answer a repeated question. "Penelope? If I am disturbing your thoughts, I will be quiet."

Startled, she returned to the conversation. "I'm sorry, Guy, I'm just tired and not very good company. You should have stayed with Dolly."

"Fustian. She has so many admirers she won't miss an old man like me. What is it, Penelope? You are worrying about something."

"No, nothing, really. It's just . . ." She threw up her hands, unable to explain.

"It's Trev, isn't it? I could tell he was building up to a fury last night, but I didn't know how to stop it. Why ever did he choose to make such a public debut? There should have been an easier way."

"It's my fault. I wanted to see Macbeth again, and he offered to take me. I really didn't think about it causing such a spectacle. The theater is dark and crowded and why should anyone notice who was there? I never meant to cause him such pain."

Guy patted her hand as the carriage pulled up in front of the house. "Trev knew what he was doing even if you didn't. It's rather like learning to swim. You have to dive in headfirst and then strike out. You can't learn by dabbling your toes in the water."

Penelope shook her head. "Perhaps, but then why would he not accompany me tonight? I wish I understood him better."

"Trev has never been readily understandable. In his youth he had wealth and title, good looks, and more talents than any one man deserved. He could have had all the women swooning at his feet and the men emulating his every action. Instead, he would disappear for months at a time playacting or shipbuilding or the devil knows what. He spent more time at his country estate than he ever spent in London, yet he knew everybody and everything that went on. I don't mind telling you he was as generous with his vices as he was with his time and money. Trev never half did *anything*. You can't possibly expect to understand a man like that."

Penelope desperately wanted to know more, but she had no right to pry, and Guy had given her enough to think on for some time to come. As the butler let them in the front door, she pressed his hand with gratitude. "Thank you, Guy. I feel less of a goose now."

Guy grinned. "Lady Trevelyan, there is nothing of the goose about you. It's that dratted gander of yours that's the problem. Threaten him with the sauce and see if he comes up to snuff."

That mixture of metaphors made Penelope wince, and she sent him off with a laugh. Leaving the butler to lock up, she hurried up both flights of stairs to check on Alexandra. Finding all well in the nursery, she returned to the floor of the master suite. With a little leap of her heart she noted a light in the library, and she hurried toward it. Perhaps Graham had waited up for her.

Gently opening the door, she gave a gasp of surprise at the sight of a dark head bent over a book in Graham's favorite chair. She had not meant to intrude upon a stranger, but as he looked up at her entrance, she had no choice but to greet him.

He was silhouetted against the firelight, and she could distinguish little of his features as he turned toward her. His long dark hair fell in disheveled curls upon a wide forehead, and the candlelight threw shadows over a long line scarring his cheek. She could not quite see the scar's beginning or end, but it gave the ruggedly handsome face a look of distinction it might not otherwise have possessed.

As he stood, she noticed he wore his clothes as carelessly as Graham. Although he still had his coat on, his cravat hung loose and he had apparently discarded his formal shirt collar. Penelope could tell by the flicker of the firelight that his waistcoat was unbuttoned, also. Despite his casualness, his clothes reflected a quiet elegance that spoke of wealth and good taste.

She felt only curiosity as she approached him. "I didn't mean to intrude. I saw the light and thought my husband might be up. He did not warn me to expect a guest."

The stranger closed his book and came around the table, his gaze sweeping appreciatively over his hostess. "I hope I did not startle you. Lady Trevelyan, is it not? Trev retired for the evening, but he warned me to expect you. I am Clifton Chadwell, a cousin of Graham's."

"Very pleased to meet you, Mr. Chadwell. Will you

be staying with us for a while? I hope the maids have made up your room to your satisfaction.''

Chadwell bowed politely over her hand but did not relinquish it immediately. His gaze seemed to study her with interest. "I have become accustomed to Graham's bachelor existence and have made myself at home. He is generous enough to give me full run of his house when I am in the city. I hope my odd coming and goings will not disturb your routine?''

"No, of course not. You must behave as if nothing has changed. I have tried not to disrupt Graham's habits too greatly. Are you comfortable, then?''

"I would be much more comfortable should you stay a while. Do you play chess, Lady Trevelyan? Trev's early hours make him a most useless companion.''

A trick of the firelight or candlelight caught the gleam of Chadwell's eyes briefly, and Penelope felt mesmerized by their piercing intensity. Shaken by the impact of his stare and his touch, she backed away.

"I have not played in a while. Perhaps some other time. It is quite late . . .'' She didn't know how to make her escape. She felt as if some powerful magnet held her in place, and she could only stare helplessly into his eyes and wait for release.

"Tomorrow, then,'' his deep voice urged. "Trev says you have not yet seen the city. I have the use of his carriage. Why don't we see the sights tomorrow after luncheon?''

"I could not. I mean, I visit with Alexandra in the afternoons, and Graham expects me at tea. I do not know if there is time . . .''

"We will start early and be back in plenty of time for Alexandra and tea. I am certain Graham will have no objection.'' Chadwell continued holding her hand as he gazed down upon her.

"No, of course not,'' she answered distractedly. How could Graham object? He had all but thrown her into the arms of society in hopes she would find a lover to keep her occupied. He certainly couldn't object if she entertained his own cousin. She was the one petrified at the thought, and she didn't know why.

Taking this for agreement, Chadwell lifted her hand and brushed his lips across her knuckles. "Till to-morrow, then."

Penelope curled her fingers into her palm and with the briefest of farewells, fled the room. She had never felt such an entire goose in her life. Trevelyan had not terrified her so much when he had appeared from the fog. In these last few days she had met lords and ladies and sophisticated gentlemen by the score, but other than nervousness, she had never felt like a schoolroom miss in their presence. Why, then, did this man shatter her composure so easily?

As she entered her chambers, she glanced at the closed door to Graham's room. If only she could talk with him, but she did not dare encroach upon his privacy. Part of their agreement was that she not interfere with his habits. She was being foolish. There could be nothing wrong in entertaining his cousin.

If only Clifton Chadwell didn't have eyes that seemed to see right into her heart.

It wasn't just his eyes, Penelope realized the next day, much too late to do anything about it. Clifton Chadwell's touch turned her into jelly, his wit deci-mated her defenses, and his smile melted any protests she could raise.

Not that she didn't try to keep him at a distance. She made him take the barouche and sit on the oppo-site seat while he pointed out White Hall and the Tower and the various offices of notables. When he insisted that they descend from the carriage to view the lions and to inspect Westminster, she very properly touched only a gloved hand to the arm of his coat. But by the time they had indulged in lemon ices, decorated them-selves in pinks from a flower girl, and ruined their gloves with the sticky juices of fresh strawberries in the fruit market, propriety had fled.

Giggling as Chadwell mourned the demise of his stained glove and decorated it with flowers from his lapel in a funeral arrangement, Penelope chanted a psalm over the glove's grave—an overgrown jardiniere on the steps of an imposing edifice—and added her own flowers to the corpse. Then, gloveless and laughing, they returned to the carriage where their myriad purchases of the day reposed on the far seat, necessitating that they sit together.

Not until he had dropped her off at home and drove off on business of his own did Penelope reflect on the scandalousness of her behavior. Had anyone seen them, they would have become subject of rumor for half the gossips in town. Graham would never forgive her.

Worrying at her stained gloves, she hurried upstairs to change before visiting Alexandra. She would simply have to avoid Clifton Chadwell from now on. He was not the kind of gentleman she should be seen with. In fact, she greatly suspected he was a rake.

Alexandra bounced in bed as Penelope hurried in to hug her. "I want to go riding. When can we go riding? I am all better now. Please, Penelope, *please*."

"You must rest until the spots are all gone. Just think of this as a holiday from your lessons and a chance to lie about and have everyone play with you. You'll be up and about in no time."

Alexandra pouted at this news, but she delved eagerly into the games Penelope taught her and finally fell asleep while being read a fairy tale. Penelope kissed her forehead and slipped away, eager to see if Graham would come down for tea.

She smiled happily as she entered the small salon to find Graham waiting for her. His hair stood out about his forehead, and she had the urge to trim it properly, but otherwise he looked magnificent standing there in a frock coat cut away at the waist to reveal his trim figure, his shoulders straining at the tailored seams as he rose to greet her. Except for his injuries, he compared quite favorably with his rakehell cousin. In fact, she preferred Graham's quiet kindness.

He seemed surprised at her welcome, but he took her hand to assist her to the chair beside the tea tray. "I take it you have left Alexandra in good health and spirits."

"And sound asleep. I shall have to allow her to be

out of bed for short periods soon. She is quite likely to drive Mrs. Henwood and the nursemaids into quitting if she is confined much longer.''

"That would make her happy. Then she would be with you all day long. Perhaps you had better let her out of bed. You are much too valuable to spend all of your time closeted in the nursery.''

"On the contrary," Penelope objected, "that is my idea of heaven, surrounded by children. I should have taken up the profession of nursery maid.''

Graham regarded her with curiosity. "You would make a most extraordinary nursery maid. The children would love you but I suspect you would terrify the parents. You exert a little too much authority for a maid.''

"Oh, dear, that does not sound very ladylike. Am I a terrible ogre?" Penelope handed him the delicate Stoke porcelain teacup and wondered at the direction of this conversation.

"Ogress, wouldn't it be? I believe I am the ogre in this family. You are just as you should be. I don't think I have told you how much I appreciate the way you have taken over the ordering of this household. I did not realize how out of hand things had become until you put it back in order again.''

Amazement crossed her face at this unexpected compliment. "I thank you for your kind words, but I have done little enough in exchange for all you have given me. Is this leading up to something?''

Graham settled comfortably into his chair and sipped from the painfully small cup while eyeing his wife with pleasure. She behaved with regal composure in company, but he knew the playful humor lurking beneath that stately grace. He had never suspected such a rare combination when he had asked her to marry him. He had only known that children loved and respected her and that had been enough. Now he knew there were facets to her that he could spend a lifetime exploring and he didn't know where or how to begin. He feared that she would despise him should she learn all the truths about him, but he was willing to risk all for just a chance at winning her favor. All he had to do was decide on how to go about it.

"Not a thing, my dear. I just didn't want you to think you are unappreciated. I hear you've met Cliff. What do you think of him?" He maintained his appearance of disinterest as Penelope's cup clattered and she set it aside to pass the cakes.

"Your cousin rather startled me last night. Does he stay with us long?"

"What? Are you ready to be rid of him already? Has he behaved disagreeably?"

"No, or course not, but he is very . . . How should I say it? Sure of himself?"

Graham spluttered in his tea at this innocuous description. "Arrogant? Quite possibly. But I thought the two of you might amuse yourselves for a while. He doesn't visit often, and as an American, he hasn't been introduced to society and has little interest in cultivating such an introduction. As a matter of fact, he is better known in a society I would prefer you did not know."

Penelope grimaced slightly. "He is much in the petticoat line, I imagine. Well, it is not to be helped. I daresay you did not behave much better in your youth."

Graham had to call upon all his talents to choke back a roar of laughter. He had set himself up for that one. In his youth! What a delightful innocent he had managed to shackle himself to. He must have had maggots in his head when he thought he could carry this off.

"Nor in my dotage, either," he managed to mutter through a mouthful of crumbs.

Penelope sent him a sharp look but did not expound upon this comment. "Do you wish me to provide some entertainment for him? I could put together a card party, perhaps. A small dinner or two. I don't think I am adept enough to manage more than that yet."

Controlling his laughter, Graham answered solemnly, "Cliff provides his own entertainment. Pray, do not try to introduce him to what few friends I have left. He is not about much, in any case. Have you ordered your gown for the Larchmont ball?''

This change of topic caught Penelope off guard, and she had to stop and rearrange her thoughts before replying. ''There is the gold sarcenet I have not yet worn. It should be quite suitable. Are you certain you still wish to go?''

''Of course. I would not miss terrorizing the entire *haut ton* all at once. The occasion is much too rare to miss, unless you object?'' He raised a quizzical brow.

''Oh, no, I have ever wanted to terrorize all of London. By all means. Perhaps I should order a new gown,'' she answered faintly, while Graham chuckled.

His sense of humor would almost certainly be the death of her.

Chapter 10

THE dark closed in thickly in these narrow streets of tottering buildings that leaned to block out the light of the stars above. Cloaked from head to toe in heavy black broadcloth that blended with the darkness but did not disguise the fact that his athletic build and proud carriage did not belong in these slums of the East End, Chadwell listened to Nellie with patience. When she finished her tale, he shook his head in sympathy.

"Still, I cannot see what I can do. Between looking for these scoundrels and rescuing your brats, I have my hands full. Bow Street is where you need to go with your tale. The lady who was murdered was not of my acquaintance. I cannot know who her gentlemen friends might be."

Nellie gave him an exasperated look. Though she was in her mid-twenties and had been on these streets since a child, she retained much of her plump, blond good looks. She had enough intelligence to avoid gin and brothels and men with fancy promises and sufficient beauty to attract the likes of Chadwell, so she fared well. It was only when she opened her mouth that the gutter betrayed her.

She spoke in a harsh, nasal whine that no amount of beauty could disguise. "Ye've only to make *enqueeries*, Cliff. No Bow Street pimp knows whose to arsk oncet they get past St. James. She was a *friend*, Cliff, even iv she warn't no better than she should be. There's plenty of them what comes down to use them rooms. It ain't right that murderin' rogue walkin' about wi'out nobody doin' nothin'."

Cliff winced but nodded his head in vague agreement. She didn't understand he had little or no contact with the people she wanted interrogated, but he could keep his ears open. She had served him well enough these past years. It was little enough to do for her.

"I'll see what I can do, Nell, but don't expect too much. My time is not my own, anymore."

Nellie's grin grew broad enough to expose her missing back tooth, the one other flaw in her beauty. "Aye, and I've seen the miss. Yer won't be comin' to see me with the likes of that one around. Done yerself pretty, ain't ye?" Since this description of Penelope only produced silence, she changed the subject. "And 'ow's my Jack doin'? You seen 'im?"

This was a topic he could expound upon, and Chadwell nodded. "He's flourishing, Nell, you needn't worry. I was in Hampshire a month ago. The family he's with is quite proud of him."

Knowing him well, Nellie frowned. "Which of the little buggers up and run away?" There was no other way the guv'nor would have left the city.

"It's to be expected, Nell. Country life doesn't suit everyone. I can only find them homes and hope for the best. It's the younger ones that stand the best chance."

"Pippin, I wager. 'E's a right one, 'e is." She shrugged off the subject. "Whatcher gonna do 'bout that letter from your fancy gennulman? Want I should carry a message back?"

Chadwell tapped the letter in his pocket and shook his head. "He's playing with a marked deck, Nellie. We'll let the gentleman wait awhile. Thanks for holding it. I'll send word when I need you again."

Nellie made a rude noise and watched as Chadwell blended into the darkness and disappeared down the narrow street. He was one of the good sort, but the money he paid her wasn't for the services she usually rendered. 'Twas a pity. He was a rare, fine-looking gentleman, and she wouldn't mind knowing what he was like under the sheets.

When Penelope returned from the evening at Almack's, she glanced warily toward the library after checking on Alexandra. Alexandra was fine, and the library lamp was off, and she breathed a sigh of relief. It would be much simpler dealing with the arrogant American in the daytime when she had all her wits about her.

She had told her maid not to wait up for her, so the lamp burning in her chamber was a pleasant surprise—until she pushed the door open to discover she was no longer alone.

"You! What are you doing here? This is infamous! Take your leave at once, sir." Penelope stepped aside and pointed to the doorway she had just entered.

Chadwell rose from the chair he had appropriated, but made no attempt to do as told. He bowed politely and resting one large hand on the back of the chair, gave her simple ivory cambric an appreciative look.

"I will have to admit, the simple style suits you as well as the extravagant. The ladies of Almack's should heartily approve."

Penelope clenched her fan in her fist and tried not to succumb to his powerful charm. Gritting her teeth, she ignored his flattery and demanded again, "What are you doing in here?"

He smiled placatingly. "If I had waited in the library, would you have come in there?" The question didn't need an answer. They both knew she would avoid him. "This way, the presumption is all mine, and you can continue to believe you behaved properly. You said you play chess. Couldn't you indulge me in one game?"

"In here!" Equal parts confused and horrified, Penelope sought some sensibility in the situation. She enjoyed Chadwell's company much too much. She would willingly play him chess or jackstraws without preference had they been in the parlor surrounded by people. In her bedchamber, alone, was beyond her capability.

"What could be more innocent?" was his astonishing reply. "Graham is not a jealous man, but even the most demanding of husbands would not imagine I could seduce you a few steps from where he sleeps. I will open the connecting door if you prefer. What better chaperon would you have? I thought you would be pleased with my circumspection.''

She had never heard anything more preposterous in all her life, but he said it with such a boyish charm she could not remain angry. He had discarded his coat and loosened his neck cloth and made himself comfortable just as Graham had done when he courted her, and the resemblance made her smile. ''You are not only arrogant, but incorrigible. Bring your chessboard to the parlor after brunch, and I will play with you. That is the best I can offer.''

''That will not do. Shall I wake Graham and insist that he sit up to chaperon us? I will, you know.'' When she began to look defiant, Chadwell backed down a smidgen. ''All right, chess in the parlor tomorrow, but surely a quick game of backgammon tonight would not be harmful? Just one game and I will go away peaceably.''

She knew better than to agree. It was quite insane even to contemplate it. No man had ever affected her in this way, and she did not like the curious loss of control she suffered in his presence. He came in and took over and she willingly submitted to his every suggestion. No wonder she felt a perfect goose after he left. But while he was here, she felt admired and needed and the center of attention. No one had ever treated her like that before, and she found it a hard combination to resist.

''One game? Promise?'' She continued to cling to the wall as she rashly accepted this compromise.

''Promise.'' Chadwell opened the drawer of the game table as if completely at home here and began removing the pieces while Penelope ventured farther into her room.

When she had crossed just half the distance and seemed reluctant to continue, Chadwell came forward and took her elbow. The heat of his hand against her bare flesh startled her, but before she could pull away, he firmly guided her toward the chair he had arranged on the other side of the table.

There seemed nothing to do but oblige. He leaned against the back of the chair as he arranged the pieces for her, and the intimacy of this gesture took her breath away. He seemed so sure of himself, so confident of his place that she could not seem to raise the voice to object. In fact, the sensation was so pleasant, she could almost wish it to continue.

Almost casually his hand brushed against the wisps of hair at her nape as he straightened to take his seat. Penelope did not dare look up as he settled his virile frame into the chair across from her. Just the sight of his loosened neck cloth dangling between the edges of his opened waistcoat made her too aware of his masculinity. She could not bear to meet his eyes.

Of course, by the end of the game he had charmed her into laughing with him, and she felt no fear as he trounced her soundly then stood up obediently to leave as promised. She took his hand willingly enough to stand before him to wish him good evening. It was only when she looked up into the molten gold of his eyes that she knew her mistake.

He did not give her time to think, no less to run. His hand circled her head to support her as he swooped down to take what she had not promised. He held her firmly, without pressure, as his lips moved persuasively across hers.

The shock of his touch held Penelope paralyzed. Her hands came up between them to push him away, but the promise of his kiss put an end to that initiative. With wonder she felt his subtle assault, and her heart increased its pace until she felt certain it would leap from her chest. Too terrified to return the kiss, she did not resist it, either.

Chadwell apparently took the latter as permission to continue, and his kiss deepened, teasing at her lips and drawing her into his need as a whirlpool drowns its victims. The hand at the back of her head tightened, and his other hand went to her waist, pulling her closer with a gentleness meant to reassure.

Penelope felt herself weakening, giving into the strange sensations inundating her body as she rested in this man's arms. She bent easily into his embrace and her hand rested against his solid chest without protest while his lips plundered hers and hers began to respond. Only when he became too confident and tightened his grip did she panic and push away.

Too embarrassed even to face him, she turned away and hid her face in her hands. "Go away. Just go away. And don't come back."

Chadwell touched the porcelain smoothness of her bare shoulder with a sadness she could not see. "I won't be able to keep away. Goodnight, my lady."

Why did he have to make even the title sound like an intimate caress? Penelope swung around to give him a scold, but the door was already closing behind him. With a sob she threw herself face first across the bed.

By the night of the Larchmont ball Penelope's normal composure had suffered a severe setback. She saw little of Graham, and by the time Dolly appeared for tea, she had forgotten the news about her brother. She forgot Dolly's disappointment when Graham did not appear. Even Alexandra complained of her lack of concentration when she beat Penelope several games in a row at jackstraws. And it was all because of Clifton Chadwell.

He behaved with perfect propriety when he appeared in the parlor for their afternoon game of chess. The fact that maids scurried in and out would have dampened the attentions of the most amorous of men. But though Penelope could not complain of his behavior, she cursed his thoughts. Every time she looked up at him, she felt the quiet warmth of his gaze, and it shattered her thought processes. Surely he could not believe she meant anything by a single kiss? But the possessiveness of his touch as he took her hand at game's end spoke differently.

She ordered her maid to stay up for her that night, but Chadwell lay in wait in the front room when Penelope let herself in. No footman lingered in the halls as he caught her hand and drew her into the shadowed darkness of the ornate salon.

He offered no word of apology or explanation but wrapped her into his arms and continued where he had left off the prior night as if to satisfy his disbelief. The same magic touched them, dropping a velvet mantle over their shoulders to protect them from the prying eyes of the rest of the world. It was as if time and place disappeared and the only reality was this touch of their lips and hands.

Shaken to the core by the intensity of her response, Penelope turned away first. There was no point in even arguing. Picking up her skirts, she fled before he could see the tears welling up in her eyes. She did not know what Chadwell was doing to her, but she knew enough to avoid it with all her might.

She did not see Chadwell the day of the ball, and it was with relief that she greeted her husband's stolid appearance in her chamber that evening. Wickedly he wore an eye patch of the same dark blue of his swallow-tailed coat, and Penelope summoned a brave grin at the sight of his scarred face.

"The Beau approved your sartorial choice then?" she inquired mildly, lightly touching her fingers to the drawn cheek just below the patch.

Graham moved his head away from her touch, and she carefully removed her hand, cursing her foolishness. It was another man's face she wished to caress. If Clifton hadn't so thoroughly destroyed her wits, she would have kept the careful distance Graham had established between them.

"I decided my wife's taste took precedence. Will all the ladies admire it?" he asked with a casualness that belied the brief tension springing up between them.

"Not if you scowl at them. Your problem is that you look much too strong to be a helpless invalid they could pet and make over. Can't you contrive to look pathetic?" she asked dryly.

Graham roared his approval of this jibe and continued chuckling as he inspected the daring gold gossamer of Penelope's gown. "I fear I shall look quite pathetic by evening's end when I am left standing all alone in the corner while you are being whirled about the floor by every eager young blade in the house. That gown should distract every eye in the room."

"It ought, considering what you paid for it," Penelope replied brashly. "It was your eye I hoped to distract, however. I thought if I could hold your attention, you would not be so inclined to terrorize the guests. I do owe the countess the same consideration she has shown me."

"Which is why I have agreed to attend her ball. Lady Larchmont will be thoroughly delighted if I terrorize her guests. It will make her the talk of the town. She quite considers herself a lioness of society, and I must admit she is a good deal more dashing than those harpies Jersey and Lieven. Matilda will certainly not serve us stale cake and watery lemonade."

Penelope relaxed as she realized he viewed the evening's chore with humor. She had feared he had agreed to go out of some misguided sense of obligation, but he seemed quite eager to meet the public again. Perhaps he grew bored of his own company and was ready to shed his isolated state.

The sensation they caused as the butler announced their arrival to a room already filled with glittering pillars of society was enough to decimate what remained of Penelope's composure. All eyes turned to stare as they descended the stairway into the ballroom. As those close enough to hear the announcement turned to whisper to those behind them, the cacophony of multitudinous voices plummeted to a wave of murmuring quiet. Penelope clung to Graham's arm as they stepped down into virtual silence.

The shocked stares were worse than the silence as heads craned to see the twisted wreck of the once handsome viscount. Blessedly Guy Hamilton hurried forward to distract them with his welcome, and Dolly Reardon did not linger long at her mother's side, but ran after him.

The countess had remained behind to greet late arriving guests, but at the ominous lack of sound from her ballroom, she coaxed her bemused husband into escorting her to join the company. The elderly earl detested dancing and gossiping and was eager to begin the card games in the anteroom, but he obligingly led his wife to the crowded dance floor. He was quite fond of Viscount Trevelyan, and though he hadn't quite made the association between the maimed man and the handsome young lord, he was quite prepared to follow his wife's orders on the matter.

"Graham, you and your lovely wife are sensational!" The countess sailed up to the quartet of young people and wrapped her fingers around Graham's sleeve. "I never thought to see the day when all the flapping tongues in town would be stopped at once, but you have quite marvelously accomplished it just for me. Pity it couldn't last." This caustic comment came about with the growing roar of everyone apparently beginning to speak at once.

Graham lifted a wry eyebrow. "Pleasure to be of assistance. I see the years have not dulled your sharp tongue, Matilda."

"Nor has it yours, Trevelyan." Lady Larchmont turned to Penelope, her dark eyes roving assessingly over the younger woman who appeared nervous but bore no sign of fainting at their reception. "Gray and I go back a long way, so you will excuse us if we do not observe the courtesies, Lady Trevelyan. You have more gumption than I expected if you are responsible for dragging the lion from his lair. I thank you."

Penelope returned the countess's stare bravely though her mind continued to whirl with the confusion of these last impossible days. Lady Larchmont appeared twenty years younger than her lanky earl, but she was still not a young woman. If her chestnut hair held hints of gray, she had succeeded in concealing them, but she could not hide the fine lines etched at the corners of her eyes and lips. Still, the countess was an attractive woman, and with her new found awareness of sexual tension, Penelope understood some of the relation between Graham and her hostess. At one time or another they had shared a liaison. Whether of short or long duration, she was not prepared to speculate. Just the knowledge of it shook her secure world a little more. Graham had told her things were different in his world, but she had not felt the impact personally until now.

"Graham is not one to be led about by a woman, I fear," Penelope managed to murmur in response. "My influence on the matter was slight."

The countess spared them both a charming smile. "You don't deserve her, Trev. You are going to favor us later this evening with all the sordid details of how she nursed you back to health, aren't you?"

"I'll do no such thing, Matilda," Graham answered calmly. "We have provided enough sensation for one evening." He turned to the earl. "With your permission, sir, I will lead your lady on the floor. I know you are eager for your game."

"Quite right. Quite right. But I'll help do the honor. Lady Trevelyan?" He tilted precariously in Penelope's direction.

Penelope took his bony arm and they followed Graham and Lady Larchmont onto the floor. She knew Guy and Dolly brought up the rear, but she felt strangely isolated at the head of the ballroom as the musicians struck up a quadrille. The feeling didn't last long as the floor began to fill, but she knew their foursome was the focus of attention for those remaining along the walls.

Graham's lame leg made his dancing a good deal less than graceful, but in white gloves and formal frock coat he appeared more formidable than fearsome. He winked at her as they passed in the pattern of the dance, and her spirits lifted another notch. If he could find humor in the spectacle they were creating, she had no reason to complain.

The evening barreled along after that. Guy claimed her hand for the next dance and any number of acquaintances clamored for others. She had no fear of being a wallflower, but she almost thought she would prefer to be. She listened politely to their chatter, but seldom did they strike on subjects of interest to her. She scarcely knew half the names they mentioned and did not care much for the information imparted about those she knew. She had little knowledge of fashion and could not discourse for long on the advantages or disadvantages of Bath and Brighton. It was with great relief that she found Graham holding out a demanding hand to her when a waltz began.

"I am certainly entitled to one dance with my wife, am I not?" he growled in reply to protests from several gentlemen waiting for a chance at Penelope's hand.

Beneath Graham's fierce stare they melted into the crowd, and Penelope's fingers closed gratefully around his. "It is kind of you to come to my rescue, but you do not need to exert yourself upon my account." She gazed up at him hopefully. "I would be quite content to sit somewhere and talk of something other than the weather or the Regent's wardrobe." She had noticed Graham had not made another attempt to dance since that first one, and she offered a respite for both of them.

One corner of his mouth turned up in a rueful smile. "I am quite out of practice, I'll admit. The waltz was considered very daring when I last trod the dance floor. But I'm willing if you are."

Penelope glanced toward the draperies she knew concealed French doors to the terrace, then back to Graham. "Could we . . . Do you think we would be noticed if we went outside? I have avoided the waltz because it is never danced at assemblies at home, and I'm not at all certain I can remember how to do it. I've practiced with some of the girls at home, but . . ." She let the sentence die away as Graham's eye took on a gleam of approval.

"If anyone dares follow, I shall scowl at them and send them running." He offered his arm and they boldly threw back the draperies to step outside.

By leaving the doors open, they could hear the music plainly. The warm May night smelled fresh after breathing the various stenches of heavy perfumes, powders, and pomades inside. Graham wrapped his arm around Penelope's waist and caught her hand, and stiffly they began to move in time to the music.

In no time at all they were moving quite creditably, if not gliding gracefully, across the flagstone terrace. Penelope found herself easily following Graham's lead, and she relaxed and began to enjoy the sensation of dancing and being held by her husband. At this easing of the stiffness between them, Graham pulled her closer, and Penelope found herself strangely reluctant to part when the music ended.

"Now I begin to remember why I used to attend these functions. The pleasure of holding a beautiful woman in my arms exceeds the boredom of chattering with empty-headed misses." Graham continued to hold her hand as he led her back toward the ballroom.

Penelope glanced wistfully up at the night sky. "I would be content to remain out here. I miss my garden. Do you think we might go to the country for just a little while when the Season ends? I'm certain Alexandra would enjoy it also."

Graham bent her a quizzical look. "You have only just arrived in the city. Surely you are not ready to abandon it?"

"Oh, it is very amusing, and I have met some fascinating people, but I suppose I'm just a wee bit homesick. I would like to see Augusta again, and the twins, and all of them. Have you never lived anywhere else but the city?" She turned her head up to read his expression.

She touched on a subject too close to his heart, and he deliberately kept his expression closed. "Perhaps when I have completed my business here, we will go to visit my sister for a while. Will that suit?"

His aloofness took some of the pleasure from his reply, but Penelope nodded agreement. "Yes, that would be lovely. She seems to be a very pleasant person."

Once inside the ballroom they were caught up in the crowd rushing for the newly opened doors to the buffet. Not quite willing to relinquish his wife to the gallants forming around her, Graham stayed at her side as they entered the supper room. His massive size made it easy for him to clear a path to the table and provide Penelope with all the choicest tidbits he could find. The crowd opened up before them as if by magic, and Penelope had to laugh at the ease with which Graham appropriated whatever he wanted.

As they sampled the elegant fare laid out before them, Graham introduced her to those of his acquaintance who dared come forward and greet them amicably. Penelope felt as if he might be really enjoying himself, and she greeted these friends of his with warmth.

She knew few of the people Graham discussed with these new faces, and she took no real notice of his reaction when someone mentioned that they had seen Deauville last week. She was more interested in the fact that this Deauville had been in the Caribbean. She knew of no one who had visited such exotic places, and she hoped they might run into him sometime so she could hear firsthand about the fascinating islands. Graham's lack of interest in the subject that so fascinated her was a disappointment, but Graham seldom allowed conversation to be dull, and she was soon caught up in another.

The musicians stuck up a *contra-danse,* and the crowd began to flow back toward the dance floor. Penelope found herself carried into the lively tune, and completely at home with the steps she joined in gaily.

When the music came to an end, she had lost sight of Graham. Assuming he had joined his companions in another room, she allowed herself to be led back on the floor again. When Guy came to claim her after that, she turned to him for assistance.

"Have you seen Graham? He is so very difficult to misplace, but I have not seen him this age or more."

Guy's long, handsome face smiled down at her reassuringly. "Do not worry, my lady. You are in capable hands. He wasn't feeling quite the thing, and he left early, with many apologies to you. You are to enjoy yourself thoroughly, and I am to escort you home when you are ready.''

Alarm immediately replaced her earlier well-being. ''He seemed fine earlier. I hope it is nothing he has eaten. I'm sorry, Guy, but I must leave. Perhaps he has caught Alexandra's measles. Do you know if he has ever had measles?'' She hurried toward the foyer, scarcely giving Guy time to answer.

''You are being overly concerned, Penelope,'' Guy admonished, but he did not attempt to stop her. He, too, wondered at Trevelyan's abrupt departure, but his reasons were of a different nature.

When they reached the Trevelyan mansion, Guy insisted on coming in with her, but all seemed quiet. The footman sleepily guarding the door said the master had gone off to bed, and Guy had no other choice but to plead his farewells.

Before the door had securely closed behind him, Penelope was running up the stairs. It was not like Graham to be ill, however much he played the invalid. True, he kept country hours more often than not, and it was past his usual time for retiring, but he would not have feigned illness to go home to sleep. He must truly be unwell, but there seemed no evidence that a physician had been called.

Bracing herself, she rapped sharply on the door connecting their chambers. She had never entered Graham's bedroom, but she knew his manservant often guarded the door. He would know how serious Graham's illness might be.

When John opened the door, he appeared surprised to see her and a little bit wary. ''My lady?''

''I would like to see Graham, John. If he is ill, a physician must be sent for.''

She had donned the cloak of authority she wielded so well, but though John appeared nervous at refusing her orders, he did not relent. ''I'm sorry, my lady. His lordship's gone to sleep and asked not to be disturbed. I can't go against his orders, my lady. He'll be right and fine in the morning, I'm certain.''

The door closed in her face and Penelope stared at

it in confusion. It was as if a solid brick wall came between them whenever they entered this suite. Why had Graham married her when he so obviously did not want a wife?

Chadwell sat in the darkened corner of one of the more sordid gambling hells off Whitechapel. The few oil lamps in the walls sent off more smoke than light and guttered gradually lower as the hours ticked by. Only the cheap tallow candles on the tables offered illumination for the cardplayers. Chadwell's table sported no candle, and he sipped at his drink, unnoticed.

It hadn't taken Deauville long to return to his old haunts and acquaintances. It had been a simple matter to track him down. A few inquiries of former club mates eager to disassociate themselves from the bounder had produced a wealth of information, and Chadwell frowned as he observed the truth of their replies.

The devil had been warned in plenitude. He had been given the opportunity for a second chance, but there he was, swindling the young fool on his right while using his mother's jewels as bait. The jewels would be lost by morning despite the winnings from the young fool. There were better cheats at that table than Deauville.

Chadwell eyed the rest of the company around the card table. He had thought DeVere reformed and attempting a respectable living, but he should have known the man's perverted tastes would not be fed on a diplomat's salary. His animosity toward the older man had developed over a lifetime, but DeVere had given him no direct cause to challenge him. The diplomat would have to hang himself; Chadwell was out for a different game tonight.

There went the jewels. That should end the game for Deauville. Chadwell did not express any satisfaction at the rightness of his deduction as the dissipated rake pushed away from the table. The result had been inevitable. The fool had brought about his own destruction. He needed only a devil's advocate to make him see the way.

He grunted in disgust as the diplomat gestured toward one of the doxies leaning against the wall and sent her after the departing cardplayer. If Deauville weren't diseased by now, he would be by night's end. As Chadwell slipped from his table to follow, he wondered idly if DeVere still held his investment in that bordello across the street. His new respectability shouldn't allow for that.

In the gloomy upstairs hallway it wasn't difficult to part the drunken Deauville from his companion. The woman took Chadwell's coin gratefully enough and disappeared down the back stairs without a word. The cardplayer stared at his new companion through bloodshot, uncomprehending eyes, until Chadwell produced his pistol.

"Let's chat awhile, shall we?" He gestured toward the room the couple was about to enter.

The rail-thin man stared at Chadwell as if he were the devil himself. "You! You're dead! Go away. Leave me alone."

Chadwell smiled unpleasantly and gestured again with the weapon. "You have been sadly misinformed, my friend. Now let us go inside and speak privately or all the ears behind these doors will know your troubles."

Having no other choice, Deauville did as told. Sobered somewhat by the sight of the pistol, he watched warily as Chadwell shut the door behind them.

"Now, let us speak of the paste necklace presently residing in your mother's jewel case. How many others have gone the same way?" Chadwell leaned casually against the door, the weapon drooping from his finger.

"I don't know what you're talking about," Deauville replied sullenly.

"You may deny it to me all you like, it's no skin off my nose. Of course, in the morning, when your mother receives an anonymous note asking that she have her jewelry appraised . . . Your uncle has already mentioned Newgate, I believe?"

"My God, you wouldn't! I'll replace them, I swear it! It's just the luck's been bad these last few nights . . ."

"These last few years, I'd say. You've lost the plantation, haven't you? And has your uncle heard of the murder warrant yet? That rather eliminates returning to France. I'd say you have quite neatly narrowed your choices to none. Was it worth it, Deauville? I let you go once. Do you think I ought to do it again? Instead of one woman dead, now there's two. And half your family's fortune gone, if not more. What do you think, Deauville? Do you think I ought to let you go again?"

The bloodshot eyes filled with fear as he heard the ominous tone of these quiet words. He knew the man behind the gun too well to doubt the hatred in his eyes. How was it no one saw the specter of death behind that disguise? Why hadn't DeVere warned him their old nemesis still walked the streets? Surely he wasn't fooled by his changed appearance?

Deauville stammered for some reply. "I told you, I'd replace the jewels. I can't bring back the dead. They were accidents. You know they were. We were only out for a bit of fun. We didn't know it was Marilee. You know that. Devil take it, man, let me go. I'll go back to the islands. Anything you say."

"Oh, no, it's too late for that. It wasn't an accident, Deauville. Don't forget, I was there. You may have killed the wrong person, but you meant to kill. If it had been an accident, you would have gone for help. But you didn't, did you? You ran like rabbits and left her there to die in agony. I hope your little bit of fun was worth it, Deauville. If you'd been a decent man, you would have seen the error of your ways then, but you didn't. We're all only given one second chance. You've had yours. The note will be in your mother's hands by morning. A copy of the note and the warrant for your arrest will be in your uncle's hands at the same time. There's only one way you can retrieve any of your honor, save your family from shame." Chadwell waited with disinterest as the other man's gaze lit with hope.

"What? What is it? Name anything. Money? I'll find it. I have friends . . ."

"Not anymore, you don't." Chadwell removed several silver objects from his breast pocket and dropped them in the empty washbasin beside the door. Then taking the barrel of the empty pistol, he handed the butt end to Deauville. "I think you know how to load it. It's the one you used that night to scare the horses. Put it to a better purpose this time. Goodnight."

As Deauville incredulously took the offered weapon, Chadwell tipped his elegant beaver hat and stepped out the door.

Chapter 11

STEELING herself for another confrontation the next morning, Penelope balanced a breakfast tray in one hand and rapped again at Graham's door. She would not be shut out of his life so easily, particularly if he needed her.

Again, John answered the rap. His coat was rumpled and his hair untidy, and his eyes did not appear ready to open as he greeted Lady Trevelyan once more. His look of weariness hid any trace of dismay he may have felt.

"Is Graham any better this morning? I've brought up some tea and things so he need not rise immediately." She waited patiently for the servant to move out of the way.

John held out his hands for the tray. "He is still sleeping, my lady, but I will set this beside the bed in case he wakes."

As he bent slightly to heft the tray from her hands, Penelope caught a glimpse of the massive bed behind him. The curtains were pulled back to allow air from the open window to circulate, and she thought she caught a glimpse of Graham sprawled across the pillows. That relieved one nagging fear that she had not admitted even to herself, but it gave cause for wonder.

"The hour is late, John. How can he sleep so long? That does not seem at all healthy. I still think a physician should be summoned."

Her ladyship's determined expression did not bode well, and the servant hastily improvised, "It's the laudanum, my lady. He sleeps off the pain, and then he's right as a trivet again."

Laudanum? Why hadn't she thought of that before? Penelope allowed the door to be closed in her face again as she added one more piece to the puzzle that was her husband. Of course they would have given him laudanum after that terrible accident. And if he still suffered pain from those old injuries, it would be natural to turn to it for relief.

She frowned, remembering one of her father's elderly parishioners who had been given laudanum at the onset of illness. Soon, she had required a drink every night just to sleep, and as the weeks went by, she grew increasingly more feeble. Penelope had tried to persuade her from taking so much of the medicine, but the woman had cried and wept the whole night through when denied it. At the end, she had been barely lucid, and Penelope blamed it entirely on the medicine.

Perhaps there were better doses of the liquid than her patient had taken. Surely a doctor wise enough to cure wounds as serious as Graham's would not prescribe something dangerous. Still, she worried, and a small frown puckered the bridge of her nose as she went about her daily tasks.

To Penelope's relief, Graham came downstairs in early afternoon to catch her teaching Alexandra backgammon in the parlor. He appeared quite hale and hearty, and she sent him a smile of pleasure as he entered.

Knowing from John that she had come home early on his account, Graham had thought to scold her for interfering where he had not asked, but Penelope's smile robbed his tongue of its sharp edge. Sitting there with the glow of the afternoon sun turning the loose curls at her nape to spun gold, violet eyes wide with love and laughter, he could no more say a cross word to her than he could to his daughter, whose dark eyes watched him with suspicion as he entered the room.

"You look like truants from the schoolroom. Where is Mrs. Henwood? Shouldn't you be learning something a little more valuable than backgammon?" He tugged lightly on a strand of Alexandra's ebony hair, but his touch and tone of voice showed more affection than concern over lost lessons.

Alexandra sent her father's piratical face a fierce look. "Penny said I could. *And* she said we might go out in the carriage tomorrow." She did not add "So there!" but the words were in her inflection.

Penelope nearly laughed aloud at the startlement leaping to Graham's eye, but he recovered quickly.

"Penny is quite right. A little fresh air should be good for you after so many days inside."

The defiant expression disappeared and Alexandra beamed with her usual mischievousness. "Penny told Mrs. Henwood I need not start on my books or my sewing all day yet. She said I am still re-coop—" She glanced to Penelope for aid. Supplied with the word, she finished in triumph. "I am re-coop-er-ating, and I should not do too much at once."

"Very wise, I'm sure," Graham answered gravely, exchanging a laughing glance with Penelope over his daughter's head. "When you are quite done with entertaining our Penny, I would like to borrow her for a while, if you would not mind."

A delicious shiver cascaded down Penelope's back for no apparent reason at these words. He could merely wish to discuss this evening's invitations or the high cost of the candles she had ordered, but just her husband's wish to be with her seemed to have a pleasurable effect.

She had little time to ponder at this oddity. Sharp words in the foyer intruded upon their tête-à-tête, and a moment later Guy burst into the room, a tabloid clutched in his hand. Ignoring Penelope and Alexandra and the footman running after him, the baronet focused furiously on Graham, waving the paper under his nose.

"Trevelyan, I will not have it! This cannot go on! Deauville's only just got back, it cannot be coincidence!"

"Hamilton, you will take hold of yourself or I shall have you carried out." Graham did not disdain to touch the newspaper being shaken violently under his nose, but turned formally to the astonished occupants at the game table. "You will excuse us, my lady?"

Before Graham could lead him out, Guy turned desperately to Penelope. "Tell me he was here when you came home last night."

Puzzled and frightened, she looked to both men before answering. Finding no answer in either expression, she answered as truthfully as she was able. "Of course. He was sound asleep. Why?"

For a moment, Guy looked relieved, but another thought seemed to strike him and he continued frantically, "All night? Was he with you all night?"

"Guy!" That bordered on the impertinent. Not wishing to reveal the state of their marriage, Penelope hid her embarrassment behind indignation.

"That's quite enough." Graham grabbed Guy's elbow and all but flung him through the doorway. The paper fell from Guy's hand as the parlor door slammed behind them.

Alexandra's expression was once more fraught with fear, and Penelope's did not reflect great calm. Carefully, she rose to retrieve the tabloid from the floor. Oblivious to Alexandra's cautious scrutiny, she perused the narrow lines and columns on the page Guy had left open.

It took a minute before she found the article, but the frown of earlier returned as she found the name "Deauville." The article gave his birthplace as Hampstead, but called him a Caribbean planter recently returned to London. It then went on to describe his suicide by a "bullet through the brain" and ended with a list of his survivors, including a mother and two sisters.

Penelope curled the paper in her hand and stared at the parlor door. A black pinprick of fear took root somewhere inside, but she knew not its source or solution. Why would Guy come here in a fury over the suicide of a man who had not lived here in years?

Graham asked the same question when he slammed the door of the study and turned to face his irate friend.

"Don't play the innocent with me, Trevelyan! I

know what happened that night. You cannot tell me it is coincidence that the moment Deauville returns to London he blows his brains out. What can you get out of seeking revenge after all these years?''

Graham limped to his desk chair and with the aid of his walking stick, eased himself to a sitting position. He stared at Hamilton's stubbornly set square jaw with displeasure. ''You have become quite single-minded in your beliefs. I cannot fathom how you imagine I raised myself from my sickbed to limp downtown and persuade a man I haven't seen in years to put a pistol to his head. You give me too much credit.''

''Then you knew about it?'' Guy demanded.

''Of course I knew about it. I know about many things. I know Deauville's reputation on Martinique turned out as unsavory as it promised here. I know he was practically bankrupt when he returned, and his uncle threw him out when he went home looking for funds. I know he has been living in a brothel and working in a gambling hell since he returned to London. It sounds to me as if our friend had every reason in the world to blow his brains out.'' Graham leaned back in his chair and crossed his walking stick over his legs as he regarded Guy calmly.

''And I know damned well that the toplofty sapskull thought too well of himself to put his spoon in the wall on purpose! Devil take it, Trev, you can't act as a one man tribunal of justice. They killed Marilee, I know, but you can't say they *meant* it to happen. You cannot bring her back with revenge. You have Penelope now. Why risk what you have over the worthless lives of these vermin, particularly since it was *my* life they sought, and not yours? If there is revenge to be taken, it is my place to do.''

''Hamilton, you're exercising your jaw for naught. As well you know, Marilee was lost to me *before* the accident. Your opinion of your old club mates has little to do with me. Those that caused the accident were a worthless lot then and remain a worthless lot now. I am ashamed that I was ever associated with them in any way. And if you don't mind your manners, I'll forget that you tried to warn me of their danger. Now I suggest you go back and apologize to Penelope. You have no doubt frightened her into hysterics, and I must say your manner of questioning was quite insulting. I don't think you're likely to earn her forgiveness anytime soon.''

Penelope had sent Alexandra back to the nursery by the time the two men returned to the parlor. The tabloid lay on the table where she sat mending a tear in one of Graham's neck cloths. He gave the item of apparel in her hand a wary look but made no comment on it. His eyebrow lifted in Guy's direction.

The baronet bowed stiffly from the waist. "My apologies, Lady Trevelyan, for my untimely and rude intrusion."

The formality lifted Penelope's eyebrows, and his evasion of his true rudeness put a sympathetic twinkle behind long lashes as she glanced up to Graham's forbidding stature. "That is very pretty of you, Guy, but I'm not likely to accept apologies without explanations. Graham?"

She held herself as regally as any princess, more regally, Graham amended, remembering Princess Caroline's particularly blowsy informality. He couldn't help but admire her stiff-necked pride, even if it was a damned nuisance. Any other woman would have been dissolved in tears or hysterically ranting by now. One or two might have meekly accepted Guy's pitiable apology. Penelope, however, had singled out the real cause of the earlier scene and nailed the perpetrator.

Graham had no intention of falling victim to his wife's perspicacity. He returned the hot potato to Guy. "Well, Hamilton, what explanation would you like to give?"

Guy set his lips stubbornly. "I am sorry, Penelope, but it is no concern of yours. If I have frightened you, I did not mean to do so, and I apologize. I beg you will consider me sincere and accept it without further explanation."

All trace of sympathy left her face and jabbing her

needle into the soft cloth, she replied coldly. "You are right. It is none of my concern. Apology accepted."

It was as neat a dismissal as Graham had ever seen. Unable to catch his wife's eye, he steered the stricken baronet from the room.

"She is angry." Guy accepted his hat and gloves from the butler while watching Graham with curiosity.

The mobile half of the viscount's face showed as little expression as the stiff half. "It would seem so. She does not anger easily. I told you to keep her out of this."

"I'll not apologize to you. You've brought it on yourself, and nothing will convince me otherwise. I never took you for a fool, Trev, but I'm seriously considering revising my opinion." He spun around and stalked out.

Graham pondered whether or not his friend was right, but it was too late to change course now. He was not one for leaving things half done, but his increasing regard for Penelope caused him to question what he had once taken for granted. He didn't like uncertainties. He preferred action to sitting around discussing pro's and con's, and he had no means of resolving the dilemma readily.

Shrugging his big shoulders in unaccustomed confusion, Graham returned to the parlor. Penelope refused to look up from her mending. He contemplated her bent head in dismay. He had no knowledge at all of how to deal with Penelope's anger since he had never seen it displayed before.

"I will not endure a fit of the sulks, Penelope. It does not become you." That sounded sufficiently stern to be convincing. Graham rested on his cane and waited.

She sent him a scathing look. "Neither do my high-necked muslins, you tell me, but you married me anyway. Obviously becoming was not one of the attributes you require in a wife."

That was a singularly odd tack to take, and Graham contemplated her line of reasoning. "You are well aware of why I married you. I have given you no reason to inquire into my affairs."

"No, you are quite right in that." Penelope stood haughtily, throwing down the neatly mended neck cloth on the table between them. "So I will not ask how that was torn after you left me unattended at the ball last night."

Graham caught her arm as she tried to pass by him. "I do not remember how it was torn, Penelope. It is of no significance."

"And neither am I. I tell you, I understand my position completely, my lord. You have made yourself clear from the first. May I go now?"

Graham turned her so she had to face him, and an unexpected tension forced out his next words. "Are you unhappy with our arrangement, Penelope? Would you have any part of our marriage changed?"

The grip on her arm was almost bruising, but the electricity of Graham's stare held her more thoroughly than his hand. She felt his tension in the pit of her stomach, but there was no other reply she could make.

"You have given me more than I ever dared dream, my lord. I could never ask for more."

He felt the disappointment washing over him and cursed himself for a fool. What did he think she would answer? He released his grip on her arm and replied more formally than before.

"I came down here earlier to apologize for deserting you last evening, and to ask if I might make it up to you by taking you for a ride this afternoon. I have just quarreled with my best friend. I do not wish to quarrel with you. Will you go with me?"

"Is that your wish, my lord?" she asked coolly, her anger unsoftened by his plea.

"My wish, yes, but not my command. Is there not somewhere you would particularly like to go, someplace you would like to see?"

Penelope turned her head away to hide the tears springing to her eyes at the soft tone of his voice. She did not understand any of this. He ordered her to stay out of his business, not inquire into his affairs, and said out loud that theirs was naught but a marriage of convenience. Why, then, did he go out of his way to make her happy and look at her as a man does when he admires a woman? Perhaps she only imagined that light in his eye. Perhaps his soft touches and gentle words were the same as he bestowed upon Alexandra. Perhaps she was running from Chadwell and hiding behind Graham.

With a slight nod, she agreed. "I promised Alexandra new ribbons for her bonnet tomorrow. And the hems have been let out of her smocks as far as they will go. I thought we might have a new muslin or two made up for her."

Graham gazed at the back of her head and his mouth quirked wryly upward at one corner. "I had thought to let you indulge yourself in a bonnet or two. I should have known Alexandra would be the only reason you accompany me."

Penelope turned to glance back up at him. "You can indulge me with a membership in the lending library, if you like. Your library is no doubt educational, but since I read neither Greek nor Latin and have little understanding of agriculture or philosophy, I am left with a few novelists from prior centuries. Admittedly, they should not be ignored, but they are rather heavy reading for a rainy day."

"Penelope, you need not be so clutch-fisted with my money!" Graham stared at this prim vicar's daughter he had somehow taken to wife. "You can go down to the bookseller's and buy out the store and stop at the printer's and have them send over every new volume off the press if that is what you like. Do you think me such an ogre that I would complain of a few books?"

Penelope's lips finally turned up at this exaggeration. "I think you would believe I set myself up in a new profession as librarian should you see bills for all that. I am not clutch-fisted, but sensible. The books I would like to read are not necessarily ones I would ever look at but once. The lending library suffices. When should I be ready?"

Graham surrendered the argument. "Go get your bonnet. I'll have Harley call the phaeton."

Penelope hesitated. "The phaeton? Are you certain? I do not want to cause you undue discomfort—"

"*Hoi polloi* may grow accustomed to my face in slow stages. I'll order the hood put up," he answered shortly.

She didn't know the Greek but grasped his meaning. Giving his face a quick search, she nodded and left the room with her heart beating at an inexplicably rapid rate.

He must have a reason for showing himself in public, at last. She had no reason to believe it had anything to do with a desire to please her, but she was pleased, anyway. So there.

Chapter 12

THE seat beside the driver was piled high with packages. Ribbons had led to laces and then necessarily to a delightful little girl's bonnet the milliner had just made up. One or two muslins had led to the need for new chemises and a pretty pair of ruffled pantalets to peek out from beneath the eyelet summer frock Graham had declared perfect for his daughter. Of course, that meant new stockings and shoes, and the pink ribbons exactly matched a miniature parasol in the bow window of one of the shops on St. James, and that, naturally, meant new lace mittens.

Graham held his peace as his wife pricked the balloon of inflated prices on the various wares on display and obtained Alexandra's wardrobe at the more reasonable rates the shopkeepers would have paid themselves. To his surprise he found no boredom in making the rounds of shops with Penelope. He enjoyed watching her outwit the shopkeepers, enjoyed the admiration he saw in their eyes as they packaged her purchases, and even enjoyed choosing colors and styles for his daughter, since Penelope requested his opinion. The surreptitious stares of the clerks failed to annoy him, and since no one wished to offend a viscount with a large purse, he met with no screams of horror.

All in all, their first outing could be named a success, Graham decided as the driver turned the phaeton back toward home. Penelope had recovered from her anger, he had assuaged another restless afternoon, and though Guy's accusations still rankled, he saw no point in changing his ways now. He had undoubtedly created a gallery of problems by marrying Penelope, but gazing down at her serene smile as she sat happily holding his hand, he couldn't repent a minute of it.

That thought led to further contemplations Graham did not yet wish to consider, so when Penelope's face lit with a sudden joy, he followed the path of her gaze. One of the more enterprising farmers from the outskirts of the city had interspersed the scanty produce of his vegetable cart with colorful bouquets of May flowers. Admittedly, it made a splendid sight, and Graham called for the driver to halt.

Penelope gasped with surprise as Graham caught her waist and swung her down from the carriage, but the warmth of his gaze as he set her down on the cobbled street brought a blush to her cheek. She smiled uncertainly in response, then looked away. Graham's strong left hand continued to linger at her waist as they turned toward the vendor. The thin muslin of her gown did little to disguise the pressure of his fingers as she bent to admire a bouquet of tulips.

They argued laughingly over the merits of wild bluebells against cultured daffodils, and in the end, Penelope's arms were filled to overflowing with an assortment of every flower in the vendor's stock. Happy with these reminders of her garden at home, Penelope glanced up to discover they stood in front of a particularly enchanting old church surrounded by towering hedges. Such happiness deserved to be shared, and instead of returning to the carriage with her prizes, she swerved and headed up the walkway to the church.

Swinging his walking stick, Graham came up beside her. To other eyes they may have made an incongruous couple—the excessively large and ferocious looking gentleman in his tailored frock coat and eye patch limping beside the graceful lady carrying an arm load of spring flowers—but appearances didn't concern them as they approached the church.

Unfortunately appearances influence the world of nature, and Penelope's flowers made an inviting garden for one busy worker bee. Penelope gave a cry of alarm as it dived for one of her daffodils. Jerking the flowers away, she only distracted his flight, and the misguided bee alighted on the neckline of her yellow muslin, to which she gave another cry of fright.

Graham gallantly raced to the rescue, trying to dislodge the bee with one hand and the flowers with the other, succeeding only in sending the bee into the safety of Penelope's bodice.

Penelope's cry of pain as the irritated bee found no escape and took its vengeance on a vulnerably soft spot severed Graham's patience with nature. Flinging the flowers to the ground, he jerked the drawstring of her gown, tore at the frail lawn of her chemise, and dived for the severely stunned nuisance.

Luckily for Penelope, no one observed this little scene within the confines of the high hedges, for Graham's frantic chase for the bee left her with little modesty. The shock of his unparalleled intimacy hit them as Graham's fingers brushed her breast in order to release the bee. Even through her tears and pain she felt the warm sensation of his hands where they had no right to be, and still clutching desperately at one bouquet, she looked up to catch Graham's dazed look. She made no attempt to elude the strength of the arm supporting her, but numbly, she made some attempt to pull her bodice back together. The gentle touch of his fingers on hers stopped her like a jolt of electricity.

Without a word Graham parted her lacy chemise and sought the damage to tender skin. The angry red welt swelling on the inside of one fair breast brought a fierce frown to his brow.

Penelope quivered as Graham's fingers sought the poisonous stinger. She shut her eyes in embarrassment, but the sudden heat spreading through her center at this intimate touch burned more than the bee's sting. Her eyes flew open again as he removed the barb, and she found herself staring into Graham's face.

They remained rooted there for what seemed like eternity, Graham's bare hand resting on her breast, his gloved one holding her so close she feared to breathe. If she had been able to breathe. The look in Graham's eye robbed her of any such ability, and Penelope held her breath as his cool fingers caressed the pain. She didn't want him to stop, and he seemed strangely reluctant to do so.

"I don't know the proper remedy for bee stings." His voice, when it came, was gruff.

"A little flour paste, and I don't carry such about." Penelope wasn't certain how she managed to speak, but the sensible words belied her state of near panic.

"Then we shall have to get you home and find you some." His voice was low and deep and as caressing as his touch as his gaze followed the path of his fingers. Without warning, he scooped Penelope up in his arms and began stalking determinedly toward the carriage, leaving the flower-strewn steps of the church behind.

"Graham, what are you doing? Put me down," Penelope whispered frantically as they emerged from the privacy of the hedgerow into the crowded street. He had not bothered to adjust her torn chemise or retie her bodice, and the sun fell warmly on her exposed flesh.

"I don't think I will." With some deliberation, Graham pulled himself up into the carriage without losing his grip on his slender burden.

When he continued to hold her in his lap as he ordered the driver home, Penelope turned bewildered eyes upward while her heart pounded strange music against her ribs. "Graham? I'm quite fine. We can't ride about like this."

With a satisfied upturn of the corner of his mouth, Graham adjusted her more comfortably against his thighs and settled her head against his shoulder. "Yes, we can. White knights and conquering heroes are allowed some privileges for their daring deeds."

When she should have been horrified, Penelope giggled. She liked the sensation of being held in his arms, and though she had a vague idea that her reaction was unspeakably wanton, she longed for Graham to move his fingers a little higher from where they rested at her waist. She had never felt such a fiery sensation as his hands had created, and she wanted to know more of it.

"Jousting with bees does not seem to rate the recompense of abducting the heroine, my lord."

"Devil take the bee," Graham warned her with a bold look that encompassed the tempting glimpse of white breasts beneath nearly sheer muslin. "I claim my reward for not carrying you off into the hedges and ravishing you right there."

"Graham!" Feeling the first faint stirrings of alarm, Penelope hastily attempted to pull together her chemise or at least retie her drawstrings.

"Oh, no, that's part of my reward." He caught her hands and held them, his one golden eye holding her mesmerized. "Cover yourself and I will be forced to take desperate measures we both may regret later. Like this." He released her hands and slid his fingers along the neckline of the gown, releasing the loose folds of muslin to slide downward until they almost threatened to fall off altogether.

His fingers scorched where they touched her skin, and Penelope understood then the import of his words through this sensation, if nothing else. Let him look his fill, for touching led to desire for more touching, and even her limited knowledge could figure the result of that.

She glanced uncertainly at the determined set of his jaw. "I think the hero of this tale is behaving with ungentlemanly rashness."

"Perhaps." Graham looked down at her and quirked an eyebrow. "But the sting would feel much better this way than buried under all that cloth, wouldn't it?"

Amusement flickered behind lowered lashes. "Perhaps. But would you have a heroine who behaves so shockingly?"

"Better a brazen hussy than one of these modern day henwits who faint at the sight of their shadow," he decided with satisfaction. Silently he gave thanks to Penelope's sense of humor. The tension that had sprung up between them could have had only one other conclusion, and he wanted to spare her that humiliation. She was only beginning to discover needs he knew too well. He would not quench her healthy desires by too sudden an acquaintance with his unwholesome visage.

When they came within sight of the house, he reluctantly returned her to the seat beside him while Penelope hastily tied the drawstring to hide her torn chemise. The closeness that had drawn them together did not disappear with this separation but lingered. As the phaeton stopped, Graham ignored the footmen running to assist them in alighting. He jumped down and turned to lift Penelope as if she were an extension of himself from which he could not be parted.

Half frightened by the intensity of her own emotions and his attentions, Penelope allowed Graham to sweep her into his arms and down to the street. She came to rest facing him and stared wonderingly into his scarred face as he continued to hold his hands at her waist. As if satisfied with what he found in her eyes, Graham touched a finger to her nose and led her into the house.

The opportunity to find out what would happen next was lost when they met head on with Lady Reardon and Dolly preparing to leave. Dolly's cries of delight distracted any notice of the electric tension between the couple holding hands in the hall. Understanding the plea leaping to Penelope's eyes, Graham graciously asked the women to join him for tea, and Penelope hastily excused herself to change her clothing.

When she returned to the parlor, the Reardons were entertaining Graham with descriptions of the exciting events of these last few weeks of the Season. He did not seem exceptionally intrigued by the prospect, and remembering the news Dolly had imparted some nights ago, Penelope gently inserted it into the conversation.

"And your brother, Arthur, have you heard from him again?"

Both Reardons responded excitedly to this topic, and only Penelope noticed Graham's sudden silence. Obviously no one had repeated this particular piece of gossip to him, and he seemed oddly stunned by the news.

With a smoothness that belied his interest, he inquired, "Arthur joined the army? I know I have been out of touch, but why didn't I hear of this before?"

Forgetting Graham's frightening appearance and remembering only that he had been a good friend of her younger son, Lady Reardon turned excitedly in his direction. "We none of us knew it! He ran off and left a letter to his father saying he wished to make his own way in the world, and other than an occasional note telling us he was alive and well, we knew nothing of him. And we hadn't even had a note in the longest time!"

Dolly jumped in to explain. "It seems he joined as an *enlisted* man under an assumed name! Can you imagine that? And then when he was injured no one had a family name to send word to and the announcement in the paper meant nothing to us. Only when he was well enough to write did we hear from him. Henry is on his way over now."

Graham set his cup aside. "Henry will be bringing him home then? Do you know when?"

Penelope could only attribute his interest to concern for an injured friend, but she felt a vague uneasiness at the flatness of his voice. When Guy had returned, she had heard the excitement in her husband's greeting. But Graham's tone now did not sound as if he were inquiring out of politeness or joy.

"It depends on the extent of his injuries. We'll be taking him to Surrey to recuperate as soon as he is able to be moved. I do hope you will come to visit. I am sure it will mean a lot to him."

Graham calmly held his cup out for Penelope to refill. "We were thinking of adjourning to the Hall for the summer ourselves. We will certainly avail ourselves of your kind invitation."

If Penelope's hand jerked slightly as she poured the tea, no one noticed. Graham had never said anything of going to Surrey earlier. He had mentioned his sister's place in Hampshire. What was the Hall? The Reardons apparently knew, for they launched into an excited commentary of the jaunts and picnics they had planned that would now include the Trevelyans.

Not wishing to reveal her ignorance, Penelope kept quiet, smiling in agreement with Dolly's plans and letting Graham control the conversation. Her mind whirled with all the events and emotions of this day, and she wished heartily that she were back home in the vicarage with only the humdrum happenings of the village to disturb her peace. Every time she felt as if she were coming to some understanding with Graham, something happened to throw her back into the dark again.

If she could only look at him as one thing or another: husband, employer, friend; it would make things easier. But he shifted so rapidly from one role to the other that he left her head spinning. This morning he had told her she had no right to inquire into his affairs. This afternoon he had treated her as wife and mother of his daughter. And now he was revealing that she knew nothing at all of him. She might as well be the governess she had envisioned herself as.

As the Reardons prepared to leave, Charles DeVere arrived. His darkly handsome visage appeared agitated as he followed the footman into the parlor, but he made his bows smoothly with the polish of a practiced politician. Pleasantries exchanged, the Reardons departed and DeVere faced Trevelyan with ill-concealed disgust.

"It's been awhile, Trevelyan. I'd heard you'd recovered."

"So they say." Graham remained standing, and Penelope hesitated, uncertain whether to call for more tea or excuse herself from the room.

Whatever animosity he harbored toward the viscount, DeVere managed to overcome it. With a polite nod toward Penelope, he inquired briskly of them both, "Is your cousin Chadwell about? I have some business with him."

"You'll more likely find him in some gambling hell on the East End than here," Graham responded coolly. "He does not reside with us."

Penelope bit her tongue. She did not understand what game Graham played by disclaiming his cousin, and it was not her business to interfere. She could only feel the tension between these two and wonder at the agitation beneath DeVere's suave exterior.

"It is imperative that I speak with him. You must know how to reach him. I know we have seldom seen alike on many things in our past, Trevelyan, but this is an issue exceedingly crucial to our nation. The streets will be filled with immensely important dignitaries in a few short days. Should anything happen to any one of those people, it will be an embarrassment to the Regent, to the government, to everyone of us. That bloody American cousin of yours has no right to keep such secrets to himself."

He spoke as if Graham ought to know what he was speaking about, as he seemed to do, Penelope noted with wonder. How could a man who seldom ventured beyond his own portals be aware of visiting dignitaries and state secrets? And what on earth did a rakehell like Clifton Chadwell have to do with it?

Graham leaned on his cane and delivered a piercing look to his visitor. "It is of no matter to me whether you rise to the upper echelons of government or sink to a hell of your own making, DeVere. Cliff will do as he sees best under the circumstances. I'd suggest if your real concern is for the safety of the czar and his company and the well-being of the Regency, you speak to the powers that be and warn them to listen carefully should an American come to them with talk of treason."

DeVere appeared to stifle an explosion of temper only by the sight of Penelope rising from her chair. Both men turned to watch her as she made a polite curtsy and moved toward the doorway.

"I do not think this discussion has aught to do with me, gentlemen. I bid you adieu."

She closed the door behind her with a calmness she did not feel. May the saints have mercy on her, but she did not have the strength or presence of mind to deal with treason after all that had happened this day.

What had possessed her to think that marriage to Graham would provide a lifetime of peace and security?

Later that evening Graham found her staring contemplatively at the shelves in his library containing his few condescensions to novels. Guiltily he remembered they had not stopped for the one thing she had requested, membership in the lending library.

Remembering the reason they had been distracted from this goal, his heart pounded a little faster as he advanced cautiously into the room. The flickering firelight illumined the shadows of long legs beneath the frail gauze of her gown, or so Graham imagined. His thoughts were ready for distraction, and Penelope provided the allure he needed. She was an innocent, he knew, and for that reason he had avoided confronting her with his desires. But her responses this afternoon gave him reason to hope she would not completely scorn his advances. His greatest fear was that she would be horrified and repulsed by his physical appearance. Perhaps he had worried for naught.

Rather than debating the merits of Swift over Voltaire, Penelope was lost in contemplation of the day's events and did not hear Graham enter. How could the gentle man she knew as husband and father to Alexandra inspire the fury and antagonism of men like Guy and DeVere? What did he hide from her that others saw?

The touch of a strong hand upon her shoulder brought her abruptly back to the present, and she jumped nervously. Glancing up to find Graham's ravaged visage illuminated by the red and gold flickering lights of the fire and hovering over her like some demon from her dreams, she shuddered as if her thoughts had conjured up a ghost.

Graham saw only the terror in her eyes, read into them the disgust he felt for himself, and with a tearing pain at his insides, stepped away.

He deserved that look of wide-eyed horror. It was a good thing one of them had come to their senses in time. Stifling the tentative hopes and desires of just a moment ago, Graham uttered some polite phrases and hastily retreated, hiding the unexpected anguish filling his soul.

Chapter 13

THE promised day of celebration for the end of hostilities with France plus the arrival of the czar of Russia and king of Prussia with their assorted, colorful retinues kept the Season in full swing despite the growing warmth of June.

On any given day the location of the exotic royalty could be discerned by the masses swarming outside whichever residence they had chosen to visit. Their carriages were followed through the streets by excited parades of people eager to glimpse the foreigners in their splendid robes and furs and jewels. Just the sight of the handsome czar sent many a maid into a swoon, and cries of adulation and excitement filled the air anywhere in his vicinity.

Like everyone else, Penelope was eager for a glimpse of people from another world. Never having traveled any farther than London, she felt her education sadly lacking if she did not take advantage of this once in a lifetime opportunity. When Lord Higdon offered to conduct her to a soiree in honor of the dignitaries, Penelope eagerly accepted.

Judging the callow young lordling to be less of a danger than the sophisticated Guy Hamilton, Graham offered no objection. He had kept a careful distance between himself and Penelope since that day he had let his wishes overrule his senses. As always, Penelope obediently fell into the role he assigned her, although he felt her puzzled stare on more than one occasion. Comforting himself with the thought that she would despise him should she ever discover his secret, he managed to control his tongue and actions.

He could not control his thoughts, however. Watching his wife laughing and playing with Alexandra, flirting with the various gentlemen who cast her speculative glances, and garbed in the revealing silks and satins he bought for her, Graham cursed the cruelty of fate. Just as he had almost accomplished his goals, temptation like this danced in his way. It had never occurred to him that the quiet vicar's daughter had the ability to dispel the ghosts shadowing his life, but for the first time in years, he contemplated the future instead of the past.

He had a choice, such as it was. He could give up his goals, the work of these past few years, the reason he had found for living, and reveal himself to Penelope in hopes that she might forgive his deceit and accept him as husband. He had never quit at anything in his life, but he had to admit the temptation was great if he thought he had a chance of winning happiness. But the possibility of his proud, inconceivably honest, and morally upright wife accepting his explanations and learning to love him threatened the bounds of logic. He had already made his path. There was no sense in diverting from it at this late date.

So he watched Penelope smile tentatively at him as she spun around in the extravagantly pleated blue faille with the lace ruffles covering the bodice, and let the young lordling proudly bear her off without a word to indicate the devastation she wreaked in his heart.

Trevelyan did not have long to contemplate the way violet eyes clouded over at his callous disregard of her need to please. As he climbed the stairs to find the lonely company of his books, a racket in the kitchens caught his attention. He recognized the raised voices of the kitchen staff, the formidable curses of his French cook, and waited patiently for John to settle the matter by bringing it to him. It was amazing how much of this discord had disappeared with the advent of Penelope. He couldn't remember how he had managed before she came.

When John finally stalked stiffly into the hallway, hauling a filthy, tattered street urchin by the collar,

Graham was grateful Penelope was not here to witness this.

The boy cringed at Graham's fearsome appearance, but within minutes, the viscount had pried the message from the terrified youth. Cursing, he strode rapidly up the stairs, flinging orders to his manservant scurrying behind him.

Caught in the crush of elegant gowns and tailored coats with little knowledge of their human contents, Penelope grew bored and restless with the evening's entertainment. The Czar Alexander appeared to be every bit as handsome as promised, but equally arrogant and pretentious. The grand duchess looked positively ferocious, and Penelope had no desire to make her acquaintance. While many of their retinue seemed to be interesting people and much more approachable, Penelope's deplorable French kept her from attempting conversation. Left to her own devices by the immature and easily distracted Lord Higdon, she sought fruitlessly for some pleasant companionship. It became increasingly evident that there was no place more lonely than in the midst of a crowd.

Not accustomed to feeling so out of sorts with her surroundings, Penelope allowed the crush to push her to the edges of the room. Crystal-cut chandeliers shone brilliantly over the array of silks and satins, and a thousand voices tinkled merrily beneath the kind candlelight. Penelope glanced speculatively at the heavy velvet draperies interspersed about the walls, wondering if escape hid behind any one of them.

Escape came in a surprising form. A tall footman in powdered wig and red livery that displayed an amazingly well-developed length of leg bore down upon her with a silver platter in his upturned hand. Penelope hid her smile as she realized the remarkable path of her thoughts. She knew she had been in worldly London too long when she began to notice the turn of a servant's leg.

"Lady Trevelyan?" The young man bowed stiffly before her.

"How did you know?" The question showed her country curiosity. A respectably bred viscountess would have expected the servants to know her identity.

"The gentleman described you." The footman appeared visibly embarrassed at the remembrance of the description and hastily presented the folded note upon the platter.

"That must have been a fascinating description to find me in all this crush. What words did he use?" she asked idly, more interested in the note than the reply. She glanced to the hastily scrawled signature and bemused, listened more carefully than anticipated.

"My lady, I could not . . ." At the sudden haughty straightening of her posture, the footman thought better of contradicting his betters. "He said I was to look for the goddess garbed in sky and clouds with eyes to match my lover's violets and honeyed tresses that brushed alabaster shoulders dusted with gold." The words came in a breathless rush as he tried to remember each extravagant detail. He ended with an air of satisfaction. "I reckoned you had to be young and wearing blue and probably had freckles. Not too many in here fit the description."

Penelope choked back her laughter at the plunge Chadwell's airy phrases took with this translation, and she glanced hastily at the scribbled note in her hands. This was a most unlikely place to discover Graham's rakehell cousin, but she was eager for any friendly face.

Her laughter quickly fled as she digested the contents of the note. She glanced up as if expecting to see Chadwell somewhere behind this tall young footman, but of course, he was not. Groping for a plan of action, she asked, "Can you lead me to him?"

"Of course, my lady." The servant gave her suddenly pale face a quizzical look. It was not the reaction he expected to a love note, but he adroitly led her to a nearby drapery to indicate the way.

She hesitated, throwing a nervous glance over her

shoulder. "Can you get a message to Lord Higdon? I cannot describe him so poetically . . ."

The footman nodded in understanding. "I will make inquiries, my lady."

"Good. Then tell him I was called home and give him my apologies, if you please." Relieved of that concern, she followed the footman down a passageway to an anteroom. The footman opened the door, bowed, and withdrew.

The small room was lit only by a brace of candles, but she recognized Chadwell's tall, broad-shouldered figure easily. Wearing black frock coat and pantaloons, he paced the floor restlessly and swung around at the sound of the door. Instead of smiling, he frowned as Penelope entered, but it was a thoughtful frown.

"I must be mad. I should never have come here." He strode across the room and caught her hand, bringing it to his lips for a lingering tribute before gazing down into questioning eyes. "But you are the only one I know to come to."

"The note said it is urgent. What is wrong? Is it Graham? Is he all right?" The heat of his palm burned against her skin, and she clung to the pleasant warmth as she searched his set face. Those golden eyes so close to Graham's own made her tremble.

The look in them now was singular as he answered her fears. "He is fine, but useless. I need someone familiar with the servants, someone who can recommend a good, stout-hearted girl to help someone in distress. The details are not for a lady's ears, but I will admit there is an element of danger. Perhaps a maid with a questionable reputation?"

Penelope abruptly withdrew her hand from his. "I do not employ servants with questionable reputations, and even if I should, I would not lend them to your assignations. Really, Clifton, you are quite about in your head to consider it."

Her cold tones only served to increase his vehemence. "Penelope, you have it wrong! You see before you a desperate man. Do not think I would have come

yond his surface sophistication and aplomb. His friend apparently meant a great deal to him to disturb his usual nonchalant demeanor.

"If that is the way you feel, I am sorry I can be of no further use to you. I will not send my servants where I dare not go." Firmly, she turned around and started for the door. It really would be better if she did not get involved in any of Cliff's escapades. Graham most certainly would not approve. And the talk of those murdered women in the streets of the East End—the papers had been full of dreadful details. She had no place going down there. It would be best not to get involved. Surely Cliff could find some better means of helping his friend.

Chadwell's low cry brought Penelope to a halt, and she turned slowly to explore his passionate look of distress.

"Penny, she is nearly the only friend I have. It is because of me that she is in danger. I have to help her. I could take pistols and sword and storm the place, but there is no promise I will come through alive, and I have discovered lately that I very much want to live. Could you not reconsider?"

His words struck a dart through her heart, and the plea in his eyes said things she dared not hear. He asked her to help rescue his mistress. That should be the only thing she should hear in his plea. She had always known Chadwell for what he was. A man like that always kept a mistress, maybe two. That he had the temerity to come to her for help spoke volumes, but she had no wish to look deeply into the matter. Another human being was in trouble. She could not let pride stand in the way of his call for help.

"If you have pistol and sword, I should be safe enough. Let us go, Clifton. If the danger is great, we have no time to quarrel further."

Penelope thought he would refuse once more, but seeing her determination, Chadwell checked his violent opposition. He could not afford to have her walk away.

"I will hate myself for the rest of my life for this,"

he muttered, sweeping up the cloak he had thrown over a chair back. "But mercifully, my life will most likely be a short one. Let us get your pelisse."

Penelope did not tell him she had worn only a shawl. True, the intricately woven cashmere confection probably had more yards of material in it than any cloak or pelisse, but she sensed it was not the ideal covering for a sojourn into the depths of iniquity. She hurried after his long strides.

Chadwell scowled as the shawl was produced at the front entrance, but it was already too late. Penelope hurried down the marble steps to the quiet street and waited expectantly for him to direct her. A whistle produced a hired hack waiting down the drive, and Chadwell hurriedly lifted her into the dimly lighted interior.

Penelope watched in amazement as he argued with the driver and finally succeeded in talking the coat off the driver's back. He threw the rumpled redingote onto the seat and swung up to join her as the coach jolted to a start.

"You don't mean me to wear that horrible thing?" she demanded as he slid into the seat beside her. The poor springs gave way beneath the combination of Chadwell's weight and the coach's motion, and she ended up in his arms before the horses reached the street.

"You may have mine," he offered courteously. "It's a trifle cleaner." He swung his cloak from his shoulders and extracted himself from the folds, then carefully set it about Penelope's much smaller frame. "I'll not risk having to fight you out of the place, too."

Penelope nervously clutched the heavy material and tried to read his pale face in the darkness. The scar on his cheek seemed to stand out against the darkness. "Will you tell me what we are to do?"

Chadwell's arm lingered about her shoulder as he stared down into wide, curious eyes. "I had not thought the risk so great until now. Penelope, this is foolish. Let me take you home. I will find some other means of helping Nell."

The other woman's name made her wince, but she bravely demanded the facts. "Let me hear what you mean to do, and I will decide if it is too risky."

She could not quite fathom the sudden intensity of his gaze, but she read the meaning of his hard hug well enough. He removed his arm quickly before she could reprimand him, but its strength lingered, abetted by the clinging masculine scent of the cloak around her.

"Even when I explain, you will not understand the dangerousness of the situation. It is not just poverty that rules the place where we are going, but evil. How much do you know of evil, Penelope?"

Penelope considered the question carefully. She knew of men in the village who beat their wives, and worse. She knew of women who beat their children until they could not stand. She knew behind closed doors much worse might be done, but she could not honestly say she knew of evil. She knew only poverty and wretchedness and cruelty, and that not firsthand. She had led a protected and comfortable life in comparison.

"Very little, I'm afraid; only that it exists." She pulled the cloak tighter and stared out at the empty streets. It was past midnight, and all sane people stayed behind locked doors. Only occasionally did another carriage clip-clop hurriedly past, or a lone figure dart across the street and into the shadows again. They were passing the smaller shops on the outskirts of the business district. No theaters or brightly lighted mansions added gaiety to this night scene.

"Perhaps it is better if you remain innocent," Chadwell replied thoughtfully. "I do not think I wish to be the one to enlighten you. I'll simply explain what I mean to do, and if you agree, you must promise to do exactly as I say, without question. Agreed?"

Penelope nodded her head, afraid her tongue would reveal her nervousness.

Chadwell caught the motion and continued hurriedly. "I have succeeded in making a very dangerous man mad at me. It's my own fault for dealing with the b—, the wretch, but you don't need to know the details. He thinks to get information from me by holding Nell in a place that caters to the needs of men. I wish you did not need to understand me in this, but you must understand Nell's danger. She is not a lady, but she does not belong in a place like that, or deserve the treatment she will receive there.''

He hesitated, taking Penelope's gloved hand and trying to read her expression in the dim light of the lamp. She kept her face averted, but made a nod of understanding. Chadwell accepted that as permission to continue.

''Fortunately for me, this place has also become—I hesitate to say fashionable, but people of society are known to come there for various,'' he fought for polite words to describe the sordid business of this bordello, ''assignations. When we enter, they will simply think us a clandestine couple seeking a room for a few hours' privacy.''

Penelope shivered and Chadwell longed to pull her closer, to offer his protection, but he could not. He had no right to do so, and she must understand fully what she went into.

''How will this help Nell?'' she asked quietly when he seemed reluctant to continue.

''Once inside, I can look for the room they keep her in. You should be safe enough behind barred doors while I look. I had meant to take Nell out with me and leave the person to stay behind to leave alone, but you are too recognizable as a lady of quality to walk alone in such a place. We will have to disguise Nell somehow and send her out first, then follow shortly after. It's a ramshackle plan, I realize, but it is the best I can do in haste. I do not wish to imagine what would become of her if I left her for any length of time in that man's hands. If evil exists, he invented it.''

Clifton's harsh tone as he said this last jerked Penelope back to the real world. It was very well to set out on a romantic rescue mission, but he was talking of a man who would torture helpless women to get his way. What else would he be capable of?

"If he took Nell because of something you did, won't he be waiting for you to show up to rescue her? Shouldn't someone else go in your place?"

Her perspicacity caught him by surprise, though it shouldn't have, he realized. Penelope's streak of practicality had kept the rent paid and the larder filled for longer than he cared to imagine. He nodded agreement with her assessment of the situation.

"That would be so if he expected me to find Nell this quickly, but he does not understand the swiftness of my informants. He thinks to hold her ransom for the information he wants from me. He does not expect me to know where she is, not yet. That is another reason I have not a moment to lose."

Cliff had said she could refuse this role if she wished, but he spoke now as if it had been decided. Even as they talked, the carriage turned down narrow streets unlit by so much as the strength of a candle. She was aware of more movement here, furtive shadows darting from door to door, leaning from windows, weaving drunkenly near the carriage wheels. The faces she glimpsed were but blurs of humanity glaring through rheumy eyes at the hack, or so lost to thought as to ignore the presence of the carriage entirely. The garish clothes glimpsed hastily in doorways did not seem to blend with the filthy rags of those misfortunates in the gutters, but Penelope sensed there were not many steps from one to the other.

Shuddering, she turned her attention back to Chadwell. "How will you find her? Surely you cannot go about knocking on doors?"

The carriage halted in a narrow lane lined by tall, blank-looking edifices that once might have housed clean, respectable shops and their owners but now had fallen to a state of decay and disuse that bordered on abandonment. Candlelight flickered somewhere from the depths of the building beside them, but otherwise it appeared uninhabited.

Chadwell donned his beaver hat and picked up the driver's redingote and threw it around his shoulders. In this light Penelope's hair lost its golden glow, and with her wide eyes staring up at him expectantly, she appeared a forlorn waif. He did not want her to look at him like that. It made it too easy for him to take advantage.

"Let me tell the driver to take you home. I will find some other way of getting Nell out."

Penelope hastily pulled the hood of the cloak over her hair and took his arm. "It would be sinful to let another human being suffer for none of her own fault. Let us be quick about it." She did not question again how he intended to make this work. She feared she did not want to know.

Chadwell glanced at her uncertainly, looked back to the dark house with its hidden evils, and throwing caution to the winds, climbed out and lifted Penelope to the ground. The hack rattled away as they turned toward the once brightly painted doors of the bordello.

Chapter 14

ONCE beyond the peeling paint of the front door, they entered a narrow wooden lobby with rooms to either side. Penelope tried not to gaze into the smoky interiors of these salons but focused on the hard arm beneath her fingers and the splintered wood of the floor she must cross before reaching the darkened stairs in the rear. She did not look up even to observe the voluptuous figure leaning against the newel post. She just knew the woman was there.

Chadwell showed no such hesitation. He blatantly admired the dark-haired beauty's full-blown charms while sliding his arm around Penelope's waist and drawing her closer. His act was as much to give her strength as it was for show. He could feel her tremors through the folds of the cloak.

"What can I do for you, sweetheart?" The woman's deep-throated voice murmured huskily over the other sounds emanating from behind thin walls.

Penelope jumped nervously at the sound of a manic cackle from one of the salons, but that noise was better than the low moans she detected from somewhere above them. Deep male voices resounded clearly above all else, and pinpricks of fear began to rise along her arms.

"A room, madame, if you have one to spare. My lady and I have need of a few hours' respite." Chadwell winked knowingly at the blowsy creature and drew his "paramour" for the evening closer, until Penelope was practically wrapped in his arms.

The woman looked doubtfully at Penelope's hidden slenderness and back to the towering, deep-chested

gentleman. "She don't look too willing, if you ask
me. The likes of you will crush her like a sparrow, no
doubt. Why don't you find a real woman?"

The whore moved boldly forward, swinging her am-
ple charms. Garbed in a tinselly red dress that wrinkled at the waist and sagged too low at the top, she
made quite a spectacle of female pulchritude, and once
within Penelope's field of vision she could not help
but stare. She had never seen another woman quite so
naked before, and she wanted to kick Cliff's shins as
he continued to admire the majestic peaks displayed
before him. Penelope had the vicious vision of a cow
with swollen udders, but obviously men preferred this
sight.

Sensing Penelope's stiff stance, Chadwell hurriedly
brought the interview to a conclusion. With a wicked
leer he tipped Penelope's chin up with his finger so
he could look beneath her hood without the other
woman seeing her face. "The lady has little choice in
the matter, does she now? That's what adds spice to
life."

Penelope read the devilment in his eyes and had the
sense to keep her lips closed. She would hate to truly
be forced into his service. His arm felt like an iron
band wrapped around her middle.

The woman shrugged and held out her hand for the
toll. "Just don't leave her remains behind unless
they're in working condition. We can always use a new
girl, particularly the quality kind."

Hard eyes revealed she had not missed a thing. Beneath Penelope's concealing cloak a satin slipper
peeped, and glimpses of blue finery glimmered with
her movements. Coupled with the way she held her
head and moved gracefully at the gentleman's side, the
evidence was clear that the lady was no ordinary
streetwalker.

Chadwell agreeably handed over the required coins,
and the woman stepped out of their way. Her gaze
followed them as they rapidly strode up the narrow
back stairs.

Penelope scarcely had time to recover from that en-

counter before the next loomed into view. An African
in purple silk and billowing pantaloons rose from the
floor as they reached the top of the stairs. Penelope
gasped and tried not to stare. The silk shirt appeared
to have no fastenings and lay open to his waist. She
had never seen skin so black, and her fascination almost overcame her fear.

Irked by the path of Penelope's gaze, Chadwell
spoke sharply to the servant. "We've paid for a room.
Show us a clean one."

The man bowed and led them down a hall past doors
once decorated in an array of colors. Several panels
seemed to have exotic scenes painted upon them, but
Chadwell jerked Penelope past these before she could
interpret the peeling blur of fleshy pinks and browns.

She could not avoid the scene painted upon the door
the servant led them to, however. Even though the colors had faded and cracked, she could discern the image of a woman in a full ball gown of the prior century,
except the gown appeared to have no bodice. The top-
less gown did not cause her to crimson so much as
what the woman was doing and who she was doing it
with. The paintings she had seen in the museum had
never shown completely naked males, and her eyes
grew wide at the sight of such masculine endowments.

Chadwell bit back a curse, shoved the door open,
and handed the servant a coin before pushing Penelope
inside and closing the door behind them.

They had been provided a single candle, and even
in its flickering light he could see how pale she had
become. Her eyes were like huge, wounded pansies
staring up at him tremulously. So much for innocence.

"I warned you," he observed harshly, fighting back
his own guilt. "It's too late to cry off now."

Penelope nodded her understanding, unable to move
her thickened tongue. She had no idea of the contents
of the room beyond the circle of light in Clifton's hand.
That circle betrayed enough of her fears without imagining her surroundings. Surely the painting was a car-
toon exaggeration. This man standing here in elegant
velvet and white linen could not look like that without

his clothes. Yet for the first time, she felt her awareness of his overt masculinity and had some understanding of the sensation.

Not daring to touch her, Chadwell raised the candle
to distinguish the room's contents. A sagging bed, a
washstand with a chipped porcelain bowl and pot, and
a threadbare armchair with straight wooden legs were
the extent of the furnishings. He found another can-
dlestick and lit the short stub, throwing the bed into
instant clarity.

Distracted by this movement, Penelope rolled up her
nose in disgust at the untidy covers and blackened pillow casing thus revealed. "Surely people do not really
sleep here. I have seen cleaner inns."

Chadwell looked at her oddly and almost chuckled
as he caught a glimpse of her distaste. "Few people
come here to sleep, my darling. The air of sordidness
adds a certain excitement, don't you agree?"

She gave him an incredulous look that should have
frozen the hair off his eyebrows. Clifton had to bite
back his laughter. Outraged innocence had never been
so diverting.

"I'm sorry, Penny. I will try not to leave you here
too long. Do you think you can manage until I get
back?"

Penelope frowned worriedly. "I do not see what
you can do with that . . . that creature sitting right
down the hall. He's not going to let you search the
place. And if this Nell is being held prisoner, surely
she will be locked in. It is impossible."

"Only to the uninformed, my dear. The 'creature'
at the end of the hall is paid to keep quiet. I can bribe
him to hold you here while I go out and dally with the
other ladies, and he will not find it at all shocking
should I return with one or two more." He refrained
from mentioning that he could return with one or two
more men or women without stirring a comment from
the African. Let her retain some innocence from this
night. "I will find my way around as quickly as I
might. I expect Nell is being offered for sale upstairs.
Coins open every door in this place."

That unexpected crudity shocked Penelope into silence. The hardness in his eyes frightened her. She had placed herself very much at his mercy if what he said was true. She could only rely on Chadwell's inherent gentlemanliness to come out of this without harm, and she very much suspected Clifton was a gentleman only when he felt like it.

Seeing her fear turn toward him, Chadwell turned his mouth up grimly. "Good. You are beginning to understand how dangerous your innocence is. If you are to live in this city, you had better learn to be a little more aware of what can happen to attractive women on their own. It was foolish of you to accompany me."

"I cannot go about distrusting everyone," she whispered hoarsely, praying her instincts were right.

"But you need not be quite so trusting, either." Chadwell pulled the cloak from her shoulders and let it fall to the floor while his gaze boldly admired the delicate beauty of creamy skin framed by the diaphanous gown. There was nothing lush or voluptuous about Penelope's slender figure, but she had the proper curves to make a man ache to hold her.

His hand went out to touch her waist, and before he knew what he was doing, he pulled her into his embrace and bent to mold her full lips to his.

A riot of emotions instantly erupted within Penelope as she fought his grasp and succumbed to Cliff's heated kiss at the same time. Her body wanted what he was doing now, longed to be held close against his long, powerful frame, needed the passion of his lips plying hers into surrender. She had wanted this from the minute she had walked into that anteroom a million years ago. She devoured the taste of wine on his tongue, drank in the musky scent of his skin, marveled at the rough scratch of his beard as he clung desperately to her lips and sought succor there. Her fingers slid over the velvet of his coat, sublimely aware of the tension in the straining muscles beneath the disguising material.

Yet she knew it was wrong, knew it with every fiber

of her being, and her heart and soul clamored to be heard. She was a married woman, and a rake like this had no place in her life. It had been pure madness to allow him to bring her here. She had practically assisted in her own seduction. The thought of being taken in this den of iniquity repulsed her until she gained the strength to push away.

Breathless, she backed away, covering her mouth with the back of her hand as she stared at Chadwell in gasping apprehension. She had no escape, but she still could not believe he would force her.

As if reading her thoughts, Chadwell shrugged wryly. "I would be inclined to try, my lady, had we been anywhere else or under any other circumstances. As it is, your virtue is safe with me. I will make haste to find Nell, then we'll depart promptly."

He swung around and walked out the door.

Penelope stared at the closed wooden panel in sudden terror, then rushed to throw the bar. She had no desire to discover what other perversions haunted the halls of this wicked house.

With Chadwell gone, her senses became attuned to the night around her. She glanced nervously around at the sound of mice scampering between the walls. She touched her fingers to the chafed skin around her lips where Chadwell's beard had scraped. She could still taste the sweet wine of his kiss, and her legs nearly crumpled at the flood of desire sweeping through her.

Fearfully lowering herself to the torn cushion of the chair, she strained to see around her. The darkness made it impossible to decipher details, but enhanced the overexcited path of her imagination. On the other side of the wall a woman moaned and a man cursed. She heard the distinct sound of a slap, but could not quite determine the source of the fierce thumping noises that followed.

Other cries penetrated the walls, weird wails that did not quite seem to be those of one in pain or fear, throaty masculine sounds that tightened her stomach into a hard coil. After a while, she felt as if she had entered one of the first circles of hell, and her teeth clenched nervously to keep from chattering.

She wanted Chadwell to return. She should never have come here. What if something happened to him? How would she escape? Graham would never understand. She desperately needed his strong arms around her, holding her, hiding her from these indecent noises, protecting her illusions.

Exclaiming over her foolishness, Penelope rose and began to pace the room. The night was warm and she did not need both cloak and shawl, but she wrapped them around her, anyway. Immediately, Chadwell's masculine scent drifted from the encompassing cloak and she clung to it, enjoying the slightly spicy aroma of his shaving soap. The tight ball in her center flowered open, leaving a gaping hunger she could not ignore.

She paced faster, starting at the sound of Clifton's voice somewhere above her. He did not seem troubled, and she had to assume he was safe. She just wished he would hurry.

A man like that would probably think nothing of making love to his mistress and several of the prostitutes before deciding to call it a night, she thought bitterly at the night dragged longer. Those passionate moans overhead could be the lovely, misguided Nell. The man's low murmurs could be Clifton's loving phrases. He was generous with his pretty compliments and sweet endearments. He had probably turned many a poor maid's head. How many innocents had his charming good looks brought to ruin? The hapless Nell was no doubt one of many.

Penelope had worked herself into such a state by the time the knock rapped at the door that she almost refused to answer it. Recovering herself, she raced to throw back the bolt before remembering to ask who was there. Luckily, she heard Clifton's murmured voice before the door swung open.

He caught her by the waist as soon as the door opened, and Penelope gave a startled cry. With a look of satisfaction, Chadwell stepped aside to allow another figure to slip through. He threw the bolt and bent a fierce kiss to Penelope's lips before straightening and releasing her.

"Very good, my love. Now let us have a scream of outrage. You will have to take off that pretty gown and slippers, too." Without waiting for Penelope's protest, he gestured to the scantily garbed woman hiding in the shadows. "Off with yours, too, Nellie. We must make this convincing. You are much of a size, I think. The cloaks will keep anyone from noticing the differences."

Penelope stared at his broad face as if he had gone mad. Impatiently he reached to swing her around, and his fingers easily located the ties of her bodice. "Quickly, Penny. Scream. Give us an argument."

"You are mad! You are quite insane! Let me go!" Penelope attempted to jerk from his hands, but his grasp was unbreakable. She could feel the folds of her bodice begin to separate, and she squirmed helplessly to avoid his nimble fingers.

"Very good. A little louder, please," Clifton murmured irrepressibly. In a rough voice he yelled, "Stop it, you silly chit! What do you think we came here for?"

In her corner Nellie began to giggle at the sight of the handsomely dressed gentleman rapidly unfrocking the furious lady. The combination of fear and nervousness she had endured this day had seriously undermined her usual good-natured complacency, but under Chadwell's protection, she began to recover somewhat. She quickly began to remove the tawdry satin that she had been wearing when she was abducted.

"You can't do this! You have no right!" Penelope gave a cry of dismay as her lovely gown fell to the floor, leaving her clad only in a thin chemise and stockings. Her arms instinctively wrapped over her breasts, but then she couldn't reach for her gown.

Penny's ladylike cries did not echo quite so loudly as he would like, but they would have to do. Chadwell turned to grab Nell's gown from her hands. "I'll damned well do what I want! You owe me this one. What do you think you are going to do about it?'' he hollered as he jerked the full skirt over Penelope's honey-colored tresses.

With a grin he caught her scantily clad waist and bodily lifted her from the floor, extracting a satisfactory scream as Nell bent and grabbed the fancy gown from beneath Penelope's feet.

"Give me a loud slap, sir," Nell whispered fiercely, presenting her well-rounded bottom for his target.

Understanding, Chadwell gave her a wallop that resounded nicely, though done with cupped hand and little pain.

Penelope screamed at this idiocy, although comprehension finally began to dawn as she struggled into the gown so clumsily flung over her head. With dismay she discovered the old-fashioned, low-cut bodice nearly fell off her, and she was scarcely better covered than in her chemise. Clifton's appraising glance quickly took note of this situation, but he did nothing more than grin at the sight revealed.

Nell was having a little more trouble struggling into Penelope's snugly formed bodice, and Clifton hastened to help. With a gesture he ordered more screaming to cover the delay.

With great pleasure Penelope reached for the wretched washbowl and heaved it at his head with a furious crash. "You lying oaf!" She flung the pot next, hearing it splintering against the wall with great effect. "You rutting bounder! I'll have you give me Spanish coin! The devil take you, I'll not be made a cake of!" Running out of ammunition and curses, she turned the washstand over with a satisfactory slam.

Chadwell grinned his appreciation as he swept the cloak from the floor and flung it over Nell, hiding the fact that he could not quite tie the bodice. "Don't cut up stiff with me, my little Cyprian. If the color of my coin isn't good enough, you can take yourself out of here. I'll be damned if I'll escort you!"

He gave Nell a shove toward the door. She didn't need to be told twice. With Penelope's scream of outrage echoing down the hall, she slammed the door and ran, clattering down the stairs as fast as she could go.

Clifton threw off his coat and cravat and raced after her, shaking his fist and cursing until she was well down the stairs and out the door. Not until he knew Nell was safe and on the way to his well-paid hack driver did he turn around and produce a sheepish look for the audience now peering out from behind half a dozen doors. With a mild shrug of his broad shoulders, he explained to staring faces, ''Fellow's got a right to get what he pays for, ain't he?''

With a swagger that nearly sent Penelope into convulsions, he returned to the room and his new paramour.

''Now what?'' she hissed as he slammed the door and reached for his discarded clothes.

''We get you the hell out of here before you start talking cant any more fluently.'' He jerked his coat on and flung his cravat loosely around his neck as he regarded Penelope with a mixture of admiration and confusion.

Now that the worst was over, the rush of excitement fled, leaving her drained and nervous. She clutched at her gaping bodice and tried to avoid his eyes. ''How can I go out like this? They'll think me a . . .''

''A whore? Very good. That's what I want them to think.'' He tugged a shiny curl to fall to her bare shoulder, creating an enchantingly disheveled look with the strands of hair flying loose elsewhere from his rough handling. ''I'm sorry, poppet, but this is the only way to get us out of here. It's quite obvious you're not Nell, or one of their own. They'll have to let us pass.''

His hand lingered a second too long on her shoulder, and Penelope held her breath as she felt the heated path of his gaze. The upper curve of her breasts burned beneath the intensity of his look, and a tingle of desire took root in her center and began to grow as her hunger reacted to his. She felt her nipples rise achingly against the slippery satin, and she knew he could see their outline clearly through the thin layers of material.

She literally ached when he moved away without touching her.

"One more performance, my pretty Penny," he whispered hoarsely, flinging his redingote over his arm. "One more performance and we'll be home."

He took her elbow and gently steered her toward the door. He pried her grip loose from the bodice and draped the loose material to show as little as possible, though the daring cleavage revealed marked her clearly as a woman of few morals.

"You must smile at me, Penelope. Cling to my arm and act as if I've just promised you all the queen's jewels."

She stared at him in disbelief, but the hard line at the corner of Chadwell's mouth made it clear this was not over. Gulping, she offered a tremulous smile and leaned farther against him.

"Where's the lionhearted girl who dared call me a rutting bounder and fling a chamber pot at my head?" he whispered tauntingly in her ear, wrapping his arm strongly about her waist.

"She is cursing the day she ever saw your face, sir." Calling up a particularly vapid look she remembered from a loose-witted girl back home, she clung to his arm and beamed vacantly up at him.

Clifton choked and spluttered, then grinned weakly. "Very good, my dear. Just hold that pose until we get outside."

The hall was quiet again. Only the African remained at his post, and he showed no curiosity as the gentleman left with a common streetwalker instead of the elegant lady he had arrived with. Going down the stairs they could see several new arrivals in the lobby staring up at them with curiosity, but the bold beauty had apparently found a companion for the evening.

Penelope felt her smile freeze on her face as Chadwell genially greeted the men openly ogling her nearly bare bosom. She longed to wrap the shawl on her arm over her shoulders, but that would be out of character. Only ladies wealthy enough to own such an expensive garment knew how to wield the yards of material well.

She clung tighter to Clifton's arm and continued beaming witlessly at the dark shadow of his jaw as he exchanged words with a man who appeared to be the proprietor. The man scowled at her but said nothing as Cliff donned his hat and they stepped out into the night.

The hack had left with Nell, carrying her to safety but abandoning them to this dark alley. Wordlessly they hurried toward a wider thoroughfare where transportation might be found. Penelope never felt more grateful for Chadwell's frighteningly muscular size than she did now. The denizens of these streets backed away as he rushed her along beside him. Their extreme wariness this night might have aught to do with the rumors of the beast who stalked these streets murdering women. Chadwell looked fearsome enough to fit such a role.

When they reached a wider street and still saw no sign of a hack, Penelope's teeth began to chatter. Chadwell took the shawl from her and wrapped it around her bare arms, but the foggy night air had little to do with her chill.

As ease for her sorely frayed nerves, she began to talk. "How did you find her? Was it difficult?"

Keeping his arm firmly around her waist, Chadwell hurried her down still another street. "Not at all. Nell comes from these streets and can take care of herself. She nearly decapitated the first man who tried to touch her. She hurt another so badly he won't be able to touch another woman for a long time. When they thought to drug her into senselessness, she flung the plate in their faces. By the time I came along they had decided to starve her into submission. They thought it would be amusing to see what she would do to a gentleman, I suspect. When I went in and didn't come out, they got bored and left only one guard to wait for me. He should get a good night's sleep before they find him."

The way he said this made Penelope shiver more. She glanced up at the taut line of his jaw and chose to change the subject. She didn't want to know what means he had used to put the guard to sleep.

"Where did you tell Nell to go? Surely she won't be safe wherever you've been keeping her?"

Chadwell gave a jerk and nearly came to a halt as he stared incredulously into Penelope's curious expression. "Keeping her? Keeping Nell? Do you mean to say you went in that place back there thinking you helped me to rescue my mistress? Penelope, you are the most caper-witted gudgeon I ever care to meet!"

Before she could make an indignant reply, Chadwell gave an ear-piercing whistle and flagged a weary hack heading home for the night. The driver looked nervously at his immense size and lifted the whip to urge his horses faster, but Chadwell grabbed the door, jerked it open, and jumped on the step to grab the reins from the man's hands. Before the terrified driver could jump from his seat in terror, Chadwell threw him a bag of coins and gave him Graham's address. Then he stepped down and lifted Penelope into the coach and clambered up after her before the man could have second thoughts.

As the coach jerked into motion, Chadwell exuberantly gathered Penelope into his arms and kissed her cheeks. "I think I could learn to love a gudgeon like you, pretty Penny. Tell me you love me, too."

"I'll do no such of a thing!" Indignantly Penelope attempted to extricate herself from his embrace, but he happily wrapped his arm around her shoulders and pulled her to his side. "What was I supposed to think? That Nell was your sister?"

"Two of a kind we might be, but she's not my sister." He grinned foolishly into furious violet eyes, nearly giddy with relief at bringing her to safety, at last. "I have no mistress at the moment, my lady. Would you accept the position?"

His laughter boomed through the streets as Penelope wrenched an arm free and tried to slap him.

The next minute, quiet reigned as he wrapped her in his arms and drowned her protests with the fierceness of his kiss.

Chapter 15

ALL the evening's fears and excitements were released by just the touch of his lips on hers. All thought
fled as Penelope succumbed to the urgent hunger of
Chadwell's kiss and the demands of her pent-up emotions. The thrill of his chiseled lips molding to hers
prevented conscious thought, and her hands went instinctively to his chest as Cliff pulled her closer.

With more tenderness than that first, fierce encounter, he began to ply her lips with butterfly touches that
shot tremors of desire through her. Penelope breathed
deeply and the masculine scent of his skin intoxicated
her further. Her mouth began feverishly to seek his,
to hold him, and when he obliged, her lips parted almost in relief.

The touch of his tongue was a warning she ignored,
so absorbed had she become in the sensations sweeping through her. As his kiss deepened, beckoning her
closer, she bent further into his embrace until her
breasts were pressing against the coarse cloth of his
cloak. Her hands rose instinctively to his shoulders,
and Chadwell groaned achingly against her mouth and
pulled her across his knees.

It all happened much too fast after that, although at
the time it seemed a long, sweet escape into heaven.
The shawl fell away as Penelope leaned back against
Cliff's shoulder, and the overlarge bodice offered little
protection against his caressing hands.

The heat of his kisses as he fled her mouth branded
the sensitive skin behind her ear. From there, they led
a burning trail down her throat, confusing Penelope as

she sought to return his kiss but found herself helpless beneath the inexorable invasion of her senses.

The broad hand at her waist flattened to engulf the concave expanse of her waist and belly. That touch alone engendered all manner of wild fires within her. While she attempted to conquer these, the hand moved higher, gently stroking the underside of her breasts as Chadwell's kisses wreaked havoc across her throat. A strange lassitude replaced her fears, and Penelope's head fell back against his shoulder as Cliff gained his goal, sliding the loose bodice from her breast and gently claiming the peak with his fingers. Shivers of excitement began to course through her veins, rushing through her middle and finding a center low in her groin as her body responded to the gentle pressure of his fingers.

Cliff's mouth returned to hers, invading and claiming the right with all the triumph of a conquering hero. Penelope's arms slid behind his neck and her fingers buried in his hair as she gladly gave herself up to this intimacy. The cool night air blew across the heated skin of her uncovered bosom, but the sensation did nothing to cool her impassioned reaction to this man's demands.

Before she understood what she had given up, Cliff moved his lips from her mouth to the taut crest of her breast, and Penelope cried out her surprise and joy. Never had she known it would be like this, and as the heat of his mouth drew her closer into his hold and she arched eagerly to meet his hungry tongue, she took no notice of his hand resting upon her ankle and slowly rising higher.

He was so much more experienced than she, so wise in the ways of love, that he took unfair advantage and knew it, but he could not help himself. Each tentative kiss she offered nearly drove him insane in his quest for more. Her joyous wonder as he taught her the sensations of her lovely body made it impossible to stop. By the time the coach rattled down the silent street to stand before the gargoyle-protected stairs, the demands of Chadwell's body cried out for release.

As Cliff's hand slid from the relative safety of her stockinged calf to the bare skin above her garter, the carriage rolled to a halt. The shocking touch of his heated palm upon her thigh at the same time as he raised his head to observe their location propelled Penelope violently from her lethargy. All the wonderful, exciting new sensations fled beneath the flood of shame, and she abruptly shoved herself from Cliff's lap.

Before he could even open the door for her, she grabbed her shawl and opened it herself, hopping down and flying up the walkway without looking back. Disheveled curls streamed down her back as she ran, and she had to lift her overlarge skirt above her ankles to negotiate the stairs. Chadwell groaned as the door opened and closed behind her, and his body achingly reminded him of its needs. He could run after her, but the result would inevitably be rape. She deserved better than that.

Penelope fled past the sleepy footman, the guttering lamps on the stairs, and into the relative security of the small salon that joined her chamber with Graham's. Frantically she glanced at his closed doors, and with swift decision she turned to her own. She could not go to him looking like this.

With the haste of madness Penelope stripped the cheap satin from her burning body, feverishly pulled the pins from her hair, and slipped into the lovely lace nightgown Augusta had sewn for her wedding night. Heart pounding fiercely, she advanced upon the door separating her from her husband.

As always, John answered her scratch, but this time, Penelope was prepared for him. Already disheveled and frantic, she had little performing to do as she pointed at the darkened far corner of her room.

"A rat! A huge, hairy rat! John, get him please!" she cried with real anguish to the sleepy manservant.

John rubbed his eyes, stared at her with disbelief, and his chivalry finally waking, he grabbed a poker from the fireplace and advanced into the room in the direction indicated.

Triumphantly Penelope sailed into Graham's chambers and toward the safety of her husband's arms. By morning, she would be wife in more than name, and Chadwell's charms would no longer have an effect on her.

Not daring to hesitate lest her determination waver, Penelope approached the heavily draped, massive bed on flying feet. Throwing back one of the heavy velvet drapes, she prepared to launch into rapid explanations.

The bed was empty. Untouched.

Penelope's mouth dropped open at the sight of that bank of umblemished pillows. Before her mind could even fly to reasons, John appeared disapprovingly in the doorway, and a light knock rapped at her chamber door.

She wanted to run and hide and disappear into the wainscoting, never to be seen again, but she could not. She was the Viscountess Trevelyan, Baroness Wycliffe, and she had to hold her head up high and keep on living, whatever happened to her heart and soul.

Feeling her insides shredding into little pieces, Penelope marched past John and flung open her chamber door.

Chadwell stood there, his forearm leaning against the door frame as his gaze swiftly took in Penelope's delicate nightdress, then swept beyond to find John clutching a poker in a tense stance of disapproval. Cliff's already pale features drained to a shade of gray as he slowly returned his gaze to Penelope's flushed face.

"Penelope, if you'll just let me in, I'll—"

She slammed the door in his face, hoping it hit his perfect, aristocratically long nose. With vengeance in her eyes she flung around and pointed at Graham's open door. "Out, get out! All of you, out!"

Uncertain who that "all" encompassed, but understanding the command, John ran for cover. He darted into Graham's chamber and carefully, very gently, closed the door. A flying object flew against the wooden panel as it closed, and he instinctively ducked before realizing he was safe.

Emotions unexorcised by this reprehensible fall from decorum, Penelope flung herself against her silken sheets and wept as she had never wept before.

The next day dawned without any material improvement in her humor. Eyes red and puffy from crying, Penelope ordered her maid to go away before the poor creature could even enter with a tray of hot chocolate. Her body ached as if it had really been molested; she could feel the rawness of her skin in every place that Chadwell had touched with his lips, and shame flooded through her in pounding waves.

Burying her face in the pillow, she tried to shut out the memory of last night, but humiliation brought the images alive to play over and over again in her head. She kept seeing that obscene door with its portrayal of virile masculinity superimposed on the image of Chadwell standing before her in his velvet frock coat. Then she saw herself naked in his arms, his hands and lips touching her in unspeakable places, and she felt as if she would shrivel up and die of shame. She could never come out and face him again. Never.

Then her memory would fly back to Graham's empty chamber and rage would replace humiliation. Where did he go at night when she thought him ill and resting under the effects of laudanum? For she knew, without a shadow of a doubt, that this was not the first time Graham had left her alone.

He had told her to find lovers, not to interfere in his life, that this was a marriage of convenience. Why had she not believed him? In her pride and arrogance had she thought she would be the only woman he would set his eyes on? Had she thought no other woman would have him and that he was hers to do with as she wished? Fool, unadulterated fool!

This was London. This was society. She could have surrendered her virtue to Graham's cousin last night and no one would have waggled an eyebrow. No one would praise her for her sheltered loyalty to her husband, or would they condemn her for her shameless surrender to Chadwell's seduction. No one cared. No one gave a damn one way or another.

A combination of fury and humiliation and pride finally brought Penelope to her feet. She would not let this degrading world bring her to her knees. She would hold her head up and go about as usual and do what she should have done from the first—pretend Graham was a casual friend and his cousin a devil straight from hell.

Donning the brightest yellow gown she could find, tying the sash herself, Penelope swept down to brunch. Blessedly there was no one about but herself, and she sifted through the morning's flood of invitations as she ate.

Deciding she was not prepared to confront either of the male occupants of this house as yet, Penelope sent for her bonnet and gloves and set out to walk to Dolly Reardon's. The fresh air would be healthy for her lungs if it could not heal her soul.

Pulling on her gloves and fastening them as she strode down the front stairs, Penelope took little notice of her surroundings. Any fog left from the prior evening had burned off in the warm June sun, and she made up her mind to stroll in the park before returning home. She missed her garden in the country.

Not planning on wandering out of the wealthy enclave of towering mansions and manicured lawns, she felt safe in not bringing her maid along. After last night, she felt more secure in the full eye of the public than behind any of these elegantly polished front doors. Perhaps that was a foolish reaction, but she could not help how she felt.

As she passed beyond the high wrought-iron gate at the end of the drive, Penelope looked up for the first time. A shiny black phaeton rolled by under the guidance of a haughty driver in maroon livery, the high-stepping grays politely waiting until they reached the corner before marring the cobblestones with their droppings. The sun glinted off windows polished by countless maids up and down the street and sparkled to you like this elsewise. A friend of mine is in serious trouble. I need a decoy, someone I can trust, but the task is of such a questionable nature that I dare not risk the reputation of an innocent. Please, Penny, give it some thought. Perhaps one of the maids has a friend. Let us go back to the house and ask. They will listen to you."

A puzzled frown formed above her nose as she realized Chadwell was serious. She shook her head slowly as she considered his question. "No, Cliff, I really cannot send one of the maids with you. They would feel obligated to obey and it would be on my hands should anything happen to them. The same with their friends. Put yourself in their position. How could they refuse? It will not do at all. If it is so very desperate, why can't I help you? There is little that I have not seen. I'm really not so very innocent as you would think."

Chadwell gave a start at that declaration, but seeing the seriousness of her really very innocent face, he managed a faint smile. "You would have me believe you are fast, Lady Trevelyan? If so, you have certainly concealed it from me until now. No, it would not do. London's East End is not the place for a lady."

"If you can go there, so can I," she replied a trifle tartly. "You think I am not acquainted with poverty and all that entails? If you are serious about helping your friend, I am your only hope. Take me home, and I will change into something a little more suitable."

"Penelope, you could put on one of your bloody high-necked muslins and it would not hide who you are! We are not talking of hovels in the back alleys of Northampton. We are talking of brothels and bordellos and gambling hells! It will not suit." Visibly distracted by her impossible suggestion, Chadwell started to run his hand through his artfully disheveled black hair, thought better of it, and looked about as if in hopes of discovering a decanter of something strong.

His choice of words and unusual vehemence gave her cause to glance at Graham's cousin questioningly, but she realized she knew very little of this man be-on marble doorsteps that had been swept and scrubbed before the gentry rose. The rows of houses reflected quiet elegance, centuries of gently bred good taste, and immaculate and orderly efficiency.

So the heap of grimy rags cluttering the base of the gatepost, hidden from Harley's watchful eye by a carefully tended ornamental shrub, stood out like a screeching mynah in a cage of canaries. Even as Penelope spotted it, a watchman hurried forward to remove the offense from her delicate gaze.

To her surprise the bundle of rags darted from the gatepost and ran into the courtyard, frantically searching for hiding or some escape route. Beneath the grime Penelope detected a young boy, but she found nothing terrified in his defiant dark eyes when they encountered her.

"Excuse me, milady. I'll be disposing of the young ruffian for you." The watchman strode through the gate in pursuit of the stray.

Desperate, the boy cried out to the only friendly face in sight. "Mr. Chad, miss! I gots to see Mr. Chad!"

Grimly recognizing the probability that this might be one of Chadwell's valuable informants, perhaps with word of Nell, Penelope stepped in to interfere.

"I'm sorry, officer. The boy is expected here. I'll show him the way to the kitchen gate. Thank you so much for your quick assistance."

The man already had the urchin by the scruff of the neck and was hesitant to release his quarry, but under the lady's relentless glare, he shrugged and scraped a bow. The boy insolently retaliated by spitting on his polished boot. A cuff to a filthy ear was prevented by the simple expedient of Penelope stepping between them.

"If you will step around to the kitchen, one of the maids will take care of that for you, officer, and tell her I said you were to have a cup of tea and a bite to eat while you wait." Penelope quietly restrained the hostile youngster by clinging to his collar until the guard was out of sight.

Then leaning over and staring directly into narrowed brown eyes, she chastised the young offender. "The man was doing what he gets paid to do. If Mr. Chadwell intends you to visit here with any frequence, you might inform him you will need a new suit of clothes and a bath."

"Gor blimey!" As the scent of Penelope's soft cologne enveloped him, and he realized he was neither to be beat nor struck, the boy relaxed into amazed adulation.

Penelope released his collar and straightened. "A simple 'Yes, ma'am,' will suffice." She waited patiently.

"Yes, ma'am," he responded eagerly, waiting to see what that would bring him.

"Very good. Is Mr. Chadwell expecting you?"

Instantly caution leapt to his eyes. "Not per'zactly, mum." He tacked on the latter after a moment's hesitation. Penelope's inquiring stare forced him to continue. "I ain't made out for the country, mum. I can't 'ardly breathe what wi' all 'em flowers in the air and all. And I reckon I rightly rather take on old Boozer 'ere than one of 'em blitherin' cows. So's I came to arsk Mr. Chad for a position 'ere in the city, where me family is." His speech gained momentum under Penelope's patient attention.

Not quite understanding this garbled message or what it meant to Chadwell, she did grasp the fact that the boy was covered with bruises and scratches as well as dirt and that he appeared more than half starved. Not wishing to send him in the same direction as the watchman and not knowing what else to do with him, she picked up her skirt and started toward the door.

"Come. We will see if Mr. Chadwell is at home."

The boy gaped in astonishment as she marched up the spotless stairs as if she meant him to follow. When she turned to lift that inquiring eyebrow at him, he responded with the same alacrity he awarded Mr. Chadwell when that gentleman spoke sharply. He leapt to the stair beside Penelope and followed as obediently as a puppy at her heels.

Harley opened the door with a expression of horror already imprinted upon his haughty features. Penelope swept past him and signaled her follower to do the same, her flashing eyes daring the butler to utter a word of protest. No fool he, his mouth snapped closed as the urchin scampered across the threshold and scattered dust across the marble foyer.

"If Mr. Chadwell is at home, please inform him he has a caller. Meanwhile, show our guest to a bathtub and some food. In that order."

A squeal almost of pain emitted from the small ruffian at the word "bath," and he glanced frantically for escape as Penelope finished speaking. Deciding the glassy hallway provided the only hope, he made a dash for it.

Harley uttered a less than calm curse, a footman hovering in the background gave chase, and Penelope sent an authoritative command after the urchin's back, all to no effect. He slipped and slid across polished floors, scattered rugs, and almost gained the dining room before sprawling in a rather abrupt head forward manner and sliding to a stop beneath the fragile legs of a Chippendale hall table adorned with a valuable Chinese vase and its bouquet of blooming cherry blossoms.

Penelope caught her breath as he raised his head to within inches of the folded leaf, but her gaze also caught another motion at the same time, and she spoke sharply. "Alexandra, come out here at once!"

The little imp appeared at the same time as Graham's study door opened and Chadwell staggered into the fray. All eyes turned to his bleary-eyed, excessively rumpled state, including that of the urchin beneath the table, who sat up with a sound like, "Coo, blimey!" followed by the toppling of the table.

With elfin swiftness Alexandra caught the vase before it toppled to the ground, but the resultant splash of water and cherry blossoms drenched her new muslin gown. In disgust she dumped the remains over the youth howling his pain at her feet.

"Nasty boy! Look what you made me do!" she cried

indignantly, glancing down at her once beautiful new frock.

"You maggot-brained little—" The urchin prepared to launch into a tirade between hiccups of self-pity, but Chadwell had finally aroused himself to a semblance of authority.

"Pippin, shut up and go quietly with Harley. I'll deal with you shortly. Harley, get that ruffian to the kitchen immediately. Jones, quit gawking and clean up that mess." He turned a sardonic eye to Penelope in her bright bonnet and gown. "I believe the other urchin is your responsibility."

Without raising her voice, Penelope directed Alexandra. "Thank you for saving the vase, Alex. Set it down and Jones will take care of it. Mrs. Henwood will find you a new frock, and the maids will clean that one. Why were you not in the nursery where you belong?"

"It's too pretty out to sew silly stitches. I was looking for you. Is he going to stay here? And who's that?" Alexandra peeped around the corner of the newel post at the decidedly disreputable gentleman lounging in the study doorway.

"Your cousin. Now upstairs, Alexandra. We will go riding this afternoon and not sooner."

"My cousin?" Alexandra gave Chadwell a look of doubt that encompassed his unshaven face, his untidy hair, and his lack of coat or cravat, and sniffed audibly. "That nasty boy's father, I suppose." Nose in the air, she swayed primly up the graceful staircase in her best Mrs. Henwood manner.

Penelope gave Chadwell a bleak look of surprise and chagrin as she realized the possibility that the youngster could very much be right, then marched out the front door without looking back.

Chapter 16

THE look in Penelope's eyes nearly smote what remained of Chadwell's senses as those violet orbs practically accused him of fathering that starveling child. As the front door slammed behind her, he glanced over his shoulder to the nearly empty brandy decanter on the desk, wondering if he ought to take the rest of it up to bed with him.

The caterwauling from the kitchen made him grimace, and he looked up in time to catch the accusing look on the manservant's eyes as John came down the stairs to investigate the disturbance. One more black mark in his book to live down, and that was even before John discovered the state of the velvet frock coat lying on the study floor. How in hell had he got himself into this hole in the first place?

Remembering he had to do something with the orphan in the kitchen before he could find oblivion in a brandy bottle, Chadwell resolutely faced the task of climbing the stairs to his chambers. Penelope's accusing eyes followed him with every step. Woman molester. Child abuser. Drunkard. Scapegrace. Rake. Each step brought another fitting appellation to mind. Liar. Deceiver. Abuser of trust.

All of these. He was all of these and more, although perhaps not in the way she imagined. It didn't matter, though. Once she found out the truth, it was all over. He had thought it wouldn't matter. He had thought if she ever discovered the truth, he could go on as before without disturbing his life, but now he could see that was a fool's dream.

He needed her beside him to drive away this veil of

bitter loneliness, to brighten his days and nights with her smile, to caress his fears and worries with her soft, eminently practical words. But to have her, he would have to tell her the truth, and the truth would destroy whatever hopes he held of winning her trust. Either way, he lost.

The brandy had brought him to that bitter conclusion last night. The broad light of day did not improve his outlook. Swearing softly to himself, he proceeded to his chambers and a much needed shave.

Dolly leapt up and ran to her as Penelope entered the salon where Lady Reardon entertained her morning callers. "Come, let us take a walk. The sun is too nice to stay inside."

"Delphinia, what has come over you? Bring Lady Trevelyan in at once. Lady Northrup and Mrs. Simmons haven't had a chance to say hello." Lady Reardon reprimanded her irrepressible youngest child before greeting Penelope benevolently. "Do come in, Penelope. Delphinia has been over-excited since learning of Arthur's return."

Removing her bonnet, Penelope entered the room, nodding a greeting to the guests and returning the dowager's smile of joy with one of her own. "How very happy for you ! Is he here now? How is he?"

"Henry has taken him to our home in the country. We will be leaving shortly to join him. He is seriously injured, but the physicians give him every chance of surviving."

This good news did not seem to lighten Dolly's eyes as it ought, but caught in the trap of etiquette, Penelope could not excuse herself to find out what troubled her friend. The other women immediately carried her into the conversation. and as other callers arrived, it seemed impossible to extricate herself.

Her thoughts far away from the chitchat around her, Penelope took little notice of the furtive glances and whispered asides when the others thought her back turned to them. With very little self-consciousness, she would not have believed them directed at herself even had she noticed, but Graham's name mentioned in a tone of loathing and fear caught her attention faster than anything else.

Dolly attempted to intervene before Penelope could turn and find the speaker. Sitting down beside her on the love seat, she touched Penelope's hand and began to chat animatedly about the pleasures of the Surrey countryside.

It was not a topic that required much concentration, and soon Penelope was rewarded with another scrap of conversation that Dolly's chatter did not hide.

"The description is the same! The whole world knows it is. It is only because of his name and title that no one has stepped forward to accuse him."

The voice was the same as the one who had mentioned Graham's name, but Penelope could not see any connection. Perhaps their conversation had moved on to other subjects.

Desperately Dolly attempted to distract her by handing Penelope a cup of chocolate. "This is the very best I have ever had. Mother found it in a little shop behind Bond Street. They have the most extraordinary bird in the window . . ."

Whatever else Dolly had to say was lost to Penelope as the voice obviously interrupted another in a loud reprimand. "Who else do you know who wears eye patches and is large enough to halt a carriage and drag a female from inside?"

The words seemed to silence the whole room. Paling, Penelope turned to find the speaker.

The hapless Mrs. Simmons met her gaze with some semblance of defiance. A tall, stout woman of an age to affect a turban and wear a voluminous flowered print that would have done credit to a chair, she held herself as erect as her old family name allowed and met Penelope's stare without qualms.

"My husband wears eye patches, Mrs. Simmons," Penelope commented calmly, sipping on her chocolate. "Do you speak of him?"

Lady Reardon rushed to divert this direct challenge. "That was the most dashing patch he wore the other night, cut to match his coat, if I'm not mistaken. All the ladies found the effect quite remarkable.''

"But Mrs. Simmons was saying?" Already in a mood that required no assistance for igniting, Penelope forced the gossip into the open.

The old lady responded readily to the challenge. "I was saying your husband exactly matches the description of the brute who dragged a woman from her carriage last night and bludgeoned her to death right there on the street.''

Penelope refused to acknowledge the iciness forming around the cavern where her heart had been. Steadfastly she met the other woman's sharpness with cool aplomb. "How very interesting. I have never heard Graham described as a brute before. Crippled and maimed are the usual epithets he receives. I am certain he will be pleased to know he has been raised to the nobility of brute." Penelope gently set her cup upon the tray and deliberately ignoring the distress of her hostess, she rose from her seat. "I had not realized the time. If you will excuse me, I must return home before my husband discovers my absence. He will most likely beat me within an inch of my life for my neglect.''

Head held high, she stormed out of the room, her irony falling on deaf ears. The gossip was much too good to be erased by logic.

She met Guy about to enter the Reardons', but seeing her pale cheeks and flashing eyes, he did a quick about face and fell into step beside her.

"Penelope, what's wrong? You look as if you've just challenged someone to a duel." Guy's lively eyes steadied as he observed the flush rising in her cheeks.

"I believe I have. I expect her seconds to arrive at any moment. People are so thoughtlessly cruel," she added as an afterthought, which Guy had no hope of following.

"It's something to do with Trev, isn't it? Not Dolly, surely . . .'' He glanced at her hesitantly, taking her arm as they started across the street.

"Of course not." Suddenly weary of everything,

Penelope allowed her shoulders to slump just a little bit beneath the sympathetic gaze of this one friend. Graham had indicated that Guy was a rake and not to be trusted, but she found his company comfortable and not exciting. His extravagant handsomeness had no effect on her heart, but the warm pressure of his hand offered solace. That was not the effect of a rake in her book.

Guy waited for her to continue, and when she did not, he tried to pry the pieces of the puzzle from her. "No, it was not Dolly, or not Trev?"

"Not either. It's just gossip. You would think I'd have heard enough gossip to know better by now. But every time it cuts a little bit crueler." Recovering slightly from her momentary depression, Penelope glanced gratefully to Guy's pensive profile. "I am sorry to bore you with my dismals. Do not let me lead you astray. I am certain Dolly is waiting expectantly for you."

"She is no such of a thing. I only meant to call to inquire after Arthur. What have the biddies been gossiping about now that has so overset you?"

"That would be spreading the gossip now, wouldn't it? I'd suggest if you owe Graham any loyalty at all, you will stay away from your clubs for a while, though. He would not find it amusing to lose you to a duel in his name. Perhaps you can come in and persuade him it is time for all of us to retire to the country to lick our wounds and gather our strength?"

They lingered at the gates to the mansion, Hamilton holding Penelope's hand and gazing worriedly down into her eyes. "I do not normally make a cake of myself in front of others, my lady, but for you I will admit that I would give my life for Graham, if need be. Can you not tell me what is happening?"

As she had no explanation at all, Penelope shook her head and smiled sadly as she touched his lean cheek. "I am glad he has you. Don't let him drive you away."

From the windows above Graham watched this tender scene with a wrenching heart. Guy's handsome visage had once more won the heart that should have been his, and as usual, he had only himself to blame.

Fiercely holding back the cry of anguish and despair that threatened to rip from his tattered soul, Graham turned away from the window. His hunched shoulders straightened to broad wings and his leonine head rose to a ferocious angle. He had other purposes for living. God had given him this second life for some reason, and he intended to carry it out.

Unaware that Graham was up and about, Penelope returned to her usual routine without inquiring after the men in her life. Men only complicated matters, she decided firmly. It would be much better to keep her distance from all of them.

Still, she could not keep from worrying over that evil piece of gossip. Just because Graham was large and wore an eye patch did not give them reason to believe he would be the killer stalking the streets of the East End. It was ludicrous to imagine a cripple with a maimed hand capable of hauling a woman from a carriage and beating her to death before anyone could stop him. Anyone would have to be desperate for excitement to imagine such a thing.

Unfortunately, Penelope remembered too well Graham's mysterious ability to throw his walking stick aside and carry her to the carriage. The memory brought a pleasant flush to her face before she stifled the feeling, remembering also that Graham had not been home last night. She would not believe him capable of murdering a woman, but she wished she had not learned he kept a mistress rather than coming to her. That he would prefer some ladybird to herself was demeaning, in the extreme least.

Penelope stayed home that evening, sending her regrets to the Larchmonts. It was not that she feared facing society after the scene in Lady Reardon's parlor, but that she had not the strength to confront Graham or Chadwell should she venture from her chambers. Asking for her dinner to be sent upstairs, she locked her doors and spent a relaxing evening writing to her friends back in Hampshire.

Discovering Penelope neither ventured out that night nor ate her dinner with him, Graham allowed his fears to overcome his senses and instantly returned to their suite. Confronted with her locked door, he stared at it as a man does when he cannot believe his own eyes. Never had she kept that door barred to him or denied him the right to come and go from her chambers as he pleased. He had known he had hurt her, that he was in all probability losing her, but he had not come to terms with what that would mean in the strictest practical sense. To be relegated to some essential, impersonal tool such as Jones, the footman, irked him to the very depths of his soul.

Yet he turned away without a word.

Not knowing the havoc she had created in her husband's heart, Penelope descended the stairs the next day in a much better frame of mind than the previous one. Graham had promised that they might go to Hampshire soon, and she would think pleasant thoughts of this journey instead of worrying over things she could not control. It was not as if she were penniless and searching for the means to pay the rent as she had so many times in the past. Gossip could not take the food from the table, and Chadwell could not throw her from her home. She would learn to endure.

Instead of sending someone to fetch the carriage for her, Penelope wandered around to the carriage house herself. The cherry tree blooming in the kitchen yard was particularly beautiful for this late in the season, and she had a mind to inquire about the waif she had brought into the house yesterday. She assumed Chadwell had known him and knew what to do with him. She refused to contemplate the possibility that even a rakehell like Chadwell could treat his own child in such a manner. No, the urchin had something to do with his nefarious doings in the slums of London. Perhaps she could find out how Nell fared. The men in the stable were much less formal than the servants in the house she had discovered. They would tell her anything she asked.

She did not need to ask, in any case. As her slippered feet touched the rough gravel of the drive, a skinny lad of ten or eleven popped out from the open stable door with buckets in hand. His dark forelock fell over a face pale from lack of sun, but also from lack of grime, she observed. He hurried to the pump, the buckets bumping against his too thin legs.

She watched as he pumped manfully at the recalcitrant handle until he produced a satisfactory stream of water. Not seeing Penelope, he grinned in triumph at his small accomplishment. Filling the buckets, he strained to lift both before making a slow return to the stables, carefully avoiding sloshing too much water from the wooden rims.

He seemed pathetically eager to work, and Penelope's heart went out to his brave struggle. Even had he food enough in his stomach to produce the muscle needed for such a task, he was not large enough to carry those great, heavy buckets. She hurried forward to take one from his hand.

"It has been a long time since I held one of these. Let me see if I can still do it."

The boy stared in disbelief at the fashionable lady in lilac ribbons and bows as she hefted a heavy water bucket into her gentle white hands. He had never seen the like, and his astonishment came out in his usual phrase, "Gor blimey!"

Penelope made a small moue of distaste and shook her dark honeyed curls at him. "That is an ugly noise for such a beautiful morning. Try, 'Thank you, my lady.' "

" 'Ank ye, m'lady," he responded promptly, his brown eyes round as saucers as she preceded him toward the stable. "But I'll likely gets me ears boxed iffen ye go in 'ere like 'at."

"We'll see whose ears get boxed," she answered airily, her eyes narrowing in definite warning as she stepped through the open doors.

The great heaving hulks of men lounging about on sacks of grain and bundles of straw leapt to their feet as the viscountess entered their dimly lit abode. Far from looking like a delicate Marie Antoinette playing at milkmaid, Penelope bore all the appearance of an avenging angel as she swung her heavy bucket at her side. They had never seen a lady swinging a water bucket before, and they stared nervously.

"Is there some here too old or crippled to properly carry a water bucket anymore? His lordship would not care to mistreat his valuable help by making them perform tasks of which they are no longer capable." Penelope's tone was decidedly ominous as her gaze swept from the lanky young groom to the burly stable lads to the more mature but still physically able driver. Each wriggled nervously as her stare came to rest upon them. Her ladyship seldom had a harsh word for anyone, but they were quickly learning the sharp edge her tongue could take beneath sweet words.

"Well, m'lady, he ain't much use for aught else," the groom finally boldly risked saying.

"Nor will he be if his back is broken at an early age," Penelope replied acidly. "Do none of you remember what it is to be young and eager to learn? Can you not remember what lessons you learned first? Or are you too much above yourselves to teach what you all must have humbly learned at some other man's feet?"

Her scorn stung, and the men dropped their heads, unable to meet her eyes. Whatever they remembered of their upbringing, the harsh words, the rod and strap, or the kindness of some understanding older man, they all remembered how it felt to be young and discouraged. That hurt look in her ladyship's eyes brought that back to them.

"I'll show him where the grain is, milady," one of the younger stable lads offered.

"Good." Penelope looked down at the pitifully thin face staring up at her in awe. "Pippin, is it not?" At his nod, she continued, "Have you eaten? Has Mr. Chadwell seen that you were given a bed?"

The child nodded his head eagerly. "I ates so much my belly blew up—blooey!" he spurted with pride and colorfulness that made his meaning entirely clear.

Penelope smiled faintly. "I will tell Cook what

foods will be good for you so that does not happen again. You must eat whatever he gives you so you will be strong enough to carry both buckets like the other men. Is this what you wanted when you came looking for Mr. Chadwell?''

"Yes, mum." He nodded with great enthusiasm. " 'Em horses are smack up to all the rigs, they is. Ain't nuffink like 'em cows.''

"Very good. Then if you are certain you are happy here, we must let your family know you are safe. Is there some way I can get word to them?'' The devil made her ask this. She was not such a great fool as to think a child whose family cared about him would let him go about as he had, but she wanted to know more of his connection with Chadwell, and she could think of no better way to do it.

The peaked face grew suddenly tough and stern and the defiant expression of yesterday returned. "Don't 'ave no family, mum. None 'cept my baby sister, and I reckon she'll forget 'bout me soon enough.''

The way he said that warned he was on the brink of tears and fighting the shame in front of these men. Penelope nodded understanding, turned to go, then casually glanced over her shoulder in afterthought. "You know, there are some old clothes up in the attic that just might fit you. You'd better come along for a minute and let the seamstress measure you.'' She glanced up to the men who had listened to her every word while seemingly busying themselves with their morning chores. "I will send Pippin directly back to learn his place, but I think you can spare him for just this morning.''

The boy warily followed her out, perhaps afraid another bath was in the offing. Penelope reassured him by stepping well out of the way of prying eyes and eavesdropping ears. "Where is your sister, Pippin?''

He stared at her warily, looked away from her frank gaze, scuffed his toe in the gravel, and muttered, "Wi' me da.''

"With your father?'' She started to admonish him for lying about having no family, but she could see his defenses rising already. There were times when she had considered herself without family, too. "Then she is safe and you need not worry about her?" She made it a question, well aware his tears denied the words.

He squirmed, stuffing his hands in his pockets. He knew the gentry were different, that he had no right speaking out to this fine lady, but he was still little boy enough to believe in miracles. After all, Mr. Chadwell had rescued him when his da was about to split his head in two for talking back to him. Anything could happen when the gentry were around.

" 'E'll sell 'er, mum," he muttered apologetically. "She's 'is fav'rite now, but I seen 'im feedin' 'er the gin. 'E'll sell 'er, just like all the others. 'E needs the gin, 'e do, an' so will she. She won't cry for nuffink when the gin's in 'er. 'E ain't got me to steal for 'im now, so 'e's got to sell 'er."

Appalled as much by what he did not say as what he did, Penelope could only stare at him. She had heard of people selling their babies. Desperate poverty made desperate people, and perhaps the children were better off with families who wanted them. That was what she had told herself until now. Pippin's unspoken words and the tale of gin to render an infant unconscious spoke of unspeakable crimes she could not dare imagine. She shuddered, then looked grim.

Holding her hand out, she ordered, "Come with me, Pippin. We will find your father and I will buy your baby sister."

Hope springs eternal, and the child leapt to do her bidding. The fate of his sister concerned him more than the fate of this seemingly invincible lady.

Chapter 17

EVEN in the bright light of a marvelous June day the streets they traversed seemed gray. Judging by the filth running through the gutter and the precarious tilt of narrow buildings in even narrower lanes, this was much the same part of London that Chadwell had taken her to just two nights before. Penelope had hoped never to see such sin again, but her errand of mercy made her brave, or foolish.

Penelope stared out the coach window at the dull, gray faces in the dull, gray streets. At least at night there had been an occasional flash of color, a light, a raucous laugh. By day, after they left the markets behind, there was nothing but the empty stares of people with no where to go and nothing to do when they got there.

They had to take a hack for this last leg of their journey. Trev's driver had refused to take her any further into the warrens of the slum, and she had to make a hasty exit before he turned around and took her home. And now it appeared as if the hack had reached the end of its course. The muddy path that lay ahead would not allow the passing of a vehicle. They would have to walk.

Even the boy began to look grave when it appeared the lady intended to descend into the mire of the street that had been his home these past ten years. Perched on the opposite seat so he could watch his world go by from the grandeur of the cracked paper at the window, he suddenly came back to reality at the thought of the lady stepping into that world.

"No, mum, you mustn't. It ain't safe. I'll go find me da. You stay 'ere.''

Penelope looked uncertain. She was hesitant about sending the boy out where she could not find him should anything happen to prevent his return. She was equally hesitant of going where she feared she herself might disappear and never be seen again. It had been insane to think she could do this alone, but she had been too proud to ask help of Graham or Chadwell. Pride had ever been her downfall.

The boy answered her dilemma. Quicker than she could think, he leapt from the coach and disappeared in an alley between two buildings she would have thought impossible to enter. She gazed after him with misgiving, but the appearance of two sinister men in the doorway of another building kept her from attempting to follow.

With a word to the driver she closed the coach door and prepared to wait. The driver had not been pleased with this route and he was even less so at being forced to wait here, but the lady's coins paid him for a week's work. He could not afford not to oblige.

The stink of the river joined the stink of the gutter to permeate the air through the cracks of the ramshackle carriage. Penelope held a perfumed handkerchief to her nose as she contrived to stay as far out of sight as she could. The two men continued to stand on the crumbling stairs, staring at the hack through narrowed eyes, and fear seeped in with the same pervasiveness as the smell.

She shouldn't let her imagination play games with her. Just because one of the men had long, unwashed hair and his hand in his coat pocket did not mean he carried a pistol or knife there. And the gap-toothed grin of the sandy-haired fellow as he seemed to stare right into her eyes probably meant he was enjoying an idle jest and not contemplating mayhem. She should know better than to judge by appearances. Where would she be now if she had judged Graham by his terrifying appearance?

Gradually Penelope became aware of other faces

craning to see inside the hack, of idle figures lounging against buildings and in doorways. Surely they must have more to do on a day like this than wonder at a hack stopped in a lane? But seemingly they didn't, and her nervousness began to grow with the size of the crowd.

So did the driver's. His argument grew vehement, and Penelope felt she would soon lose before she spied the small figure of Pippin darting between legs and dodging down the street. She breathed a sigh of relief and pointed him out to the driver who reluctantly agreed to wait.

The coach door flew open and wide, brown eyes stared up at her with a relief akin to her own. " 'E's comin', mum, m'lady," he amended hurriedly. " 'E's bringin' 'er."

Penelope glanced out to see a short, rotund man waddling rapidly down the street carrying what appeared to be a bundle of rags, except that a mass of golden curls spilled out the top. The man's heavy jowls did not disguise the meanness of his mouth, nor did his heavy lids hide the reddened signs of debauchery in his eyes. She shuddered at the cruelty she saw in that face. How could a man like that breed innocents? It seemed they would have to inherit the evil.

Perhaps their mother or mothers had been decent women. Certainly she saw no sign of cruelty or degeneration in Pippin's worried eyes, and when the man stopped outside the door, she could see no signs of anything in the blank blue eyes of the infant. No intelligence, no life, no heart or soul shone from those mirrored eyes. Penelope nearly wept at the sight of that lovely vacuous face, but when she looked up to the father, her eyes hardened to angry pools of violet.

She waited, not daring to speak first. By all rights she ought to rip the child from his hands and order the carriage to flee, but the man was the child's father and the tired hack horses couldn't outrun an angry man. She would wait and see what happened.

"The boy says ye 'ave an intr'st in me Goldie?" He spoke in a nasal whine, his gaze darting all about as he took in Penelope's fashionable gown, the golden ring on her finger, the fresh youth of her face. He seemed to grow more confident as he hugged the infant closer. " 'Er mum's dead, ye see, an' I can't rightly take care of the two of 'em. Pippin says ye're mighty good to 'im. but 'e's a big boy and looks arter 'imself, ye see. Goldie 'ere, she's mighty special to me. Just like 'er mum, she is.''

"I haven't time to dicker with you, sir. The child needs food and fresh air and a good home. I will provide her that. Will a sovereign be sufficient to convince you to give her up to better things?''

The man's eyes gleamed as Penelope produced the shiny coin from a small purse in her reticule, but he continued to clutch his silent bundle. "I orter, I really orter, but she's all I got now that my boy's off on 'is own. I can't bear to part wi' 'er, and that's a fact.''

Accustomed to bargaining to pinch every penny she could, Penelope knew this ploy, but she found it difficult to argue over the cost of a child's life. Her lips grew thin as she gestured for Pippin to climb in.

"It's time we go, Pippin.'' Producing a second coin, Penelope held it temptingly in her palm. "Two sovereigns or we'll be gone. I wish to make Pippin happy, but there is a limit to my generosity.''

The man whined a protest, eyeing the purse still bulging with other coins. Terrified the lady meant what she said, Pippin acted with more haste than wisdom. Catching his father entirely by surprise, he reached up and grabbed the bundle from his hands, then leapt into the carriage, slamming the door behind him.

" 'Ere, mum, let's get on wi' it.'' He shoved the child into Penelope's arms and rapped hastily for the driver to leave.

Of course, there was no chance of such a scheme working. The hack could not turn down the next lane quickly enough to escape, nor jerk to a start fast enough to throw off the screaming, furious man clinging to the door. But it was enough to bring the gathering crowd streaming into the street to join the action.

Penelope screamed as the fat man jerked open the coach door and reached into the interior to retrieve the infant. Someone else climbed to the other side of the carriage and punched out the cracked and yellowing paper of the window to reach in and grab whatever was available. Others were scrambling up over the back of the coach as if it were an adventurous mountain to climb, while more surrounded the horses, screaming curses and preventing escape.

Pippin beat wildly with his fists at the man reaching through the windows for a fistful of Penelope's hair. Penelope screamed and clung tightly to the infant in her arms, kicking with slippered feet at the cruel man blocking the doorway. The driver outside had no more protection than his whip, and he swung it wildly, missing his aim more often than not and succeeding only in infuriating his captors to stronger jeers and feats.

The coach began to rock in the tumult, and Penelope had all visions of being cast out into the streets and stripped to the bones by the carrion closing in for the kill. Still, she could not surrender the child.

The sound of a horse galloping down the muddy street caused exclamations behind her, but before her assailants could determine if the comer were friend or foe, he was upon them, flailing whip to and fro with much greater success than the driver. Cries of pain and curses rang out, and the coach stopped its ominous rocking as the men in back scampered out of range of the stinging lash.

With one one last desperate lunge, the rotund man in the doorway grabbed for his daughter, only to be struck down with a vicious blow across his shoulders from a walking stick greatly resembling a bludgeon. Penelope gasped in recognition of the weapon and glanced out to see the wildly furious features of her husband striking out at the men hampering her escape. Cloak flung back to reveal the deadly strength of broad chest and bulging shoulders, Graham swung whip in one hand and stick with the other. To Penelope's dismay, she caught the glimmer of silver at the cane's end and realized it had become a deadly sword in Graham's hands. More than one of her attackers discovered this too late and whirled away, blood flowing between their fingers as they grabbed in amazement at their wounds.

She had only time to glimpse the livid fury of that scarred face, the burning anger of one golden eye as he glanced inside to ascertain her safety, and then the carriage jerked forward, forced from captivity by Graham's violent actions. That one glance was sufficient to set her trembling with a fear she had not felt minutes earlier. Her husband in full rage was more terrifying than a ship full of pirates. The scrawny scarecrows she had just encountered were no comparison.

Filled with awe at the sight of the giant beast upon the huge stallion valiantly clearing a way for the lady's rescue, Pippin kneeled on the seat and stared out the window as long as he could watch the scene. When the carriage rattled around the corner and out of sight, he gave a huge sigh and settled down to stare at Penelope with wide eyes, not daring to utter a word.

Too terrified herself to offer explanations, Penelope glanced down at the infant in her arms. Wide blue eyes had shuttered closed. The child slept.

It was almost too much for her shattered nerves. She wanted to laugh, but it would be the laugh of hysteria. Tears pricked behind her eyes, and she rocked back and forth in the seat, consoling herself if not the infant.

They heard the sound of the horse galloping up and Pippin strained to see the ferocious rider once more, but he stayed behind the jolting, rocking carriage all the way back to the manicured streets of the West End. Penelope heard the hooves like the drums of doom and knew she had escaped one terrible fate to face another. There had been nothing gentle in Graham's face when he had looked in at her.

She was right. Before footmen could come tumbling out of the house to open the door and let her out, Graham's roar was echoing up and down the drive. He cursed the coachman as he paid him for the damage to his coach, swearing he would cut his throat if he ever dared take another lady to those streets again. He cursed the footmen for their clumsiness in opening the door and retrieving Penelope. He ignored Pippin, but he bellowed his rage at the butler who had allowed Penelope to leave without finding out her destination. Had his coach driver not been the one to return and warn Graham of his wife's intentions, he would have flattened the fellow and thrown him out on his ear. Instead, he merely roared his fury with orders never to take her out again without his permission. He cursed the maids who peered around corners to see what the uproar was about and then he sent all the servants flying from the hall with bellowed orders until he was left alone with Penelope and her bundle of rags.

Swinging open the study door, he pointed a command for her to enter, his anger still raging too strong to speak to her as the glitter in his one golden eye warned too well. Drawing on her reserve of calm, Penelope held her head high and did as directed, but her insides trembled violently. Graham was a massive man, and his anger would be terrifying in the best of worlds. In this one, where she had no idea where she stood, whether on quicksand or solid ground or air, his anger had the power to petrify her. She clung to the silent child for the security of her righteousness.

The door slammed and she could feel his scathing gaze burning a hole through her back, but his words, when they came, were soft and full of anguish.

"Why, Penelope? Why did you feel you had to risk your life for this pestilent child? My God, she is probably ridden with lice, besotted with gin, and rotted by pox! What do you intend to do with her? Are you that desperate for a child of your own that you would steal one from the streets?"

The tears fell then, tears she had been too terrified to let fall earlier, tears she had been too proud to let anyone see. Her shoulders shook with the force of her sobs, but still, she could not turn to face him. He would never understand, nay, could not, for he was a man and incapable of feeling the emotions of a woman for a child.

Graham watched helplessly as her sobs rendered

speech impossible. He could not comfort her. He had denied himself that right. There was nothing he could say or do to give her back the comfortable life he had stolen from her. He had hoped his wealth could make her happy, but he could see now that Penelope had never craved wealth. What she wanted was someone's love, and that he did not have it in him to give.

"It's all right, Penelope." He tried to soothe her with words. "I won't take the child away from you. We will clean her up and call a physician to look at her and if she is well enough, we will put her in the nursery with Alexandra."

Penelope shook her head vehemently, gulping back sobs so she could find the words. "I didn't mean her for myself. I didn't mean for you to have to take her in. I just could not *leave* her there. Don't you see?"

Anger tinged his voice again. "You mean to say you traveled those treacherous streets, risked your life or worse, for an infant you had never seen and do not want? Are you mad, Penelope? Do you have any idea what could have happened back there? Are you so innocent as not to understand what goes on in those places?"

She knew what she had risked. She had seen it in the hungry eyes of those men back there. She had done just what those other unlucky women had done, only she had gone in the broad light of day, thinking that would make it safe. The others had been murdered after dark by a man who resembled her husband. She has been lucky enough to be saved by a madman. She turned slowly to meet the rising ire in Graham's eye.

"I am sorry I frightened you, but I could have done nothing else. I know a childless couple in the village who will be happy to have her. You need not concern yourself any further."

The proud defiance in her eyes caused as much pain as her earlier tears. Did she see him as some kind of monster who would throw the infant out on the streets and beat her for her waywardness? Perhaps it would be better if she thought of him that way. It would make things easier for her when she discovered the truth.

"I forbid you to go back to that end of town again. I will see to it that you don't. My driver already has instructions not to take you out without my permission. Harley will report to me if you should try to go anywhere alone. You will begin arranging to close the house for the summer. I have given orders for the Hall to be opened for our arrival. That should curb your ability to try to save the entirety of the East End for the nonce."

Ignoring the fury building in Penelope's normally obedient demeanor, Graham continued, "I will make one concession. You may have an allowance for charitable works to spend as you choose. I will not make any inquiry into how it is spent. It may go on jewels and furs if you prefer, but I am happy to give you those should you ask. This will be cash in your hand, not credit, but there is one string attached. If I should ever find you have placed yourself in such a dangerous situation again, you will never have another penny from me for any cause but the clothes on your back. You will be able to save those souls that money can buy or none at all. Is that understood?"

Torn between more emotions than she had suffered in a lifetime, Penelope glared at Graham through tears, unable to express any of those things that needed to be said. Perhaps he was as confused as she about her place in the order of things. He railed at her as he would the servants, ordered her about like a child, offered her money and jewels like a mistress, and occasionally, just occasionally, spoke to her as if he really cared somewhere deep down in that barrel chest.

She was too confused herself to know the appropriate response. Luckily the child in her arms began to squirm and whimper, finally showing some sign of life, and Penelope averted her attention to this more immediate need rather than her husband's harsh face.

Had she looked up again, she would have caught his expression soften as he watched her comfort the child. Tears still wet on her cheeks, she turned shining eyes to the tiny form in her hands, cradling the infant expertly as she cooed and caressed pale cheeks and calmed the infant's cries. With her tousled hair falling in soft waves against her heated cheeks, she could have posed as a Madonna for any artist he knew. Graham would have given all his wealth for the opportunity to give her a child of her own to love and caress as she did this one, as she did his own. The thought that he would comfort himself in so doing did not cross his mind.

"I will bathe her in the kitchen and keep her from Alexandra until the physician says it is safe," Penelope murmured, refusing to look up to his angry eyes again. Without acknowledging any other of his commands than that, she left the room, turning her back on the man who needed her far more than he would ever admit.

Chapter 18

"I AM NOT!"

"You are so! Nasty, nasty, nasty little boy!" Alexandra chanted triumphantly, hands on tiny hips as she glared defiantly at the taller youth in the stable doorway.

"Alexandra Melissa Trevelyan, what are you doing?" Penelope sailed down the drive, the bright blue ribbons of her bonnet flying in the breeze, her white sprigged muslin catching the first winds of the coming storm as she came around the corner of the house.

Alexandra's defiance fled, but she set her jaw with a look of determination that seemed hauntingly familiar, and Penelope nearly gasped at her sudden resemblance to Chadwell. It was the black hair that did it, she quickly decided, for Alexandra's heart-shaped face could never resemble the hard square jaw of the cousin's. She would have to quit shocking herself like that. Just because she had learned the world was a wicked place gave no reason to assume everything in it was tinged with wickedness.

"Alexandra, your father is waiting for you. The carriages are leaving now. Whatever are you about?"

"Pippin says my daddy isn't my daddy. He says ferocious beasts eat little girls and can't be daddies. Tell him that nasty Mr. Chadwell is not my daddy!"

Penelope would gladly have knocked both their angelic little heads together for repeating what she had only just thought of. Children had naught to do but observe their elders, though they understood little. They would never see Graham's true visage beneath that scarred and patched surface, no more than they

could see his resemblance to Chadwell. They only saw
Graham's fierceness and Chadwell's dissolution and
came up with their own interpretation.

"Pippin, you are to be ashamed of yourself! Mr.
Chadwell may have found you this position, but it is
Lord Trevelyan who pays your wages and Lord Trevelyan who is helping me carry Goldie to her new
home. Do you think I would leave your sister in the
care of a beast who eats little girls?"

Pippin stuck his chin out. "She called me a nasty
little boy. I ain't little. I'm twicet as big as 'er!"

"Which is why you should be nice to her and not
tell her scary stories. Big boys should protect those
smaller than themselves. Now tell Alexandra you made
it all up and both of you say good-bye politely. We
won't be seeing each other for some while."

The boy looked suspiciously as if he would cry, but
bravely, under Penelope's gentle command, he held
his grubby paw out. Alexandra stuck her tongue out in
reply.

Penelope sighed in exasperation and caught her
daughter by her tiny gloved hand. "You would do
better to make friends than enemies, Alexandra Trevelyan. Now say good-bye. We must go."

Happy at having achieved the last "word," Alexandra waved and called a merry farewell and skipped
along at Penelope's side, leaving the bereft orphan behind without a qualm. Her nose had been seriously out
of joint these last few days with the advent of the infant
in the nursery, but the adventure of an excursion into
the country had relegated her jealousy to the past. She
was quite content to be drawn into Penelope's haste.

Penelope wished she could be so serene. Graham
had held himself aloof these past few days as she had
ordered trunks packed and holland covers thrown out
while running up and down to calm the uproar in the
nursery. Alexandra's jealousy had been as nothing to
the infant's withdrawal from the diet of gin, and her
screams had put the entire household on edge for days.

But things were finally settling down. She almost
wished she could see Chadwell one more time before

they left. The haunting look of hunger and need he had given her that last night coupled with his shocking state of the next morning left her feeling guilty. Perhaps even rakes had a conscience of some sort, and perhaps he was not quite so lost to sin that he could not be saved. Now she would not have the chance to know.

Graham waited impatiently at the door to the elegant barouche with its quietly decorated coat of arms on the door. The matched thoroughbreds pranced and snorted in the traces, much as she felt her husband was doing as he threw open the door before the footmen could do so. Whatever else he might be, Graham Trevelyan was the epitome of a well-bred nobleman. His tailored, earth-colored riding coat sat perfectly across the broad expanse of his shoulders. His starched white linen lay smoothly against his wide chest. His immaculate cravat stood stark against the swarthier coloring of his skin. The only problem with the image was that his ferocious attitude and leonine figure did not match the pale, bored elegance of the modern noble, but more aptly belonged to the days of Sir Francis Drake or Walter Raleigh. Penelope did not wait for him to spread his cloak beneath her feet.

The storm broke before they were scarcely out of the limits of the city. Alexandra's squeals of fear at being in open country with lightning zigzagging overhead reached Graham's ears as he rode alongside the carriage. With a signal, he sent the carriage into the relative protection of a nearby barn. Once the horses were situated, he shook off his cloak and left it outside to climb into the seat across from Penelope.

Alexandra immediately scrambled into the security of her father's protective embrace, burying her head against his coat while Penelope gently rocked the wide-eyed infant in her arms. Across the small gulf between the seats their gazes met and once again, Penelope realized why she had married this man. The love and gratitude in that one fierce eye melted all her reserve all over again, and she offered a gentle smile in return. That she could give him Alexandra back repaid some small part of the debt she owed him. But the look in his eyes spoke of more than that, and she had to turn her head away to prevent the excited churning of her insides. She must be a wanton to think of those things Chadwell had done to her while looking in her husband's face.

Graham watched sadly as she turned away from him. He kept deluding himself into thinking that something magical would happen to dissolve the beast in him and make the maiden love him as he was. He wanted it so much that he saw it in her every gesture, every look. They sat together peacefully like this, like the family he desired, but it was all a fraud, an illusion. What did he have to do to chase away the witch's spell and uncover the true beauty he desired?

Remembering his purpose in making this journey, Graham took a deep breath and drove away such thoughts. She would hate him soon enough. The witch's spell did not hide true beauty but ugliness so raw and deep she would never forgive him. He clung to Alexandra and leaned his head back against the seat while the thunder rolled in the skies overhead, proving the god's anger.

The summer storm passed as quickly as it had arrived, and the carriages were soon rumbling down the familiar roads of Surrey. The inhabitants of the village closest to Trevelyan Hall came out to stare at the grand carriage with the noble crest they had not seen in years, and Penelope gazed back at them with a mixture of hope and despair. She had lived in a cottage much like that charming one over there. Would Graham ever permit her to know the inhabitants?

Such thought disappeared with the confusion of their arrival at the Hall. Alexandra had fallen asleep in her father's arms, and Graham stepped out of the carriage first bearing his precious burden. Footmen came running to lower the steps for Penelope, to fling open the door for his lordship, to unload the boxes and trunks and servants they had brought with them from London.

The entire household turned out to greet the new

mistress, and their eyes widened at the sight of the infant in Penelope's arms. Backstairs gossip quickly put an end to any rumors arising from Goldie's presence, but the state of confusion at their arrival kept the house in a turmoil for hours.

An elderly butler and housekeeper apparently controlled the staff, and these two greeted Graham and his daughter with tears in their eyes, exclaiming over Alexandra's delicate beauty and avoiding the scarred visage that had replaced their master's handsome face. Graham introduced them to Penelope, and because they assumed she was the reason Graham had finally returned to his home, they beamed at her with gratitude and welcome.

By the time everyone and everything was restored to some facsimile of their proper place, Penelope was weary unto tears. The last days had been hectic and full of confusion. She had scarcely had a chance to make her farewells to the few people she had come to know in London, and now she had a whole new set of faces to learn. She simply didn't have the strength to cope with it the first evening.

Discovering Penelope had given word that she would dine in her chambers that evening, Graham gave the same order for his repast, then climbed the stairs to the upper story where they had adjoining chambers. The Hall obtained its name from the great hall of the old keep that formed the towering, drafty foyer and public room. From there, the house had been added on to, higgledy-piggledy, for generations until there was no rhyme or reason to the pattern of its rooms and hallways. He had chosen the most modern, comfortable rooms for his own chambers with his first marriage. The servants had automatically installed them in the same ones upon their arrival. He would have to consult Penelope to see if this arrangement was satisfactory.

Their suite had no polite parlor and no bath chamber, only small alcoves on opposite ends for their personal servants and a small room at the rear for their wardrobes. A connecting door led from the master chamber to Penelope's smaller room, and for some reason, the arrangement seemed much more intimate than the equally huge chambers with their connecting parlor in London.

Penelope was too tired to take notice of this fact immediately. She could tell her room had been recently aired but little used. The fragile bed in the room's center boasted no draperies, only a delicately carved tester. The silver counterpane still had wrinkles from where it had been folded away in some drawer, and it did not quite seem to match the ancient midnight blue velvet of the window hangings. But she realized Graham had not lived here since the accident, and she certainly didn't mind what was, after all, luxury compared to the house she had grown up in.

The knock on the hall door startled her. She had sent her maid away to her own supper and was rather enjoying the peace of solitude. She gave a tentative call and turned from her unpacking to stare in amazement as her husband entered.

From that very first night Graham had come and gone from her chambers as if they were his own. He seldom knocked, and if he did, he entered without waiting. That he not only knocked but used the public door instead of their private one put an ominous note to their relationship. She stared at him with anxiety.

"The housekeeper said you had ordered dinner in your room. Are you not feeling well?" Graham's gruff voice hid his concern as his gaze took in Penelope's pallor and the shadows beneath her eyes.

That seemed an odd question from an invalid who seldom ate his own meals downstairs, but Penelope answered it politely. "I thought you would retire early, my lord, and I did not want to weary myself or the staff by insisting on formality. It has been a long day."

"So it has." Graham made no pretense of leaning on his walking stick but held it casually in one hand as he turned his head to examine the room with his one good eye. "Not a very hospitable homecoming with a chamber like this. You will have to order it decorated to suit your taste." He eyed the narrow bed with misgiving. "That should be replaced. There are larger ones to be had in half the rooms of the house."

Penelope withheld her bewilderment as she rose and came forward to touch the smooth wood of one fragile poster. "It is old, but quite lovely. If we are to stay here only in the summer months, it should not need draperies. I am certain there are more important things that need your attention after all these years."

Graham's head gave an involuntary jerk of surprise as he realized how far his thoughts had diverted from his wife's. Marilee had seldom slept in that bed except when indisposed, until those last unhappy weeks; that was why she had never bothered to adorn this room properly. He had kept her warm through the winter months in the big bed on the other side of that wall. This bed was too small to comfortably hold him, and he had always hated it when Marilee had escaped in here. But for Penelope, it wasn't an escape. It was what she expected. It had never crossed her mind that he could not join her there.

"Perhaps you are right," he sighed, returning to the present. This whole house had too much of the past in it to be comfortable. That was why he had avoided it for so long, one of the reasons, anyway. The servants who knew him too well were another part of the reason, but that part was almost over. In a little while, it would not matter what they saw or did not see. He drew his attention back to Penelope.

"Perhaps there are other chambers you would prefer. Explore the house as you will. I have no preference one way or the other where we sleep." The Hall held no hidden passages, no secrets. It was as honest and unpretentious as Penelope herself. His only objection would be if she situated herself on the opposite end of the house from himself. He was not ready to give up all hope quite yet.

The oddity of Graham's behavior struck Penelope more than his words. He seemed nervous and ill at ease with his own home. Or was it with her? The words "where *we* sleep" had not escaped her, and the sudden realization that he must have left his mistress behind in London made her swallow whatever reply might have come to her tongue. London was not so far that he couldn't make the journey when he wished, but why then did he take such an interest in her rooms?

Deciding he was only bored and still out of sorts after her escapade into the slums, Penelope sought some manner of healing the breach. "Perhaps sometime we could go over the house together and decide what would be best. Will you have time?"

As best as she could tell behind that immobile mask of his face, he seemed pleased with this suggestion. He nodded a curt agreement and turned to go.

"My lord?" When Graham turned back to regard her quizzically, Penelope took a deep breath and plunged in. "Would you care to share your dinner with me in here? It seems foolish to each dine alone on other sides of the wall."

The taut muscles of his face seemed to relax. "Quite right." He glanced around at the nearly barren room. "But I think we had best use my room. At least there is a table in there."

That thought had not occurred to Penelope, and if it had, she would never have made the suggestion. It was too late now to withdraw the offer, and he seemed so pleased with it that she could do no more than agree with him.

When their dinner arrived on silver trays, Graham greeted her wearing only a loose satin lounging jacket over his buckskin breeches and open-necked shirt. She could not help but notice the coarse hair curling just above the V of his shirt, and she quickly cast her eyes downward as she entered the room. This had not been a good idea at all.

As Graham seated her at the small fireside table, Penelope glanced around this room that was his. It was much smaller than the London chamber, which was odd considering the comparative size of the two houses, but this one seemed much homier. The bed did not sit isolated on a dais in the empty center of the chamber but nestled next to a bow window overlooking the gardens. Perhaps in winter, draperies engulfed both bed and window, but for now, only a forest green counterpane draped the bed, and shutters partially closed out the night. He had arranged the chairs near the hearth, leaving only a Queen Anne dresser against the far wall. A Brussels carpet in various shades of green and ivory and brown completed the decor.

Amused, Graham watched her perusal of his quarters. After forbidding her entrance to his London chambers, this change must have aroused her curiosity, but she made no comment on the difference.

"Do you approve?" he finally asked when she directed her attention to the plates being uncovered.

Startled into looking up, Penelope regretted it instantly. They had really not sat so close except in the carriage since he was courting her. The candlelight threw the scarred side of his face into shadow, but she could read the warmth in his eye well enough.

"It suits you." She found her tongue long enough to answer.

Graham dismissed the servant hovering over them, and they were left alone with the crystal and the china and the tantalizing scents of warm bread and delicately poached fish. Penelope discovered she was starved.

Graham at his best could have enchanted a princess, and he was on his best behavior this night. He gently skirted the issue of Goldie and the other abused children of London's back streets, encouraged Penelope's tentative plans for using her allowance on a suitable foundling home, and listened carefully to her opinions on Alexandra's care and upbringing. He offered little of himself, but answered what questions he could concerning the Hall and its tenants. As the meal came to its end, he had her laughing at carefully selected anecdotes of his childhood.

In this setting, without the strain of being in the public eye, and without the interminable household interruptions, they could just be themselves, as they had those first few weeks before they married. Penelope forgot she was his wife, forgot Chadwell, forgot Graham's mistress and all the rumors and mysteries that separated them, and fell under the spell of her husband's wit and wisdom. They could talk companionably on so many topics as she could not with the idle fops of London or the village folk at home. It was as if they truly were equals, and his interest flattered her more than all of Chadwell's physical attentions.

By evening's end, however, physical awareness became as much a part of the enchantment as the laughter and the conversation. Despite the premature silver of his hair and the wrinkled scar of his face, Graham was a superbly built man in the prime of life, and Penelope was too much a woman not to notice. His low, deep voice had the power to raise the hair at the nape of her neck when he looked at her as he was doing now. A light flush rose between her breasts when she sensed that was the direction his gaze took. He didn't even need to touch her to make her feel as if he had just kissed her thoroughly.

When it finally came time to say goodnight, Graham took her hand to help her rise and continued to hold it as he walked her to the door. The heat of his ungloved palm as his fingers entwined with hers sent a flood of warmth through Penelope's veins.

"I know you are tired, my love. Do you wish to postpone our journey into Hampshire a while longer? I can send a message to my sister . . ."

Penelope shook her head. "I will be fine in the morning." She hesitated, not certain whether to blurt out her real feelings or not, but the intimacy he had allowed these last few hours gave her enough confidence to reveal this one small thing. "I fear if I keep Goldie too long, I will become too attached to her. It is better that I take her to her new parents right away. They are waiting eagerly for her."

A thoughtful frown formed over the bridge of Graham's nose as he looked down into Penelope's trusting violet eyes. He really did not deserve someone so good and innocent, but Alexandra did, he reminded himself. Some compromise would have to be reached, and soon, before he drowned in the deep wells of those eyes.

With his gloved hand he touched her upturned face.

"Sleep late, then. The journey is not a long one, and since we will be taking the roads instead of cutting across other people's orchards, we should not get lost."

A wry smile at his own expense bent one corner of his mouth, and Penelope's stomach did a funny flip-flop. "I can find my way from the orchard," she reminded him mischievously.

"So you can. But would I ever pry you away from the vicarage and all your admirers?" he taunted mildly. Then shocking her totally, he lifted the palm of her hand to his lips and pressed a kiss to it before letting her go. "Goodnight, my pretty Penny."

The kiss seemed to burn a path straight to her heart, defying all anatomical routes. Penelope curled her fingers around the burning brand he left and stared, lost, into the depths of that one gold, almost amber eye. Without a word, unable to pry one from her tongue, she nodded and slipped through the door to safety.

Chapter 19

IT rained all the way to Hampshire. Rather than face the elements alone, Graham joined Penelope and the children in the carriage. He had offered to take two carriages so the governess and a nursemaid could endure the demands of an infant and a bored, lively, six-year-old, but Penelope preferred the company of the children to riding in elegant silence. With Graham filling much of the interior, the limited space became even closer and more lively.

By the time they reached Stanhope Manor, he had succeeded in teaching Alexandra how to make a cat's cradle out of Penelope's hair ribbon, taught her the slightly edited lyrics of a rowdy song whose chorus seemed to be repeated at longer and louder lengths with each rendition, and kept them all laughing with jests that seemed to spring from an unlimited receptacle behind his mighty brow. There was no time for boredom to set in.

The noisy trio and their fretful bundle arrived well after the manor's country dinner hour. Lady Adelaide and her husband, Sir Brian, greeted them in the salon, and Adelaide's eyes lit at the sight of the infant in Penelope's arms. Apparently several months along in pregnancy, she gazed worshipfully at the blond infant while making polite greetings to her amused brother and his wife. Not neglecting Alexandra, Adelaide knelt and swept the little girl into her arms with genuine affection and a plenitude of promises. When Penelope suggested she needed to take the children to their beds, Adelaide insisted on doing the honors. She appropriated Goldie, took Alexandra by the hand, and left Penelope to trail along behind as best she might.

Relegating the maids to the impersonal tasks of warming damp sheets and unpacking tiny dresses, Adelaide indulged herself in the delights of undressing and bathing the little girls, with Penelope's help. It took only a few soapy suds in the eyes and squeals of childish delight to bond the two women in the first links of friendship.

By the time Graham and Sir Brian climbed the stairs to see what took so long, Penelope and Adelaide were chattering away as if they had known each other all their lives. The children tucked soundly in their beds, the two women had drifted to the chamber where a maid unpacked Penelope's trunks, and both were gasping with laughter at Adelaide's description of her big brother's first encounter with a surfeit of fermented grapes.

Graham bent a quizzical eyebrow as they erupted into renewed giggles at his appearance, but he suffered their mirth with great aplomb while admiring the flush of rose in Penelope's pale cheeks. Steamed by the children's bath, tendrils of hair curled about her forehead, and her eyes seemed to shine with a liveliness he had not seen in weeks. The heat rising in his groin had little to do with the first stirrings of other long dead emotions, however, and his gaze seldom strayed from Penelope's face as the talk flowed on around them.

Finally taking notice of her brother's unusual silence and the direction of his gaze, Adelaide nudged her unobservant husband and inquired politely of her guests, "Have you eaten? I am certain we can summon up a cold collation if you care . . ."

Graham cut her off with a gesture. "We stopped at the Golden Goose. Do not let us keep you from your country hours any longer. The journey has been a long one, and I fear Penelope may be overtired."

Adelaide looked to her new friend with laughter at this description of the short hop from Surrey to Hampshire, but Penelope appeared to be nervously contemplating a flickering lamp upon the wall. With a smile to herself at the little baroness's modesty under her husband's lustful gaze, Adelaide hastened the good-nights and ushered her husband out the door leaving Graham and Penelope alone in the chamber she meant for them to share.

Graham watched as the color fled Penelope's cheeks once the door closed. Not looking at him, she hurried to her trunks, only to find them already unpacked and the contents neatly stowed away. The thought that his sister would necessarily chamber him with his bride had not occurred to Graham before; rather a telling lack of foresight, he decided.

"Penelope." He spoke without knowing what to say.

She turned from her aimless search of the wardrobe to stare at him. As usual, he had thrown off his coat and loosened his cravat. His quietly elegant waistcoat of pale gold brocade hid nothing of wide shoulders encased in flowing white linen, and in the dim light he appeared more than ever a pirate. Strange, though, how she wished to touch the coarse cut of his silver hair. Why did he insist on wearing it in that poorly trimmed manner?

"I will tell Adelaide my snoring disturbs you and ask for a separate chamber. There are rooms enough aplenty in this place." He had not known he meant to say it until the words were out of his mouth. He cursed to himself as Penelope's eyes lit with relief. Then they glazed over thoughtfully, and she shook her head.

"No, I suspect your sister would take exception to that. Unless my presence will disturb you, we had best learn to deal with each other as husband and wife. We cannot always ask for separate chambers wherever we go."

The joy soaring through him almost brought an exuberant grin to Graham's face, but remembering himself in time, he gave a solemn nod of agreement. Her presence would annoy the very devil out of him since he knew she meant this sharing of a bed to be a chaste one, but it was one step closer than he had been before. While there was yet life in him, there was hope.

Penelope eyed his nod askance, but seeing he made no suggestion or objection, she gathered up her night rail and disappeared behind the dressing screen. Apparently Adelaide did not think a personal maid called for on this occasion. She would have to unbutton her own bodice.

She could hear Graham moving restlessly about the room, and she blushed at the thought of him undressing just on the other side of this flimsy screen. She had fully meant her vows when she had taken them in church, but Graham had made it so convenient to forget them. He had every right to do as he wished with her; she just could not know what he wished. He had managed to ignore her so thoroughly and so long that she could not feel he had any husbandly desire for her. Yet there were times when he made her feel as if his thoughts had taken the same direction as his cousin's inevitably did. She had no notion of which Graham she would meet outside this screen.

She had no notion which Graham she *wanted* to meet, she realized as she finally tied the sash to her silken robe. She had not brought the nightgown Augusta had made for her, but sensible linen ones that covered the shadows of her body as the thin muslin did not. Not knowing whether to be relieved or displeased at this lack of foresight, Penelope took a deep breath and stepped from behind the screen. She might look the part of spinster, but her heart was beating faster than any maiden's.

Graham had divested himself of all but his trousers but he had thoughtfully donned his robe to cover the full extent of his nakedness. He turned as Penelope stepped from hiding, and his heart lurched and lodged in his throat. In her high-necked linen with the trailing robe wrapped primly beneath her breasts, and her long honey-brown hair streaming to her waist, she appeared no more than a child, and he knew he could not lightly take advantage of such innocence.

"We should do this more often," he offered in jest and was rewarded with a small tilt of lovely pale lips at this gesture of appreciation. "You first. I'll douse the lamps."

Gratefully Penelope slid beneath the manor's best bed covers and surreptitiously slipped her wrapper off as Graham strode about the room, returning the night to darkness. She could not help but admire his pantherlike grace. It seemed behind closed doors he lost all need for limp and walking stick, or did he suffer the pain rather than lower himself in her eyes? It did not matter. She felt a rush of warmth at either thought and did not dare look him in the eyes as he bent to put out the lamp beside the bed.

His nearness was almost suffocating. As the last light flickered out, the darkness wrapped around them like a shroud and Penelope's other senses sharpened in consequence. She could feel the heat emanating from Graham's muscular chest as he bent over the bed. A cool draft drifted across her skin as he straightened to discard his robe. Before she had time to panic, he was beside her, his heavy weight drawing the feather mattress downward awkwardly.

She hurriedly buried herself deeper in her own side, drawing the covers up to her chin and securing them around her so she could not feel any part of him against her. She did not want to know if he had discarded more than his robe.

Not unobservant, Graham noted his wife's frozen stance and made no move in her direction. Staring toward the ceiling, he ruefully considered his choices. He had no idea what her reaction would be should he turn and pull her toward him, although every fiber in his body longed to do just that. Rubbing an exploratory hand over the immobile, scarred portion of his cheek and mouth, he could only imagine her reaction to a kiss by such as that. He had not thought this through at all.

He could possibly persuade her to it; he was canny enough to sense that. The vicar's daughter would not deny her husband his rights, however much it disgusted her. But that was not what he wanted. He wanted her warm and willing and eager, as she had been that night when she came to his room, and he had not been there.

Cursing himself for the impossible situation he had created, Graham remained motionless on the lonely island that was his side of the bed. "Penelope, you need never fear me. You know that, don't you?"

The familiar sound of his deep baritone washed over her with relief, and she relaxed. "I know," she managed to whisper.

"What it must be like to be such a saint as to know no fear," he murmured, rolling his eyes heavenward.

Penelope giggled, well aware of the exasperated expression he would wear. "Angels will watch over your sleep, my lord."

"They're likely to be exceedingly shocked, if so," he grumbled, and without further explanation, he turned his back toward her.

Quite content to share the closeness of her husband's bed without any of the discomfort, Penelope rolled on her side, tucked her hand beneath her cheek, and fell soundly asleep.

Their days in Hampshire were too short.

Their first venture of the journey was to deliver Goldie to her expectant adoptive parents. Penelope turned away from the awe-filled delight of the couple with tears in her eyes. As they departed in the midst of much gratitude and well-wishing, Graham surreptitiously handed her his large handkerchief and watched her with curiosity.

When they were in the carriage and rolling away again, he questioned her softly. "Are you sorry to give her up?"

Penelope wiped a tear from her eye, and summoned a watery smile for his benefit. "Yes, I am sorry to give her up, for all that I know she will be in good hands. But I cry because they are so happy. They are good people, and they have waited so long to have a child. I'm afraid such power to change lives will make me quite giddy."

Graham grumped a noncommittal reply and stared

out the carriage window. The power to change lives made a person more than giddy, it changed their own, but he would not reveal that piece of information to her just yet. He would have a hard time explaining the source of his knowledge.

Augusta's cries of welcome brought more tears, Graham observed as the two women hugged each other and both launched into excited chatter at the same time. When it came time for refreshments, he calmly solved Penelope's dilemma by rising from his chair at the grate and moving to one by the kitchen fire. Resting his stiff leg in front of him and sipping at his tea from his lowly seat, he continued to watch as the two women settled into a cozy chat over the ancient and much battered kitchen table. Penelope seemed as much at home here as in his brother-in-law's grandiose dining hall.

He enjoyed watching her fingers flying as she talked. Wisps of hair continually escaped whatever coiffure she attempted, and her long, graceful fingers were always brushing them back from her eyes, or twisting them thoughtfully at her nape. He wanted the right to capture that flying hand and hold it against the table in proud possession. He wanted the right to nuzzle the curls at her nape and kiss the ones on her forehead. He wanted much more than he deserved or she expected. In this constant proximity it would soon become an obsession.

He wasn't new to obsessions. He had a clear, calm, logical outlook on life. He knew Penelope wasn't beautiful in the conventional sense, for instance. Her features were pleasantly even, her figure moderately good. But he had seen those unremarkable eyes widen into rain-drenched pools and startling storms and sunlit summer days. He had seen those tender lips tremble with both fear and passion, turn up in joy and laughter, and he knew them to be the most beautiful lips he would ever see. He wanted just to touch them, to feel their life and love, and this was obsession, for he knew he could not, and still, he watched and waited.

Back at the manor he watched as she slipped easily

into the elegant, indolent life of his sister and her husband. She did not set out to charm or impress or any of those things many another stranger to this life might do. Not his Penelope. She scolded Brian for not insisting that his pregnant wife get her exercise by walking about the gardens every day. She laughed at Adelaide's insistence that she was entitled to have the Wycliffe crest on Graham's carriage. She chased Alexandra through the house in rousing games of hide-and-seek and blithely treated the starchy servants as if they were all Augustas. She did absolutely everything wrong and made everything enchantingly right.

Graham's powerful fingers clenched the wide doorjamb as he visibly restrained himself upon entering their shared chamber to find Penelope bent over the grate, stirring the embers. She had not yet donned her wrapper, and the fire outlined every curve of her body through the loose linen of her gown. That was the hardest part of this enforced proximity.

As much as he admired her character, enjoyed her spirit, thrived on her wit, he still wanted her body. Even knowing he could destroy everything he admired about her by taking her, he could not help imagining what it would be like to bury himself in her softness until she cried out with pleasure. For he knew the passionate nature Penelope concealed beneath that welcoming smile and wide-eyed innocence. He wanted to be the one to wake those passions, to arouse her into the awareness of the way his body was meant for hers, and to see her wonder as she succumbed to these delights.

Cursing mightily to himself, Graham released the doorjamb and strode into the room with a purposeful tread that made Penelope jump and turn around. She stared in horror at the angry twitch of his taut jaw and retreated before the passionate intensity of that one golden eye.

"Is there something wrong, my lord?" Penelope grabbed for her robe and hastily wrapped it around her. Graham in the full throes of anger could be a terrifying sight, but she was learning the anger was more frequently directed at himself and offered her no danger.

Still, she could not help watching warily as the mobile side of his face tautened and jerked angrily over one high cheekbone. Doffing his frock coat and tearing at his confining cravat, the broad muscles of his shoulder and chest strained against the tailored seams of his shirt. His waistcoat narrowed to a flat, powerful abdomen encased in tight breeches, and the strong muscles of his legs bulged against the soft cloth. She could find little sign of lameness or ill health in his athletic frame, and she wondered once more about this enigma who was her husband.

"I am impatient to be off. There is much I have to do. Will you be ready to leave on the morrow?" Graham scowled as his hasty jerks knotted the carefully tied cravat Brian's valet had fashioned for him this morning.

They had only been here three days and Penelope wasn't the least bit ready to leave, but she could understand his haste to return to the Hall. It had been sorely neglected in his absence, and there would be much to do.

"I can be ready anytime you are." She came forward and pushed away his browned fingers and the black-gloved hand from his cravat. With casual competence, she unknotted the starched linen for him, then stepped back. The intensity of his gaze burned against her hair. Why did he keep staring at her like that?

"Good. We'll break the news to Adelaide in the morning." Graham turned his back to finish his undressing and heard Penelope quietly steal into their mutual bed. He could control his lust one more night, but not much longer. It was time to get back to the final task he had set himself.

More tears were expended at parting, leaving Graham to ruefully decide that things would be much more cheerful if the women didn't enjoy themselves so much. When Adelaide pulled him aside for a private farewell, he went reluctantly.

Taller than Penelope, she could meet his gaze on a

more equal basis. She didn't flinch at the scowl forming across his scarred forehead, but brushed aside a straying hair. "The little baroness has been good for you, big brother. You look handsome and healthy again, and I've even seen you laugh a time or two. I had thought you decided on a marriage of convenience, but I can see it has turned out elsewise."

Graham scowled irascibly. "Do not be playing Cupid with my wife, 'Laidie. Penelope is a good, sensible girl and an ideal mother for Alexandra. She is content with that. Do not be expecting more."

Adelaide made a rude face at him. "Next you will be telling me you encourage her admirers so you need not be burdened with the responsibilities of a husband. Fie on you, Trev. She is more beautiful inside and out than Marilee ever was, and you were so jealous of her you wouldn't let her out of your sight. I know you too well. I don't know what game this is you are playing, but Penelope is too good to be hurt by it. Keep her safe, Trev. Her life has been much too hard in the past to have to suffer more."

That much was only too true, and as Graham kissed his sister farewell, he resolved to listen to that much of her advice. Whatever choices he had to make from here on, he would have to take Penelope into consideration first. She deserved that much.

Chapter 20

GRAHAM dived so seriously into the work waiting at the Hall, Penelope began to wonder if it were herself or old ghosts that he sought to drive away. Without consulting her, he ordered old draperies and tapestries brought down and cleaned and only the best returned to their proper place. Moldering furniture was thrown out without thought to its value or restorable potential unless Penelope came upon it and salvaged it from the rubbish heap. Carpets were taken up and beaten and floors scrubbed and polished. Carpenters and painters and artists were called in to repair leaking, drafty windows, crumbling plaster, damaged wainscoting, and to paint the walls with bright new colors and murals.

Once the house was full to overflowing with workmen painting, pounding, and scraping, Graham turned his attentions to the park and fields beyond. Penelope breathed a sigh of relief when he rode out and immediately set about restoring the house to order. Whatever he hoped to accomplish by turning his home upside down, she would complete by making it into a welcome haven to return to at the end of his day. Whatever ghosts lingered would have to take up residence elsewhere, preferably with the workmen. By vetoing preposterous murals of Egyptian sphinxes, walls of Oriental red, and any suggestion of rearranging the current structure, she succeeded in removing the workmen at an amazing rate.

With satisfaction Penelope saw the last of the gold-and-white brocade draperies installed in the main salon. With the floors polished to a brilliant gleam and decorated with a scattering of new Aubusson carpets of similar shades, and the lovely old Queen Anne pieces cleaned and polished and arranged to invite conversation, the salon was ready to accept visitors. The workmen had been sent to the nether portions of the house, and Penelope could almost hear herself think again.

As if knowing she was ready for him, Guy appeared that afternoon. Instead of being perched sedately in her newly refurbished salon, however, Penelope was out on the front lawn chasing Alexandra through the shrubbery in a merry game of tag. They both spied their visitor at the same time and ran toward the drive, Penelope hastily shoving straying hair into pins and Alexandra yelling excitedly.

Grinning at this welcome reception, Guy swung down from his horse and caught Alexandra up in his arms. His lean, dark face lit with pleasure as the little girl kissed his cheek, and he glanced over her head to the not much older girl smiling up at him. "Don't I get a kiss for the other cheek?" He raised a mocking eyebrow to Penelope's flushed face.

"I don't need to resort to bribery when I want to go riding." Penelope brushed a stray strand of hair from her cheek and tried not to place much consequence on the admiration shining from the deep blue of his eyes. Guy was born to flatter women.

Guy laughed and tugged Alexandra's curls. "You scamp. Is that all you want of me? Hasn't Penny taught you it's naughty to trade kisses for favors?"

Alexandra ignored this admonition. "Penny said we might go riding before tea if Papa comes home, but you can take us, can't you?"

Guy glanced over her head to Penelope. "Graham's not at home?"

"He's out seeing to some neglected field or other. Apparently the manager he left in charge did not do his duties to Graham's satisfaction. Did you need to see him? Surely you have not come all the way from London in hopes of catching him?"

Guy set Alexandra down. In his chocolate riding coat and tight-fitting breeches, he appeared exceptionally handsome this day. Golden hair fell down over his bronzed forehead, and laugh lines crinkled at the corners of his eyes as he held Alexandra's hand and smiled at Penelope.

"I wouldn't give the old curmudgeon the satisfaction. Did he not tell you my home is just a few miles from here? Or that the Reardons live just beyond my place? Did he think he could keep you all to himself all summer?"

"I believe Dolly mentioned it, but we have been so caught up in work that it completely escaped my mind. Won't you come in? Graham will probably not be back for some hours, but I would be glad to have you for tea."

"Then the least I can do is take you ladies riding. Shall we?" Guy grinned as Alexandra sent a pleading look to Penelope. He had given her little choice in the matter.

Seeing no harm in a short jaunt with Alexandra in accompaniment, Penelope agreed. Not bothering to change into her fashionable riding habit, she allowed Guy to seat her as she was. The rumpled day dress of brown and gold could not be any more soiled than it already was after chasing Alexandra through the park, and she had no need to impress Guy with her elegance.

The little jaunt turned into a much longer one than anticipated. Guy's lively tales of how he and Graham had spent their summers swimming and fishing in the stream, stealing apples from the orchard, and terrorizing the neighboring gentry necessitated a tour of all the scenes of crime, and laughter prevented their keeping a close watch on time.

The sound of a horse galloping down the path behind them jarred Penelope into realizing how far the sun had sank in the sky, and her gaze jerked up to meet Guy's with the same thought. Their horses slowed to a halt as they turned to gaze behind them, in the direction of the hard-riding hoofbeats.

Graham and his massive stallion soon galloped into view. From this distance his expression could not be seen, but as he caught sight of them, the set of his shoulders seemed to relax, and he approached with the casual grace of an experienced rider.

Alexandra cried a greeting and set her pony to its paces, showing off her prowess. The corner of Graham's mouth tilted upward appreciatively at this performance before he lifted his gaze to meet Penelope's. Before she could greet him, his gaze traveled on to Guy.

Guy's grin did not quite reach his eyes as he took in his friend's impassive expression. "The ladies grow bored if left alone too long, old sport. You'd best beware lest some charming leprechaun spirit them away one day."

Alexandra giggled at this nonsense, but sensing some undercurrent she did not understand, Penelope remained silent.

"I certainly hope my ladies have more sense than to be charmed by a leprechaun, or any other rogue." Graham turned a reflective eye to his wife. "Do you suffer from neglect, my dear?"

"I never suffer from neglect," Penelope replied in her primmest manner. "Sometimes, I even welcome it." With an arched eyebrow directed toward both men, she spurred her mount toward home.

As Alexandra hurried to follow, the two men exchanged glances, each waiting for the other to respond to this enigmatic remark. A small quirk appeared at the corner of Guy's lips. Graham controlled a grin, and they both broke out laughing at the same time.

"You are lucky to find a Penny like that one, sapskull." Guy urged his horse into a canter beside Graham's as they trailed the two females. "She has a mind of her own."

"Rather eccentric of her, really," Graham agreed with characteristic understatement.

Guy sent his friend a sidelong look. In the saddle Graham appeared the perfect specimen of rude health. He controlled his spirited stallion with nonchalant ease, using only one hand. His broad shoulders and thick chest strained at the old riding coat he wore, and there seemed nothing wasted about the powerful thighs clamping the stallion's side. In fact, he looked healthier than he remembered him from before the accident, with the exception of the disfiguring scar. Guy frowned.

"Leg not bothering you when you ride like that?" He feigned concern.

"Don't make an old man of me yet. I've got a young wife, if you'll remember." Graham deftly avoided the topic. His gaze followed the sway of Penelope's slim waist ahead. The flimsy piece of scarf she had tucked in her bodice for modesty had come loose, and he tried not to imagine how she would look if he caught up with her. The high-waisted gown had been cut low across the bosom if he remembered correctly. He eased his stallion to a faster trot.

"I'd be happier if you remembered that fact more frequently. When are you going to take her to visit the Reardons?"

A scowl began to form on Graham's face. "Who sent you to ask that?"

"Not Arthur. He's about as communicative as you these days. He nearly stuck his spoon in the wall, Trev, and he's younger than both of us. Don't you think you ought to hear his case?"

"Explanations don't bring back the dead. Stay out of it, Hamilton. I'll take Penelope to visit if she likes. Do not ask more of me."

Relieved at receiving a rational reply for the first time since he had returned home, Guy pressed his luck a little further. "He's already said he had no part in what happened to me, and I believe him. He was just a young pup, and DeVere used him for an errand boy. The guilt lies with the eldest of us who allowed the bastards to go too far."

"Speak for yourself." Curtly Graham sent his horse ahead, leaving Guy behind in a curtain of dust.

Penelope looked up as Graham reined in beside her, and she flushed as she noted the path of his gaze. Her equestrian talents did not lead to riding without hands while she secured her tucker, but she attempted pushing a straying edge into her bodice.

"I like a woman who is not afraid to show she is a woman." Graham curbed his impatient stallion as he turned his full attention upon his embarrassed wife.

Penelope had no practice at this kind of flirtation or studied flattery. Only the fact that the gentleman at her side was her husband kept her from flying into the boughs altogether. She expected such talk from Chadwell, but not Graham.

"Show is one thing, flaunt is quite another." Flustered, she replied a little more curtly than necessary.

To her surprise he answered with a hint of admiration. "You may be right at that. I would feel much better about your riding out with Hamilton were you wrapped in velvet and linen up to your neck."

That statement nearly left her speechless, and Penelope greatly feared she gaped at him before recovering herself. This from a man who had told her she might take a lover as she chose! Did the witch's spell wear off gradually then? Perhaps the beast did not become the handsome prince overnight, but in stages.

Restored from shock by her sense of humor, Penelope answered sedately. "Then I should have to forego his company all summer or suffer from heat rash. Which is your wish, master?"

Graham managed a half grin as he reached out to catch the straying scarf again, daringly tucking it more firmly than she had done. "I like your freckles just as they are. A rash would not become you. And since it is futile to forbid a rogue like Guy the door, I will leave the matter to your own good taste."

"My lord is most kind," she said wryly, but the twinkle in her eye as she urged her mount to run after Alexandra took the sting from her sarcasm.

True to his promise, Graham took Penelope to visit the Reardons the very next day. Dolly gave an ecstatic cry and only by an admonition from her mother refrained from dragging her friend to another chamber for a private coze. Instead they wandered out to join the other guests and the remainder of the household in the gardens.

Graham fell into serious discussion with Henry, Lord Reardon, Dolly's eldest brother over the condition of the bridge adjoining their properties. Charles DeVere became bored with this pragmatic discussion and wandered over to join the ladies. Guy wasn't in sight, but Dolly said he had promised to stop in before tea.

Penelope had never had opportunity to study the Honorable Charles DeVere at any length. He was not so fashionably handsome as Guy, but had a sharp, striking face marred most often by the mockery in his smile. From his remarks she gathered he had over-ample intelligence and practiced charm, but little true sensitivity of nature. He drew Dolly out, enchanted her by speaking to her as if her opinion mattered, then completely forgot she existed when another target for his wit or charm appeared.

Penelope resisted his efforts to draw her out on the subject of Graham's injuries or his cousin's business in England. She didn't wish to appear unfriendly, but neither did she have Dolly's need to impress, and the subjects were personal ones better directed to Graham. Finding her monosyllabic replies unedifying, DeVere turned his attention to Lady Reardon and the conversation drifted to the convalescent patient in one of the upstairs rooms.

Graham had the misfortune to appear at Penelope's side just as this topic opened and at the same time as the butler led Guy onto the terrace to join them. After the first greetings Guy immediately asked after Arthur's health, and Graham was trapped.

Penelope noted his withdrawal and wondered at it. Perhaps he had overexerted himself yesterday and his leg pained him. Surreptitiously, she entwined her fingers with his and sent him a quiet, questioning look. Graham squeezed her hand and continued to hold it, but he did not meet her gaze.

As the tales of Arthur's foolish bravery in running away to join the army and live the life of an unheralded soldier unfolded, Penelope watched the other participants in this drama. The Reardons told the tales in rounds, each adding his own bit to the story. Guy prodded them with questions he obviously already knew the answer to while carefully avoiding Graham's eye. DeVere, on the other hand, seemed intent on watching Graham's reaction to the point of ignoring all else.

It was becoming more and more obvious to Penelope that there was something between these three men that only they knew about and perhaps, the missing Arthur. Since they would not speak of it among themselves, she doubted if they would reveal it to her, but the mysteries haunting her husband's life left her with the constant feeling of living on the edge of a precipice. Why would he tell her nothing of himself?

Inevitably the Reardons suggested that Graham go up to visit, since Guy and DeVere had already been and the patient could deal with only one visitor at a time. Penelope felt Graham's hand tighten until she feared he would crack her bones, but nothing of his anger or tension appeared on his face as he bowed politely to Lady Reardon's request.

"I cannot feel I would be an encouraging visage for an invalid to look upon. Perhaps, when he is stronger . . ."

"Don't be such a nodcock, Trevelyan. You might offer something of a shock to strangers, but to those of us who know you well, the difference disappears. Arthur has seen worse, I wager." Henry's blunt manner would set teeth on edge had he not been so obviously good-natured.

Graham clenched his teeth and the muscle over his jaw tightened, but he bowed to the task. Excusing himself from the company, he followed Henry into the house, leaving the others to continue the conversation.

"Arthur used to think Graham some kind of a god," Dolly whispered confidentially to Penelope as Lady Reardon commanded the attention of her daughter's suitors. "Henry is nigh onto ten years older than Arthur, and he was already married and producing babes, but Guy and Graham were men about town when Arthur first came down from school. I can remember watching them from the upstairs hallway when they attended the Christmas Ball. You never saw such handsome men in your life! They were all the girls talked about when they came up the stairs.''

''Guy is still available,'' Penelope teased, lapsing into this lighter conversation. It did not pay to worry about Graham. She kept forgetting he was a grown man who could take care of himself better in this world than she could. He certainly didn't need her to mother him as she did Alexandra.

''Oh, but he thinks I'm a silly goose, and he disapproves of me, very rightly so.'' Dolly's eyes widened earnestly, surprised that the observant Penelope had not noticed. ''He is all the time scolding me as if he were one of my brothers.''

Penelope smiled at this blindness. ''You treat him as one of your brothers. I suspect that is one of the reasons you have so many admirers. It makes you very accessible, but a man like Guy isn't quite used to that kind of treatment. He thinks he's too old for you.''

''Too old!'' The words popped out of Dolly's mouth with such an exclamation that the others turned to stare at her. She reddened at the quizzical lift of Guy's mocking eyebrow and hurriedly explained, ''The wine. Penelope thinks Graham's wine cellar is too old.''

Guy turned a suspiciously laughing gaze to the amused upturn of Penelope's lips. ''When you get ready to throw it out, throw it my way, Penny. I'll be happy to dispose of it for you.''

''Dolly has just been explaining to me that wine improves with age. As I understand it, you and Graham are the equivalent of a good Madeira.''

Guy's whoops and Lady Reardon's cries of reproval brought any further attempt at private conversation to an end. The chatter became general, leaving Penelope to return to worrying over Graham.

She had good cause to worry. Left alone with the man in the upstairs chamber, Graham stared with fierce contempt at the familiar face on the pillow. Once it had been a youthful boy's face, but the years had brought it to hardened manhood, and judging by the expression, little compassion or wisdom had been learned with the years. The darkened features of a man who had spent many months under a Spanish sun tightened into an implacable expression beneath Graham's gaze.

"All these years, I'd thought you dead. I should have known you were too damned proud to die in such a manner. I kept waiting for your ghost to haunt me, but I can see you'd rather do it in person." Arthur coughed violently as if the task of speaking had depleted his breath. The white bandage around his usually dark crop of hair provided sharp contrast to the healthy coloring of his skin. He had apparently been lying atop the bed covers, reading, when Graham entered. His book lay cast aside beside the stiff leg wrapped in heavy bandages.

"If Marilee's ghost doesn't haunt you, none will. I prefer more physical vengeance, myself." Graham leaned on his walking stick and glared at the enemy who had once been his youngest friend.

"Fine. You with one eye and me with one leg. A fair fight by any standards. Will you send your seconds?"

"If that's the way you want it, but I've waited this long, I can wait a little longer. I've had five years to recuperate. You'll not need that long. Just don't think you can escape me."

Arthur's fists clenched against the counterpane, and for a brief moment, sorrow flashed across his dark eyes. "You will accept no explanations, will you?"

"Save them for Marilee when you meet her. All I hear are her screams of pain when I look at you." The stark hatred and bitter pain in Graham's eye as he said this prevented argument.

With a sigh Arthur lifted his hand and let it fall again in agreement. "You are right. No explanation will right that night. Send your seconds whenever you are ready."

"I'm glad to see the charioteer still has some honor in him." With that parting remark Graham strode out.

Chapter 21

UNAWARE of the black cloud hovering over her lovely summer days, Penelope thrived in her new home. The grounds offered all the gardening opportunities she could desire, the people were much of a sort as her home, the company was to her taste, and the freedom to ride about as she desired without carriage and a battery of footmen relieved her beyond measure.

Graham watched as she shed her prim facade for that of a happy, normal woman. He would have rejoiced at the change had he not also noticed the increasing frequency with which Hamilton and DeVere appeared at their doorstep. To add insult to injury, she had taken to visiting Arthur Reardon at his bedside. Admittedly she was always in the company of Dolly, but the wound still festered. Every man in the neighborhood had the right to pursue her except himself. That thought gnawed at his soul more than any other. Since Penelope thought they were friends, he could not forbid her to see them. And to warn the others to stay away from her would reveal the state of his mind. He was trapped in a torment of his own making.

Try as he might, he could not go to her like this. Pride prevented him from discovering her distaste; honor prevented him from stealing her innocence under false pretenses. If he could hold himself aloof long enough, she would find other lovers and he would be free of these wasted longings. It would be easy enough to see her as any other woman once she shed that captivating aura of innocence, he decided. It was her honesty and total guilelessness demanding the same in return that kept him away.

Once more Penelope found the door between them closed. She mourned the lack of closeness that she had thought they were developing, but she could do nothing to breach the barriers. Graham had not married her for companionship. Apparently, he had no need of companionship. He even ignored his friends when they called, leaving them to her care while he went about setting the estate in good working order again.

Pensively Penelope watched Graham's wide shoulders as he strode away from her, knowing Guy Hamilton waited in the front room. What had happened to the man who had all but admitted jealousy of Guy's attentions? The man who had slept in the bed beside her and looked at her as if she were a woman he could admire? Where did that man go when this gruff stranger entered?

And why did it matter to her? Was she so desperate for attention that she must demand it of a man who had enough to think about beside herself? She had never needed a man's flattery or admiring gazes before. Why should she feel mistreated if she did not receive them now?

Deciding she must be growing unacceptably vain, she hurried to greet Guy and tell him that once more Graham had escaped their company.

"Why do we not ride over and find Dolly? She enjoys an outing more than anyone, and she spends so much time cooped up inside entertaining Arthur."

Guy's eyes darkened to a deeper blue as he regarded his hostess, but he bowed acceptance of this decision. "She has shown a remarkable degree of sensibility in caring for her brother that I had not expected of her. If you do not mind adding a third party, I am willing."

"Three is a crowd? Shame on you, Guy. And what makes you think Dolly is not sensible? She is young and she has been much spoiled, but she is not lacking for sense or affection." Penelope tied the ribbons of her hat and pulled on her riding gloves as they stepped out into the sunshine.

"And you are so very old that you can call a chit like Dolly young? You have some very strange notions, my dear Penelope. It is not the difference in your ages that make you a model of all that a man admires. I hope Trev knows how very lucky he is." Guy held her horse as she used a mounting block to reach the saddle, but his gaze was solely on her.

Penelope sent him a mocking look. "Sir Percival, if you do not show more sense than that, I shall abandon you entirely and retreat to the nursery for intelligent conversation. Graham tolerates me because we are much of a kind, both practical, logical-minded individuals unswayed by strong emotions. You and Dolly, however, are impulsive, laughing, loving creatures who light up the lives of others. Why do you ridicule what is good in you and admire what is dull in me?"

"Because I need a good, sensible partner who will keep me on the right path and make my house a welcome place as you have done the Hall. I am tired of the bachelor life. It is time I settled down."

"Would you not enjoy settling down more with someone you love? It is all very well to decide on a sensible wife who will put pretty flowers in your vases, but what if she whines when she talks? Or sneezes without using a handkerchief? Or nags? Love might be blind to such faults, but without love, they would make every day an irritation. Do you think you can find a woman without faults?"

"Are you saying you and Graham married for love or are perfect?" Guy asked sardonically.

"You do not think we love each other?" Penelope returned the question quietly, wondering what had made him ask.

"I have known Graham all my life. He is my best friend, but I am not blind to his faults. Since the accident, I cannot know him at all. He does not comport himself in a manner to invite love. No, I think he has taken advantage of you and for whatever reasons, you have allowed it."

"Perhaps so, but as I said, we are very much alike. We do not have the need for strong passion, so we swim along quite nicely. I do not think you can say the same for yourself. You would not be content to let me go my own way as Graham does.''

''No, by Jupiter, I would not!'' Guy responded vehemently. ''And neither should Graham! One does not throw a rare gem down on a common table and leave it there for all to pick up and admire as they will. The man has taken leave of what few senses he has remaining. When I see DeVere and his ilk hovering over you like vultures, I think I do not know the man at all. I'd as lief think him to be the crazed madman loose in London as to think he would allow you to fall in the hands of the likes of DeVere.''

Penelope heard this outburst with amazement, but in all fairness, she had to defend Graham. ''You must have an exceptional picture of me. I am no rare jewel, but as common as any other female and quite capable of looking after myself, thank you. I do not know what you hold against Mr. DeVere, but I'm not likely to fall into his hands or anyone else's. Graham knows that. I think you are developing an imagination as overactive as Dolly's. And what is this of a madman in London? Have there been more murders?''

Guy ran his hand distractedly through his hair. ''What? No. Not lately. It's just the description sounded so much like Graham that people are talking, but nobody really believes it's him. That's not the point.''

But Penelope was tired of this talk of herself and more interested in the talk of Graham. ''What description do they give?''

Exasperated with himself for mentioning the subject, Guy answered curtly. ''Tall. Broad-shouldered. Wears a cloak. Carries a cane. Some have mentioned an eye patch. The only difference is the hair color. None see it as gray.''

Penelope made a dismissive gesture. ''That could as easily be Chadwell or any number of other men in London. And anyone can feign an eye patch.''

''Scar on the cheek, too. Who's Chadwell?'' Guy's glance was decidedly suspicious.

"Graham's cousin. Have you not met him? He is something of the family black sheep, I gather. He has a scar on his cheek, too. Not like Graham's, of course. But after such a war, can you imagine the number of men with scars?"

Guy wasn't listening to the debate over the elusive madman. His attention fastened on this mention of a hitherto unknown cousin. "I didn't know Graham had a cousin. Chadwell? Is that his surname?"

"Clifton Chadwell, from America. I have not traced the family tree, but the resemblance is there. But if there have been no murders, someone must have caught the man, or scared him off. Thank goodness. Graham does not need people staring at him as if he were a fiend of some sort. Can you not see how that would change a person?"

Guy wasn't satisfied, but they had arrived at the Reardons' and the subject dropped. Later, he heard DeVere inquire of Penelope about Chadwell's whereabouts, and Guy remembered the conversation. He listened to her reply but received no satisfaction from Penelope's disinterested shrug indicating ignorance. If Graham had an American cousin, he must be so many times removed as to be a total stranger. Guy vowed to question his friend at the first opportunity.

When talk turned to the upcoming church festival, Guy lost any further chance to enlarge his knowledge of this elusive cousin. Both Penelope and Dolly had agreed to help in the festivities, and before the day was out, they had recruited most of their male acquaintances. Even Arthur, who was now able to hobble his way downstairs, was given the assignment of compiling lists of events and judges. Only the promise that their jobs would be brief and the remainder of the day could be spent in the company of their gentle commanders kept the men from escaping with groans of dismay.

When Graham discovered he had been volunteered to judge several of the events, he bent a severe look upon his noble wife. "You expect me to do *what?*"

The candle in his study had nearly burned to the stick, but there was sufficient light to judge his surprise.

Penelope knitted her fingers together in front of her and confronted him with false bravado. "Judge the horses. Guy said you are a very good judge of horses. And then of course there are the ceremonials where you will have to present the prize, but that is not so very difficult. The vicar is thrilled to death that you will be able to attend. It means so much to the villagers, and it won't hurt you any to give a little of your time."

"My money is not enough?" he inquired dryly, moving away from his desk to find another candle or lamp. Discovering what he wanted, he lit it at the small fire in the grate, then turned to better see Penelope. "Unless they are offering a horror show, I cannot believe they need me there to scare the children and frighten the hens from laying."

Penelope placed her hands on her hips and frowned at this great, hulking bear of a man who feared to face the people who knew him better than any. He had grown up here, and she already knew the people remembered him with fondness. She had spent these last days fielding eager and curious questions. It was time he answered them on his own.

"Do you intend to spend the rest of your life hiding from those who know you? If you can endure the stares of strangers, why not those with whom you must live? And the stares will go away once they grow accustomed to the change. It is only a scar, after all. There are others who must suffer much worse."

Leave it to Penelope to humble him and make him face the facts. If she had been around five years ago, he would not be where he was right now. He studied the glow of her innocent beauty and wondered once again how a cynical villain such as himself had the luck to win such a pristine soul as his wife, and he surrendered. The devil had owned him for too long. The delights he wanted were right here on this earth, embodied in the angel standing before him.

"We'll talk about suffering later, after this thing is

done," he growled. "Then I'll exact the price from your pretty hide."

"Yes, master," Penelope replied meekly, but the grin tugging at the corners of her mouth told she was not fooled by his irascible reply. "I shall go tell the Cook to fix your favorite strawberry tart, and then I shall sit in the coal dust and eat my swill until you call for me." She bounced a pretty curtsy and swept out, leaving Graham to struggle to control his laughter.

The day of the festival dawned magnificently, remarkably clear. Alexandra was up at dawn, rushing to the windows to see if the promised jugglers were coming down the road, fleeing Mrs. Henwood to escape to the kitchens to lick the icing bowls for the cakes the Hall would donate for the bake sale. Penelope captured her with promises of new flowers for her bonnet, and by the time the carriage was ready, Alexandra was appropriately gowned in white dimity and lace with an enormous pink sash and a rose bedecked bonnet to match.

Penelope chose a pale spring green organdy with puff sleeves and yellow ribbons entwined through the gathered bodice. With no other ornament but the matching ribbons in her honey brown hair, the attire had a country simplicity striking to the eye, but even more so when she moved, for the gauzy material clung and fluttered and made every step a graceful art.

Blessed with this sight the moment he crossed the threshold while his wife chased his daughter across the verdant stretch of lawn, Graham nearly called a halt to the whole proceedings. With the wind plastering the frail gown to every curve and the sun shining on bare arms and shoulders, Penelope appeared more nymph than angel, and Graham regarded the sight jealously. The urge to catch her and hold her against him and feel her body mold to his nearly crippled him, and he could only stand and watch helplessly from the steps until they discovered his presence.

Penelope saw him first. Allowing Alexandra to escape, she stopped her wild chase to nervously brush the folds of her gown back into place. Graham stood so tall and straight and forbidding, very much the lord of the manor, and here she played the part of hoyden. He had obligingly decked himself out in glowing white linen, a gold brocade waistcoat that rivaled the sun's shine, fawn doeskin breeches, and a dark green frock coat cut short across the waist to reveal the muscular planes of his flat abdomen. A gold watch fob glittered beneath the coat's button, and even his mahogany walking stick appeared polished to a high shine. Remembering the deadly sword concealed inside that deceptive stick, Penelope concealed a shudder. All that glitters is not gold, and she did not fool herself into thinking her husband the genial country squire he chose to portray this day. Whatever he was, she admired him for it, however, and she approached him with a lighthearted step.

"You will have to hide in the horse ring with the men, my lord, or you will not be able to move for the ladies clinging to your coattails."

Graham caught her gloved hand and lifted her to the step beneath him. He noted appreciatively the faint dusting of freckles above her bodice, then raised his gaze to the startling violet of her eyes.

"I think I am big enough to deal with the ladies. How do you intend to fend off the gentlemen?"

At the warm look in his eye, a slow blush crept into Penelope's cheeks, but she did not look away. "I suppose I must choose a protector. Would you do me that honor?"

Graham couldn't help but grin at this sauce. "Did you know the recompense a protector asks you would not think it an honor. But if you must insist on parading about as a forest sprite in little or nothing, I will assign myself the duty of looking after you, providing I do not need to flit about as you do with yon heathen." He nodded over her shoulder to where Alexandra braved the coachman's dire threats by standing beneath the noses of the carriage horses, alternately crooning a little song to them and patting their dark manes.

Penelope rolled up her eyes at the danger the little scamp put herself in, but the horses were growing accustomed to it. She was her father's daughter in this; no amount of scolding would keep her from the animals.

"Mrs. Henwood will be here shortly. I am not at all certain that is any guarantee Alexandra will arrive home in the same state that she left, but the festival comes but once a year. She can come to small harm among friends and neighbors."

Graham did not feel called upon to inform her that even the innocence of the countryside hid dark secrets. Let her think the day as brilliant as it seemed. He touched his fingers to the soft, warm skin of her cheek. "Then let us mingle with the populace, my dear. I am eager to begin slaying dragons."

Chapter 22

PENELOPE sampled the last of the strawberry jams and consulted with the vicar's wife in low whispers while a dozen eager jam-makers watched anxiously and rolled their hands in their aprons—all except the one Penelope finally pinned the blue ribbon on, that is. A spry, elderly lady with a serene smile and a halo of silver hair, she had beamed confidently throughout the judging.

"That's very unfair of you," Penelope murmured close to the woman's ear as she fastened the gaudy bow to the winner's collar. "The others will never guess your secret."

The woman looked vaguely startled and scrutinized Lady Trevelyan with nearsighted gaze. The lord's new lady was just as young and pretty as she could be, but what did she know of making jams? Regaining her confidence, she inquired innocently, "What secret? It's good strawberries that make the jam."

"And a currant or two for tartness." Penelope grinned as the old lady looked taken aback at her knowledge. "I'll enter my own jam next year and we'll see who comes out ahead."

The woman broke out in a broad, beaming smile, took Penelope's hand and patted it approvingly. "Lord love you, honey, then I'll just have to enter the baking competition. You won't know the secret of my plum cake."

They laughed and the other disappointed losers joined in, hearing enough of this last to hope they had a chance in the following year. Penelope moved about as if one of them for a lifetime, and Guy had difficulty extricating her from the clatter of conversation.

"The horse judging contest is next. Graham sent me to find you. Said he wasn't going to make a fool of himself unless you're by his side." Appropriating Penelope's gloved hand, he tucked it in the crook of his arm and steered her out of the jam booth and through the colorful throng.

Children whooped and hollered and dashed in and out among the legs of their elders, and Penelope cast a prayer to heaven that one of them was not Alexandra. The aroma of meat pies sizzling in their earthen oven competed with the sugary scents of the confectionery table and was lost entirely by the time they passed the booth selling fried pies. Penelope held a hand to her stomach and stared wishfully at the treats as Guy hurried her along.

"How can you make me smell horses when there is all this to sample out here?" she complained as Guy rudely informed her food would have to wait.

"Because I've got my nag in one division and Graham will give the prize to O'Donalson if I don't bring you as ordered. You've just done your job overwell, my sweet. He's going to be the most officious judge in all the kingdom. Plead my case, Penny. I've got a few pounds riding on the outcome."

This was said as Guy led her up to the judge's stand at the ring. Dolly came running up to join them, her chiffon scarf blowing delectably in the breeze as she clamped her overlarge hat to her head. DeVere straggled along behind, his impassive gaze following everything.

Graham stepped out of the stand to claim Penelope, his hand clasping hers possessively as he greeted his friends and neighbors. His stiff stance and formidable features made him difficult to approach, but his manner with Penelope revealed his more human nature. Even as Guy and the others drifted off to examine the competition, the other judges and observers lingered to hear the viscount's opinions and be drawn in by Penelope's eager questioning.

Before the end of the competition, the men were arguing as vociferously with Graham as they did among themselves. The furious glare of one golden eye did not quell these men who had known him since he was a lad. The taut drawn muscle of his scarred face might momentarily terrify, and did often enough, but the lady on Trevelyan's arm punctured these moments effectively. Who could fear a man whose wife dared stick her tongue out at him? Or a man who lost his own tongue when trying to explain why the gelding was better suited to the wagon pull than the stallion?

The teasing she received after that made it obvious her ignorance was not needed through the rest of the events. Leaving Graham to debate the merits of Guy's roan over O'Donalson's gray, she excused herself to join the judging of the baby contest.

Bored with the horses, Dolly joined her. They indulged themselves in sticky taffy from the confectioner's booth, found Alexandra scaling a tree on a dare from a group of young ruffians no older than herself, rescued her, and fed her candy while locating the terrified Mrs. Henwood, then wandered on to the booth where the mothers gathered to show off their youngest.

Graham found her there sometime later, a baby in each arm, a child clinging to her skirt, and a wide smile on her face. The broad faces of the young women around her indicated their enchantment with the new viscountess, and Graham feared a general squall would ensue should he invade this feminine territory.

At his side Guy gave a groan of dismay at the sight, for Dolly had entangled herself in a group of urchins who seemed to be as fascinated with her glorious hair as the tales she told.

"Look at them! What is it about women surrounded with children that makes a man think of bankruptcy?" Guy shoved his hands in his pockets in a gesture of dismay.

Graham couldn't tear his gaze away from the scene. With irony he answered, "Is that what you think of? Strange, that's not what comes to my mind."

Guy gave a hoot of laughter and turned to regard

his friend's impassive expression. "Then you're not dead yet, old fellow. I was beginning to wonder." As Graham continued to stand there beneath the tree instead of moving forward to claim his prize, Guy grew curious. "What are you waiting for? She's ready and you're willing. Has some law been passed that you can no longer enjoy yourself?"

At that moment Penelope glanced up. Her gaze locked with Graham's, and a slow blush began to suffuse her cheeks under the intensity of his stare. If she were as imaginative as Dolly, she would see longing in that look, but that could not be. Whatever it was, she could feel it warm her blood all the way to her bones.

Surrendering the babes, she hurriedly extricated herself from this final contest. Nervously tucking straying strands of hair back into their pins, she approached the men beneath the tree. Graham stepped out to claim her, and she completely forgot that Dolly and Guy were about.

"My turn now, is it not?" Graham demanded, catching her hand and holding it captive.

She did not need to inquire into his meaning. With an uncertain nod she agreed and caught her breath at the blaze lighting her husband's eye. That blaze did not signify anger, she knew, because it was accompanied by his half smile and not the tightening of his jaw. She did not dare contemplate what it did mean. She was content to know he was pleased.

The afternoon sped by swiftly on wings of sunshine and golden laughter. They sampled the wares of all the food booths, dripping hot gravy down their fingers and ringing their mouths with sugar. Despite the disadvantage of one eye, Graham won the archery contest but gallantly forfeited the prize to his runner-up. Guy gambled on the pea beneath the shells and to everyone's surprise, won the pot. Graham pointed out the fact that the next pots doubled and tripled what he had won as everyone pressed around to try their luck after seeing someone win, but that didn't damp his friend's delight. He insisted on spending his winnings on an outrageously gaudy brooch to hold Dolly's scarf in place.

They saw a sleepy Alexandra carried off by a bedraggled and exhausted Mrs. Henwood and laughed as the polished DeVere fell victim to a mud-ball fight. The day was wearing to an end, but no one was eager to acknowledge it. The four young people were greeted with enthusiasm wherever they went, a far cry from the formal politeness of London's society.

Graham scarcely heeded his need for a walking stick but swung it jauntily, using it to ward off running little boys who might topple them in their haste and to rap Penelope's fingers whenever she reached for another excruciatingly ugly object created by some eager if not talented hand.

Finally in a rare moment of self-defense, Penelope caught the stick and tugged it away from him. The surprise on Graham's face brought laughter all around, but the gleam leaping to his eye warned of the punishment to come, and Penelope whirled around and fled, stick in hand.

In the rapidly growing dusk she caused little stir among the weary holiday crowd. Laughing as she heard Graham's heavy footsteps thundering after her, she dodged between the booths and headed for the church. She had no illusion of outrunning him, but planned on claiming sanctuary once within the hallowed interior.

Graham caught up with her just as she slipped through the side doors into the unlit gloom of the first pews. His powerful arm wrapped around her waist and literally lifted her from the floor, pulling her back against his strong frame. Penelope gasped and giggled as she held the stick out in front of her and Graham reached around her to grab it. In one last frantic struggle he twisted it from her hand.

The second the stick left her hand, all interest in it died. Penelope felt her heart thudding against Graham's hard arm and squirmed to break his grasp. At the same time Graham lowered her to her feet and broke his grip to turn her around. She remained within the circle of his arms, staring up into his face without thought of fleeing as she felt his muscles flex to draw her closer.

Without a word of warning, Graham bent his leonine head and touched his lips to hers. A tingle of mixed alarm and joy fled through her body, but Penelope did not resist. Instead she bent closer to the warmth of his broad chest, resting her hands there as she turned her mouth up to sample more of this pleasure he offered.

And pleasure it undoubtedly was. It took root in her toes and spread upward at an alarming rate that quickly encompassed her entire body. Her fingers twisted in the smooth fabric of his waistcoast as his kiss grew warmer. His lips moved tantalizingly across hers, sampling every curve and ridge, finding the corners and tasting them before returning to cling fiercely and with an ardor that stole Penelope's breath from her lungs.

Incredibly she found herself responding, pressing eagerly for more, standing on her toes and wrapping her arms around his neck in ardent invitation that Graham did not mistake. With a groan he slid his hands up and down her slender back, fearing to frighten her with the extent of his need, unable to let her go. His mouth closed tightly, possessively over hers, drinking wantonly of the wine she so innocently offered and growing intoxicated with heady response.

Only when she felt his tongue trace teasingly between her lips did Penelope realize where this led. Her experience with Chadwell had taught her much, and terrified of making such a cake of herself again, she tore away. This was a church, after all. What they did here had no place in a house of worship, although her body ached for the touch that would soon follow.

Before Graham could recover himself, she was off again, not out the door they had entered, but through another. He heard her breathless laughter and relieved, he gave chase.

The door led to a winding staircase and Graham took the stairs as agilely as a mountain goat. The glow of the setting sun lit the interior of the belltower as he climbed through the hatch, and he halted in the opening to admire the scenery.

Penelope stood outlined against the last rays of the sunset, her hair lit in a coronet of gold that trailed in silken streamers down her long, slender throat. Her breasts rose and fell rapidly as she gasped for air after her flight, and the clinging cloth of her gown neatly outlined full curves and slender waist. As she leaned back against the wall, the gown clung to rounded thighs, and the blood thundered in Graham's brain.

Raising himself slowly into the belfry, he reached for the nearest bell rope. Before Penelope could cry out her astonishment, the bell began to peal in long, sonorous notes. Quite methodically Graham reached for the second rope, and a matching accompaniment rang out over the darkening grounds.

Eyes round but laughter bubbling to her lips, Penelope grasped the third rope. Her tug did not have quite the success of Graham's, but he generously reached over her head and pulled that one, too.

With all three bells pealing madly, the crowd on the commons began to run for the church. Penelope glanced down at the antlike brown figures scurrying across the lawns and back to Graham's shadowed face. Without a word he grabbed her hand and led her hastily back down the stairs.

They could hear the questioning cries of the crowd approaching as they ran through the nave, and as one, they dropped into the nearest pew. When the first torches burst into the church, they lit only the lord and his lady kneeling piously with looks of devout wonder on their faces as they faced the altar.

The vicar pushed his way through the crowd and glanced suspiciously up the stairway, then back to Lord and Lady Trevelyan rising from their prayers. Graham's massive figure gently lifted his lovely wife to her feet, and in the hearing of those closest, he murmured, "Our prayers have been answered, my dear, you will see."

Penelope choked back an hysterical laugh as the

vicar's mouth shut with a snap. The tears in her eyes came naturally as she tried to smother her mirth, but the stories that flew about town the next day had any number of radically different interpretations. Remembering Penelope's way with children, the women instantly declared she cried because she had not yet been blessed with a child, and the bells signified the Lord's answer to her prayer. The men remarked that if she was not yet with child, it had more to do with the accident and her lord's crippled state, and they placed a much less pious interpretation on Graham's remark. But even as the rumors grew with each repeating, no one dared come out and speculate that the lord and his lady might have set the bells to ringing themselves. Even those who knew Graham in his younger days were hesitant at casting his new wife in the same mold. What purpose would there be in Lady Trevelyan soiling her dainty slippers in the filthy bell tower?

Penelope pondered that point not much later as she soaked in a tub of hot, bubbly water and contemplated her ruined shoes on the floor near the grate. Her maid had nearly cried in distress at their state, but Penelope could not bring herself to throw them out. She could not bear to part with a single memory of this day, so she had sent the maid away and lay cozily in the warm bath, reliving each and every scene all over again.

The part where Graham kissed her came in for more replay than any other. He had caught her completely by surprise. Never had he done more than hold her hand. She had assumed him entirely indifferent to her. But this day he had kissed her as Chadwell had, held her as if he did not mean to let go. Her heart took on a quicker pace as she considered the consequences of this new development. Graham had not been in London for some weeks. Perhaps without his mistress he grew hungry for a woman, any woman. She did not have enough knowledge of men to know whether this was possible. Surely he must kiss his mistress in the same manner. It did not mean anything, not really. It was exciting to know he might consider her desirable but was that all she wanted from him?

It was certainly better than nothing. Remembering the way he had held her, the way his mouth had felt against hers, Penelope reached abruptly for the soap. It would not do to build up hopes.

Just as her fingers touched the soap, the door from Graham's room swung open, and she gave a cry of surprise. The shock of her husband's entrance at this untimely moment caused temporary paralysis, but recovering quickly, she grabbed for her towel. Gravely Graham bent to retrieve it from the floor and hand it to her.

He wore only a long dressing robe that did nothing to conceal the broad expanse of his chest as he straightened up again. He wore his hair neatly brushed back from his forehead with only a few strands escaping and gleaming silver against his darker skin. The black patch had a particularly sinister effect this night, perhaps because she read the gleam in his eye too easily. His scar tautened over his cheek as he saw the fear leaping to her eyes, but he made no effort to leave.

"I apologize for intruding. I had thought you done by now. Do you need some assistance?"

The blush deepened on her cheeks as Penelope tried futilely to slide further into the water and cover herself with the towel at the same time. "If you would not mind, my lord, you could be of most assistance if you would turn your back."

Graham studied the tangles of light brown hair dangling against her cheek and throat, then allowed his gaze to rove downward. The color rose attractively from the valley between her breasts to spread upward and he had the sudden urge to plunge his hands in the water and lift her out to see if she colored all over. Gallantly resisting this urge, he turned his back and crossed the room to lean against the bedpost.

"I thought it time we had a little talk, Penelope." He listened to the sound of water splashing and imagined her slim, straight-backed form emerging from the water. She would have her back toward him, of course, and he tried to picture the exact curve of the derriere she would not think tempting enough to cover.

"You are displeased? I thought you enjoyed today. I know I do not play the part of noble lady well, but you must admit that you behaved less than nobly at the least." Penelope hastily dried herself, leaving streams of water running down the hard-to-reach part of her back as she reached for her wrapper.

He heard her stepping from the bath and guessing correctly that she had donned her robe and now dried her feet, he swung around. The sight of a shapely calf propped on the tub's edge held his admiration until Penelope looked up to see why he did not answer. She quickly straightened and nervously adjusted the sash of her robe.

"As I am behaving less than lordly now. You need not be so blunt with my faults, Penelope. I know them all. And no, I am not displeased with you. I cannot remember a day I have enjoyed more."

Relieved, Penelope wandered distractedly to the dressing table and began to remove the pins from her hair. The mirror revealed an image flushed with heat and embarrassment and framed in disheveled tangles of impossible hair. Her high-waisted robe of pale blue satin exposed an unconscionable amount of bare skin when worn without a chemise or gown. She tried not to think of that as she tried to fathom the meaning of his appearance here tonight.

"I am glad. You need to laugh more. I like to hear you laugh."

Graham smiled at the guilelessness of her reply. He knew she simply spoke her thoughts without attempt to flatter or charm. One more facet of his intriguing wife that he had begun to enjoy.

"I shall remember to laugh more often." He stood up and crossed the room to poke at the few glowing embers in the grate. "Penelope, answer me truly in this. Have you found anyone who catches your fancy? Has anyone yet claimed your heart? Do not be shy about answering. I know you and Guy have been much together . . ."

Penelope swung around and stared at him with perplexity. He sounded so serious, as if the fate of the world relied on her answer. She could have understood if he asked in jest, but like this . . . She shook her head in bewilderment.

"Guy is a good friend, nothing more. I have told you I am not of a romantical turn of mind. I enjoy being with people, I like some better than others, but I cannot say one has captured my heart."

Graham looked up and studied her. "Not even Chadwell? Out of sight, out of mind?"

She had the grace to blush. "What he wants has little to do with the state of my heart. You do me no favors by leaving me in his company."

Graham drew a rueful face as he stepped closer. "You know you are under no obligation to be faithful to me. Under the circumstances I could not blame you for seeking a man like Chadwell."

Penelope watched his face with an ill-concealed mixture of wistfulness and indignation. "I am sorry, Graham. When you first told me that, I did not understand, and I was too frightened to question. Now I must tell you that I can never be that kind of wife. I do not mean to disappoint you, but I grew up with provincial ways and cannot change now. When we said those vows before the altar, I meant them. I am willing to obey you in all else, but I cannot step outside those vows."

He stood directly in front of her, the candlelight making shadowed hollows of his harsh lineaments as he studied her face intently. For once, his expression was neither deliberately impassive nor openly mocking. If she had only the power to read minds, she could see directly into his, and there would be no need for speech. As it was, she could only wait helplessly for his verdict upon her rash words. Had she been bold, she would have lifted her hand to stroke his face, but he had rejected that gesture once, and she had not the temerity to try it again.

"You may regret those words," he warned. "You were made to have children. Even if your heart remains free, you will feel the longing for what you have missed."

In these last few months she had learned enough of herself to suspect the truth of this, but she also knew the strength of her convictions. She shook her head slowly. "I have Alexandra. She has the spirit of half a dozen children. That is more than I ever imagined happening to me."

"Penelope . . ." The name escaped Graham's lips almost as a groan as he reached to touch one of her fallen tresses. Then remembering himself, he dropped his hand and strode rapidly toward the hearth. Bracing one hand against the mantel and staring into the dying embers, he tried again. "I have not dared approach you for fear you would be frightened of a visage like mine. I cannot believe my good fortune in winning you, and I have no wish to push my luck too far and so risk what we have now."

He hesitated, searching for other words. Bewildered, but acting on some instinct she had not known she possessed, Penelope came up beside him. The shadows made his hunched shoulders broader than seemed possible, but she knew the gentleness of his great strength, and she had no fear of him. Gently she touched his arms, making him raise his head to look at her.

"I would not have married a man I feared, Graham. Why do you hurt yourself so by painting us both as we are not?"

Because he knew more than she, knew better than anyone that he did not deserve his great good fortune, but he could not explain that to those trusting violet eyes. He only dared what he did now because he could see that she would be unhappy in the future, and more than anything else he wanted to bring her some small happiness. If it also came mixed with disappointment and disillusion, he could not spare her that. He could only hope the one outweighed the other.

He stood up and did as he had wanted earlier. He rubbed a gentle finger along her soft cheek and wrapped it in a strand of silken hair. "It is human nature to believe the worst, Penelope. So I believe you are not quite human, since you see only the best in everyone. Tell me, my precocious angel, what would you say if I asked you to be my wife in truth?''

Penelope thought her heart must have stopped, for when she felt it again, it was beating frantically as if to catch up lost time. Graham's solemn stare held her powerless. She could only look up into that wounded face and know he had offered her all his pride and left her the choice of destroying it or returning it bandaged but intact. She knew her answer without thought, she just had difficulty articulating it. How long had it been since she had given up hope of ever hearing those words? She did not possess the practiced phrases of a society matron but had to speak straight from the heart. Her heart was too simple to offer elaborate speeches.

She held his gaze and replied, ''I would say yes.''

Chapter 23

STILL he resisted. He had been taught to be a gentleman, although these last few years belied the fact. Even now, in withholding the truth, he was being less than gentlemanly, but he had to consider her happiness. Sometimes the truth could only hurt. Yet he had to make her think.

"I would give you time to consider your answer, Penelope. You need not reply immediately for my sake. Sometimes a generous heart is not the kindest or the wisest."

Graham held himself aloof, the shadows of the fire widening the distance between them. Penelope had no knowledge of the means women used to entice a man or engage his affections. Frustrated at her inability to make him kiss her again so he could understand the truth of her reply, she turned her fingernails into her palms and prayed honesty would serve.

"Graham, you mistake me if you think me an angel. I am a woman just as any other. I told you on our wedding night before I even knew aught of you that I expected to honor our vows. Now that you have given me this time to come to know you and respect you, I can say it with even more confidence. You have given me months to consider, Graham. My answer will not change."

He could read the truth in her eyes, and his heart gave an unexpected lurch. He wanted her in the way a man wants a woman, and he wanted her for the solace he knew she offered to his self-esteem. He had not expected more than that, but something warned he was about to lose as much as he gained. He did not hesitate to make the exchange.

Raising his hand to cup the back of her head, he bent to capture her lips with his.

Knowing she had just surrendered herself to a man who could not love her, Penelope sought satisfaction in the hungry joy of his kiss. She had been fooling herself to think she had not wanted love like everyone else, and a bittersweet sorrow flavored this first taste of passion's joy. But the heady excitement of Graham's kiss soon removed all thought of might-have-beens. Her hands slid to his shoulder as her lips trembled eagerly beneath the onslaught of his kiss.

"Ah, Penelope, there should be champagne to ease you past your wedding night." Graham wrapped her closer into his embrace, spreading his kisses across her jaw to the vulnerable hollow beneath her ear.

Before she could reply, he lifted her from the floor and caught her by the knees. She gave a cry of alarm as she felt herself weightless and powerless in his arms, but the faint grin on his lips as he observed the way her satin robe fell open took away any protest. Clinging with one hand to his shoulder, Penelope tried to cover herself with the other as he effortlessly carried her across the room to his own.

Only a brace of candles lit this dark chamber, and Penelope sighed with relief. She had expected to come to her husband respectably garbed from head to foot in her relatively modest muslin night shift. The scandalous looseness of just a sash to protect her from her husband's gaze made her exquisitely nervous. The places Graham's hands rested as he set her on the floor gave room for all manner of frightening sensations, and she could not look him in the eye as she felt herself sandwiched between the bed and Graham.

The candles on the bedside table sent gleams of light along her robe but hid her blush. Graham tipped her chin up with his finger, and unable to resist the trusting plea of her eyes, he bent to ply her lips into soft surrender.

This time, when his tongue flicked gently along her

mouth, her lips parted willingly. It did not matter that this was not the handsome Chadwell seducing her. The sensation was the same, magnificently terrifying and alarmingly exciting as Graham's kiss deepened to take possession with an expertise that gave her no hope of resisting.

Bent helplessly in his embrace, she could do naught but rest her hands against his broad chest and give herself to the racing, pounding sensations this invasion produced. When his hand slid around to brush aside the opening of her robe and caress her breast, she melted against him as if she had no strength of her own. His large hand cupped the fullness of her breast and began to play tantalizing games with the rising crest until she did not know if it was his moan or her own when he raised his head to look upon her.

Before she knew what he did, Graham untied her sash and parted her robe completely. The flickering light danced across the white satin of firm, upturned breasts, the shadowed hollow of her taut abdomen, and the dark honeyed curls below. Gasping, Penelope reached to pull the robe around her again.

Graham stayed her hand. "No. Before I extinguish the candles, let me see what my rashness has won."

His gaze devoured her as she stood quivering and ashamed before him. But when he touched her breast with gentle reverence, a fiery joy leapt through Penelope, and the shame did not seem so bad. Wrapping his broad hands around her waist, Graham lifted her to the bed, allowing her the security of her robe for a while longer. His hand again rose to caress her breast before he turned and began pinching out the flames.

Clinging to her robe, Penelope crept between the turned down covers and listened to the sounds of Graham undressing. She did not think it would take so long to remove his robe and whatever little he wore beneath it. Perhaps he gave her time to grow used to the fact that she would shortly learn the mysteries of married life. If so, he did her no good because she grew more nervous with each passing moment. The satin fabric rubbing across her nakedness served as an ever present reminder of the sensuality he had aroused in her, a sensuality she had not known she possessed and that she feared as one does the unknown.

She was not unfamiliar with the way the bed sagged when Graham climbed upon it, but she knew this time he would not politely stay to his own side. As if to confirm her fears, he raised himself on one elbow and leaned over her, and she could feel the heat of his flesh through her flimsy covering.

"I will try to treat you gently, Penelope. Forget whatever you have heard of wedding nights and let me touch you as I have just done."

His voice sounded different somehow, closer and more tender than the throaty, gruff remarks to which she had grown accustomed. She reached to touch his face, but he caught her hand and kissing it, returned it to the pillow where he held it captive.

"Lie still and let me teach you, my lovely Penny." The caress in his voice was unmistakable, and the smooth touch of his mouth across hers silenced any protest.

Too frightened to relax, she could only allow him his way. His kisses plied skillfully at her lips until they burned for more and parted to give him entrance. The touch of his tongue deep within caused her to arch reflexively and his hand was there to catch her movement, caressing her breast through the hampering fabric of her robe and sliding beneath her to hold her captive. This closeness made her startlingly aware of his male nakedness, and Penelope tried to cringe away, but Graham had her surrounded.

A small moan died in her throat as his mouth drank thirstily of hers and his palm forced her closer, sliding down her back until it cupped her buttocks. Through the satin of her robe she could feel the heat of his hand, and she blessed the way the fabric slid between them to protect her from the man holding her so intimately.

Within minutes she was no longer capable of such conscious thought. Graham's hand came up between them and slid beneath the satin to wreak havoc with

the sensitive peak of her breast. Her breathing grew
ragged as his hand began to explore her nakedness.
When he lingered at the curve of her hip, she drew a
deep breath, only to discover her mistake when Graham bent his head to suckle the peak he had so thoroughly aroused with his caresses. Lost, completely
incapable of controlling this situation, Penelope cried
her surrender and arched against the heat of his mouth.
That movement brought her more of the ecstasy his
tongue had to offer, but it also dislodged her robe from
between them, as his hand was quick to remind her.
She felt the hard thrust of his maleness between her
thighs as he brought her into the curve of his body,
and she began to learn the first of many lessons the
night had in store for her.

Satiated with one breast, Graham lay her back
against her open robe to sample the other while his
hand continued to roam, exploring the excitements of
her body and teaching her the passion she had yet to
learn. When he tried to touch her most intimate places,
Penelope whimpered in protest, but his hand boldly
overrode her objection. She could not believe this was
right, that a man could touch a woman like so, but as
the heat of his hand stirred embers of desire within
her, she moved achingly to his caress.

He did things to her that made her blush to admit
even as he did them, but his kiss kept coming back to
smother all protest, and her body traitorously reveled
in the pleasure of his touch. When he finally parted
her thighs with his hands and moved his heavy weight
over her, she was too lost to the drug of his kisses to
understand the import. Not even when he caressed her
there until a tingling sensation made her rise against
him did she know what he was about. Not until the
piercing pain filled her to the very quick did Penelope
know what she had done.

True to his word Graham was both quick and gentle,
but the shock had drained away the pleasure. Humiliation swept over Penelope as his body entered hers and
took control, rocking to a rhythm she could not meet.
The satin of her robe received the blood of her inno-

cence, and her skin rubbed against its folds as Graham held her shoulders pinned with his hands and her hips captive with his maleness.

Not until she felt her husband's loss of control, the groan that escaped his lips as one hand slid beneath her to hold her higher, the frantic thrusts that spilled his warmth into her, did Penelope begin to feel the power of this joining. Too late, it was over, and her body ached oddly even as Graham withdrew to return her freedom.

It was only then that Graham brushed the robe from her shoulders, throwing it aside as he turned on his back and pulled her with him. His hand roved caressingly over the swell of her breasts to the deep valley of her waist, claiming her and reminding her of his claim.

The hollow pit within her belly grew tighter as Penelope realized she had given Graham full right to do this whenever he wished. Never had she dreamed how much she would have to surrender to become a full wife. It had been easy to say the words, to act on principal, but the reality was frightening to an extreme. She had known her life would no longer be her own when she had agreed to take this man as husband. She had not known that it also gave him claim to everything she called private. Only the knowledge that his seed lay planted deep within her kept her from pulling abruptly from his embrace.

"The next time will be better for you, my Penny," Graham murmured against her ear. "I think I shall enjoy teaching you what you have been missing."

"The next time?" She had just been contemplating with satisfaction the fact that he had done his duty as husband and would probably not need to do so again unless his seed did not bear fruit. This mention of next time made her rise up to try to see his face in the darkness.

Graham chuckled and ran his hand into her hair, pulling her down against his shoulder again. "You would not plant only one seed in a hill of corn, would you? If it is children you want to grow, you must tend the ground carefully and plant at the right times. To put it crudely, my love, we have just broken the earth.''

Penelope buried her face against his shoulder and conquered an overwhelming urge to sink her teeth into the smooth flesh there. Broken the earth, indeed! She had married a monster of decadence. That was the only thing she could conclude.

Still, she made no objection when his hand continued its gentle explorations, and she made no attempt to free herself when he adjusted her more comfortably against his side and wrapped her soundly in his embrace. Her lashes closed and her breathing grew regular to match the rhythm of the heartbeat against her ear. That her breasts wantonly pressed against his muscular chest and her bare leg lay shamelessly entwined with his powerful thigh made no difference to her sleep.

Chapter 24

PENELOPE woke to the light of day and the familiarity of her own room. In sleepy surprise she turned over to make sure she did not mistake, but there was no sign that Graham had even been here.

None, that is, but the fact that she was completely naked and that the soreness between her thighs remained when she moved. Remembering what Graham had done to her there, her cheeks flamed scarlet and she buried her face against the pillow. The pictures in Chadwell's house of ill repute had not lied, then. That was what happened between men and women that no one ever talked about. No wonder. No sane woman would ever marry did she know what the future held.

Although she did not think she could ever bear to face him again, Penelope could not completely blame Graham. He sought his own pleasure since his mistress was not available, that she understood. But he also sought to give her what she wanted most—a child. Perhaps he also had some latent urge to produce a son, but he would have denied himself had she not encouraged him. It was her own fault. Now she must bear the consequences.

Covering her abdomen with her hand, Penelope wondered how long it would take to know if their efforts had been successful. Remembering Graham's insinuation that it would take more than one time, she wondered if she really wanted a child that much. Imagining herself with rounding belly and all the world knowing what he had done to her, her courage failed. Was it too late to change her mind?

Practicality reared its ugly head, and she knew she

could not hide in here forever. Afraid of this new body he had given her, Penelope stepped gingerly from the bed. Just the process of using the chamber pot made her blush, and afterward she scrubbed vigorously at her private parts. The scent of Graham clung to her, and she wished desperately for another bath, fearful someone would notice.

Finally electing a liberal splash of toilet water to disguise any lingering scents, imaginary or otherwise, Penelope dressed quickly in a high-necked gown of lavender muslin. Remembering how her body responded to just a touch of her breast, she understood why Graham preferred the low-cut bodices, and she could not bear to show herself so shamelessly again.

It was late and she did not bother to call her maid to dress her hair. Graham would no doubt be on his way, and she would not entertain any callers today. Pinning the long lengths in a simple chignon, Penelope took a deep breath and prepared to reenter the world.

She nearly fled to the safety of her private chamber upon discovering Graham lingered over his breakfast. He looked up at her entrance, however, and she could not gracefully make an escape. Carefully avoiding his eye, she picked up a plate from the sideboard and selected a small piece of bacon and an egg.

Graham had politely risen from his chair at her entrance, and he chuckled now at the sight of her bent head and pink cheeks. Before she could slide into the distant seat that was properly hers, he reached out to touch her cheek, forcing her to face him.

"You look beautiful this morning, Lady Trevelyan, even if you do choose to hide much of your beauty behind your high-necked muslins." He bent a lingering kiss to her lips, ensuring her response before releasing her and pulling out the chair beside his. "Sit with me. I am almost done and I want to memorize the way you look to keep me company until I return."

"Such flattery will get you nowhere," Penelope protested as she accepted the seat offered. His kiss had made more than her lips tingle, and she wasn't at all certain how to act beneath his warm perusal. It was as if he had the ability to see her without her clothes, and she felt as if she sat eating naked before him.

"It's not flattery but truth. I can see I have my job cut out for me to teach you not to be so prudish. Your days as an untouched spinster are over, my lady. Look me in the eye and tell me you did not enjoy any part of it."

Now was her chance. She had only to look up and tell him to his face that she had changed her mind, that he would have to save his embraces for the kind of woman who enjoyed that kind of thing, or pretended to. Surely he would not force himself upon her when he understood her feelings.

But when she looked up to find Graham's familiar face frowning down on her, she could not do it. He had seemed so happy at her acquiescence, and the memory of his kiss was so strong that she could not deny him. Perhaps another time, but not now. Cursing her blush, she answered carefully, "I do not make much of a liar, my lord."

"No, you don't, and for that I am grateful." Graham leaned over and brushed her cheek with his ungloved hand. "Be patient, Penelope. I am asking much of you, but not more than you can give. By the time the corn is ripe, you will be looking forward to the planting as much as the harvesting."

He laughed at her outraged expression, pressed a kiss to her forehead, and departed on his daily tasks. Not until he was gone did she wonder why she had not noticed his glove last night, or why his scarred and partially immobile mouth seemed to melt so effortlessly against hers when they kissed under the cover of darkness. Those were topics for another day, when she had regained more of her equilibrium.

As was not unusual, Graham did not return in time for dinner that night, and Penelope retired gratefully to the privacy of her own chambers. Perhaps if given enough time, she would learn to accept her husband's marital demands. But tonight it was pleasant to return to the comfort of her empty bed.

She had no sooner fallen asleep than a familiar step crossed her floor. Fighting clouds of sleep, Penelope tried to waken, but not until she was lifted in strong arms and carried across the room did she realize where she was. In the darkness she could see nothing of his features, but she knew the feel and smell of him, and she murmured a soft, protesting "Graham" as he laid her across his bed.

Ignoring this slight objection, Graham removed his robe and leaned over his sleepy wife to waken her with a kiss. With his hands planted on either side of her head, Penelope could not resist, and his demands were slow and sensual, wakening her from more than sleep. When her lips parted beneath his insistence, he groaned his pleasure at her response and took his claim hungrily. His hand sought the soft purchase of her breast while his tongue plundered the sweet recesses laid open to him.

The soft linen of her night shift hampered his caress, and as he joined Penelope on the bed, Graham's hand caught in the hem and pulled it upward around her waist. He heard Penelope's gasp of surprise, but the urgency of his need prevented hesitancy. When she struggled against his kiss, Graham buried his hand in her hair and kissed her until they were both dizzy with desire. He felt her resistance still, and his hand began to stroke and play at the tight juncture he would win from her.

Penelope tried to fight him. She turned and twisted and writhed in an effort to avoid those insinuating fingers, but they only slid deeper, sending jolts of electricity through her until her hips began to rise and fall to the rhythm Graham commanded. Without even knowing what she did, she opened to his whispered, "Now, Penny," and she moaned a little as she felt him fill her completely.

Graham continued to murmur soothing words as his body returned her to the movement he had taught her earlier. Without need of any other caress, her body responded. This time, there was no pain, and if there was humiliation, it was lost in the burgeoning pleasure growing and swelling and blooming inside her. When she felt that she could stand no more, that surely she would burst from the intensity of these forbidden pleasures inflicted upon her, Graham gave an anguished cry and shuddered above her.

It was then that she knew the true meaning of what they did, for her body did burst as it opened and took him in until there was no separating one from the other and the liquid warmth wrapped around them, engulfing and overflowing like fields after a summer rain.

Exhausted, Graham lay momentarily atop her, pressing her into the mattress with his heavy weight, branding her forever with the heat of his flesh. Penelope slid her hands around his back and pressed small kisses into his shoulders, allowing the aftermath of loving to blind her to thought. A sensuous languor stole over her, disturbed only when Graham roused and rolled over, carrying her with him.

They said nothing, for there was nothing that could be said without stirring troubled waters. Graham idly caressed her breast while Penelope curled against his side, content to accept his strength as her pillow. The time for thought would be at the break of day. The time for adjusting to this miracle of becoming one whole was now, while no word or act separated them.

Graham waited until Penelope's breathing was light and even, then reluctantly rose from the bed and carried her back to her own chambers. He longed for the right to lay beside her throughout the night, wake to find her at his side, but he had yet to solve that dilemma. Tucking the covers around her, he kissed her forehead, and giving a growl of disappointment, returned to his lonely room.

Penelope once again woke to her empty bed. This time, she did not feel the same rush of relief, although she was reluctant to examine why this might be so. She wondered for a moment if she had not dreamed the whole thing, but the lethargy in her limbs warned it would have been a dangerous dream, had the marks on her breast not revealed the reality. She remembered clearly all Graham had done to her, and while a blush stole across her cheeks, a new sensation crept through that place where they had been joined together, and it was not at all unpleasant.

Graham did not wait for her to go downstairs this morning but joined her as soon as he heard her moving about. Already fully dressed and ready for the day's activities, he appeared all the more impressive to Penelope's newly opened eyes. She felt naked and disheveled in the chemise she had drawn on before he entered, but the look in his eye indicated his impression was not quite the same.

"I trust you are feeling no ill effects after last night? I fear I may have been a little too rough with you."

He seemed sincerely penitent and worried, and because she had suffered only pleasure at his hands, Penelope had to forgive him. She pulled on a robe the maid had laid out the night before and daringly approached him, touching his cravat since he allowed no caress of his face.

"You frightened me, but with time, I will learn not to fear your touch." Shyly she studied his expression, trying to find what she wanted in the half smile on his lips and the unreadable light of his eye.

Graham brushed a strand of hair from her cheek, then let his hand wander where it would—along the slender column of her throat, down the neckline of her robe, to the knot of her sash. His hand hesitated there, then simply slid beneath the robe to seek the taut peak of her breast straining against the chemise. With interest he noted she continued to stare up at him, although he was well aware her body was already responding to his touch.

"You learn quickly, my pretty Penny. I hope you do not learn so fast that you go seeking others for these pleasures. I find I am rather jealous of my right to teach you physical love."

"Good, then you will not go seeking your mistress any time soon. I do not know enough yet to enjoy sharing you with others."

"My mistress?" Startled, Graham frowned down at her trusting expression. Certainly she did not challenge him with intent to make a scene, but he could see no other reason for introducing this mythical creature. Then remembering the night she had found his chamber empty, he realized the conclusion she had drawn, and he offered a wry smile at his own expense. If it made her happy to think that, it was better than the truth.

"That's fair. As long as I have you, I need no other. Now kiss me and I will leave you alone until tonight."

Her cheeks colored at his tone, but obligingly, she stood on her toes to reach his lips. Graham caught her against him and took more than a simple kiss before he set her down.

Leaving her flushed and confused, he departed. There was much work to be done after five years of neglect, but the reward waiting for him when he returned home was well worth the effort.

He came to her again in darkness that night and all the others of that fortnight. When Graham worked in the study, Penelope tried to wait up for him, but he never came until her eyes closed and the candle guttered out. Then he would lift her into his arms and carry her to his bed and teach her all those things her body longed to know, although sometimes against her will. He won all these battles and more, until just a touch of his hand or his movement told her what he wanted, and she gave willingly. Once certain that he had tended his field thoroughly, he carried her back to her own bed and parted with a kiss.

To Penelope's surprise and relief, no one noticed the difference in her. She helped Dolly address invitations to a rout Lady Reardon decided to give. She walked patiently around the Reardon garden as Arthur tested his mending leg. She rode out with Dolly and Guy to visit other neighboring homes. And no one remarked on her new worldliness. It seemed odd that such a major change in her life could not be seen by others, but it made it easier to face the light of day.

Graham had not forgotten the charitable allowance he had promised her, and in the excitement of these past few weeks, Penelope had not forgotten the enormous sum locked away in her writing desk. Such wealth had the power to change more lives than Goldie's or young Pippin's. She had to plan carefully to prevent doing more harm than good. With Graham gone much of the day and with the slower pace of country society, she had time to ponder its uses carefully.

She had meant to consult Graham with her plans as soon as he seemed to have a spare minute, but that opportunity did not come. DeVere had shown up several times at the Hall looking for Graham and leaving messages for him, but Graham never seemed to respond and showed no interest in meeting with him. So both their hopes of consulting with the viscount disappeared when Penelope returned home from the Reardons one day to find DeVere in the salon, Pippin and Alexandra fighting in the garden, and the house in an uproar over Graham's hasty departure.

As she climbed out of the carriage, Alexandra came running up with Pippin following close after, both yelling incomprehensible phrases into the wind. Penelope stood in the drive and waited for them to quiet, although curiosity over Pippin's presence nearly led her to shout a command for silence.

Once they realized there would be no response until they spoke one at a time, they bit their tongues and glanced at each other before making small bobs of greeting to Penelope.

"Very good. Now what is this of ponies?" She held up a hand as both tried to speak again. "Ladies before gentlemen. Alexandra, what has happened to cause you to behave in such an unladylike manner?"

Alexandra stuck her chin out defiantly. "He rode my pony. I didn't say he could ride my pony. He could have *hurt* him."

Penelope tried to disguise her surprise at the city-bred orphan riding all the way out here. It did not seem likely. She turned to Pippin and offered him a turn. "Did you ride the pony here, Pippin?"

"Yes, mum." He stuck his lower lip out petulantly

and threw Alexandra a malevolent look. "I daren't take one of 'em great critters, but Nell said 'twas important and I 'ad to get word to the master someways."

Nell! That did not bode well at all. Perhaps something had happened to Chadwell. They had left only a skeleton staff in London, and none would know much of Chadwell or Nell. The boy shouldn't have come alone, but he was impetuous. She took both children by the hand and started up the steps.

"Have you seen Lord Trevelyan yet? Does he know you're here?" Penelope ignored Alexandra's angry tug.

" 'E done up and gone. Took 'at great black critter of 'is and left soon's I gave 'im the letter."

Penelope didn't like the sound of that at all, but she couldn't let the children see her fright. Entering the house, she led them down the hall toward the kitchen. "Then we must find some other way of getting you back to London. That's too long a ride to make alone." She gave Alexandra a severe look. "Now I want you to thank Pippin for bringing your pony out for you to ride. He must have been terribly afraid to ride all that way by himself. Remember how scared you were when the lightning flashed? And you had your papa with you."

She squeezed Pippin's hand when he seemed about to protest, and he kept silent while Alexandra peeped around Penelope's skirts with awe. "Did lightning hit you?"

Pippin shrugged nonchalantly. "Oncet or twicet. Not so much's to notice."

Penelope rolled her eyes heavenward, but this bold-faced lie seemed to please Alexandra. She began to chatter excitedly about the other parts of the journey while Pippin invented one tale after another to feed her curiosity. Seeing Harley waiting patiently for her attention, Penelope sent the youngsters off to the kitchen for biscuits and milk and turned an inquiring look to the butler.

"There's a gentleman in the first salon, my lady; a

Mr. DeVere to see Lord Trevelyan. What shall I tell him?''

"Then his lordship has left for London?" At the butler's stiff nod, Penelope pursed her lips in perplexity. "Did he leave any message for me?"

"He was in a great hurry, my lady. John had to fetch him from the fields, and he rode off without his baggage."

That told her nothing. He had clothes and toiletries in London should he decide to stay, but she hoped it meant the stay would be brief. She nodded absently at the news.

"I will see to Mr. DeVere, then, Harley. Thank you."

When she entered the first salon, however, there was no one there. Puzzled, she glanced around, but he did not stand at the pianoforte or behind the column with a bust of Diana. She checked the window nooks and found several of the sashes open to let in fresh air, but DeVere did not hide here. Shrugging, she turned and left the room.

Had she looked more carefully out of the window, she would have seen the dust thrown up by the galloping hooves of someone's racing horse down the drive, but she did not.

Chapter 25

WHEN DeVere reached the Trevelyan London town house, there was no sign that Graham had arrived, but DeVere was not a man to jump to hasty conclusions. Graham had a fairly good head start and undoubtedly a better mount. He could have been here some time ahead of him.

Lingering in the long shadows of the houses across the street, he idly patted his pockets in pantomime of a man searching for a lost or misplaced object. While he searched, he noted the drive gates were open, and the recent calling card of a horse still lay steaming upon the road. He was certain Graham had arrived, but he could not know if he were still there.

Deciding to wait just a little longer before approaching the house, he was rewarded with the sight of the man he had really come to see—Chadwell. DeVere watched in satisfaction as the dark-haired American climbed into the carriage pulling around from the stable before he sauntered down the street to find his own mount. The carriage would be easily followed.

On the basis of a hastily scribbled letter signed by Lord Trevelyan and affixed with his seal, Chadwell gained entrance through one of the private doors of a mansion only slightly less opulent than Carlton House. A gentleman apparently awaiting him took his arm and whispering hastily in his ear, led him through long corridors adorned with statues of Greek deities and velvet draperies.

Not in the least nonplussed to discover Chadwell's destination, DeVere dismounted, dusted himself off, and with a word and a coin to a liveried servant, entered the mansion at a different entrance. Once inside, for the first time, he hesitated. He was not attired for a formal court function, and he cursed himself for not registering what the American wore beneath his cloak. Now that he knew the destination, he realized Chadwell had been wearing stockings and a dress sword. He had to have been in court attire.

Thinking quickly, DeVere mentioned a well-known name to another liveried servant and found himself quickly whisked upstairs. There, he waited in a private parlor until the servant left, then crept out to gain a third floor and the quarters of a startled maid. Nervously she nodded at his commands, and within minutes she was scurrying to do his bidding. The American was not the only one who had eyes and ears in numerous places.

Meanwhile, Chadwell slid quietly into a grand ballroom, joining a huge press of people milling and surging about tables lined with sumptuous foods, had he been close enough to partake of them. Occasionally he caught a glimpse of a swan carved from ice, a golden fountain pouring what appeared suspiciously like champagne, and platters stacked high with grapes and other fruits obviously imported from someone's orangery. But though his stomach grumbled in protest, he was not here to indulge in the buffet.

At the far end of the room on a raised dais mingled an assortment of royalty and their dignitaries garbed in the vivid regalia of their various countries. Gold braid, sashes, and medals abounded, but Chadwell had no time for such as these, either. Whispering to the gentleman at his side, he gestured toward the window nooks and private alcoves along the walls. His companion nodded, said a few words to a third man lingering behind them, then steered Chadwell toward the dais.

Now garbed appropriately in black satin knee breeches and frock coat, a jeweled sword clattering awkwardly against his stockinged knees, DeVere entered the ballroom. If any paid attention, it could be seen that his breeches sagged instead of fitting tightly and that his coat hung loosely over his trim abdomen, but he held himself with enough dignity to avoid careful observance.

It took some while to locate Chadwell, but DeVere's clever mind had already deduced the occasion bringing the American to these rarefied circles, and the path of his thoughts narrowly followed Chadwell's. There was too much riding on this event for DeVere to make any mistakes. He inched toward the front of the room and was rewarded with the sight of his prey bent to speak to a slender, fox-faced man in gray.

Chadwell scowled and remonstrated with this official. "He's here, I tell you. My sources wouldn't lie. There may be more than one of them, and they have pistols. If I knew who their target was, we could set a trap, but I couldn't get a name. Unless you want to search every person in the room, you're going to have to get his royal highness and his guests out of here or cordon off the dais. I might recognize one or two of the villains, but in this crush, I'm not likely to see them in time."

"The Regent won't hear of it. This will be the last public occasion for his guests to get together, and there are important topics being discussed. Rumors of assassins will only make him laugh. This affair is by invitation only. The type you are speaking of could not possibly have entered."

"I did," Chadwell reminded him.

The other man frowned. "And the person responsible will be severely reprimanded, I assure you. He is overzealous in his duties."

"Damn you, man! Can you not see . . ." He broke off abruptly and stared over the shorter man's shoulder, then hastily shoved him aside and gestured at the man who had escorted him thus far.

Without further ado he drew his rapier and jumped into the crowd, causing screams of fright from those around him. The fox-faced man gave an angry shout and signaled his men mingling among the guests, but they were too far distant to stop Chadwell's mad dash.

As a man near the dais drew a long-barreled pistol and took aim, shrieks split the crowd and people pushed and shoved to avoid the weapon. In the few seconds in which everything occurred, there was no time for thought, only reaction. Some of the braver gentlemen, assuming Chadwell to be the danger, threw themselves in his path. Another of the assassins, knowing he was not one of them, pulled a second pistol and took aim at the sword-wielding American. DeVere, hearing the screams, tugged out his own weapon and leapt toward the fray.

Chadwell's rapier flashed in a bright arc and a gun exploded, sending the stink of sulfur over the hysterical mob. DeVere screamed his rage and dived toward the wounded assassin just as Chadwell swung to confront the second pistol.

Struck by DeVere's lunge, Chadwell lost his footing. The rapier blow meant to disarm his opponent went wild at the same time as the second pistol fired. Burning pain pierced Chadwell's thigh as he fell forward, and his rapier buried itself in his attacker.

DeVere's lunge had already had its effect. The first assassin now lay sprawled across the ballroom floor, his life's blood pouring from a wound in his back. The fox-faced man gave DeVere a look of disgust and shouted orders for the gunmen to be hauled away. It was obvious that whatever the assassins might have told of their plans would be buried with them. DeVere's ill-fated lunge had seen to that.

Chadwell, on the other hand, did more than give the polished diplomat a look of disgust. Pure loathing crossed his face as he clutched his thigh and shook off offers of assistance. Jerking his rapier from the still body on the floor, he pointed it at DeVere.

"The minute I find evidence that you planned this, you bastard, I'll see you drawn and quartered. I had not thought even you could go this far." His fury so violent he feared he would not control it, Chadwell swung around and limped after the men carrying out the bodies.

In the confusion behind him he managed to escape

without being showered in the royal gratitude he so richly deserved for this act. Considering his other activities, he would have been a hypocrite to accept it. Dragging himself into the carriage, Chadwell collapsed against the seat as the horses bolted into the street.

Penelope frowned at the closed door between her bedroom and Graham's. It had been nearly a week since he had left, and she had no other word from him than the message the carriage driver carried after returning Pippin to the city. It was good to know he was well and conducting business that needed his attention, but she felt as if they were back where they had started, with the door closed between them.

She had made few improvements to the small chamber that was hers. Perhaps it was time to stop fooling herself and set about making herself comfortable here. Even in that blissful time when Graham had taken her to his bed, he had always returned her here. He meant to keep the distance between them. She had no right to imagine that they would ever be closer. Love might exist in the minds of poets, but it seldom occurred in the real world that she knew. She should be satisfied that she gave her husband some small measure of happiness.

She didn't feel particularly satisfied, however. She had a lovely home and comfort and security, and Alexandra was a joy and a blessing. She ought to be on her knees in prayers of thanksgiving. Instead she felt as if she had traded one set of responsibilities for another, with no improvement in the loneliness that filled her nights. She was only human, and she craved love, the love that her mother's death and her father's absence had denied her, the love that a husband should have offered.

Chastising herself for such selfishness, Penelope set about doing what she had learned to do long ago when she felt out of sorts—finding something worthwhile to do. She had already worked out some ideas for the charity money. If Graham didn't have time to help her,

Guy seemed to have plenty to spare. Not being accustomed to wealth, she wasn't certain of her judgment. She wanted a second opinion.

Guy found the enterprise she had in mind mildly amusing, but he agreed to be silent about it. They rode out one morning to inspect the property she was considering and to talk terms with the owners. By the time they rode back that evening, Penelope was all but bouncing in her saddle as she talked of all the plans that had come to her just through the course of one day.

Guy's laughing eyes watched her with as much admiration as humor. She had not really needed him for this trip. She had known the value of the property and had dealt firmly with the owner, ridiculing his first outrageous offers until the man realized he did not deal with an empty-headed female with more money than wits. Guy had simply given his support and allowed the owner to save face by giving credit for the lady's knowledge to the man who accompanied her.

As they came around the bend to the Hall, Penelope spotted a vaguely familiar carriage in the drive, and her thoughts instantly turned to Graham. Perhaps he had rode home with a friend, or perhaps the driver carried a message. She hastened the pace of her mount.

By the time they came abreast of the gleaming equipage, Penelope had placed it. Adelaide! She and Brian had said they might venture out for a visit once the newlyweds had time to settle in, but she had forgotten the generous invitation she had made them. She hoped one of the guest bedrooms had been sufficiently set to order.

Alexandra was already dragging her laughing aunt down the steps when Guy and Penelope rode up. Adelaide gave Guy a curious look as he helped Penelope from her sidesaddle, but she greeted him with the warmth of an old friend. Alexandra in the meantime excitedly grabbed Penelope's hand and tried to pull her toward the stables.

"Come see what Aunt Adelaide brought for me! I put him with my pony so they could keep each other company. She said I mustn't let him in the house, but he's so little, Mama, couldn't we please? Just until he gets bigger?''

Bewildered but overwhelmed that Alexandra had called her "mama" for the first time, Penelope glanced up in dismay to Adelaide for explanation. Graham's sister smiled in satisfaction at the way Alexandra clung to her adopted mother, and she reached out to give Penelope a hug of greeting.

"I have missed you already. The kitten was a good excuse to come before you could possibly be ready for us. I hope you do not mind. We will sleep anywhere. It does not matter. I was growing restless and needed the company.''

Kitten! Well, that explained a good deal, and Penelope's mouth curled upward as she returned her sister-in-law's hug. "I told you that you are welcome anytime. We might even find beds for you. Is Brian here?'' At Adelaide's nod, she continued, "Of course, he would not let you out of his sight now, would he?'' She glanced laughingly at Adelaide's rounding figure.

Then stooping to hug Alexandra, she brushed the little girl's wild mane of black hair from her forehead. "I'd love to see the kitten, love, but I must take Sir Percival in for some tea and see that your aunt has a room ready for her. Would you help me? Then we can go see about your pet.''

After seeing everyone settled and admiring the kitten and admitting that perhaps he might be happier in the kitchen for a while, Penelope gladly sat down to tea with her favorite people. Guy and Brian appeared to be in familiar accord, leaving Penelope and Adelaide to coze quietly in the corner.

"Isn't Graham coming home to tea?'' Adelaide demanded at once.

"He was called to London on some pressing business. I expect him any day now.'' Penelope sipped from her cup and tried not to show her fears.

"Business!'' Adelaide turned up her pretty nose. "He's up to some mischief, no doubt. I never saw one for gallivanting about the countryside as much as Graham. I hoped he had finally taken a notion to settle down. This is the first time that I know of that he's set foot in this place since the accident. I thought it a good sign.''

''I thought the physician who tended him came from around here? Surely Graham stayed in his own home while he was recuperating?''

Adelaide shook her head vigorously. ''The accident happened on the other side of the county and he was taken to a friend's home there. When he was well enough to be moved, he insisted on opening up that museum piece in London and moving there. I could not object, for it was the Season and the time for my come out, but I have always loved the Hall. It seemed strange not to come here in the summers.''

''I had hoped to drive the ghosts away. He did seem to enjoy being back. I am certain it is just some unfinished business that keeps him in London.'' Penelope spoke with more assurance than she felt.

''I'm just glad you didn't go with him. The things I hear of those murders make my hair stand on end.'' Adelaide shook her head cheerfully as if her hair standing on end gave her great pleasure.

''I thought they stopped some time ago?'' Penelope made no claim to clairvoyance, but a chill ran down her spine at this mention of the ghastly events that had taken place in the East End last spring. Since she had seen how the people lived there, she could imagine the horror of being trapped in such a place with a madman on the prowl. Graham had been right to be angry with her for going there.

''They did, but I just received a letter in the post from a friend of mine who was forced by politics to dally there a while longer. There's been no end of scandals with assassins running rampant through the halls of parliament or whatever, but some even say the madman was in the prince's ballroom, and now he roams the streets at all hours. It is horrible. I vow, I'll not feel safe to return until he is caught.''

Adelaide's manner of rattling on past the facts to her opinions left the subject scantily addressed, but it was sufficient to make Penelope nervous for Graham's safety. "Surely it is just conjecture? You know how rumors start. A lady faints, a bystander screams, and the whole town panics."

Guy and Brian had begun listening with the introduction of this topic. Guy appeared amused at Penelope's description of mob hysteria, but Brian shook his head in disagreement. "I only wish it were that, my lady, but I have had it from very reliable sources that two women have been killed this week alone. Graham is right to leave you here. I'll not allow Adelaide back to town until the monster is caught."

Guy brushed back a lock of hair and frowned. "They think it is the same man? How can they know?"

Brian looked at the women's anxious faces and shook his head. "It's best not spoken of in front of the ladies. But witnesses have given a remarkably similar description. They have all seen a cloaked man in the vicinity. He is said to be of well above average height and quite strong-looking. They all agree his hair is dark, and he sports a scar on one cheek." For Penelope's benefit, he added, "There has been no talk of the eye patch this time as there was this spring. It cannot be proved that such a man is the killer, I suppose, but it does seem remarkable coincidence that he is always in the area where one of these murders occurs."

Looking at Penelope, who seemed to grow pale before his eyes, Guy answered lightly. "Well, then, we can excuse Graham. He not only doesn't fit the description any longer, but he's not been in London to give gossips something to talk about."

Brian and Adelaide laughed, but Penelope kept silent. She was relieved that no one would accuse Graham of such horrendous crimes, but she knew of one other person who accurately fit that description and frequented that end of town. The terror that Graham had gone to town on some mission concerning Chadwell ate at her insides, but she could see no way of mentioning her suspicions to her friends.

Chapter 26

WITH guests to entertain, Penelope feared she would have to set aside her plans for the foundling home she meant to establish, but Guy handily eradicated that problem. By mentioning her favorite charity to Adelaide and taking Sir Brian under his wing, he effectively took care of both of them. Adelaide threw herself into the project with wholehearted enthusiasm, and Sir Brian agreed that he and Guy should circulate among the neighbors to raise funds for the cause.

Penelope made them promise her name would not be mentioned in the project except as a sponsor along with everyone else. Since she had not yet had time to discuss this charity with Graham, she did not wish to offend him with her forwardness. Nor did she wish the extent of her charity to be known. She had always felt these things were better kept to oneself, and the men agreed to abide by her wishes.

Plans to transform the old farmhouse into sleeping and teaching quarters for a dozen little girls necessitated the services of numerous workmen. Adelaide knew the neighborhood and knew the people to be hired. Between them, they went over the house from top to bottom and planned what needed to be done with the new foreman. He made suggestions as to the practicality of some of their ideas, but on the whole, they worked well together. Penelope was grateful for the assistance. On her own she would have been fearful of making as many changes as were finally decided upon.

Although her days were full, she could not help worrying about Graham every minute when she was left alone with her thoughts. She felt foolish worrying about a grown man who seemed quite adequately able to fend for himself, but that did not stop her remembering the horrors of London that Chadwell had introduced her to and fearing Graham might somehow be caught in that sordid world of his cousin's. The fact that even after they had shared so much she knew really very little about her husband did not ease Penelope's mind. She knew there was much he kept from her, and she had to accept being thus excluded, but she did not have to like it.

With all her fears and worries Graham's arrival came as something of an anticlimax. Dolly and Guy were visiting to discuss the rout Lady Reardon planned. Involved in the commonplace discussion of themes and colors, Penelope thought little of the arrival of a carriage until Sir Brian idly peered out the window to mention Graham had finally ventured to put in an appearance.

Penelope's heart made a flying leap to her throat as she glanced eagerly toward the drawing room doors. Their meal had already been cleared from the table, but she sent a footman scurrying back to the kitchen to warm something for his lordship. Adelaide watched all this with a small smile. Her brother might speak of marriages of convenience, but her eyes told her otherwise.

When Graham did not immediately come to the drawing room, Penelope excused herself and slipped out into the hall. She caught him as he was about to start up the stairs. At the sound of her footsteps, he swung around. The movement made him wince slightly, but he made a graceful bow as she hurried toward him.

He appeared worn and weary, and Penelope ached to caress the tired lines around his eyes. Instead, she just gave him a worried look. "You look quite done in, my lord. I will not keep you. Shall you have a warm bath before Cook sends up your supper?"

Graham looked relieved as he touched a hand to her

rounded chin. "That will be fine. Do we have guests?"
He nodded toward the lighted drawing room.

"Your sister and Sir Brian have come to visit, and I
asked Dolly Reardon and Guy for dinner. I will give
them your excuses. They will understand."

He nodded, seemed on the point of saying something, then with a shrug of his large shoulders, he
turned to make his way up the long staircase. Penelope
watched in consternation as he leaned more heavily
than ever on his walking stick. The fact that he had
not kissed her or offered words of happiness at being
home had not escaped her, but her concern for his
health took precedence. Whatever had he been doing
to return home in such a state when he had seemed to
be doing so much better before he left?

She sent servants scurrying for both water and tow-
els and orders that the meal should be kept warm, then
returned to her guests. They appeared curious that
Graham would not come greet them with news of London, but no one demanded explanations. Instead,
thoughtfully, Guy escorted Dolly home a short time
later, and Adelaide declared herself quite weary and
demanded Sir Brian take her up to bed.

Within the hour Penelope was able to hasten up the
stairs to see how Graham fared. The door between
their rooms was closed as usual, but boldly, she rapped
upon it. He had taken her as wife. Surely that entitled
her to some rights.

Graham, himself, answered. That seemed to bode
well for a change. Garbed in a maroon velvet dressing
robe, his chest still damp with water droplets, he
looked much more the man who had left here a few
weeks before. Penelope kept her relief in check as he
showed no inclination to invite her in.

Puzzled by this return to coldness, she spoke with
more formality than she would have done otherwise.
"Is there aught I can do for you, Graham? If your leg
is giving you much pain, perhaps I could wrap it in
warm linen . . ."

Graham wrapped his fingers around the door frame
and stared down into Penelope's innocent face. She

had dressed her hair in fashionable swoops and curls, and several dangled wispily about her cheeks and throat. The urge to touch flooded through him, but he knew where that would lead, and he could not allow it without revealing all. He should not have come home so soon knowing what pain he would cause her, but he had not been able to stay away. Somehow, he had hoped he could smooth this over and make it come out right in the end without telling her any of it. Wearily he could see now that he asked the impossible.

"I am fine, Penelope; mother Alexandra, not me. It's been a long day. If you do not need me for anything, will you excuse me? I'd like to get some rest."

She had worried herself frantic for weeks, prayed eagerly for his return, wanted nothing more than to be held in his arms once again, and he treated her as one of his more pestilential servants! He acted as if he had never taken her to his bed and made lavish love to her, acted as if they were nearly strangers. She would not tolerate being shoved back into that role once again. Pride rebelled, and instead of meekly obeying his commands, for the first time, Penelope asserted herself.

"I need to talk with you. Have you seen your cousin Chadwell? Is he still in London?"

These unexpected questions caught him by surprise, and Graham frowned, an expression that drew his eye patch down in a most formidable manner. "Yes, he is still there. What makes you ask?"

Penelope bravely stood her ground. "I know he is your cousin and that your sense of duty protects him, but I fear he will cause you great harm by staying. You must tell him to return to his own home. That would be best for everyone."

"What mad bee do you have in your bonnet now?" Nothing short of astounded at this declaration at this late date, Graham could only stare at her with incomprehension.

Penelope was on shakier ground here, but she had already set foot on the path and must continue with it. "You have as much as said that he has not a good reputation, and I know he frequents low places and has a loose way with women. Now these rumors of a madman stalking the streets of London describe him exactly, and I cannot tolerate thinking he has access to Alexandra and the maids. It will not do. Even if the rumors are false, you must see how it looks. Send him away, Graham.''

For a moment he thought he had gone quite mad. The whole world turned upside down and he was looking at it from behind the mask that he had worn so long it came second nature to him. He almost laughed at the thought of being trapped behind it forever. Just desserts, that would be called, and he deserved it. To keep her, she would condemn him to a life of falsehoods.

Catching himself before he succumbed to exhausted hysteria, Graham replied curtly, "You know nothing of which you speak, my lady. I bid you good night."

He closed the door, gently perhaps, but closed nonetheless. Penelope stared at the thick oak panel with disbelief and growing anger. He could not do this! He could not simply ignore her, pretend she did not exist, that she had no self or opinion of her own!

The anger was better than the pain, the heartrending anguish that welled up within her at this harsh rejection. She had dared to offer him some small part of herself, opened her heart to him, gave him her trust, and he had thrown them back in her face as if they were naught but dirty dishwater. She could not quite believe it hurt so much, that she had been fool enough to let down her defenses that far, so she let the anger replace clear thought.

It was with anger that she slammed the bolt home on their connecting doors and anger turned the key in the lock in the hall door. Not tonight would he sneak into her room like some petty thief and carry her off. Not tonight or any other night. She had offered and he had scorned her. Never again. Her fragile defenses could not withstand another such blow. She would give him what he bargained for in the first place—a marriage of convenience only. She would do her duty by

Alexandra, use his extravagant wealth for the charity she could never afford on her own, and leave him to rot in whatever hell he was bent on creating for himself.

She would not think of Chadwell and the danger he represented. She would set aside such money as she thought necessary from her allowance to escape to Hampshire with Alexandra should the worst befall the house of Trevelyan. Beyond that she could not plan.

Beyond the next minute she could not plan. Going to bed knowing Graham was just on the other side of that wall drove all hope of sleep from her mind. She had not realized how much she had hoped for his return so she could again enjoy the comfort and excitement of sharing his bed for whatever few hours he allotted. She had secretly hoped that this enforced absence would renew his ardor to such a degree that he would allow her the night. What a henwit she must be! To think they had a marriage just because his lust had overcome his self-absorption for a few brief days! He had probably regretted it ever since. Well, she would render him the service of preventing such discomfort from henceforth.

The anger might make the pain a modicum easier to bear, but it did not help her sleep. Penelope tossed in her down-filled bed all night, waking at every sound, fighting the urge to weep as the hours ticked slowly by and she knew of a certainty that Graham did not even intend to try the door. She did not even have that satisfaction to comfort her lonely hours.

By morning she had dark circles beneath her eyes, and unwilling to admit to anyone that anything was wrong, Penelope set out at dawn to examine what work had been done on the orphanage the prior day.

After a restless night battling his conscience, Graham's humor had not improved greatly. When he came down to find his wife departed to unknown regions and his guests looking expectantly to him for news and entertainment, he became deplorably irascible.

Accustomed to her brother's moods, Adelaide quickly removed herself and her husband from his vicinity, leaving Graham in the grandeur of his loneliness. Even Alexandra failed to amuse him when she escaped down the back stairs from the nursery and demanded to be placed on his lap and fed a sweet roll. His leg would not allow the additional weight, and he was forced to command her to sit on a chair like a proper lady. She pouted and regarded him sulkily until Mrs. Henwood came to recover her.

Even in his worst humor Graham was quick to discover how empty the rambling Hall could be without the expectation of finding Penelope smiling up at him whenever he walked into a room. He stayed in his study, catching up on neglected work, but he never heard his wife's voice floating through the halls, or the light patter of her feet on the parquet. No laughter brightened the day, no childish games interrupted his concentration. He was to be punished for his transgressions by cold, icy silence.

By day's end Graham was cursing himself for his stupidity and was prepared to promise almost anything in return for Penelope's forgiveness. He had missed her savagely for weeks, longed to return to her arms, and knew it was time to make things right. Now that he was here, he should not have to go on suffering. He didn't know where to start or how to begin, but he would make amends somehow. The prospect of facing gentle Penelope's wrath was too daunting to imagine.

When Graham came down to dinner, however, he found himself dining alone. Harley informed him that Lady Trevelyan had sent word she would be dining with the Reardons this evening, and that the Stanhopes had been promised for another engagement elsewhere. Graham cursed the splendor of his long, candlelit table and failed to taste a bite of the carefully prepared dishes the cook sent up for his delectation.

He looked in on Alexandra before she retired for the night, and she rewarded him with a kiss that would have to hold until his wife returned with something stronger. The memory of Penelope's passionately vulnerable kisses returned some of Graham's humor. He could not offer her lovemaking just yet, not until this tangle was straightened out and he could explain, but he could indulge himself in a few stolen kisses.

He wandered into the library and selected a dusty tome for perusing while he waited, but he could not concentrate. By the devil he did not know how he had come to this state, but it was a mixed blessing at best. Not since his youth had he been so beset with such fears and worries. How could one small female succeed in turning his life inside out? He had not anticipated this at all when he had first sought her out.

He had to admit that despite everything, it had all turned out much better than he had expected. He could no longer imagine the cold, empty marriage he had planned on last spring. True, last spring he had expected his own demise at any moment and meant only to plan for Alexandra's future, but living had become increasingly pleasant to contemplate. He had only one more distasteful chore ahead of him, and he hoped that could be resolved in some other manner than originally intended. He did not want to risk Penelope's displeasure any more than he had. The past was too full of mistakes he didn't wish to repeat, and the future held too many pleasant possibilities to jeopardize what they were just beginning to build together.

He heard Adelaide and Brian return and sauntered out to greet them. They seemed surprised that Penelope was not with him but did not linger to keep him company. The hour was late and Adelaide's pregnancy was beginning to slow her down. Graham wished them a good night and returned to his study to wait some more.

A carriage pulled up the drive not much after that, and Graham listened with relief as he heard Penelope's voice greeting the footman at the door. He frowned as he recognized Guy's low voice making his farewells, but he told himself that it was sensible for Penelope to have an escort on these country lanes at night. Not willing to greet his old friend at this hour, Graham waited until he heard him depart before stepping out in the corridor to meet Penelope.

He had hoped she would see the light and come to

him, but he supposed that was too much to ask after last night. He did not know how he would explain that away, but an explanation would come to him with time. For the moment he had desperate need of a simple, loving kiss and the approval of violet eyes. He hurried into the foyer only to find Penelope disappearing at the top of the stairs.

Cursing his lameness, Graham hobbled after her as fast as he could, his great frame lurching awkwardly up the elongated stairway, probably providing much amusement for the footman below. Not caring about the spectacle he created, he hurried after his wife.

She had already entered the bedroom by the time he reached their wing of the house. Deciding that was probably best after all, Graham entered his own chambers and threw aside his encumbering frock coat and cravat. Feeling like a new bridegroom all over again, he inspected his face to make certain another shave wouldn't be required. Grimacing at the sight revealed in the mirror, Graham felt his hopes gutter a little, but he crossed to their connecting door with confidence. A good-night kiss was all he asked. He could persuade her to that no matter how angry she might be.

When he encountered the bolted door, Graham could not believe the truth of his senses. Penelope had shut him out only that once, and that he had convinced himself had only been an accident. Even when she had her maidenly modesty to protect, she had given him full freedom of her chambers. Her generosity in this as much as any other factor had convinced him she would not object to him as husband in truth. To find the door bolted now, after all that had passed between them, was too incredible to accept.

Forcing himself to admit that he may have hurt her more than he knew, Graham took his punishment like a man. He endured the humiliation of having to knock for admission at the door of his wife's chambers. He knocked lightly and waited. No response. Thinking she had already retired, he knocked louder. And waited.

It was only when he noticed the faint light from

beneath the door flicker and go out that Graham realized Penelope had no intention of answering. He wanted to roar his anguish for all to hear, but he did not. He had spent too many nights hiding his pain to lapse from the habit now. If she could not withstand his company any longer, he would not force her.

With shoulders slumped, Graham blew out the candle and retired to his massive bed, alone.

Chapter 27

PENELOPE disappeared again the next day without a word to Graham, but this time he did not linger about the house in hopes of seeing her. He greeted his guests affably, assured himself that they would be sufficiently entertained for the day, and rode out on his own business for the day. The pain in his leg as he spent the better part of the day on horseback disguised the greater pain in his heart quite effectively.

By evening, Graham was too stiff to do more than retire early. Since that had been his habit for years, Adelaide and Brian took little notice of it. Penelope returned in time to make the evening interesting, and none was the wiser of this new estrangement between the viscount and his lady, although Adelaide puzzled slightly over their habits.

When they finally did meet over dinner the next day, they both played the practiced parts of host and hostess without making it obvious that they seldom exchanged two words with each other. Penelope found she could not even look toward the other end of the table without suffering a rending sensation in the vicinity of her heart that caused such pain it brought tears to her eyes. Graham sat there so cool and imperturbable as he engaged his family in casual conversation; it was as if she did not even exist.

Penelope fought her feelings with every weapon she could devise. If she tried not to think of him and kept busy, the feelings would eventually go away, she knew that. The hurt her father had caused by riding off to London without looking back had eventually faded until it had become just a sore place that hurt only when touched. Surely her feelings for Graham could not have developed to such a strength that they would take years to eradicate.

If she could just stay away from him long enough that she did not have the overwhelming urge to touch his hand whenever he was about, or to sit there praying that he would suddenly look up at her with love and joy in his eyes as if nothing had ever happened, or until she no longer needed his kiss or caress, or any of those other things he had used to enslave her—then she would be safe enough to act natural in his company. Perhaps.

But since she could do none of those things, she stayed away from him whenever reasonably possible. Graham made it easy for her by avoiding her with equal intensity. Without exchanging a single harsh word, without a cold glance or act of hostility, they managed to quite civilly and respectfully estrange themselves totally from each other. It was painful, but not so painful as admitting feelings that could only bring further rejection.

The invitations to the Reardon rout finally arrived, but Penelope did not bother mentioning it to Graham. She had promised to come but could not bear to do so in his company. They had managed a dinner or two together where they would not be seated in proximity and might mingle with others through the evening, but the rout would inevitably call for Graham to attend to his lady. This was not London. A husband did not desert his wife publicly on these occasions. So it would be better if he did not go at all. She would excuse him for health reasons, and Guy would have to suffer as her escort. Or perhaps Arthur. His leg was improving slowly; he might do the honors. That would be perfectly respectable under the circumstances.

By the week of the rout it had become apparent to Adelaide that something was seriously wrong between her brother and his bride, but she could not quite put her finger on it. They both behaved unfailingly polite in each other's company. Neither said an unkind word about the other when they were not. It was those things that were not done that started to add up. They never shared a smile together, a touch, a secret look of longing as they had before. Although both of them had an extraordinary ability to sense the moment the other entered the room, or even the house, they never seemed to meet. Adelaide didn't understand it, and what she didn't understand, she didn't like.

Guy, too, noticed the difference, although in different ways. Instead of talking excitedly about what Graham might think if she did this or that, Penelope seldom mentioned his name at all. When she wanted an opinion on something she wished to do at the orphanage, she asked Guy instead of Graham. When someone suggested that they both come to dinner or for cards or for a picnic, Penelope always begged off for one or the other of them. Graham, Guy could not get near enough to watch. His friend had shut him out completely.

Had he known that Graham had seen Penelope riding out with him early one morning and kept track of all the other occasions when they were alone, Guy would have understood the distance and put an end to it. But wrapped up in his own affairs and knowing Penelope to be only a good and loyal companion, he did not see the significance. Penelope needed help with the project she had undertaken, and if Graham did not care to help, someone needed to make the attempt. Guy trustingly lent his hand.

Thus, after hearing from one of his tenants that Guy had been seen riding toward the Hall, Graham sent his mount toward home early one day, setting off a train of events that should otherwise never have happened.

The day was so fine that Adelaide had decided they needed to take tea on the terrace. The walled, stone structure overlooked the vast expanse of the park at the side of the yard and conveniently gave a glimpse of the carriage road to the house. Resting her maternal plumpness in the glory of the summer sun, Adelaide smiled beatifically upon the world at large as she set aside her cup and engaged Penelope in a desultory discussion of boys' names. Today she had decided the child was definitely a boy.

Brian watched her with such love and amusement that Penelope felt a stab of longing so severe she could almost label it jealousy. She had callously dismissed the word "love" as an affectation of adolescents and poets, but she could think of no other word that described the look exchanged between these two. When Adelaide touched a hand to her swollen stomach and glanced toward her husband, a fire leapt to his eyes and he bent from his seat on the wall to take her hand. The silent communication was so obvious, it was almost as if they had spoken aloud. Penelope felt excluded from a world she could never attain, as she had been excluded from so many other pleasures in the past. Tears crept unbidden to her eyes and she looked hastily away to observe the cloud of dust rising from the road indicating a carriage approached.

Guy had joined them on the terrace earlier, and now he raised his cup to his lips as he followed Penelope's gaze. His own hopes kept him from noticing Penelope's sorrow, and he watched the approaching vehicle with an eagerness he could no longer deny.

"I was not expecting Lady Reardon today. Do you suppose Dolly has ventured out on her own?" Penelope speculated as she recognized the phaeton. Dolly's laughter would ease some of the tension she felt at having to act merry for her guests when all she felt inclined to do was weep. The affection growing between the creative young redhead and her more mature suitor had its amusing moments, also, but they only added to her own misery at the moment. She refused to think that everyone around her had found love but herself. That was the worst kind of self-pity and she refused to succumb to it.

So Penelope smiled and tripped lightly down the steps and crossed the yard to meet the newcomers as their carriage rattled near. Having already noticed that the Hall's inhabitants were sunning themselves on the terrace, the carriage driver had considerately pulled around so his passengers need not traipse through the front portals and the entire west wing to reach them.

The reason for this informality became quite clear when a footman threw open the door and a male figure stepped out. Penelope halted her progress in amazement as Arthur stiffly turned and offered a helping hand to his sister. He then limped determinedly toward his hostess, Dolly clinging ferociously to his arm.

At the sight of the young man's brave effort to maneuver the uneven surface of the lawn without crutch or stick, Penelope ran to greet them. Several years younger than Guy or Graham, Arthur still wore the mark of harsh experience in his weather-beaten face. Perhaps once his gray eyes had laughed like Dolly's and his tawny hair had fallen over even features laced with boredom or humor, but no longer. A shadow hid behind a face worn lean from hard living, and a strong character had eroded the softness of youth.

Arthur took Penelope's hand and bowed over it, but he refused her aid in continuing to make his way across the yard to join the others. She and Dolly exchanged a brief, worried glance, but there was pride behind Dolly's expression.

Guy and Brian rose politely to greet the latest guests. Arthur made a small fuss over Adelaide propped in her chair, while to Penelope's amusement, Guy completely appropriated the task of welcoming Dolly. So thoroughly was everyone enjoying this unexpected event that they failed to notice another small cloud of dust rising along the drive.

Arthur had not yet taken a chair to relieve his uncertain leg when Penelope looked up and caught sight of the rider galloping headlong around the bend. She did not need to see his face to know the rider's identity. That proudly erect form racing at a mad pace on a black animal large enough to come straight from hell could only be one person. Graham.

Remembering the antipathy Graham had shown for his young neighbor, Penelope felt a small qualm of worry, but surely even Graham would not be rude to a guest in his own house. She hoped he would just enter the house and ignore the party out here entirely. That would be more like him.

But of course, he did not. Flinging his reins to a footman who came running from the house, Graham swung his stiff leg over the stallion's back and strode with great halting lengths across the lawn. The difference between Arthur's fragile, uncertain gait and Graham's strong, jerking strides was apparent to everyone.

There was no mistaking the malice glittering in his uncovered eye, either, as he took note of the composition of the small party on his terrace. The men remained standing as he approached, but Penelope laid a restraining hand on Guy's arm as he seemed prepared to intervene.

Graham noted that proprietary gesture with as much venom as he noted Arthur's presence. These last years of isolation had put him out of practice in managing the facade of false politeness, and his wrath had a source too great to allow such pretense. Ignoring the others, he turned his glare on Arthur first.

"I did not think you would be so brazen as to set foot on my property, Reardon." Graham hitched his game leg up the stair until he towered over the defiant youth, then with nonchalant ease, he settled himself comfortably on the garden wall. Ignoring the gasps of horror at his rudeness, he removed his felt hat, brushed it off, and lifted his formidable one-eyed glare in anticipation of Arthur's reaction.

"I had come to show you I am quite well and ready whenever you are," Arthur replied coldly, although quite inexplicably to all his listeners but one.

"Oh?" Graham raised a mocking eyebrow. "It appears to me as if you could not stand in a strong wind. I would recommend a long, healing journey in a distant climate as beneficial to your health." With deliberate abruptness, he stood just as Arthur clenched his fists and stepped forward.

The effect of Graham's abrupt motion on Arthur's uncertain leg was immediate. He tried to halt, staggered, came down hard on the bad leg at an awkward angle, and fell.

286 · *Patricia Rice*

The women screamed. Guy, being closest, leapt to break the fall. Graham simply crossed his powerful arms across his chest and waited.

Penelope could not believe she had witnessed this scene. In all her anger at his selfish, single-minded behavior, she had never believed Graham to be the beast others claimed him to be. With his silver hair standing out about his head and his one unpatched eye gleaming golden in wrath, he appeared fierce and invincible. But she had seen him melt at one of Alexandra's smiles, had been the victim of his tenderness, and knew he had always meant well even when he roared the loudest. For him to deliberately insult and harm a neighbor and guest was beyond her comprehension and knowledge of this man she called husband.

"That was uncalled for, Trev," Guy muttered in a low voice as he helped Arthur regain his feet.

Irate, Dolly tried to throw herself between the men and protect her brother, but Guy caught her by the waist and unceremoniously shoved her toward Penelope. Knowing enough not to interfere with that which she did not understand, Penelope held onto Dolly while the men continued to glare at each other, although admittedly Graham no longer seemed to be glaring but waiting with tired impatience.

"I'm not running again, Graham. I repeat, I am ready any time you are." Pale-faced but stoic, Arthur shook off Guy's steadying hand and met Graham's stare boldly.

A hint of admiration flickered briefly and disappeared in the storm of Graham's fury. "You are a fool, then." With a cold look to Guy, he indicated the waiting carriage. "Send the young whelp home. For his own sake, persuade him of the benefits of a lengthy journey."

Without the formality of a polite greeting to the remainder of his guests, Graham stalked into the house and disappeared, leaving fury, revulsion, and bewilderment behind.

In all her wide experience of dealing with people

and uncomfortable, emotional situations, Penelope had never encountered one quite like this. Had it not been for Adelaide at her side, she would have been tempted to flee the scene herself. Instead, between the two of them, they managed to convey their sympathy and bewilderment to the young Reardons. While not quite pacifying the irate Guy, they did see them all off without further harsh words. Dolly was too shaken to do more than cling to Guy's hand, but Arthur made polite bows to his hostess and her sister-in-law.

"I apologize that my appearance has ruined your lovely day. I will not let it happen again."

There was something so brave and lonely in the way he pulled himself up into the carriage that Penelope found a tear creeping down her cheek. How could Graham judge this poor boy so harshly? It did not seem credible.

Penelope took the coward's way out and retired to her chambers with a headache after that. If only there were some way she could sit in the silence of her room and think through the jumble of her thoughts and emotions to come to some understanding of Graham's behavior, but she could not. Even those who loved him and had known him all their lives seemed bewildered by his irrational moods. How could she hope to understand what they did not?

To make matters worse, Alexandra slipped from the nursery to perch like an elf upon Penelope's bed and regard her with solemn eyes. Uncannily aware of the adult tension in the house, she attempted to offer her own solutions.

"Take me riding, Penny. Riding always makes me feel better. And Papa will come, too, if I ask him. We can go to the pond and watch the ducks. I like watching the ducks, don't you?"

Penelope gathered the little girl in her arms and held her head against her shoulder. "I like riding and ducks, too. And I love little girls with pretty black hair that gets in their eyes." She lifted an offending strand and tickled Alexandra's nose with it. "But sometimes I just need to be by myself, don't you?"

Dark, soulful eyes stared up at her sadly. "Don't you love my papa anymore? You won't go away, will you? Papa isn't happy unless you are around."

Penelope sighed and cuddled the child on her lap. "I don't want to go away, Alexandra. I love you, and people don't like to go away and leave the ones they love. I think your papa would be happy if you were with him, though."

"Does that mean you don't love my papa?" Alexandra persisted.

Penelope sought for words to explain to a little girl what she could not explain to herself. Why was it Graham she thought of night and day and not the amorous Chadwell or the amusing Guy or any of the other men she had met these past months? Why was it she continued to defend Graham to others even when he behaved as reprehensibly as he had today? And was it not her desire to defend him now that tore her apart, because she could not find the reason or excuse to give herself? How could she explain those feelings to a child, reduce them to the lowest common denominator?

In only one way. Hugging Alexandra as her father would not allow her to do to him, Penelope replied gently, "Of course I love your papa, Alex. It's just sometimes hard to show it."

The child nodded wisely. "I know. I try to hug my kitten Aunt Adelaide gave me, but it wriggles loose and runs away. But I love him anyway. I'm glad Papa brought you home, Penelope. I can love you even when I'm bad."

Penelope laughed, and reassured that her world would not tilt anytime soon, Alexandra departed for other adventures. Sometime later, Penelope looked out the window to see Graham tying ropes to a low tree limb and fitting a seat to them under Alexandra's direction. With a painful tug at her heartstrings she watched as Graham gently set his daughter in the swing and pushed her carefully so she would not fall, not an easy task for one of his strength. How could she ever have doubted that she loved him?

But women had loved unwisely throughout history. It did not change the situation any, only made it more dangerous to her emotional well-being. Obviously Graham neither craved nor needed her affections. In fact, she thought he would be more dismayed than anything else should he discover them. So she would continue to enforce this distance between them until it became habit, and she could breathe again when he entered a room.

Chapter 28

HEAD pounding after a lonely and foolish bout with the brandy decanter the night before, Graham descended the stairs and entered the dining room cautiously. He found his sister pensively contemplating the morning's post, but the look she gave him when he entered made him wince and think twice about breaking his fast. It might be easier to grab a hunk of bread and cheese from the kitchen and keep on going.

Wearily deciding he had no desire to be driven from his own table by a female half his size, Graham filled his plate and sat down silently. Adelaide sipped her hot chocolate and continued to regard him with the same lack of emotion as she had the mail earlier.

"It is customary to say 'good morning' when one enters the room," she remarked idly, watching her brother's scowl deepen.

"I'll try to remember that." Defiantly he bit into his toast and picked up his own stack of letters.

"Why does Penelope not join us for breakfast any longer? She always seemed to enjoy it when she was with us."

"Maybe she tires of the company," Graham responded rudely, casting aside one letter and opening the next.

"I certainly would if I had to look at that scowl every morning," Adelaide said tartly. "But then, the little baroness shows astonishingly odd taste in marrying you. I hope the price of saving her home was not greater than she expected."

Graham threw down the letter and glared at his sister. "And just exactly what is that supposed to mean?"

Adelaide stared at her older brother innocently over her cup. "Why, nothing, I am sure. Penelope is a perfect widgeon for helping others. I am certain she thought she could offer you as much as you gave her when you married. She was quite right, too. She turned a surly, crotchety old invalid into a human being again. For a while, anyway. The task of perpetually redoing her efforts must get a trifle tedious, though. I suppose you offer adequate recompense?"

"Addled, you are. Our parents named you wisely. If you have a thought you would like to share with me, by all means, please do. Otherwise, let me return to my reading." Graham glared at his sister. She ever was one to scramble words. He had no patience with her now.

"I only wondered if you thought paying handsomely for her house in Hampshire, buying her those lovely clothes, and bestowing a ridiculous amount of spending money on her would be sufficient to make Penelope happy for the rest of her life? Do you think your wealth sufficient payment for her love?" She added this last impatiently as Graham continued to stare at her with a baffled expression.

Finally comprehending where this conversation led, Graham gave his sister a look of disgust. "You are all about in your tiny little belfry, 'Laidie. Now be a good little girl and go run and play. I have work to do."

Adelaide snatched the letter from his hand, tore it in two, and flung it beneath the table. "That is why Guy Hamilton escorts her out every morning or brings her home every evening. And that is why Guy Hamilton will be escorting her to the biggest social event of the summer, I suppose? Don't you ever learn, Graham? Isn't that the reason poor Marilee sought comfort in his arms? Or do you think both your wives so greedy they needed two men to keep them happy?"

Adelaide jumped from her chair as well as she could and turned to walk out on her addle-pated brother. Graham caught her wrist before she could escape.

"Are you trying to tell me Penelope has taken a lover? Because I won't believe it, you know." He said that through clenched teeth wanting to believe the truth of what he said, but doubting his own judgment.

Adelaide glared at her aggravating sibling. "Upon my word, Graham, you put me completely out of charity with you. Do you think you fool anyone with that pretense of nonchalance? I saw you yesterday. It was Guy you wanted to come to cuffs with, not poor Arthur. You didn't know Arthur was there until you rode that poor beast of yours into a lather and tore up half the lawn to get here. I wouldn't give you credit for the wit of a goose, big brother. I know you too well, no matter how you choose to paint your face."

With that startling remark Adelaide jerked her arm free and stalked out of the room, her beribboned curls held high and the slight train of her light muslin gown sweeping indignantly after her. Graham stared after her in astonishment and confusion and decided his head hurt more than he knew. Adelaide occasionally had that effect on people.

But her arguments stayed with him. Adelaide had not told him anything he didn't know, except for her mention of the social event of the summer. He would have to track down that reference, but it didn't signify as the others did. He knew Penelope craved a family and love. He had certainly taken advantage of that knowledge when he had made his outrageous proposal to her. He didn't think she was as young and impressionable as Marilee had been when she fell for Guy, nor were the circumstances the same. And in any case, Guy was older and more mature and knew to beware of these things—unless he was as smitten as she.

Cursing himself for allowing these doubts to encroach upon his normal logical pattern of thought, Graham gave up his effort to read the post. He knew Penelope wasn't in her chambers. The only time her doors would open to him were when she wasn't there. He had discovered that days ago. If she were in the house, he would have sensed it by now. He knew the sound of her footsteps, her laugh, even the echo of her whisper in the draftly halls. He would go out and check the stable. That would give him some idea of the truth of the matter.

To Graham's momentary relief, the stable boys told him that Penelope had ridden off this morning with one of the grooms. Adelaide's suggestion that she was out with Guy had been pure conjecture. Telling himself that Penelope had too much good sense and too many morals to dally with the likes of Guy, he mounted his own horse and started down the lane. Perhaps it was time to find some way of putting an end to this estrangement, although after his performance yesterday, it would be no easy task. Penelope had been as horrified as everyone else by his rudeness, and more curious.

With a small grunt of surprise Graham noted Guy riding toward him as he rode into the tree-lined lane leading to the Hall. They met in the center of the dirt road, both horses restive and eager to be on their way, their riders equally wary but for other reasons. Graham kept a close hold on his stallion's reins as it pranced nervously. He waited for Guy to speak.

"I want to talk with you." Guy spoke coldly, searching for some understanding in his friend's expression.

"I'm not stopping you." Graham remained noncommittal.

He had not wanted to do it here, with both horses chomping at the bit, but if Trevelyan would not invite him back to the Hall, so be it. Guy minced no words. "Arthur won't tell me what that scene was about yesterday, but I can guess. You don't really intend to challenge him, do you?"

"What difference is it to you if I do?" Graham inquired coolly.

"He's a bloody cripple, Trevelyan! It would be insane."

"One cripple against another seems fair to me." Graham shrugged and loosened his reins slightly, letting the stallion move ahead a few steps. "He's been given fair warning. I cannot do better than that."

"Graham, you have taken leave of your senses! It's

been five years. Everything has changed. You can't blame the man now for the boy of five years ago. Haven't you ever heard of forgive and forget?''

"I've told you before, Guy. You don't ever forget the sounds of your wife screaming in pain and dying in your arms. You live with the horror for the rest of your life. How can I forgive? All I can do to avenge her pain is extract the same from those who caused it.''

With that, Graham gave his horse his head and he was off, leaving Guy to stare after him in torn anguish. Finally throwing off old memories, he jerked his mount around and galloped off in another direction.

Penelope looked up in astonishment at the rider racing across the field. It certainly could not be Graham. He did not know this place existed nor that he would find her here. Besides, the horse was a roan and the rider too lean.

She wiped the beads of perspiration from her face with her apron and gazed proudly at the neat gray trim she had just completed on the farmhouse porch. The pale gray seemed to blend gently with the weathered old bricks and timber of the house. It needed only a few baskets of ferns and maybe a pot or two of geraniums to give it color, and it would offer warmth and welcome to all comers. That was what she wanted to accomplish—a place of light and warmth and open air instead of the cold, dismal, narrow lanes of London. Children could thrive in these surroundings.

Taking a rag to her hands, she approached Guy as he threw himself off of his horse. Curious about his hasty ride but content with her accomplishments, Penelope smiled serenely as he strode toward her. ''Surely you are not in such a hurry to see how my color scheme has worked?'' she asked mockingly.

Guy threw the newly repainted porch a quick look and nodded approval. ''You were right. It does work. It seems to be coming along swimmingly, but you are right again. That is not why I am here. Do you have time to talk?''

Penelope's eyes widened, but obligingly, she pulled off her apron and lay it across one of the workmen's benches. Dusting wood shavings from her old cotton gown, she finally considered herself presentable and took Guy's arm.

"Let us find somewhere out of the hustle and bustle, and then you may talk as you wish."

Guy found a cool nook beneath the shade of an apple tree next to the well house. Throwing his handkerchief down on the rickety wood bench, he seated Penelope, but he continued to pace up and down in the dust.

"I cannot know where to begin," he complained anxiously. "I do not know what Graham has told you, nor do I wish to say more than I should. I just know something has to be done and he will not listen to me. I pray that you have some influence with him."

Penelope twisted her fingers together in her lap as she watched Guy's handsome face pull taut with worry. He so seldom showed the world aught but good humor, she knew he must be extremely blue-deviled by something, and she feared she would be of little help to him.

"If you speak of Graham, then you are the only one to whom he listens, and possibly his cousin. I do not know. I am the very last person whose advice he will take unless the matter concerns Alexandra."

Guy jammed his hands into his pockets in a gesture of frustration. "He does not listen to me, by Jupiter. That much I do know." He swung on his booted heel and confronted Penelope. In her country bonnet and high-necked gown she looked every inch the vicar's daughter, but he knew the strength behind those deep violet eyes and took little note of her attire. He appealed to the baroness, not the vicar's daughter. "I do not know what has come between you two lately, but I know Graham will not refuse your request. You are everything good for him, and he knows it."

"I could wish that were so, Guy, but it is not. He has rejected me more than once for reasons I do not understand. I am the very last person you should come to.''

The sadness in her voice jarred Guy from his anxious pacing. He dropped to the bench beside her and took her hand, forcing her to look up at him, albeit with a quizzical expression. He studied the quiet hurt behind her eyes and groaned aloud. "Don't tell me that, Penny. I thought you had tamed the beast, that you, of all people, had learned to stand up to him. Don't tell me he has scared you away, too?''

Penelope watched Guy's lean, dark face, but her thoughts were elsewhere. "I do not fear Graham, no. I just don't understand him. I thought, at first, it was just the scars that made him turn his back on people, that he feared ridicule, but it is not that, is it? When we first met, he did not want to frighten me, and I think that is all that kept him from appearing in public. But then, sometimes, he grows so angry he seems to *enjoy* frightening people. That is when I don't understand him. How can he be so gentle and thoughtful sometimes, and so abominable at others?'' Her gaze finally focused on Guy, questioning him as if he would have the answer.

Guy pondered the best way to approach the problem and finally decided the beginning was the only place to start. "I cannot give you answers, Penny, but perhaps you would understand his anger better if you knew more about him. He has told you little of the accident, hasn't he?''

"He has told me nothing. What I know I have learned from others.'' Penelope retrieved her hand and primly folded it in her lap, staring at her crossed fingers as she made this admission.

"That is typical. Graham never talks of himself. Did you know he spent a summer learning to sail with Nelson?'' At Penelope's incredulous shake of her head, he continued, "Neither did anyone else at the time. It was Nelson himself who mentioned it, claimed it was a damned shame the navy lost a sailor like Graham simply because he was an only son and tied to the land. And Graham was just a boy at the time. Graham has a penchant for conquering mountains and never telling anyone. He just does it for his own enlightenment.''

"I can understand that, but why do you tell me this? Does he regret the loss of his ability to do whatever he wishes? For I do not think there is much Graham cannot do if he puts his mind to it. I have never seen a one-eyed man win a target shoot before, nor a lame man walk faster than the well, but Graham can.''

"That is something else that bothers me, but let us take one thing at a time. I was talking of the accident. Anyone else would have described every last bloody detail to any who would listen. They would have sent out militia to track down the ruffians who caused it. They might eventually grow tired of the subject, but they would certainly have mentioned it to a new wife who must look at the results for the rest of her life. But not Graham.''

Penelope bent him a puzzled look. "Someone caused the accident? How?''

Guy stood up and began to pace again. "I am not the one to be telling you this. Perhaps you should talk to Arthur, or heaven forbid, DeVere. I owe Graham my life, and in return, I cost him his wife. I was the one she was riding to that night.''

At Penelope's distressed look Guy backed up to the very beginning, though it pained him to admit his faults. "It's a long story, Penny. My father had just died and I had come into a large inheritance I did not know how to manage. I fell in with a fast crowd. I make no excuses for myself. I hope you'll never know of the kind of places I frequented.''

Penelope looked down at her hands. She could very well imagine what kind of places he spoke of, and she had difficulty fighting a blush.

Guy didn't notice this reaction, but hastily outlined his story. "I belonged to a club that started out as a fast set of whips. We caroused together as young bachelors will. Graham grew bored with it soon enough and left. The rest of us were equally bored but sought wilder pleasures together. Some new men joined who weren't adverse to disregarding the law. One thing led to another, until finally when my acquaintances took up what amounted to thievery and violence, I regained my senses and reported them to the authorities. Those who had enough influence to escape the law were quick to exact their revenge. Graham was the one who came to my rescue.''

Guy felt Penelope watching him, and he took a deep breath before continuing. ''Graham carried me to his home. He and his wife tended my wounds with their own hands and managed to make me feel a hero instead of a fool. In return I fell madly in love with Marilee. In time I learned she returned my affections.''

Penelope held her opinion to herself but tried to puzzle out how this affected her. ''So you asked her to elope with you?''

Guy shook his head and ran his hand through his hair. ''No. Never. When I realized what was happening, I left Graham and Marilee at the Hall and fled to London. Unfortunately my enemies were not aware of this. I had information that could have caused them damage, and they were determined to prevent me from revealing more. I wouldn't have because it involved close friends I'd hoped to protect, but they didn't know that. What happened after that I could only learn from the servants at the Hall.

''Graham was out when a message arrived for me. It was unsealed and Marilee was uncertain whether it should be forwarded immediately, so she read it. The note warned me my life was in danger if I did not flee the country immediately. She could not know it was meant to draw me from the safety of Graham's protection. According to the servants, she panicked, threw down the note, and ordered the phaeton.''

Sadly Guy lifted his head to meet Penelope's gaze. ''While the carriage was being readied, she packed a bag, apparently meaning to flee the country with me. She was very young and foolish. But that is neither here nor there.'' He looked away from Penelope's shocked expression.

"She drove the phaeton herself, at a reckless pace for a rainy night by all accounts. The rest I cannot know for certain, only these parts I learned from a few involved. Graham must have come home or seen the phaeton and followed. Somewhere he caught up with her and she let him in. There wasn't time for him to turn it around, and I daresay he was too furious to think of it, probably imagining to fly to London to confront me with my betrayal of his friendship. Graham and I had similar phaetons. In the driving rain that would be all that was recognizable, the size and build of the carriage. My would-be murderers probably couldn't see who was at the reins; they just expected me to be the one responding to that letter. I doubt that it would have mattered in any event. They were drunk and ready for murder and had reason to hate and fear Graham as much as myself. Their attack had to be deliberately planned for that particular spot. It was the most dangerous point along the road, and the easiest place to make it look like an accident. Only Graham knows for certain what actually happened that night; Graham and whatever few of my club mates are still alive. Somehow, they must have panicked the horses so that even Graham couldn't control them. The phaeton overturned just where they planned it, at the bridge over a ravine. Both Marilee and Graham were thrown out onto the rocks below. Graham has never told me all that happened that night, but you can imagine it for yourself. It should have been me in that carriage, but instead, it was Marilee who died for my sins."

The words tumbled from Guy's lips hastily, with a revulsion not only directed at the offenders, but himself. The pacing wasn't sufficient to rid himself of the emotion, and he ran his fingers through his hair, talking as rapidly as he was able.

"I cannot begin to tell you of the horror that spread over the countryside at that accident. No one could speak of it for too many were involved, and the circumstances were revolting to an extreme. The perpetrators disappeared quickly after that, all of them thinking Graham as dead as his wife. Knowing my guilt, I left, too. Graham was left alone with no one but his sister and his father, and his father died not long after.''

Guy came to a halt in front of Penelope and stared at her in anguish. ''Can you not see what I am saying? Graham has a right to be angry, to scorn us all. It was not fear of frightening people that has kept him from facing society, but hatred for that society. Whatever happened that night has scarred more than his face, Penelope, and I'm afraid it will come to harm you and others if he cannot be persuaded to reason.''

Penelope shook her head, not believing Guy's reasoning. Graham had friends. He had forgiven Guy. That did not sound like a man angry at the world. It did not explain his coldness to her. It told her little other than that the pain Graham carried with him must run deep, much deeper than she cared to know.

''I do not see what I can do, Guy. He would listen to me if I told him Alexandra needed a new dress or a chair needed recovering, but he is not going to sit still while I preach a sermon about the golden rule. Give me a magic wand and I would wave it, but I know of no other way of taking away his anger.''

Penelope could not help looking at Guy's tortured face with curiosity. How much had he loved Graham's first wife? Had they been lovers? Was that why Graham had objected to her seeing too much of his friend? And how could they still be friends if what Guy said was true?

She knew that people sometimes went outside their wedding vows, but she had never heard anyone actually admit to being a party to it until now. Wickedly she tried to imagine herself in Guy's arms, but she could not. How could Marilee have done it? Graham without the scars would have been an excruciatingly handsome young man, the kind she could never have dared admit aloud to admiring without people looking at her plainness and laughing in scorn. Marilee must have been beautiful and wealthy and of noble family. They would have been a perfect couple, with a lovely child. How could anyone throw all that away? It would be like waking up to a storybook dream to be given all that.

Guy sat beside her and took her hand again. "Don't let him challenge Arthur. Tell him you are ill and have him take you to Bath. Tell him someone in your family is ill. Tell him anything, but get him away from here until I can persuade Arthur to go away. If you have any love for him at all, make him see reason or get him away."

Shocked, Penelope jerked her hand away and stared at him as if he had lost his wits. Challenge Arthur? Why would Graham do such a thing? Guy shouldn't be saying these things to her, wouldn't be, she felt certain, if his love and concern for Dolly had not exceeded his reason. Love was a wretched business. She wished she hadn't got involved in it at all.

"Guy, you are all about in your head. Why would Graham challenge Arthur? He likes the Reardons, and Arthur is much too weak to provide any kind of challenge. It is a good thing, for I could not lie to Graham. You are very wicked to make me worry like this. I cannot know what you are about to try to send me up into the boughs. I have better things to do." Briskly, nervously, Penelope stood up and brushed her hands against her skirts. Guy should never have said these things.

Guy leapt up after her, catching her by the shoulder and spinning her to face him. "Arthur was *there*, Penelope. Can't you see that? Arthur was one of the men who rode out to stop the carriage that night."

Penelope stared at him in horror and disbelief. Then, breaking away from his grip, she ran back toward the farmhouse, not wanting to hear any more, not wanting to believe. Not Graham. Not Arthur. Not any of it.

Chapter 29

IT didn't take long for word of Guy's tête-à-tête with Penelope to get back to Graham. All the world might love a lover, but they seemed to take sadistic pleasure in seeing one with horns on his head, too. Graham flung the book he was reading across the room after hearing one more tittering laugh outside in the hall. Penelope was out late again.

That Guy had been seen holding Penelope's hand, arguing with her, touching her shoulder, should mean nothing at all to him. There was no law written against holding hands or arguing. Jealousy was an absurd emotion, particularly for one who had clearly told his wife she was free to do as she wished. Before. Before he had taken her to his bed. Before he had made her his wife in more than name. Before he had learned to trust her beyond all else.

Every argument he gave himself deteriorated in such a manner. What in hell was she doing meeting him in that out of the way place to start with? Where did she go each day that caused her to neglect her guests, her home, her family? Had he been so sadly mistaken in her character?

Or had he done this to her? Graham threw himself back into the chair before the fire and stared at the flames morosely. He had taught her passion. She had known nothing of it until he came along. That much was his doing. But he had denied her love. How could anyone love a visage such as he presented to the world? That was his own fault, too. How could he have expected Penelope to look forward to an evening in the arms of a man who would terrify the staunchest of soldiers? He'd been a fool from first to last. When was he going to start doing something about it?

Not tonight. Tonight he would probably kill her. Tomorrow. Tomorrow he would present his whole case and make her understand. Perhaps not his whole case. There were still things that went undone. But he would tell her enough to be honest with her, to plead his cause and win her back. At least he would take away any excuses she might have for turning to Guy. That much, he could do. Maybe.

When Penelope came home to find the light still on in the library, she contemplated it pensively. Nothing Guy had said made it any easier to understand Graham's behavior. If she went in there now, she would be asking for further rejection. But just the fact that he had waited up when he usually had to rise early to see his estates said something of his concern. It would be easier to turn her back on the light than to face her racing heartbeat and go to him, but one did not get through life by taking the easy route. She would stop and wish him a good night.

Heart pounding at this daring, she tiptoed on slippered feet to the heavy paneled door, pushing gently against the wood carving. Perhaps if he were busy she would go away without disturbing him. She really had no right to interfere in his private life. She shouldn't intrude. But she could not keep away. The door slid open silently.

Graham's great frame lay sprawled across the long sofa, his gloved hand behind his head. She thought him deliberately ignoring her, but then she saw his good eye was shut and his chest moved evenly. He slept. Smiling, she slid quietly into the room. She had never caught Graham asleep before.

His face looked much more relaxed and younger in sleep. With his head turned slightly against the pillow of his arm, she saw only his good side, and the resemblance to his cousin was so striking it made her gasp. The lashes against his cheek were dark, as was the beard shadowing his chin. Alexandra must have inherited her coloring from him. She longed to stroke the hard, angular line of his jaw, but she feared it would wake him.

How pleasant it would be if she could kneel beside him now and kiss his cheek and have him wake and take her in his arms! That's what she wanted to do. That was what she longed with all her heart to do. She would like him to make love to her here by the firelight where she could see his face and know his desire. But perhaps it had not been desire that brought him to her but a sense of duty, a need for a son? She could not afford to find out.

Sadly she picked up his coat from where he had flung it across the arm of a chair. The fire would be out soon, and he would be chilly in his shirt sleeves. Odd, how he looked just like other men as he lay there, the white cloth fluttering at his throat, his silver hair almost curling where he had let it grow slightly. No one would be frightened of him now, except herself. He looked too much like his cousin, and her feelings frightened her. Hastily she arranged the coat over his sleeping chest to keep him warm. That was all she dared to do.

As silently as she had come, she slipped away.

Penelope redoubled her efforts at the orphanage the next day. Her dreams of the night before had been restless ones, and the tension they had created had not dissipated with the morning sun. Her thoughts turned too often to Graham's masculine length sprawled across the sofa, to memories of nights he had held her in those powerful arms and she had felt him naked and warm against her. The desire was too strong to combat, but she could bury it in hard work.

So it was that Chadwell found her when he arrived at mid-morning. While carpenters hammered away somewhere in the interior of the old house, Penelope balanced herself on a precarious ladder against the crumbling bricks outside, tugging at the ivy vines creeping between the walls and window frames. She wore an old gown of inexpensive brown weave much faded with drying in the sun and let down about the hem so she looked the part of washerwoman. But she had discarded the hampering tucker that should have covered her throat and shoulders to disguise the full swell of her breasts, and no washerwoman ever appeared so nymphlike. With the morning sun threading her hair with golden highlights and her cheeks rosy with the heat of her efforts, she presented a portrait of a slightly disheveled goddess perched dangerously between heaven and earth.

Cursing under his breath, Chadwell crossed the lumber-strewn lawn with rapid strides. Before Penelope scarcely had time to take note of his arrival, he was upon her, his long arm wrapping about her waist and lifting her bodily from the ladder. Penelope gave a little shriek as her fingers parted from the ladder rungs and she found herself flying through the air, but Chadwell's hold was firm, and she soon found herself sliding down his chest until her feet touched the ground.

Stunned, she could only stare up into his handsome face, the golden eyes staring at her with a hunger so clear and strong that she could not tear her gaze away. She scarcely noticed that he continued to hold her most improperly and that she continued to lean against him, her hands resting against the textured weave of his kerseymere waistcoat.

"If you did not break it first, I think I should wring your pretty little neck for climbing up there like that. What on earth possesses you to do these things, my maggot-brained Penelope?"

His words held more astonishment than anger, and as he held her near, she could feel his breath like a caress against her cheek. There was that about the way his mouth softened to tell he meant to kiss her, but wantonly, she did not back away. She gave a satisfied sigh as his long fingers tightened at the small of her back and he drew her into the curve of his body.

His kiss was warm and inviting and washed through Penelope's veins like strong drink, warming her blood and rendering her senseless. Her head spun giddily as her lips parted and their breaths intermingled and she tasted the masculine flavors of his mouth. The desire shooting through her came as something of a shock. It needed only this kiss, this one caress to expose her folly and weakness, to reduce her to a trembling wanton in his arms. Her whole body ached for his touch, and she did not mistake the urgency of his hold as his hands slid up her back along the curves of her sides.

This was impossible, in full daylight in front of a house full of workmen who would be delighted to spread the gossip far and wide. No matter how much she hungered for this touch, needed his desire, she could not do this to Graham. Horror at what he would feel welled up in her, and she broke away, turning her face and pushing at Clifton's chest.

"Let go! Let me go, Cliff! I cannot . . ." Somehow she found the strength to elude his arms and tear free, but he was not so easily put aside.

Catching Penelope by the waist, his square-jawed face tense and unforgiving, Chadwell fought her resistance. "Don't, Penelope! Give me a chance to explain!"

She struggled more against herself than him. She wanted to listen, wanted explanations, wanted to watch the color of his eyes and the way his lips curved up in a mocking smile, wanted her own destruction. She could not believe she had come to this, that she could betray Graham in such a vile manner. There must be something gravely wrong with her to love one man and desire another. Or else the devil had spun a spell on her.

"No, Cliff! Go away!" she cried, but his hold on her became relentless, terrifying her. Where before his arms had been gentle and caressing, now they were like twin bands of steel crushing her chest. In horror, she remembered the rumors from London, the descriptions that could well be Chadwell haunting the wretched streets of the slums for victims, and panic followed quickly on the footsteps of fear. "I'll scream! I'll scream if you don't let me go!"

Fighting her would not accomplish his cause, and Chadwell reluctantly did as told, releasing the temptation of slender curves to better establish rational argument. "Penelope, please, I only want to talk to you," he pleaded as she slid from his hands.

"We have nothing to talk about! Graham should have sent you away long ago, but I am warning you now, if you do not leave London—leave England!—I will tell him what you have done. I will tell him and you will lose the best friend you have ever had!" She threw this at him defiantly, not knowing if there were a word of truth in it. Graham might not care if she fell into his cousin's arms. Graham might despise his cousin. Who was she to know anything? She just knew she had to remove him for her own safety as well as any other females fool enough to fall for his charms.

"It seems I'm about to do that in any case," Chadwell replied sadly, reaching for her arm. He could not let her run just yet. Things had gone out of hand, but he had to tell her.

The touch of his fingers on her wrist sent shock waves through Penelope's arm, nearly paralyzing her. The look in his eyes nearly tore her heart in two, but she could not let his looks influence her. He could be a madman, but he most certainly was a devil. In self-protection, she swung her free hand with all the strength she possessed.

Her palm connected squarely with his jaw with a sickening slap. Penelope winced more than Chadwell, but she had caught him by surprise and his grip loosened. Before he could catch her, she was flying into the house and the safety of the company of workmen with hammers and saws. A few minutes later she was at the upstairs window, her face a ghostly white against the large violet shadows of her eyes as she stared down at him. Chadwell stayed where he was, refusing to leave, willing her to listen.

Penelope threw open the sash and made a violent gesture. "Go! I never want to see your face again! Leave before I send the men out after you!"

In despair he stared up at her wrathful loveliness and knew he had been defeated. He was not yet ready to make his explanations to the entire world. He might never be given the opportunity to make his explanation at all. There was a very real terror in her eyes as she slammed the window closed.

Penelope's fingers dug into the sill as she watched Chadwell turn and mount his horse. She felt her heart being drawn from her as if it were attached by a string to his as he rode away. He sat the big stallion well, his broad shoulders proud and straight in the short-waisted frock coat, his fashionable beaver hat covering his dark curls at a rakish angle, his powerful thighs in their tight breeches guiding the horse with ease, but somehow, she knew he did not move with the same casual grace as he had arrived.

She didn't leave the house again until Guy arrived to escort her home. She could not take a chance that Chadwell waited somewhere out there, waiting for the workmen to leave, waiting until she had only a groom to protect her. How fortunate that Guy had promised to stop by this afternoon to see how the work progressed!

He greeted Penelope with surprise at her eager welcome as she ran down the porch stairs to meet him. She scarcely gave him a chance to inspect the work in the back stairwell the workmen had promised to finish that day. She clung nervously to his arm and agreed quickly that she ought to leave when he suggested they might meet Dolly for tea.

Glancing down with curiosity at the bent brown head at his side, Guy could not conceal his curiosity, but he held his tongue. The fingers holding his arm were trembling, and he steadied them with his other hand as they came out of the house.

They said little as they rode back toward the Hall. Lengthening shadows told of the lateness of the hour, and Guy was not surprised when Penelope mentioned a headache and begged off from visiting the Reardons. Her face had grown longer and more weary with each passing mile.

With concern Guy caught her hand before they passed through the gate to the Hall. Warm blue eyes studied hers as he spoke. ''Is all well, Penelope? Did

I speak out of turn yesterday? If so, please forgive me. I would gladly take back one wrong word.''

Penelope shook her head and looked away, her shoulders slumping despondently. "No, you only told me what I needed to know. You are wrong about Graham. He does not hate, and I cannot believe he would challenge Arthur, but then, I have not been right about very many things lately. Good night, Guy.''

She rode off without looking back. Guy followed her a short way down the drive, far enough to be certain she reached the house safely, then staring after her with perplexity for some while, he finally turned his horse and rode out again.

From the security of the trees lining the lane, Chadwell watched Guy go. On his face, had anyone been there to see, pain and despair wrote their marks in lines about his tired eyes and lips. Without a sound he turned his stallion back toward the trees.

That night Graham listened at the door as Penelope wept her woes into the pillow. The choking sobs ripped at his heart, and his gloved hand rested uneasily on the door latch. He wished desperately to go to her, but did not know what he could say even if the latch should open.

He could not let such anguish go ignored. Remembering the coat spread over him when he woke on the sofa in the early hours of the morn, Graham prayed she had not shut him out entirely. If only a door would remain open between them, perhaps some solution could be found.

The latch gave way without a hitch, and Graham breathed a sigh of relief. Pushing the door aside, he could see a single candle gleaming gently beside the bed, throwing its shadows across the sobbing figure lying there.

She did not even hear him enter. Graham stood uncertainly at the foot of the bed, wanting to take her in his arms and kiss the tears away but suspecting he was the cause of them. Deciding Penelope in her thin night rail and hair streaming down her back was more temptation than he could deal with easily, he settled himself carefully at the far end of the mattress. Here, he could only be tempted to touch the small bare toe peeping from beneath the hem of her gown. Gazing at that toe, Graham found it more enticing than any woman he had ever seen in any state of dishabille, and he doubted his wisdom in this choice of seats.

"Penelope, please, stop crying and tell me what is wrong." That was not very helpful, but he could think of nowhere else to start.

Penelope shook her head, refusing to raise her face from the pillow. Her words were muffled and faint. "Go away. Just go away and leave me be."

That sounded familiar, and Graham sighed with exasperation, crossing his arms over his chest to keep his hands from straying. From this angle he had a clear view of the round curve of her posterior, and the sudden ache in his loins reminded him of how long it had been since they had shared a bed. Shutting out such thoughts, Graham tried to find a reasonable reply.

"I cannot leave you crying like this. If it is something I have done, I would know of it, Penny. I don't mean to hurt you." Her sobs scarcely lessened. In fact, they seemed to grow worse, and he tried another tack. "Penelope, you know I would give anything to make you happy. Except my right hand, perhaps. But then, I could not afford to lose the left, either. Or any other of my appendages, come to think of it. I have grown rather attached to all of them over the years."

His efforts were rewarded with a watery giggle, but Penelope still refused to look up. Desperate times called for desperate measures, and Graham finally gave in and wrapped his hand around her foot. "Come around here and tell me what is wrong or I shall tickle you until you do."

Penelope gasped and tried to retrieve her foot, but Graham's hold was quite firm. "Don't, Graham! I'll stop. Really, I will! But my eyes are all red and ugly. Go away, do. Just for now."

That was better. Graham relaxed and began to stroke her ankle. "Shall I get you some of my eye patches?

You would make a fetching piratess, I should think.
But if you can look at this fearsome visage of mine, I
should manage a few tears and a runny nose. Sit up
now and tell me what is wrong.''

He made her feel foolish, and the heat of his hand
against her foot stirred sensations better left buried.
Reluctantly wiping her eyes, Penelope turned over,
hastily pulling her knees up to her chest and covering
her feet when he released her.

Graham solemnly handed her his handkerchief.
Wearing only an open-necked shirt and tailored buff
trousers as if he had been preparing for bed, he
dwarfed the end of her narrow mattress. She took the
cloth and wiped at her eyes, watching him warily. He
had not shown her this much concern since he had
returned from London well over a week ago.

''That is better.'' He eyed her critically as Penelope
pushed long strands of heavy brown hair from her face.
''Actually it would be a shame to cover those lovely
eyes with patches. They sparkle like the dew right now.
Adelaide's get all puffy and her face turns blotchy and
she looks a proper harridan when she cries.''

Penelope smiled wanly at his flattery. ''Adelaide is
beautiful enough not to care what she looks like. It is
only us plain people who must fuss and fret over our
looks.''

''You're angling for that one,'' he admonished. ''I
should not spoil you. You would grow more vain than
Alexandra. So I'll not tell you how beautiful you are.
And I won't mention that if all the world were as plain
as you, the sun would no longer need to shine because
it would be as bright as day already. I'll let you keep
thinking you are plain so you will not be tempted to
try your beauty on others.''

''That's doing it a shade too brown, my lord. Someone has been giving you lessons in nonsense. It really
is not necessary to practice on me. I am quite content
being plain if you do not mind it too much.'' Penelope
wiped at her eyes and hid a small smile.

Graham reached out and grabbed her ankle and
pulled it toward him, holding it tightly despite Penel-

ope's squirming protest. "Let us begin again. Why is my beautiful wife crying her eyes out alone in her bed when she could come to me? Speak, Penelope, or I shall torture it out of you." His thumb ran warningly down the sole of her foot, sending shivers up and down her leg.

"I tried to go to you," Penelope replied indignantly, fighting his sympathy with anger. "You made it quite clear that I am too foolish to understand anything, and you shut me out. Why should I tell you anything now?"

Graham's lips bent slightly in their half smile. This was progress. He seldom made Penelope angry. "Because I cannot mend my ways until I know what I have done wrong. You have punished me very severely this past week, but I do not know what I must do to earn your good graces again."

"Do you say you do not even know what you have done wrong?" she asked, incredulous. The hand on her ankle was slowly easing upward, but she tried to ignore this.

"I have been curt and rude, for which I apologize. You must understand that there are occasionally other things on my mind, and I am out of practice in being polite. It does not come so naturally as it once did."

"Curt and rude, I understand, even if others do not. But you told me I did not know what I was talking about and refused to discuss something I felt very strongly about!" Penelope did not mention he had also shut his door in her face when she very much wanted to hold him after worrying herself ill for weeks over his absence. That would give him more than he deserved. "You must decide whether you want me as wife and equal or as a paid servant who should keep her thoughts to herself!"

"The governess seduced by her evil employer and terrified of being thrown out without references?" Graham murmured wickedly, his hand exploring further, testing the curve of a rounded calf. "Is that how you see us? Then I have been cruel, and you are right to punish me, but can we not find a better way of fighting? I do not like being locked from your room.''

Penelope blushed, as much at the look in his eye as the tone of his words, but she held her ground. ''It is all right for you to shut me out, but I cannot do the same? How do I fight that? Shall I take an ax to your door? Or your head?''

Graham chuckled appreciatively at the twin spots of red upon her cheeks. ''That would get my attention assuredly. But perhaps we could find a better solution. Why don't we remove the lock so neither of us can shut the other out? I know there may be times when you would prefer to be left alone, and you must understand there are times when I would do the same, but surely we are adult enough to say these things without hurting each other?''

He made everything sound so reasonable, she was ashamed of her behavior, but he had explained nothing, and he had not said he would send Chadwell away. He seduced her in the same way his cousin did, without offering any of himself. Was that how it was meant to be between man and wife? Each going his own way except in bed? She did not think so if she could judge by Adelaide and Brian, but perhaps they were the exception to the rule.

''Removing a lock from a door will not remove the barriers between us, Graham. There are things you do not tell me, and times you will not listen. I try not to bother you with trifles, and I have no right to ask the secrets of your heart, but you cannot behave as you did with Arthur the other day without offering some explanation. Such behavior affects me as well as you, and I think I should have some right to know.''

She came too close to subjects he was not ready to dwell on, and Graham defended himself in time-honored fashion by turning to the offensive. ''I do not think I am the only one with secrets, Penelope. Would you care to tell me how you have spent the days since my return? What is so important to you that you neglect your guests and your duties? And then tell me why Guy is the one who shares these times with you?''

Penelope stared with incredulity at the tight lines of his face and the whitening scar. "You could think that of me?" she asked, disbelief plain in her tone. "How could you? What have I ever done to give you such an opinion of me? Perhaps we are very wrong for each other. I thought we might suit, that we might bump along together once we worked things out, but I have been so very wrong about other things, perhaps I was wrong in this, too. Let go of me, Graham."

She tried to shake her leg free, but far from releasing her, Graham gave a tug that pulled her from her high perch on the pillows and slid her night rail to embarrassing heights. Penelope scrambled to pull the meager cloth back, but Graham gave a triumphant grin and finally surrendered to the pleasure of riding his hand over her tempting bottom. Penelope shrieked at this invasion and threw herself at him to push his hand away, but that was the wrong move to make. One steellike arm wrapped about her waist and dragged her across his lap while his free hand continued its ardent explorations.

"Oh, we shall suit very well, my prim Penny, and shortly I will ask you again what you have been doing with your days. But not right now, I think."

With great satisfaction he bent his hand to claim protesting lips and felt her total surrender to his touch.

Perhaps their castle was still surrounded by thorns and the prince still resembled a frog, but the princess had awakened.

Chapter 30

PENELOPE woke to a bed not her own but with no one beside her. Cautiously she glanced across the semi-darkened room, remembering the placement of tables and chairs before the empty grate and the dresser and washstand against the wall. Her night rail and Graham's shirt and trousers lay in puddles of cloth upon the floor, and she buried her face in the pillow again.

How could she have let him seduce her like that? She had every right to be angry with him, to demand explanations, but she had let him sweet-talk her into his bed without a word of apology. And now he had escaped for the day and she was no further along than before, just well and truly tumbled as if she were a mistress he could discard at will.

Strangely she felt no anger, but only a languid contentment as she stretched and burrowed herself into the comfort of Graham's massive bed. At least he had not returned her to her own room as he was wont to do. She liked it here where she could still see the imprint of his head upon the pillow and smell the masculine scents that lingered on the sheets. She turned on her side and touched the indentation in the pillow, wishing the shutters on the window were open so she could see out.

A noise in the entrance to the dressing room made her glance up, and her heart did an odd tattoo against her ribs as she discovered Graham watching her. With light only from the top of the windows, he stood in shadow, but she could tell he was still only half dressed. He wore a robe wrapped around his flat middle, concealing the fresh trousers he had just donned but leaving much of his chest exposed. She knew he bore scars just below the collarbone, but she could not see them from here. She had never really seen them, only felt them in the darkness when he made love to her.

Blushing at the memory and embarrassed by the way he was looking at her now, Penelope pulled the covers up to her nose and curled up beneath his pillow. Acutely aware that she wore nothing at all, she couldn't meet his gaze. This was the first time they had shared a bed for the entire night. She had never known what it was to wake after a night of love and find her husband still beside her.

Graham contemplated her turtlelike plunge beneath the covers with mixed emotions. Admittedly it must be a little daunting to wake to a piratical visage such as his glaring down at her, and that stirred a feeling of pain and remorse. But he also had the tiniest suspicion that it was her own embarrassment she hid, and that thought brought a crooked smile to his lips.

Penelope heard him saunter into the room and gulped as he sat down upon the bed. A fresh scent similar to pine clung to him, and she realized she would recognize that scent anywhere. Daringly she peeped from beneath the pillow and felt her heart nearly stop at the look she found in his eye. She would never get any sense out of him at all when he looked at her that way. She had no thoughts but the need for him to be there.

"No more tears?" he asked gruffly, studying her pink cheeks.

"Not now." Penelope kept her pillow near at hand but boldly dared to look up at him. She could not honestly say that he was handsome, and perhaps he was not a true gentleman, but she loved him with every ounce of her heart and soul. It was hard to imagine how she could ever have thought otherwise.

"You are not afraid of me?" he asked with curiosity when she did not come out of hiding with more than one violet eye.

That brought the other eye into view as she stared at him in astonishment. "Afraid of you? Should I be?"

Graham chuckled and grabbed a fistful of hair, pulling her up from her cocoon of covers until he could at least view the slender curve of her throat and the creamy bareness of her shoulders. "You amaze me, Lady Trevelyan. You are as timid as a wild rabbit when I but wish to look upon you, yet you have no fear of my touch. Why is that?"

Penelope gave that some thought as she snuggled her shoulders into the pillows piled next to his thigh. Primly she hugged the covers over her breasts to protect her modesty. "That could be because I am accustomed to your touch, but it is always dark when you look at me. I'm not *afraid*," she offered honestly, "but I'm not accustomed to being seen without clothes. It cannot be very proper."

Graham caught her chin and turned her gaze up to him. "Propriety is for the public, not the privacy of our chambers. In here we can be ourselves, say what we think, do what we like. Don't you think that's the way it ought to be?"

He said that with such deceptive intensity that she knew he had a reason for it, but she very much wanted it to be like that for them. Warily she tested his words. "Say what we think? If I ask why you do things that hurt me and others, you will not tell me I don't understand and it's none of my business?"

"Am I allowed to ease into this with simple things first?" he asked, mocking her words of months ago.

Penelope pulled the covers back up to her nose and glared at him. "Of course, if that is your wish, but it works both ways."

Silently Graham stared at her. She had the right of it. If he could not be honest with her, she had no reason to trust in him. He would have to put an end to this dilemma, but he could not face it in the cold light of day. Tonight, when he had wooed her and won her, perhaps then she would forgive him.

With a pained half smile, he agreed. "Very well, we will do this slowly. I will take your word for it that you are not swayed by Guy's winning ways if you will believe me when I say I have never meant to hurt you or any of the innocents who stumble unwittingly against my anger. I had never thought to mend my ways when we married, but I can see now that your opinion of me is more important than anything else, and that I will be happier when I have won your approval.''

The sheet lowered to her shoulders again as Penelope stared at him in disbelief. ''I will try very hard to believe that, my lord, but you must know you don't make it easy.''

''I know,'' he said gruffly, rising to his feet. ''But I have faith in your wisdom and forgiveness. Come, let us greet the day together.'' He held out his hand to help her up.

Penelope's gaze flew from where he stood to where her night rail lay, and her cheeks began to crimson. She wanted to please him, but perhaps he forgot she wore nothing beneath these sheets. His suspicious chuckle put an end to that thought, but reluctantly, Graham reached for her wrapper and held it out—one step from her reach.

Sighing with exasperation at this childish ploy, Penelope flung back the covers and rose from the bed, snatching the night rail from his hands. Jerking it on, she stuck her tongue out at him and proceeded grandly toward her own chambers, head held high and chin up.

His roar of laughter filled the room and brought a soft smile to her lips to start the day.

By evening, the smile had disappeared. She had thrown herself into the work at the orphanage as usual, singing to herself and quite happy with the way things were progressing, but entirely forgetting the Reardons' rout that evening. When she returned home to find Adelaide dressed in all her finery and pacing the floor, her hand flew to her mouth in horror.

''I forgot! Oh, no, Graham will never forgive me. What am I to do? Guy will be here any minute.''

Adelaide's brow wrinkled with perplexity. "And Graham makes fun of the way I speak. Whatever are you about, Penny? I'm sure Graham will forgive you for forgetting, he does it often enough himself, but Guy is the one who is escorting you, is he not?"

Penelope flushed and looking longingly toward the stairs and escape. "Yes, but I forgot to tell Graham we were going," she whispered. "Is he here?"

"I heard him roaring not long ago. If he's not to go, why should it matter? Let him sulk in his own mean little world."

Penelope cast her a helpless look and hurried toward the stairs. She had to explain to him, make him understand why she had not mentioned the rout, and why Guy would be downstairs shortly to take her away when she knew very well what Graham planned for this evening.

He was not in his chamber when she reached it, and she uttered a very improper oath under her breath. He was probably in the kitchen rattling the staff for some minor misdemeanor. She would have to get dressed and wait for him.

Her maid had a bath waiting and a gown laid out. Penelope did not linger long over her ablutions but raced through the motions, all the time listening for the sound of Guy's arrival downstairs or Graham in the room next door. Guy was as late as she, thank heavens.

She donned the gold silk and waited impatiently for the maid to finish fussing with the matching ribbons twining through the elaborate loops and curls she created. Scarcely taking time to admire the effect, Penelope caught up her gloves and fan and flew down the hall toward the stairs.

To her dismay, she could hear Graham's laughing voice carrying up from the salon. She would have to face him in front of everyone else and admit her deception. Why ever had she tried to do it? She knew better than to commit even the smallest of crimes. She always got caught.

Slowly she descended the stairs, one slippered foot

reluctantly following the other until she could see down into the front hall and knew they were all standing there, waiting. Her gaze quickly searched the shadows until she found him, and her eyes widened in astonishment. Graham had dressed in his formal frock coat as if he meant to attend, also!

His appreciative gaze followed her down the last few steps, leaving Penelope even more flustered. She glanced quickly aside to Adelaide and Brian, but they saw nothing wrong in this charade. Gulping back her fear, she looked inquiringly to Graham. He merely smiled and held out his arm.

"Shall we go, my dear?"

He knew. Somehow he knew about the rout and Guy. Guy wasn't late. He wasn't coming. Not knowing whether to be terrified or happy, Penelope peeped timidly up to Graham's square-cut jaw as she took his arm.

"You are not angry?"

"Angry? No, why should I be when I know you will explain all, tonight," he leaned over to whisper wickedly in her ear, "When we are snug and warm in our bed."

Penelope gasped and cursed at the heat rising in her cheeks, but she clung tightly to his strong arm as they went out the door.

The rout was an unequivocal success from the viewpoint of almost all parties involved. When the guests insisted on an impromptu dance, Graham stayed close to Penelope's side, grudgingly allowing her to dance with others only when etiquette required that he escort his hostess and other guests onto the floor. Penelope observed as the evening drew on that Dolly's color rose to a most flattering shade of pink, particularly after Guy defied all rules by leading her out on the floor for a third and fourth dance. Lady Reardon appeared to remain remarkably calm over this breach of good manners. Either her guests kept her too busy to notice or Guy had charmed her as thoroughly as her daughter. Graham caught Penelope's laughing look and lifted a quizzical eyebrow, but he could not discern her answer when she nodded toward Guy and the young redhead. His puzzlement only made her laugh more.

The only incident to mar the evening went largely unobserved by all but the two participants. Arthur had joined his family in the receiving line for his first public occasion since returning home. He and Graham had coldly ignored each other; for the sake of appearances, neither said a word to ruin the evening. When Charles DeVere arrived at the portals, however, Arthur went white with rage and hurriedly left his place to catch the other man by the elbow before he could start down the line.

"What in hell are you doing here?" Arthur pushed the older man back in the direction of the door, keeping his voice down so the other guests would not remark upon his behavior.

"I received an invitation," DeVere returned icily. "Your family has not found me offensive in the past."

"That is because I did not see fit to give them the sordid details. A man of character would not have dared return here under any circumstances. I should have known you would act without honor. If that is the game you choose to play, I will feel free to act the same and reveal you to all and sundry."

By this time, Arthur had forcibly steered his guest back outside, and they stood concealed by shrubbery, their voices scarcely rising above the clatter of arriving carriages and clamor of excited party goers.

DeVere coldly shook off Arthur's restraining hand. "You cursed young pup! How do you think to expose me without getting yourself turned out of the house? Let the past die."

"I care not what happens to me, but I will protect the innocent with the last breath in me, as I shall soon enough, I know. Trevelyan is only biding his time before calling me out. I will go to my death without fear, but I will leave a letter behind to my brother. While I live, your secret is safe. When I die, that letter will keep you barred from every decent door in town. I'd suggest you find another place of abode, DeVere."

DeVere ground his teeth together in barely controlled rage. "How can Trevelyan know anything? You are imagining things. He was near to death that night. He could know nothing. You are playing at heroes and villains, Reardon. Wake up to the real world."

"I have. That is why I forbid you in this house," Arthur stated quietly. "I don't know how Gray learned of my involvement, but he knows, and he means to kill me for it. I don't believe your life will be a long one once he learns your involvement. I cannot give you a better warning."

"Chadwell!" DeVere hissed. "I thought it was just you he was after, but it's all of us." He slyly kept to himself the fact that the American apparently didn't know of his own involvement. It didn't pay to reveal too much. In fact, he had said too much already. Arthur looked at him oddly.

"I will go, but if you intend to outlive that rotting hulk of a neighbor of yours, you had better keep your lips sealed. He'll not challenge you or any other when I get through with him." DeVere spun on his heel and stalked off.

Only Lady Reardon noticed her son's white-lipped countenance when he returned to the house, and she placed the blame on overexertion. Arthur brushed off her attempts to send him back to his sickbed, and thoughtfully he stared out over the crowd to where Graham stood head and shoulders above everyone else. He couldn't right the wrong that had been done, but he could do everything in his power to keep it from happening again.

Penelope relaxed contentedly in the circle of Graham's arm as the carriage rattled toward home. Adelaide and Brian had left earlier, and they had the carriage to themselves, a fact Graham took full advantage of. His kisses set her skin ablaze, and the path of his hand left her eager for more. She wished the fabric of her gown would disappear so she could feel his strong fingers against her bare flesh.

Graham caressed her breast and bent to steal the honey from her parted lips. He prayed that after tonight there would be no more deception between them, and that she would not reject him coldly, as would be her right. She was so warm and vibrant in his arms, he could not imagine life without her, but he could not live this lie any longer. His kiss deepened as the carriage rolled to a halt.

The footman assigned to open the door for them stared wide-eyed at the sight revealed and hastily stepped back, allowing the door to close again. Graham chuckled against Penelope's mouth and reluctantly released her, staring down at her kiss-swollen lips.

"A few more minutes, darling, and I will have you all to myself. Are you ready?"

"I don't think I am. I don't think I will ever be. You cannot turn the little cinder girl into a princess overnight," Penelope answered breathlessly, clinging to his hand for reassurance.

Graham laughed and jumped to the ground, holding his hands out to pull Penelope from the carriage. "You don't know your own powers, princess. We shall see who changes into what before the night is over."

With that utterly nonsensical remark, he led her into the house where servants waited with lamps and warm water and all the comforts one could ask for. Penelope could still scarcely believe all this was true. Surely she would wake up one morning and find it all a dream.

When Harley came rushing forward bearing a message on a silver platter, Penelope felt her heart plummet, and the feeling of well-being immediately dissipated. No message at this time of night could be a good one. Here was the part where she would wake and find the dream was just a nightmare.

The note was addressed to her, and Graham passed it to her with a worried frown. Penelope's hands shook as she unfolded the rough, cheap stationery. She didn't recognize the jerky scrawl, but she knew the name at the bottom and her cheeks went white as she scanned the contents.

"Penelope, what is it?" Anxiously Graham watched her face, wishing to rip the paper from her hand.

"Augusta. It's Augusta. Bess tells me she is ill and is asking for me." Penelope handed the paper to her husband, her face pale and wide-eyed with distress.

Graham hastily scanned the note and felt a lump of lead form in his chest. He lifted his gaze to Penelope's and the lump solidified. "You will want to go, of course. Can you not wait and get some rest and go in the morning?"

He could tell by the look in her eyes that he asked the impossible, but Brian sauntered out of the study before she could answer. He read the tableau in the foyer with ease. "What is it? Is something wrong?"

Graham shoved the crinkled note at him but did not take his eyes from Penelope's. He didn't want to let her go. Selfishly he wanted to keep her with him, but he knew her too well. Softly he said, "I will go with you. Go pack a few things and I will call the carriage back."

Penelope shook her head. She could not ask him to leave his work and Alexandra to sit by the bedside of an old lady he scarcely knew. That was for her, alone, to do. "It would not suit, Graham. I will let you know when I get there if there is anything you can do."

"Penelope, I cannot send you out into the night—" His words were cut off by a gesture of Brian's and the appearance of Adelaide upon the stairs. She stared down at them worriedly.

"What is happening?"

Brian passed the note on to her and answered with a question. "Would you care to return home a little sooner than expected? You know we have talked of it. I agree with Graham, though. It would be better left for morning."

Adelaide hastily read the message, then glanced to Penelope's tearful expression and shook her head. "No, we had better leave at once. The maids can pack our things and send them on later. Come, Penelope, let us change and then we will be off."

Within the hour the matter was settled. The Stanhopes' carriage and fresh horses were brought around and the travelers snugly tucked in with pillows and blankets to get what rest they might while they journeyed.

Graham stood on the steps and watched them go with the feeling they were taking his heart with them. He lifted his hand in a final farewell and slowly turned toward the empty house.

Chapter 31

GRAHAM smoothed the thick vellum of Penelope's note and read it over once again, hearing her voice speak the words. The faint scent of lavender rose from the paper, and he ached to be near her, to hold her and comfort her, but she did not seem to want him there. He knew she would be staying at the cottage and that her days and nights would be occupied with her patient, but even this knowledge didn't daunt his desire to be close by in case she needed him.

The only things keeping him from packing his bags and joining her were Penelope's lack of invitation and the other letter lying on his desk. Graham glanced at this more official correspondence and grimaced. That one was more command than invitation and he had no wish to respond to it. They wanted a part of him that was over and done with, or would have been had Penelope not been called away. He had made his decision and intended to keep it, but this summons made it clear that things wouldn't be so simple as he had hoped.

Sighing, he folded both letters and slid them in his breast pocket. One more time he would play the clown, and that would be the end of it.

The fox-faced man paced up and down the elegant Aubusson carpet, ignoring the magnificent Turner and Gainsborough oils in their gilded frames, and avoiding the delicate Sheraton love seats as if they were naught but obstacles in his path. He turned to the silver-haired gentleman lounging in the large wing chair near the exquisitely carved Adams mantel and scowled.

"You do not understand the seriousness of the situation, Trevelyan! One of my own men can be a blackguard of the worst sort, or your cousin can be a murderous traitor for those bloody Americans! Damn it, man, we still have a war on our hands. You know what they do to traitors during times of war?"

"I can't imagine." Graham leaned back in his chair and gave a prodigious yawn before giving a desultory reply. "But I'll vouch for my cousin. That leaves you with the blackguard. Hang him and see if that doesn't put an end to this nonsense." He made a dismissive gesture.

The small official seemed to swell to twice his size in rage, and his face turned a mottled purple. "Damn it to bloody hell! Don't give me that idle fop pose. You have your finger in every sticky pie in this town and well I know it. I don't know how you do it, but it's your frank that got Chadwell into the Regent's ball, your signature on the deeds of those houses Chadwell operates from, your name on the notes of everyone of those men in that infernal club. Don't think I don't do my work, Trevelyan. I'm just as thorough as you, and I think we're after the same man. Now do I get your cooperation or will I have to climb over your back to get at what I want?"

Graham lifted his one uncovered eyebrow with a look approaching respect. "You do have a point there, sir. Why don't I send Cliff over to have a chat with you? I'd like to see an end to these depredations, myself. The streets of London are no longer safe with these villains about. Will that suit?"

The fox-faced man grimaced. "I need to see him now. I need to see both of you. Can't you summon him here?"

Graham smiled wanly and leaned forward on his walking stick. "Don't ask the impossible, sir. My cousin and I cannot be seen together. You, of all people, should understand that. I will send him to you this evening."

The other man gave the viscount a shrewd look, but Trevelyan's complacent expression gave no clue to his thoughts. He wasn't certain how much of Graham's pose he believed, but it would make sense that the athletic American would be the legs of this operation while the invalid viscount provided the financial side. That left one to wonder which was the brains behind it all, but he'd find that out soon enough.

Accepting the crumbs offered, he made a slight bow and stalked out.

"I will tell you one more time that I know nothing of these murders other than that someone obviously wished to implicate myself or my cousin in them. How else would you explain the mysterious stranger having an eye patch one time and none the other?" Chadwell quit stalking up and down before the cluttered desk and threw himself down into a nearby chair. "I have been working these streets for years. It's odd that the rumors started shortly after Gray first appeared in public. For what it's worth, my opinion is that his savage countenance stuck in the minds of the populace and the similarity between him and the actual murderer made them talk of ghastly scars and patches, since that's what a murderer ought to look like. The stories changed after he left town. Unless you want to lock us both up, I'd suggest you start looking for a common background in the victims' lives."

The fox-faced man scowled thoughtfully as he chewed on the nib of his pen. The blot of ink on his lip revealed he had been giving much thought to the subject before this.

"Women like those aren't easy to trace. Two were from the theater. Another had once been mistress to an earl who will remain unnamed. Another frequented a particular gambling hell I have an interest in because our friend seems to have an interest in it. They all have been seen on that end of town at one time or another. You are the only connecting link. That assassination attempt was planned by someone inside my office. How you came to know of it is of great interest to me. The fact that you are now implicated in these murders makes this even more fascinating. And what your part is in that infernal club complicates matters even further. I think you owe me a little more explanation than you have given.''

With a mocking smile, Chadwell leaned back in the leather upholstered chair and threw one leg over the arm. "You needn't worry about the club. It's been permanently disbanded. There are only two known members remaining in the area, and one of them will be leaving shortly. The other claims to have resigned his membership long ago, but he's the one who concerns us, isn't he?''

The American's arrogance brought a flush of fury to the official's face, but he restrained his temper as long as he was getting information from him. "In what way? Would you care to enlighten me?''

Chadwell narrowed his eyes and stared at the molded carving on the ceiling. The office reeked of officialdom from the solid mahogany desk and oak chair rails to the framed documents on the walls. He hadn't meant to get in this deep, but if there was any chance that there was some relationship between the assassination attempt and his own vendetta, then he had little choice in the matter. But he sure as hell wouldn't let this gentleman have the satisfaction of knowing it.

"DeVere has access to your office, he was in the room when the attempt was made, and he once belonged to that club of miscreants who terrified the countryside a few years back. As far as I am aware, DeVere dropped out of the club at the same time quite a number of others came to their senses and cut their ties with it. The remainder went on to rape and larceny and murder. Charming lot, wouldn't you say?'' Chadwell contemplated the tip of the cigar he had appropriated from the humidor on the desk. He didn't smoke the filthy things, but they did make an excellent prop.

"As far as you are aware? I'd rather thought you had become an authority on the subject. Or is it Trevelyan's knowledge you rely on? Why did so many owe money to your cousin?''

Chadwell swung the cigar airily. "Let's say I gamble a wee bit. My signature isn't worth a tinker's damn, but Gray's gleams like gold to the scum. So I wager with his markers, and I win rather frequently. I make them write their vows to Graham to cover the notes he writes for me. Paper for paper, like having my own bank. Grand scheme, ain't it?''

The fox-faced man made a grimace of disgust. "Except your victims tend to die or disappear before they ever repay him. That leaves you a small fortune ahead, doesn't it?''

Chadwell shrugged. "A man needs to live, and Gray don't begrudge the expense. You'll understand that if you're as smart as you think you are. Let us get back to the subject in question. Since Gray and I most assuredly did not murder your soiled doves, and since I am the one who stopped your bloody assassination, you will have to write us off your suspect list on both counts.''

The other man grunted his disapproval of this flummery, but he did not interfere.

Chadwell took his silence as consent to continue. "Since we have no other immediate suspects besides DeVere, it would behoove us to look a little further into his activities. I will admit, until now, I have given him little consideration. I dislike the man. I know he is capable of great treachery. I have surmised he is the owner of at least one brothel off Whitechapel, but without evidence, I have had no reason to go after him. I cannot see his profit in murdering the petticoats nor in implicating me, but if you think I am the connection, then by all means, let us go after him.''

The fox-faced man leaned forward and placed his hands against the desk. "How?''

A tear splotted against the still wet ink, smearing it across the vellum, giving rise to more tears as Penelope wadded up this disaster and threw it to join the others. Sinful waste, it was, but what did waste matter when she had lost the one person in the world who had ever truly loved her?

That thought brought renewed tears and she gave up on the letter to lay her head on her arms and weep all the tears she had been holding back all day. She wept that she hadn't been with Augusta in these last few brief months of her life. She wept for the past that was lost with her. She wept for the loss of Augusta's cheery smile and the warm kitchen of delightful smells and the homely advice. She wept for the gnarled fingers that had meticulously stitched her lovely bridal nightgown. And she wept for herself.

She should have asked Graham to come. He would have taken care of all the practical details of funerals and coffins, and she could have stayed with Augusta instead of leaving her alone and cold this whole day. He would have held her now and made her feel warm again. He would have reminded her that she could have others to love, perhaps not the same as Augusta, but not the emptiness there might have been.

She owed him so much, she hated to impose on him anymore, but she needed him now, needed him here. Gulping back a sob and crudely wiping at her eyes with her sleeve since her handkerchief was already saturated, Penelope sat up and picked up the pen once more. She would write and he would come. She couldn't go through the funeral without him.

As it was, she had to, even after the letter was sent. No reply came before the day of the funeral. Penelope ran to the window at every sound of a horse or carriage, but none was Graham. Her expression of despair tore at Adelaide's heart as Penelope turned back into the room, and she silently berated her absent brother. With a telling look to her husband, she hurried to take her sister-in-law's arm.

"Come, you will ride with us. Then you will come back to the manor. There will be no more of this sleeping alone in this empty cottage when we have that great monstrous house to keep you in. You know Graham will cut up stiff if he finds we allowed you to stay here alone."

Talking nonstop, Adelaide managed to steer Penelope toward the entrance. Brian acted as footman, handling the door of the cottage. Together, they got Penelope into the carriage and held her hands throughout the journey. But no amount of sympathy and consolation could replace her need for Graham at her side.

When she returned to the manor that night, she couldn't sleep in the overlarge bed she had once shared with Graham. Finally giving up on it, she slipped into her wrapper, and carrying blanket and pillow, curled up on the couch beneath the window. It made little logical sense, but it felt more like her bed at the Hall, and she could dream Graham would come for her during the night.

He didn't, of course, and the next day Penelope stared bleakly over the trees in the park to the road beyond. From her bedroom window she could see only a few patches of the graveled path, but she knew Graham's carriage wasn't hidden behind the trees. He wasn't coming.

It was nearly September already. Soon, the trees would turn color and coat the ground in rustling drifts. The manor had a lovely forested park. It would be nice to have a similar one at the Hall.

Sighing, Penelope turned away from the window. Staring at the tree would not salve the pain in her heart. She felt deserted by everyone she had loved. Why hadn't Graham come? Had her letter somehow been mislaid? Then why hadn't he written? Or come in a raging fury to find out why she tarried so long without writing? Silence did not reflect the man she knew, but how well did she really know him?

Not very well, at all, she surmised gloomily. He had a life he hid from her, a life that sometimes made him surly and impossible to get close to. She should not complain. When he did have the time to pay heed to her, he did it with such charm and devotion that she could almost believe he held an affection for her somewhere in the depths of his heart. She should remember the good times, the times they laughed and loved and shared together, and not complain of the bad.

When she had puttered around the cottage, giving away what would no longer be needed, tidying up, covering the few pieces of good furniture, closing the shutters and other innumerable tasks she created until it became obvious that Graham did not mean to come, Penelope finally announced she would return on her own.

Adelaide attempted to dissuade her, but reminding her of Alexandra, Penelope managed to break away. The Stanhopes insisted she travel in style, though, and they returned her in their carriage with gifts for Alex and letters to Graham.

It was twilight before she finally arrived at the Hall. The setting sun sent a rosy glow over the weathered brick wings of the rambling mansion, and they almost seemed to be reaching out to welcome her home. The windows sparkled and winked, and Penelope had to smile at her fancy that the house was happy to see her. It was her own joy at returning here she saw reflected in the welcoming panes.

As soon as the carriage door opened, she lifted her skirts and alighted, nearly running up the steps to greet Harley and look eagerly for Graham and Alexandra. Alex came bounding down the stairs with cries of delight as expected, and Penelope scooped her up in her arms and showered her with kisses. Graham would have received the same had he appeared, but he did not.

Harley assured her his lordship hadn't been feeling quite well and was simply resting, but he seemed relieved at Penelope's appearance. She played with Alexandra awhile, hoping Graham would wake and come down, but there was no sign of him by the time Alexandra was sent off to bed.

Worried, Penelope ordered a light dinner served in her room. It had been weeks since Graham had taken to his bed like this, not since London if memory served her. What had he been doing to return the pain so severely he had to resort to laudanum again? Surely that was the only reason he had not come down to greet her.

When dinner was served, she knocked lightly on the connecting door, hoping she would find him awake enough to entice him to join her. When John answered, she gaped at him in dismay.

''How is he, John? What has he done to put him back in bed again?''

John's weathered face looked more lined and weary than usual, but he offered her a small smile and shook his head. ''He'll be fine, milady, just tried to do too much at once. Just let him sleep it off.''

''Let me see him, John. He's not taking as much laudanum as before?'' Anxiously she tried to peer over John's shoulder, but the bed wasn't in view of the door here.

''He don't like nobody to see him when he's taken like this, milady. I got my orders. Just give him time, you'll see, he'll be right as a trivet again.''

Somehow he lacked his usual easy confidence, but Penelope had too much pride to go where she was not wanted. Head held stiffly, she nodded and closed the door, and felt the tears welling up inside all over again.

Her food went back to the kitchen, untouched. Like a ghost, she drifted through the halls, checking to be certain Alexandra slept soundly, drifting into the library to look for a book, staring out the windows into the empty blackness. Without Graham, the Hall had no soul; it was just a big, empty house.

She would not believe he had gone to his mistress. If she believed that, she would go out of her mind. Taking her book and going back to her own chamber, she made herself comfortable in the brocade chair and waited. He was just sleeping and when he woke, John would tell him she was home. Then he would come to her, and she would be waiting. Graham would like that.

That thought lasted until the early hours of the morning when her eyes refused to stay open and her head began to nod wearily. The candle had almost guttered out, and with a sigh Penelope blew it out. She would wait for him in bed.

She would not believe Graham had gone to his mistress because that would reduce her to the status of glorified governess again, and she could not bear it. She would tell Graham in the morning that she wanted all the rights of a wife, not just the ones he wished to bestow upon her. She could endure the knowledge that he did not love her if she at least knew he was faithful to her.

If he laughed at her, she would leave him. Her heart could not carry the burden of still another break.

Chapter 32

GRAHAM did not come to her during the night. Frightened by the possibility that he might truly be ill and furious that he would not trust her to help him, Penelope overcame her pride and pounded once more on his chamber door.

John appeared more haggard than the night before, but he was still large enough and strong enough to prevent her pushing past him. Penelope crossed her arms and looked him in the eye.

"Are you going to let me in there or am I going to have to call on Sir Percival and Lord Reardon to forcibly remove you?"

John wavered. He had never seen the mistress with the shadows of a summer storm in her eyes. She had always been quiet and polite, relying on her authority to get her way. Never had he heard her voice raised in anger but that one night when she had tricked him from his duty to find the master gone. He didn't think she would be any less angry if he allowed her to do it again, but this time was different. He felt it in his bones.

Rationalizing that his lordship would not appreciate it if his friends were witness to this domestic quarrel, John surrendered. "He isn't here, milady." He stood aside to let her see for herself.

The bed lay untouched, as it had that last time. Penelope felt her heart ripping into little pieces, but she refused to fall apart in front of the servants.

Coldly she inquired, "How long has he been gone?"

"Soon after you left, milady." John did not even try to hide the worry in his voice.

Penelope turned suspicious eyes to him at the tone of his voice. "Do you know where he went?"

"No, milady, that I don't," he answered quickly, anxious to prove himself innocent.

Penelope didn't know how to react to that. Should she assume Graham had simply gone off to his mistress and didn't inform his servant? Perhaps he had received another message from London, but surely he would have said something to John? John could be lying, or Graham could be in a ditch somewhere hurt and unable to call for help. She tried not to let panic rule her thoughts.

"Did he not say anything when he left? When he would we back? Anything?"

"He just said he had some business to take care of and he'd not be long, that if you tried to reach him, to send word to London. I did that, so I been thinking he was with you."

Penelope absorbed this information, squelching her fears by applying logic. Graham could take care of himself. He was much too big to disappear. If anything had happened to him, someone would have let her know. First, she would make a few discreet inquiries. Perhaps someone else knew where he had gone. Guy would be the most likely choice.

Trying to behave as if everything were normal, she sent word to Guy to meet her at the orphanage when he had time. She rode out shortly after breakfast to inspect the building herself. Things seemed to be progressing so smoothly she would have to start giving thought to finding someone willing to take over operations. That should not be so very difficult. Since it was meant to be a home for girls, a woman would have to manage it. She knew from her own experience that there were many women with the education and intelligence to handle a foundling home, ones forced by circumstances to make their own way in the world. She would decide on this person first, and together they would decide on what teachers would be needed. After that, they would begin looking for the girls to fill the rows of empty beds in the upstairs rooms.

Guy found her inspecting the softness of the cots that had arrived while she was gone. The pallets seemed rather thin, and she frowned. While he stood, unobserved in the doorway, the viscountess dragged one mattress from its frame and flung it over a second. Laughing as she struggled to make the unwieldy pallet lie straight, Guy stepped forward to help.

"Don't you have a footman or somebody about to help you with these whims, my lady?" Guy shifted the mattress so it lay directly on top of the other, then threw his long frame across the cot to test it for himself. Leaning against the wall and crossing his arms behind his head, he looked up at her impudently. "Care to join me?"

"Oh, Guy, won't you ever grow up?" Penelope asked crossly, walking away from his carefree exuberance. She didn't have the heart for laughter right now.

Guy instantly leapt to his feet and ran after her, catching her by the waist and swinging her around. Blue eyes studied her intently. "What is it, Penny? What has Gray done this time?"

She could feel the comforting warmth of his strong hands through the thin muslin of her light summer frock, and the sympathetic look in his eyes encouraged her to seek solace by weeping out her woes on his shoulder. Guy would always be a comfort to her. He would never leave her wondering and hurt like Graham. Why couldn't she have had the good sense to fall in love with Guy?

Penelope shook her head and pushed away from his tender hold. "Don't, Guy. Have you seen him since I left?"

He watched her walk away with a puzzled frown. "Graham? No, I thought he'd gone with you."

"No, he had to go to London on some business. I just thought maybe you'd know when he would be back." Penelope took a deep breath and tried to silence her fears before turning back to Guy. "How are you and Dolly faring these days? Since you're still alive, I can see her brothers didn't call you out for your outrageous behavior at the rout."

Guy grinned and caught her up in the posture of a waltz, swinging her around in the space between the cots. "I told you Dolly is a senseless little chit. she does not complain of my brash behavior and has convinced her suspicious brothers that my intentions are honorable."

"And are they?" Penelope lifted a quizzical eyebrow and put a stop to the impromptu dance.

Guy looked sheepish as he shoved his hands in his trouser pockets. "If she'd have me."

Penelope laughed at his transparent eagerness. "You haven't asked her yet? Coward. Do you intend to just dally at her heels until she gets bored waiting and looks elsewhere?"

"I would make an excellent cicisbeo, wouldn't I? Probably better than a husband. I'm a dozen years older, Penny. I'd be doddering around like Larchmont with my wife leading me about by the nose." He slumped down on the cot nearest the window and cast her a look of despair.

Penelope stuck to her guns. "Craven. As Alexandra so aptly puts it, coward, coward, coward. If you love her and haven't got the gumption to ask for her, you deserve whatever happens. Don't come to me for pity."

"That's easy for you to say!" Guy stood up and began to pace before the window. "All a woman has to say is no. What will I do if she says no? At least this way I can go on seeing her. If she tells me no, I couldn't bear to be near her again. I would lose my mind; I know I would. You and Graham were quite right to decide on a marriage of convenience. If you'd told him no, you could have both gone on just the same as before. It's only when these cursed emotions get in the way that things get complicated."

"Yes, rather." Without another word Penelope turned around and stalked out of the room.

Startled from his self-absorbed dilemma, Guy dashed after her, catching up with her on the stairway. "I didn't mean that the way it sounded, Penny. Forgive me. I know you love him, although the sapskull doesn't deserve it. And beneath that rough exterior, I know he loves you, too. Just give him a chance. He'll come around.''

Stiffly Penelope continued down the stairs, Guy clattering along beside her. Growing irritated with the proud lift of her chin, Guy grabbed her hand and dragged her out to the porch, out of the hearing of the workmen in the back of the house.

''The last time I saw Gray before I went away to war, he was on his deathbed. His head and chest were completely wrapped in bandages. One leg was plastered from ankle to thigh, and his hand was bandaged so thickly it looked like a pillow. He was unconscious and hadn't moved in days. Everyone was just waiting for him to die. His father even had solicitors out frantically trying to determine the succession. When I came back five years later and learned he still lived, I couldn't believe it. I expected to find some ghastly emaciated skeleton clinging to life from sheer meanness. Instead, you know how I found him. Despite his pretensions to the contrary, and do not mistake me— Gray is a skilled actor, a very talented one—he showed every sign of being a man in the best of health. A man like Graham does not choose a mousy schoolteacher for wife, no matter what story he has told you. He told you what you wanted to hear to win you because he wanted you. He would never have taken 'no' for an answer. Do you understand me, Penelope?''

He held her arm as if he would pull it off should she deny him. The intensity of his gaze darkened his eyes to almost a blue-black against the tanned shadows of his face. Penelope stared up at him as if to verify the truth of his words by the symmetry of his features.

''What makes you call him an actor, Guy? I have never found him to be less than honest with me, when he chooses to say anything.''

Guy relaxed and leaned against the porch post. ''In his younger years Trev walked the boards of many stages. Even Mrs. Siddons admitted he had talent. Many's the play we have staged at the Hall when we ran out of other entertainments. Graham played most of the parts. I'll not say that he's been less than honest with you, Penny, but I'll wager he's not offered all the truth, either. He's wooed you and won you with some flummery, and now he's scared as I am of losing his lady when he declares himself. I wish I had half his skill in knowing what a woman wants. But even if I should, I would not be able to act the part as well as he. I can't hide my love, and I couldn't hide my hurt if she tells me nay. Gray can.''

Penelope smiled faintly. "I think you credit the females of the race with more hard-heartedness than they possess. I cannot imagine any woman alive rejecting either of you. Or is it stupidity you accuse us of?''

Guy grinned, and his eyes brightened to blue again. "Not either, rather more the opposite. Women have such an understanding of what a man wants that they can wrap any man of their choice around their little fingers. I have yet to meet the man who admits to any understanding of women. We are at your gentle mercies.''

"Fie on you for a fool, then." Penelope dismissed this platitude airily. "We are left to watch and wait and hope and so see more than a man who has but to act without thought to get what he wants. If Dolly says you nay, then it is because she is a senseless chit or you have behaved abominably. And I cannot feature you behaving in such a manner to a lady.''

Guy looked at Penelope standing there with the cool breeze whipping at her thin skirt and tossing the wisps of hair about her slender throat and heard the voice of reason. His eyes lifted to her steady gaze with renewed hope.

"If a villain like Graham can win a paragon such as yourself, my lady, then surely this poor fool can persuade a certain feckless lady to the same. Wish me luck, Penelope.''

"You don't need it," she scoffed, and minutes later she watched him ride away. She had no clearer notion as to where her husband might be than before, but a very odd emotion began to grow as Guy's words replayed in her thoughts. Could there possibly be any truth to them? Could Graham truly feel more than he showed for her?

Penelope tried the Reardons later that day after ascertaining Graham still had not returned to the Hall. Dolly gave no sign that Guy had approached her with his question, but she was so bubbling over with excitement at seeing Penelope that Penelope found it difficult to get a moment alone with Arthur or Henry to make her inquiries.

Noting their guest's grave demeanor in the face of his sister's cheerful prattle, Arthus finally sent Dolly to find his walking stick. When he was left alone with their guest, he nervously twisted his teacup in his hands while he sought for words.

"I do not mean to be rude, Lady Trevelyan, but when even Dolly's foolish stories can't bring a smile to your lips, I fear some weighty matter preys upon your thoughts. Is there aught that I can do to relieve the burden? Sometimes it simply helps to talk about it."

Penelope smiled gently at this ponderous speech. Arthur was only a few years older than herself, but these last years of living a life of danger had given him a more cautious attitude than most young gentlemen of his age. She liked him for his openness, however.

"I am simply wondering why I have not heard from Graham. I know it is foolish of me, and I know that he does not confide in you, but I sense there is something the two of you share. I thought, somehow, you or your brother might know what he is about."

Arthur's gray eyes looked troubled as he set aside his cup. "You are perceptive, my lady, but in this I will disappoint you. Graham hasn't been here since the rout, and I have no notion where he could have got to. I wish I could help. Where has he gone? Did he say?"

"Do not worry yourself. He has just gone up to London on business. It's a woman's prerogative to worry when she receives no love notes while her husband is away. He will be angry with me for mentioning it, so please say nothing. He has done this before and returned safely. There is no reason for concern now."

"But you are concerned and you do not strike me as quite the same flighty creature as my sister. You would not go up into the boughs over nothing. Have you spoke with Hamilton?"

That provided a good opening for a change of subject, and Penelope leapt at it eagerly. "Yes, of course, but I think his state of mind is no better than Dolly's." She laughed and leaned to refill his cup. Before long, she would be as good at acting as Graham. "I should think a man of his experience would be able to deal with infatuation a little more maturely, but I must admit to enjoying watching his arrogance knocked cock-a-hoop by someone with no experience at all."

Arthur chuckled and darted his sister a laughing look as she dashed back into the room, empty-handed. To Penelope he confided, "I see no hope for either of them. We will need to construct a circus tent when it comes time for the ceremonials."

Dolly threw back her red-blond curls and glared at her brother suspiciously as she came up to them. "I don't know what you have done with your walking stick. I have searched everywhere you said and it is nowhere to be found. I cannot imagine how you could have lost it. And what ceremonials are you chuckling about?"

Arthur calmly continued chewing on the sandwich he had just popped into his mouth and looked at his sister with a helpless shrug. Penelope smiled at this ploy and to appease Dolly, gestured toward the fireplace implements near Arthur's chair.

"If I am not greatly mistaken, you will find his stick in there. That is one of Graham's favorite habits. And we were speaking of Graham's birthday. I thought it would be great fun to make a proper ceremony of it, but Arthur has rather rudely suggested it ought to be a circus. If you would oblige me, let me have his cane and I will beat it about his head a few times."

Arthur continued chuckling as Dolly leapt for the weapon and mockingly set about applying it to his ears. Penelope departed soon after with no new information, but Arthur continued pondering her question long after she had gone.

Riding home, Penelope tried to convince herself this time it was no different than the last when Graham had disappeared for weeks. He had come home grouchy and irritable and limping worse than ever, but he had apparently been in no danger. She really should not worry about his abrupt methods, but her argument rang hollow even to herself.

This time it was different, she sensed it in every part of her being. Graham simply would not have disappeared without a word knowing how ill Augusta was and how she would worry, especially not after he had behaved so solicitously at the rout. They had almost reached an understanding that night. He would not risk it intentionally. Not answering her letter was the final straw. Graham would never have ignored her urgent plea. Never. Something was wrong. She just didn't know how to go about finding what it was.

When she returned to the Hall, she sent her maid scurrying to find her trunk and pounded on the door of Graham's chamber. When John appeared, she informed him boldly, "If Graham does not come home tonight, we are going to London on the morrow."

Chapter 33

CHADWELL raced the black stallion across the lengthening shadows of the hedgerow. Garbed in dark-tailed frock coat and pantaloons with only an occasional glimpse of white cravat, he blended in with the shadowy green of the overgrown briars and privet. His costume was not that of a country gentleman out for a leisurely ride, however, and if the sweat beading on his brow could be seen, even a casual observer would remark upon his exertion. He raced as if the devil were on his heels, or worse yet, ahead of him.

In Chadwell's mind the latter was the case. He had cursed himself for three times a fool when he first left London. By now, he had exhausted curses as well as himself and his mount. It could not be much farther. He would have to get there in time.

He should have known better. Why would he think Arthur had changed when none of the others had? Yet still he found himself disbelieving the note he had intercepted. What would Arthur have to gain by dealing with vicious cutthroats of the type who could be hired for murder? It made no sense. True, he was the younger son, but easy-going Henry would never throw him out or let him go penniless. Where was the motive?

Chadwell's weary brain could find none, but the writing had been Arthur's. There was no mistaking it. The man must be mad. Somewhere over the years his mind must have snapped. Damn, but why hadn't he finished for him when he had the chance? And now Penelope would pay for his failure.

He couldn't let it happen. Arthur had to be stopped.

It was a trap. He sensed it, but he had no time to figure it out. Arthur couldn't have planned on his intercepting the note; he knew nothing of Chadwell. He must be planning to lure Graham out by using Penelope as bait. That was the only logic he could follow.

His mind cried out in anguish at the urgent plea of Penelope's letter. How could Arthur dare to mistreat an innocent like that? What was he thinking? He must be going as mad as Arthur. This was the same man who had stood over the twisted wreck of the phaeton knowing full well somewhere among the remains lay one of his friends, injured and probably dying, and had walked away. Walked away and ordered the others to do the same. He could not believe even the perverted DeVere could be so evil. What would have happened had they known Graham lay among those ruins instead of Guy? Would it have been different if Graham had made himself known? Could all of this have been prevented if Graham could have just summoned a loud moan from among the rocks where he had been thrown?

That agonizing question had worn itself thin long ago, but it came back with greater clarity now, beating like a violent refrain of drums in his head as he neared his destination. Penelope's life was more important than the dead and gone, but it still hinged on an action that had happened years ago. God, this was not fair. Don't let Penelope pay for the sins of others.

Just let Penelope live. He would not ask for more. Her letter had mentioned nothing of where she was or how she was being treated, but the frantic tone of her words rang in his head just as if Penelope had spoken them. Her perfect, ladylike writing could have been written by any female, but not those words. Those were Penelope's cries of fear and loneliness, he would recognize them anywhere. Only Penelope could manage to say so much in so little, write gentle, restrained language that pierced the heart without sentimentality. She should have taken up writing books. He would tell her that when he saw her again.

Because he would see her. He would find her. Arthur's note had made it evident where they had taken her. He knew these fields and valleys like a second hand. He knew where Arthur would hide her. He just had to get there before any harm was done.

In the darkness he did not see the thin wire stretched between the two trees marking the beginning of the lane. He knew only that the path to Penelope lay ahead of him, and he increased his pace. Had he been a shorter man, the wire would have cut across his throat. As it was, it caught him across the chest and he flew backward over the stallion's rump, his head coming down with a resounding crash upon the rocky field.

The man in the shadows smiled to himself at the sound, but this momentary aberration quickly turned to a frown when he stepped from the bushes to examine the prone figure on the ground. He had not expected Chadwell to answer Penelope's plea.

Kicking at the body sprawled before him, he was forced to reconsider his plan. Revenge on Chadwell was very well and good, but now he knew it was actually Graham who was his enemy. And as if knowing his role had been discovered, Graham had taken to hiding in the protection of that Gothic town house of his. He had thought the carefully forged note from Penelope would have brought him out.

Chadwell moaned and the man scowled. He had managed to intercept that one letter from Penelope with the help of one of Graham's kitchen maids, but that trick wouldn't work again. The maid had been fired, and he couldn't rely on the lady staying in the country forever. With Chadwell out of the way Graham would have to come forward, but only if his lady were truly abducted. A forgery wouldn't succeed a second time. It would have to be the real thing.

Anticipation began to flow in his veins. These last years of avoiding trouble had been dull beyond belief, even with the war to add its variety of excitements. He enjoyed a challenge, and this one stood to gain him freedom. No one but Graham would suspect him. With Graham out of the way he could do anything he pleased.

With a sardonic smile he moved to recover his horse. Getting Chadwell on the beast would be a chore, but it should be amusing to imagine the American's reaction when he woke to discover his surroundings. He would wish he had stayed in his own country to face the entire British army.

The wide street with its quietly elegant mansions was relatively empty as the carriage pulled through the gates to the Trevelyan town house. Most of the occupants of these houses had retired to their country estates for the summer, but they would be soon returning for the Little Season. Penelope paid little heed to the chimney sweep on the neighboring roof or the window washer frantically rubbing the panes across the way. Her thoughts were entirely on the reaction of the man dwelling inside the dark house when she appeared on his doorstep.

Would he be angry? She was interfering with his affairs, and he had made it plain that he did not want her involved. Of course he would be angry, but she could not tolerate the silence and suspense and suspicion any longer. She had to know where she stood in his scheme of things.

Guy's words of the day before had haunted her thoughts all night. What had he meant when he had said Graham would never have married a mousy schoolteacher? Graham had married her because of her love for children, and she certainly wasn't one of the world's greatest beauties. That made her close enough to a mousy schoolteacher in her own eyes. Was Guy telling her that Graham saw her in a different light? That did not make sense. Graham had been an invalid and practically a hermit and he had married her for Alexandra's sake and because she was not afraid of him. How could that be a pretense as Guy hinted? She could think of no earthly reason why Graham would have married her elsewhere.

And what pretense could Graham be hiding behind? She knew he was involved in something here in London. She suspected it had something to do with Chadwell and his activities on the other end of town, but she could not fathom what. There could be some pretense involved in that, but it should have naught to do with her. Guy was getting as fanciful as Dolly. Next, he would be patting the gargoyles on the head and calling them by name.

Penelope smiled up at the ugly creatures guarding the doors. They would prevent evil from entering the house, no doubt. It was a wonder they did not keep everyone from entering the house. As a servant dashed to open the door for her, she stepped eagerly over the threshold.

She knew immediately that Graham was not here. Despite John at her side, the driver with her bags, and the footman who had scurried from the back, she knew the house was empty. It echoed hollow in her ears as the foyer filled with the sounds of footsteps. Shadows flickered on the ceilings from the lamps hastily lit in the sconces on the wall. Heavy draperies hid the windows and the covered furniture remained untouched from when they had left last June. She turned her feet toward the stairs, but she knew Graham would not be there.

Minutes later as her maid laid out clean clothes and poured warm water in the basin, John knocked at her door to tell Penelope what she already sensed. Graham had come and gone.

"And Mr. Chadwell? Has he been here?" Nervously she kept her eyes on the gloves she was removing rather than John's face.

Something flickered hesitantly behind the man's eyes, but he apparently decided against revealing it. Solemnly he answered, "He's gone, too, milady. They ain't been seen since your letter arrived the maid says."

Penelope's gaze jerked back up to John's. "Then he received it. Could something have happened on the road between here and Hampshire?"

John shrugged his narrow shoulders. "There could have been an accident, milady. They say as he took that big stallion of his and left in a tearing hurry, but

clear, but what was this of being held against her will? Hands shaking, Penelope read the letter again, slowly scanning the words and feeling the impact Graham must have suffered as he read them. How could someone be so cruel, and why? Why would anyone want to make Graham think she had been abducted?

Sudden calm logic descended like a peaceful blanket, smothering all else. Chadwell would know. She had helped him when he needed it. He would help her. Nell would know where to find him. He might even be with her. All she had to do was find Nell. For that, she would need someone familiar with the East End.

Pippin. Pippin knew Chadwell. Pippin had carried his messages before. Pippin might even know Nell.

Without further thought Penelope refolded the letter and clinging to it tightly, turned her slippered feet in the direction of the stables.

Pippin watched her approach with astonishment, but he did not move from the side of the large yellow mongrel to which he clung. Penelope observed the ugly beast with amusement and stopped to scratch behind its ears.

"Where did you find him?"

" 'E followed me 'ere, 'e did," Pippin answered warily. The master had said nothing about his pet, but he probably hadn't even noticed it. The missus noticed everything.

"What do you find to feed him?" The dog's limpid eyes watched Penelope with such gratitude that she had to smile.

"There's a bloke in the kitchen what 'elps me to find scraps. 'E don't eat much, and 'e's a good dog. 'E guards the 'ouse, 'e does. Ain't no bloomin' thief goin' to get in 'ere."

"Well then, he certainly deserves his dinner, doesn't he? But dogs take a lot of care. You will have to bathe him and brush him to keep away the fleas and dirt. Will you do that?"

Reassured that the pet was his to keep, Pippin would agree to anything. He nodded eagerly. "Yes, mum. I been doin' that. One of 'em grooms, 'e been teachin' me. I do the same for Mate 'ere as 'e does for 'em 'orses.''

"Mate?"

"That's what 'is lordship calls me," Pippin answered proudly. "And 'at's what me Mate is. So's I thought if it's good 'nough for me, it's good 'nough for 'im.''

Penelope would have laughed but for this mention of Graham. Anxiously, she inquired, "When did you see his lordship, Pippin?"

The boy shrugged. "I don' know. 'E comes and 'e goes. Few days back, I reckon."

"And Mr. Chadwell? Have you seen him?"

The boy looked at her suspiciously. " 'Course. Ain't I supposed to?"

That was a curious question, but Penelope didn't linger long over it. "I need to find Mr. Chadwell. It's very important, Pippin. Do you think you could help me find him?"

He brightened momentarily, then frowned. "I can go arsk Nell, but 'is lordship said you ain't ever to go back there again. Me and Mate will go. 'E's got a good sniffer. 'E'll sniff 'im out in no time.''

Penelope dug her fingers into the dog's thick skin as her heart raced. "I need to talk to Nell if you can't find him. Can you bring her back here?"

The wariness returned to the boy's eyes, but he nodded slowly. Nell wouldn't like it, but he'd lay his life down for the lady if necessary. "I'll bring 'er. 'Ow's Goldie? 'Ave you seen 'er?"

Penelope forced herself to relax slightly. "Just a few days ago. She's doing beautifully. She had on the prettiest pink dress, and she's laughing and making noises that sound just like she's talking. We'll go to see her sometime, if you like."

"Yes, mum, milady. I'd like that. Me and Mate better gets goin'. It gets dark early now."

"You'll take the carriage. I'll not have you walking those streets alone. Let me call John."

John appeared ready to protest when commanded to seek out Chadwell's mistress with Pippin's help, but he thought better of it. He knew the men to call on to lead a search of the countryside, but they could not begin until daylight. Searching the East End had occurred to him, but he had no familiarity with those streets. The boy was better than nothing.

Penelope watched them go with trepidation. She feared to send them where she could not go herself, but she had little choice. She wished she had brought an army of footmen with her, but it had not occurred to her that she would need the staff. Perhaps she should have sent the groom and the one footman in the house. She would be safe enough alone in the mansion, but it was too late now.

She turned and walked back toward the house. The lone figure standing in the shadows inside the gate watched her progress through narrowed eyes. If Graham were in there, he would never succeed in capturing her quietly. Curse his luck that she had come now.

But something in the snatches of conversation he had caught caused him to suspect she was alone in the house. If Graham had already escaped his lair, it was all the more important to act quickly.

He watched as an upstairs drapery became illumined from within, then traced the path of the roofline near the window. Every house in London had a means of reaching the roof so a man might climb up to clean the innumerable chimneys. This one was no exception. Smiling to himself, he located the ledge that would give him access to that room.

Lady Trevelyan was in for a bit of a surprise.

Penelope gasped as the sweet smelling fumes filled her mouth and nostrils. Her eyes stung and her mouth burned and she struggled to rouse herself from sleep, but the gagging, noxious fumes suffocated every breath, and soon, she floated through a sea of darkness.

The dark figure hovering above her released the rag from her face. The substance was dangerous, not to mention volatile, but he had used it successfully before. Sometimes it was very convenient to render a victim senseless, and it was remarkably easy to do after they had their tumble in bed with one of his girls. Out like a light they would be, for as long as he needed it to empty their pockets or their houses or rifle their offices. Then they would wake and blame it on a surfeit of wine and women.

He looked down on Penelope's slender form with contempt. She had not changed out of her dark poplin traveling gown. Obviously she expected the others back soon and intended to wait up for them. Exhaustion had made dark semi-circles beneath her eyes, and her face looked pale and weary even in sleep. He had been known to bring several of his girls to the house like this, and by the time they woke, they were fully ruined, but this one would be more trouble than she was worth. He had other plans for her.

Getting her out of here would be easy. The secret passages and hiding places had been sources of great amusement since they were boys. The one to the street was always kept locked from the outside, but from in here it would provide no difficulty. Graham really should have blocked all those old tunnels long ago. It made things much too easy.

Swinging Penelope into his arms, he headed for Graham's chambers.

Chapter 34

THE cold penetrated her senses first. She shivered, then reflexively, she gasped for air. It came damp and moldy but clean of noxious fumes. She gasped again, and a warm, anxious voice whispered in her ear.

"Penny! Thank God, Penny. Wake up."

Strong arms lifted her, shaking her slightly, and her eyes fluttered. The masculine voice was so familiar, so anxious and tinged with fear, that she wanted to reach out and reassure its owner, but her arms wouldn't quite function. She felt funny all over, and her stomach was queasy. She shivered again, and he drew her into his lap. Her head rested on a broad shoulder, and she felt the coat wrapped around her, trapping the heat of his chest next to her. It felt good, and she snuggled closer, her hand instinctively rising to curl against the brocade of his waistcoat. Hard, masculine thighs warmed her bottom, and she squirmed against them, seeking a more comfortable position.

This time, a hint of laughter laced his voice. "Penny, my dear, sweet Penny, I love you dearly, I do, but if you do not soon wake I will be forced to take advantage of your helplessness. I am a starving man and you are a wickedly attractive woman and even these unfortunate circumstances cannot dampen my ardor."

His words caused sufficient clamor of alarm in her brain to wake her to the truth of them. Through his tight trousers and her thin gown she could feel the full length of his maleness pressing against her. The sensation was not unpleasant, but with wakefulness came awareness and her eyes flew open.

"Clifton!" The dim light of this damp chamber was sufficient to note disheveled dark curls and laughing eyes. Something besides laughter lurked behind those golden depths, but she could not continue staring into them. Touching the narrow scar marring his cheekbone and stopping dangerously near his eye, she slid uncertainly from his lap.

Her slippered feet touched the cold, damp floor, and her glance wavered to take in her surroundings. Chadwell rose from the narrow bench, supporting her with his arm as she absorbed the desolation of their plight.

"Where are we?" she whispered weakly, not backing away from the safety of his closeness as she stared at the rough rock walls all around them. The cubicle could be no bigger than a tall man in either length or width, and her head turned fearfully upward toward the source of light. An iron grate exposed them to the elements, and the morning sun sent shadows down the towering walls.

He answered her questioning gaze rather than her words. "He's rigged some type of winch outside and lowered you in a basket. I thought you might be safer with me, and I lifted you out. From the feel of my head, I think he just dropped me down."

"Who?" Growing alarm gradually erased the last vestige of ether, and she turned to stare up at Chadwell.

"You did not see him, either?" He searched her face, his heart tearing at the sight of her fear.

"I . . . I must have fallen asleep." She searched her memory, and the pain of Graham's disappearance returned. "Something woke me, but they'd covered my face with a rag. I don't remember anything else."

Chadwell cursed and stared up at the square of light, his jaw tensing at the unfairness of it all. He had the woman of his choice in his arms, but little hope for the future. He couldn't let her know that, though. He didn't want her to panic.

"They seem to have got things a bit backward. I came out here looking for you, but you were a little tardy in arriving." His hand slid from her shoulder down her arm. He had already explored their prison for exits. There were none. It would be pleasant to forget their plight for a while, and Penelope presented a temptation he had ever found hard to resist.

Penelope stepped away and turned to face him, her expression one of puzzlement. "I thought Graham was the one who went after me. I found the letter in the library in town. It was a forgery. They must have taken the letter I mailed from Hampshire and copied parts of it. But Graham has disappeared, too. Did he send you after me?"

The words were on the tip of his tongue right then, but as Chadwell shook his head in denial, Penelope's face brightened in excitement, and she caught his hand with renewed hope.

"You got the letter first? Then that means Graham has escaped them. Don't you see? That letter was meant to bring Graham out from wherever he is hiding, but if it never reached him, then he is still safe. John and Pippin will discover I am gone soon enough and they will send everyone out looking for us, and Graham will know what to do when he hears of it. Do you know where he is?"

Chadwell opened his mouth, closed it, then shook his head mutely. How could he destroy her hopes? He had no idea what the fates had in store for them. Let her hope a little while longer.

"I know nothing other than that letter. I should not have acted so hastily, but your words were very effective." He shrugged apologetically.

Remembering how he'd run to rescue Nell, Penelope flushed a little. "Is it the same man, do you think? The one that abducted Nell?"

"I wouldn't be surprised if he had a hand in it. I had just found out some very ugly things about him when your letter came. I'd thought he meant to hold you until he got away, but I'm afraid there may be a little more to it than that."

"But Graham knows about it, doesn't he? He can go to the authorities when he discovers us missing."

Tiredly Chadwell ran his hand through his hair. He

disliked this business of deceiving her, but he could see no good coming of telling the truth. "It will do no good to worry, Penelope. There is some bread and cheese in that basket under the bench. It seems we were not meant to starve, in any case. Why don't we have a bite to eat instead of trying to puzzle this out on empty stomachs?"

Brought back to the realization of their situation, Penelope looked around with growing dismay. They had only the narrow bench to sit or lie upon. A tin pitcher and cup hung on a piece of wood jammed between the rocks, presumably holding their supply of water, but there was no basin for washing. Worst of all, there seemed nothing suitable for a chamber pot, and she suddenly discovered this to be her most pressing need.

"Is there no way out of here?" she whispered in anguish, her gaze tracing the cold stone walls for any sign of a door.

Not understanding her sudden change in emotion, Chadwell reached out to a jagged protuberance of one rock and tried to shake it. "Solid, Penny. I have gone over them all. There used to be an old keep here. This would have been part of the dungeon. From what I understand of the times, we are fortunate not to find a skeleton. Our ancestors tended to be a murderous lot."

"Man has not changed so very much then, has he?" She shivered and crossed her arms beneath her breasts, clutching at her elbows. "I am glad they did not put us in separate chambers, but it is going to be a trifle inconvenient. How long have you been down here?"

Dimly Chadwell began to perceive her problem stemmed from his presence. He leaned against the wall farthest from her and tried to relieve her fears. "Not long enough to be so desperate as to take a lady against her will, Penelope. I was only jesting earlier, surely you know that."

Wry humor twisted her lips as she looked up into Chadwell's handsome face. He really did have quite a devastating countenance, but rape or seduction had not been the first thing on her mind. Perhaps it should have been, but she just could not believe Chadwell guilty of the crimes she had tried to pin to him.

"I should hope you were jesting, for I fear I would find any attempt at lovemaking a most uncomfortable experience despite your best efforts. If you don't mind my foolishness, have you been here long enough to discover where they hide the water closet?"

At the wry look on his modest Penelope's face, Chadwell erupted with laughter. She bore it with good humor, however, struggling to keep her own laughter from joining his. She feared hers might have a trace of hysteria in it.

Recovering quickly, Chadwell bent to retrieve the basket under the bench. "I fear I have not been very polite to our hosts. I have been making profane use of their dinnerware in return for their hospitality. Perhaps now that a lady resides here, they will be a little more considerate in their facilities."

The basket contained a long loaf of bread and a large bowl of cheese. "These came down with you last night. They haven't varied the fare, but they have increased it." He dumped the cheese into the basket and offered her the bowl. "Shall I turn my back and sing loudly?"

Penelope stared at the bowl in dismay as she realized what he meant. Never had she been reduced to such circumstances, and crimson flushed her cheeks as she gingerly accepted the bowl. "Very loudly, please," she replied meekly. "I am most uncomfortable."

Chadwell gave her a sympathetic grin and turned his back. Gallantly he launched into a booming rendition of "Ach, Johnny, I hardly knew ye," complete with all the melodramatics of voice and expression. Penelope's shoulders were shaking with laughter by the time she finished, and tears were running down her cheeks.

Her feminine voice joined the final refrain with such pathos that Chadwell's cracked with laughter. When she touched his arm, he turned and grabbed her waist.

"One good Gaelic ballad deserves another. How are you at 'Lord Kildare, My Love'?"

Understanding his need, Penelope lifted her voice as loudly as she could in the first lines of the stanza, while keeping her back to the impromptu chamber pot. Her voice was not so loud as his, and her cheeks remained flushed when Chadwell returned to her side to join the refrain with his smooth baritone.

Her giggles brought the serenade to an end, and Chadwell sent their skylight a hopeful look. "Don't you think when all the dogs in the neighborhood begin howling that someone might come investigate?"

"Either that, or fear the dead are walking and stay away." Penelope lifted the pitcher from the wall and examined its contents. "Is there any chance that someone might hear us if we keep up a continual cacophony?"

"Very little, I fear, unless they are looking for us. In which case we would hear them first. I know this place well. It is unfit for anything but rock collectors, and there are not too many of them hereabouts." Chadwell held out the tin cup so Penelope could pour a little water in it. He then produced a flask from his coat pocket and poured a generous dollop into the water. "That should warm you up a tad." He handed her the concoction.

Penelope discovered she was not only starving, but dying of thirst. It was amazing how being deprived of something made it suddenly more desirable. She settled herself on the narrow bench and sipped delicately of the brandied water before handing it to Graham's cousin. She broke off a portion of bread and puzzled over the cheese until Chadwell produced a pocketknife and neatly sliced her a slab.

"I regret the meagerness of the refreshments, my lady. Had you warned me of your impending visit, I would certainly have ordered something more suitable." Chadwell pushed the basket to sit between them and settled himself on the other end of the bench.

"If you have drunk very much of this stuff, I can

understand how you manage to be so abominably cheerful. Will it hold out until they come for us?''

Chadwell peered solemnly into the nearly empty cup. "Not at this rate. We will have to send the butler into the wine cellar. Where has that fellow got to, anyway?''

Penelope laughed at his nonsense and leaned back against the hard wall, staring up to the distant blue of the sky. Now that the day was beginning to warm outside, it did not feel so bad in here. She refused to think about the night. The man beside her strived hard to remain a gentleman, but the circumstances made everything exceedingly difficult. She kept remembering the reassuring strength of his embrace, and she had difficulty keeping her gaze from straying to the dark fur of his chest just barely visible where his shirt fell open at the throat. She still wore his coat around her shoulders, and his cravat lay loose and untied against his waistcoat. Never one for formality, Chadwell had abandoned any pretense of it here.

At her silence, Clifton turned to lift a quizzical eyebrow at her. "Your thoughts?''

Penelope turned her head just enough to see the dark stubble on his chin and the tender line of his mouth. His upper lip had a firm, chiseled look to it, but there was a sensuousness to the rounding of the lower that make it difficult to turn her gaze away. She got only as far as the dent in his square jaw and sighed. "Do you really think we will escape in time?''

Chadwell touched a finger to her chin and lifted it to meet his gaze. "Did I not, I would not be spending my last hours chivalrously resisting your charms, my lady.''

In this light his eyes were a gleaming amber, and she could not tear away from their hold. She felt his desire in the way his fingers molded to her jaw, saw it in the smoldering depths of his eyes, and knew it met his match in her own.

"Don't, Cliff. You are too much like Graham," she whispered.

"Am I?" He did not seem surprised at her words,

and he did not release her. His fingers smoothed the soft satin of her cheek and drifted down the line of her jaw to her throat. "In what way?"

Penelope jerked her head away and took a hasty gulp of their doctored water. "In every way, except that you are an incurable rake and I must believe Graham is a faithful husband."

"Must believe? Does that mean there are some doubts?" Regretfully Chadwell returned his hand to the task of dismantling his crust of bread.

"I don't know. He is so . . . enigmatic, sometimes. I had hoped we were coming closer to some understanding, but then he hied himself off to London as soon as I turned my back. I could understand if he had left some message, some word when he knew how worried I was about Augusta, but he was so eager to depart that even his servant didn't know where he was."

"How is Augusta? I am sorry I did not ask earlier. Other thoughts took precedence, I'm afraid."

Penelope could not put her tongue around the words. Any attempt to do so would reduce her to tears. She posed the answer lightly. "If only the good die young, she has gone to join all the other sinners."

To hell with good intentions. Chadwell set the basket on the floor and reached to gather Penelope into his arms. When he held her cheek securely against his shoulder, he murmured, "You know better than that. They didn't come any younger than Augusta. I'm sorry, Penny. Someone should have been with you."

He offered her all the comfort she had longed for, the gentle, understanding words, the security of his embrace, the knowledge that someone cared, and she wasn't alone. It would be so easy to take what Cliff offered, but she knew the difference between right and wrong, and this was wrong. Graham might never offer her the love she needed, but he was her husband, and she owed him her loyalty. Reluctantly she disentangled herself.

"It's all right. Adelaide and Brian were there. I just wish I knew what happened to Graham. Let us talk of

LOVE FOREVER AFTER • 363

something else. I have always wondered what America would be like. Educate me. Are the towns very much like ours?'' Clutching her arms together to keep from shivering with her need for Clifton's hold, Penelope stared at the far wall rather than her companion.

Chadwell made a sound of angry irritation. Standing up, he paced the few steps from wall to wall. He pounded a fist into his palm and seemed to choke on the words swelling up in his throat but freezing on his tongue. Penelope stared up at him wide-eyed, wondering what it was she had said.

He finally turned and leaning over her, placed his hands on either side of her head, trapping her against the wall. The muscle in his jaw worked furiously, and it was some time before he could calm himself enough to speak.

''Penny, I have so greatly wronged you already, don't ask me to lie to you any more. I want to make things right, but I don't know how to any longer. Everything I can do will only make things worse. This must be God's revenge, trapping me in a room with no escape with the woman I want more than life itself and no means of persuading her into my arms without making her hate me. What am I to do, Penelope?''

His desperation frightened her. She stared up at him without understanding, knowing only the strength of the arms concealed by loose linen and the heat reflecting from his body so close to hers. She felt only the urge to comfort, to touch his square jaw until he smiled again, to return things to normal. His intensity was beyond her comprehension.

''I am married to your cousin, Cliff. You ought not to be saying these things to me,'' she finally whispered. Chadwell's magnetism had ever been her downfall, but she had to resist. A man like Chadwell would scarcely look twice at her had they been on a dance floor with crowds of elegant people. He spoke only out of loneliness and some desperation she could not understand.

Her sensible words deflected his anger, and Chadwell collapsed beside her on the bench. Her constant he's always got his cards about him. Looks to me like someone would have let us know if they found him.''

"Thieves could have picked his pockets. Or he could have taken one of his shortcuts across the fields and no one's found him yet. We'll have to hunt everywhere.''

"Yes, milady." He didn't mention that this was the season for men to be out in their fields and that hiding a man the size of Graham would be no easy task between here and Hampshire. Had they been in Cornwall or on the moors, perhaps . . . John shook his head and set off to man a search.

A light repast was prepared for her supper, but Penelope had no stomach for it. She left it on the table and carried a candle to Graham's chamber. Perhaps he had left some evidence of where he had gone.

Finding nothing there but the massive bed they had never shared, Penelope hurried on to the library, avoiding the memories. Memories made her eyes sting and brought a galloping rush of fear to her chest. Nothing could have happened to Graham. Not Graham. He had survived that terrible accident. He could not be brought down by some petty thief. She would not believe it. They would find him, and shortly she would be in his arms again. They had a whole life ahead of them. There would be more children. The nursery would be full of laughter, and Graham would laugh with them. She refused to believe anything else.

The library had its own set of painful memories, but they all fled the instant Penelope laid eyes upon the letter lying open on the table. The paper was much the same as she had used to write to Graham. She had not used the Stanhope stationery but the few precious pieces of blank vellum she had hoarded in her desk at the cottage. Even the writing looked like hers, although a little heavier. She had never learned to press firmly on the nib. Some of the words were even the same—whole sentences, in fact. She stared at the letter in disbelief. It was hers, but not hers. How could that be?

Her plea for Graham's presence stood out loud and

proximity would drive him to madness if he did not find a solution. They could die this day, and it would be with all these lies on his head. Worse, he could die alone, and she would be left to sort out his various treacheries after he was gone. What in *hell* was he going to do to make her understand?

Resting his shoulders against the wall, he closed his eyes and crossed his arms across his chest. "Then I won't say these things to you. Let me tell you a story-book tale instead."

"Not a bedtime story, I trust." Relieved that he chose to be reasonable, Penelope replied with mockery.

Chadwell twisted his head and peered at her skeptically through one barely opened eye. "Don't laugh. By the time the sun sets you will be glad enough for my services to keep you warm. Now be a good girl and listen for a change. I promise not to put you to sleep."

That properly put her in her place, and Penelope closed her mouth. She prayed Graham would come for her soon. She very much feared Chadwell had the right of it, and she dreaded finding out.

When she made no answer, he nodded and closed his eye again. "Very good. Now, once upon a time there was a foolish young prince who thought he owned the world. Because he was so arrogant and full of himself, other foolish young men thought he must be important, and thus they did their best to emulate him. The young prince was too arrogant to even notice; he simply accepted it that if he raced phaetons, or gambled on horses, or joined a particular club, his subjects would, too. When he decided to move onto other pursuits, he assumed his subjects would do the same. He never noticed nor cared it they did not."

Somewhere during this prelude, Chadwell opened his eyes and he now glared at the far wall. "When the princeling eventually grew bored with his idle pursuits, he decided it was time to wed, and he chose a young princess whose beauty and charms momentarily pleased him. While he was occupied playing house with his new wife, his latest plaything, his subjects continued to carouse and grow more unruly. One in particular whom he knew to be a troublemaker grew rather demanding upon the kingdom's coffers until the prince cut him off without another farthing.''

Penelope kept silent, searching for the meaning she knew Chadwell hid behind his tale. She suspected he talked of himself since she did not think he was of a type to speak so unkindly of another behind his back, but he might speak so of Graham if they had once been close.

When she made no comment, Chadwell rose restlessly and began to test the rocky walls for footholds or fingerholds. He had already spent hours searching fruitlessly for some escape, but Penelope's presence made it imperative that he find one before nightfall. If their captor was the one he thought, he could not believe he would harm Penelope, but he had no desire to find out, either. He continued to speak as he methodically tested every crack and crevice.

''By this time the prince had grown bored with escorting his young princess from ball to ball, and he began looking for other challenges. His old friends seemed to be still involved with what he considered childish activities, so he continued to ignore them. He knew the troublemaker had fallen in with a dangerous lot, but he had been destined for such a fate from birth. He was old enough to take care of himself and the prince felt no responsibility for putting an end to his troublesome career. He warned his old friend of the dangers ahead and went about his own business.

''By now, the young couple knew they were to be blessed with a child, and the prince determined he would settle down and learn to be a proper husband and father and take up the responsibility of commanding his kingdom, a pastime he had hitherto neglected. The princess, being very young, resented this change from their social whirl, but with the child coming, she had little choice in the matter.''

He had to be talking of Graham and his wife. It was not the story she had heard from society, but then, what would society know of private grievances between the young couple? It saddened Penelope to think people blessed with so much could be so selfish as to spoil it all, but they might have learned better had Marilee lived. Surely Alexandra would have taught them both the delights of parenthood with time. But if the prince of this tale was Graham, where did Chadwell fit in? As the troublemaker? That seemed very likely, and she stared at his broad back with growing dismay.

"The prince threw himself into his latest challenge, finding it very much to his liking. He spent his days learning the management of his modest kingdom and his nights discussing plans and changes with his father, who was too ill to continue an active interest. The princess must have felt very left out, but the prince was too busy to notice."

Penelope frowned slightly. Chadwell was being terribly harsh on Graham. Marilee could have shown an interest in the estate and Graham would more than likely have been delighted to teach her. She wondered how much more of this tale was slanted equally harshly, and she started to speak, but Chadwell's movements prevented her.

She stared at his right hand as he found a small hole to grab at. The smallest finger stood out at an odd angle when he used it to grab the rock. It did not seem to function in coordination with the others. Why had she never noticed that before?

Perhaps because she had avoided looking at him at all. He made her uneasy and instead of confronting her fears, she avoided them, always looking away when he turned in her direction. As he continued to speak with his back turned toward her, she felt safe in observing him carefully. She was a coward, no doubt, but she could not tear her gaze away.

"The child was born with much pomp and ceremony, and for a while, everything seemed to be merry again. But then, one day, the prince received word that one of his old friends was in dire trouble. Heedless of the harm he could bring on his small family, the prince galloped off to the rescue, proving to himself, if no one else, that he had not grown old and stale. With much flourish and triumph, he carried his friend back to the kingdom to be kept safe and nursed back to health, although both he and his friend made many enemies with this act.''

Penelope knew this part of the story, although Chadwell evidently wasn't aware of the fact. Instead of concentrating on his mocking words, she watched his hands with growing fascination. He had succeeded in finding a toehold and now groped higher up the wall, where the sunlight reached. She could see now that he had some difficulty gripping with the right fingers, but he did not let the defect deter him. The sunlight revealed a thin white scar across the back of his hand, and unconsciously, she began to knead at her own hand while her thoughts groped to follow his words and search for an elusive memory at the same time.

''The arrogant prince thought he had restored his kingdom to peace until the night he came home to find his wife weeping her heart out and his friend, flown.

''Even then, the shallow cad thought things would return to normal if he pretended nothing was wrong. That was his undoing. The next night, when he returned home, it was to find the princess flown after his friend.''

Chadwell gave up the futile search for another handhold and dropped to the ground. He turned to find Penelope's gaze fixed on him with a fearful fascination, but determined to complete what he had set out to do, he did not end his tale there.

Dropping down to the bench beside her, he caught up her hand and began to play with the simple wedding band upon her finger.

''That was when the prince learned a kingdom could be lost or stolen as easily as it can be gained. He ran after her, hoping to find the glass slipper, I suppose. He caught up with her, but the princess steadfastly refused his offers. In his fury the prince continued driving the pumpkin onward instead of forcing them to go back. His mind was on the betrayal in his own ranks and not the anarchy that reined in his kingdom. It was raining. The night was black. He had no inkling of the ambush planned until the villains rode out of the bushes with murderous intent.''

Chadwell's right hand closed over Penelope's, squeezing tightly as the words seemed ripped from his throat with the greatest effort. Penny rubbed thoughtfully at the jagged scar marring the brown skin of his hand.

''They had planned this meeting well, timing it just as the carriage rode over a narrow bridge. They deliberately fired a gun in the air, panicking the racing horses. The prince might have handled them under better circumstances, but it was pouring rain, the bridge was narrow and slippery, and a light phaeton was the worst possible carriage for such a night. He tried to keep the terrified beasts on the road and aiming at the villains blocking the bridge, but even as he brought the horses under control, a wheel hit a loose plank and all was lost. At that speed the phaeton flew into the air and down the steep embankment to the rocks below, just as they had planned, although they most certainly thought it was the prince's informing friend and not himself that they destroyed.''

The strangled tone of Chadwell's voice told Penelope more than she wanted to know. She stared up at the white line marring his beard-stubbled jaw, her eyes growing round as a painful ache took root in her stomach. Unconsciously her hand moved to hold tightly to his linen-covered arm, as if to prevent him from saying what would follow next.

Trapped by his own words, Chadwell plodded doggedly forward. ''The prince must have been knocked unconscious at first, but the rain pouring down woke him. He heard the voices of the villains who had sent him over the bridge, but he could not hear his wife. He tried to call out but could not. He felt as if he were merely a ghost hovering over the scene, watching the mortals sliding down the embankment or standing on the edge, calling to each other as they examined the wreckage, searching to be certain their victim would never speak out again. In the dark and the rain and the mud, they did not search very hard, and they did not see the prince hidden beneath the carriage, but he could hear them, and he knew them by their voices. The troublemaker was not among them as he had surmised, but a man he had thought his friend rode up in a carriage directly afterward and ordered them all to leave. Instead of coming down to help, to look for the injured, or sending for help, he told them to forget it and get out before someone came along.''

The pain was still there. After all these years, the pain of that betrayal rang loud and clear, and Penelope nearly wept. She didn't understand how or why. She couldn't put her knowledge into logic or reason, but she knew it as surely as she knew the color of his eyes. The prince and the man beside her were one and the same—and they both were Graham.

Chapter 35

"DON'T," Penelope whispered. "Don't tell me any more. I know what happens. Remembering will not change it. Grief will not bring her back. Pray she is happy now, love her daughter, and know that she would want you to go on with your life."

Golden eyes turned to stare down into hers for the first time since the story began. His hand came up to smooth her cheek, to brush a tendril of hair from her face. Penelope stared back at him, fear clawing at her insides. She did not know how he had accomplished it. She did not understand why he had done it, but now that her eyes were open, she knew she had discovered the truth. The thin scar along Chadwell's cheek skirted the eye that Graham had kept patched, but the mark was in the same place. It stopped short of his lips, and she remembered the nights when she had wondered how he had kissed her so fully in the darkness when he could not during the day. Explanations for many little things flooded her mind, but she shoved them all aside to answer the hurt in his eyes. Her hand lifted to trace the scar along his cheek.

"I know it is presumptuous of me, but I love you. Could you not give my love a chance to ease the pain, if only just a little?"

He did not try to find out how much she understood, or try to explain himself at all. His need was much greater than words and cried out for the love she offered with just her look and the touch of her fingertips. Wonderingly his hand continued to explore, tracing the soft line of her cheek, sinking into the thickness of her disheveled tresses. The sun had reached its zenith and poured down on them with a benevolent light as they looked and touched as they had never been allowed before.

"You do not know what you say, my love. You have the power to ease my pain, to lighten my days and nights, to make me whole again, but I have only treachery and deceit to offer you in return."

Despite his words he could not keep from touching. Terrified he would make her fear him, he went slowly, but he could not stop. Even as his lips formed the words, they bent to brush along her lovely brow. Such a high, serene brow she had, with all the pureness of innocence upon it.

"No more. No more deceit. If we ever get out of here, we will start anew. Can't we?" Penelope pleaded with him as his kisses worked their magic. She could no longer think but only respond to the need swelling up between them.

He had taken away her hopes of rescue. There was naught else they could do but wait for their captor to return. What difference did it make now if he should spend his last hours in the arms of a woman he had wronged? He just hoped she understood when the time came.

Gently Graham covered her lips with his, and the piercing pleasure of that connection erased all else. He pulled Penelope into his arms and her hands slid behind his neck and all further decision fled from them.

Penelope clung desperately to the strength of Graham's shoulders as his tongue plundered her mouth and aroused her to aching sensations she could not name nor think to control. He eased her into his lap so his hand could roam freely, cupping her breast while his kiss deepened to steal her breath away. That wasn't enough, and wantonly, she teased his tongue with hers, and her hand strayed to find the fastenings of his shirt.

Her fingers lovingly traced the scars below his collarbone that she knew she would find, and when he loosened the drawstring of her bodice to seek the satin skin within, she felt no fear. However it came to be, this man was her husband, and she loved him.

Graham lovingly lowered her bodice and chemise and splayed his large hand along the side of her breast while just his thumb played with the rising peak. He need not disguise himself beneath the foolish glove any longer, and both hands reveled in the smoothness of the skin she offered as his alone to touch. Just the knowledge that no other man had been given this right heightened his hunger.

Penelope caught her breath as Graham's mouth moved unexpectedly from her lips to her breast, but the sudden sharp pleasure of this new sensation released all inhibition. She arched eagerly into his embrace, ran her fingers along the strong column of his throat to the hard muscled planes of his chest, and deliriously felt the rigid line of his arousal beneath her. She knew where this led and she wanted it as much as he. More, because now she could look up into his handsome face and run her fingers through his hair and know he would not reject her caressess.

As if sensing her need to look and touch, Graham returned her to the bench and helped her to pull off his shirt. Her hand was dwarfed by the broad expanse thus revealed, but he gave her little time to learn fear. The ribbons of her chemise were released and pushed downward with her gown, and with the simple expedient of lifting her with one arm about her waist, he removed gown and chemise in one swoop.

Spreading his coat across the rough bench, Graham lay her gently upon it, then stood to complete his own undressing. Penelope watched unabashedly, her desire making her shameless as she lifted her arms to welcome him.

The first touch of his heated flesh against hers sent shivers of ecstasy up and down her body, and she opened to him without hesitation. Graham lingered, however, seeking the pulse at her throat with his kiss, stroking her soft curves with his broad hands as he learned the secrets of her body in the filtered light of the sun.

Penelope read his pleasure in the way he lifted his head to look at her, in the sensual line of his mouth as he bent to kiss her again, and in the golden gleam of his eyes as he discovered her joy. She had not thought such ecstasy possible from just knowing she was the one he wanted, but any remaining doubts in her heart fled, leaving it entirely his as his lips closed tenderly over hers, sealing the promise of their passion.

They came together then, blending effortlessly, moving with a grace of equal desire and the depth of a powerful hunger. Graham's body moved within hers, wakening her to the purpose it was meant for. Swelling with the need to welcome him, Penelope moaned his name in pleasure and moved with him. Needing no further encouragement, Graham caught her to him and rocking recklessly in the cradle of her body, brought them to the precipice and over, hurtling them into an inner space that offered comfort and not pain.

Afterward, Graham moved to release her from his heavy weight, but Penelope could not bear to let him go. His hips pressed against hers, flattening her spine against the hard board beneath them, but she held him there while she could. She felt him raise up on his hands to look at her, and a small smile drifted across soft lips as she opened her eyes and looked up to him with satisfaction.

"I love you," she murmured

"There are times when I almost believe you," he muttered in wonder, caressing a long tendril of honey brown hair from her cheek. "Whatever happened to my unromantic Penelope?"

She colored slightly as both bold eyes caressed her and a mocking smile lifted both corners of his lips. Just one of Graham's golden eyes had been difficult enough to deal with. It would take some time to accept the effect of two.

"A wicked prince disguised as a beast stole her heart and taught it to love. I don't think she'll ever be the same again."

"He's still a beast," he warned. "All the fairy tales in the world won't change him."

"Oh, he's a beast, no doubt." Penelope closed her eyes and shivered with pleasure as his hand came between them to claim her breast, and she felt the tightening in his groin as she moved helplessly against him. "And it's quite possible I shall live to regret becoming his victim, but let us pretend just a little while longer."

"This part is not the pretense, Penelope," Graham whispered against her ear as his body quickened and moved inside her again. "This is the part that is real."

Ans so it was. His beard scraped against her skin wherever he kissed her. Her posterior could already feel the bruises of their cruel bed. Graham's masculine scent had a strong flavor of brandy, but Penelope would not give up one particle of the reality of their lovemaking. She knew she was not dreaming when her body arched and spun and met the driving demand of his. She could taste the perspiration rolling down his chest, see the strain of his jaw muscles as he sought his release with her own, and knew his pleasure was as real as the one erupting and exploding inside her. Whatever the outside world held, this was real.

They slept wrapped in each other's arms until the sun lowered, turning the twilight to damp. When he could no longer warm her with his heat, Graham gently swung his foolish wife into his lap and reached for her clothes.

Sleepily Penelope wriggled into chemise and gown but resisted standing up so he could pull them over her hips. She curled against his chest, quite comfortable in this position and not wanting to be disturbed.

Graham chuckled. "I do believe this is where we began this morning, my lady, although admittedly, I am enjoying it much more without my clothes."

Penelope didn't need his words to tell her that. It would be very easy to succumb to the pressure probing delicately against her thighs, but the darkness brought other fears, and she finally opened her eyes to glance speculatively at the grate above their heads.

"Will they come soon?" Obediently she stood when Graham lifted her to the floor.

"Unless they mean to starve us to death," he replied grimly, reaching for his trousers.

A faint howling sound in the distance added eerie emphasis to his words, and Penelope hugged her arms to hide a shiver of fear. There was light yet in the field above, but in this deep shaft, all was shadow. If someone came, they couldn't get them out without their cooperation. That was small consolation. Their enemies could go off and leave them to starve. What were their chances of being found in this dismal place if they refused to cooperate?

"What will they do?" That was the nearest she could come to expressing her fears. She still did not understand why they were prisoners. If they were being held for ransom, who was left to pay it? Unless, of course, their abductors did not realize Graham and Chadwell were one and the same. That would cause some consternation when no one could be found to pay their blood money.

Graham wasn't certain that he knew, but he knew better than Penelope that they had no choice in the matter. If they refused to go up when commanded, their captors had only to begin shooting pistol balls down the shaft to change their minds. He hoped a better solution would come to mind before then.

The howling came closer, and Penelope threw the grate another nervous glance while Graham shrugged into his shirt. "Surely there are no wolves in this place?"

Graham stopped fastening his cuff to listen. "No wolves, but it's rather an odd time for a fox hunt, too. I wonder if the thing is in pain?"

The staccato barks following the howl put an end to that theory. Graham hastily shoved his shirt into his trousers and fastened them.

"Give me some of that cheese."

Penelope broke off a hunk and held it while Graham sought for the toe and hand holds he had found earlier. Part way up the wall, he held out his hand for the cheese. It was an awkward position to throw from, but he heaved the hunk upward. It reached the top but toppled straight back down. Graham cursed while Penelope searched the floor for the crumb. This was their supper he was playing with. She would not waste any more of it than necessary.

His second try was more successful and he gave a grunt of satisfaction when the cheese did not come back. He dropped back to the floor. The dog's yelps were louder than before, and the faraway mumble of voices seemed to follow.

"Do dogs like cheese?" Penelope asked with some measure of doubt.

"We will hope this one does. Get ready to yell with all your might. This place is not easily seen even when you're on top of it."

"Do you really think they are looking for us?" Penelope tried to fight the excitement and hope welling up inside of her, and she clutched Graham's strong arm for support.

He circled her waist and continued staring upward. "The man or men who put us here did so in the dark of night and without the infernal commotion of a dog. I can think of no other reason why someone would be out there. Yell, Penelope, they are getting closer."

They yelled. They screamed. They laughed at the echoing sounds produced. Graham's deep roar bounced off the walls and resounded like thunder. Penelope's soprano had little chance of being heard over that fearful sound, but she joined in as fervently as he. And in minutes, the shouts of other voices came closer.

"They're coming! Oh, Graham, they're coming!" Penelope hugged him, burying her face against his broad shoulder as he pulled her tightly against him. She felt the tension of his embrace and looked up questioningly. "Will they be able to get us out?"

"If they've got a rope and a place to tie it, I'll get us out. It will be all right." His words were meant to reassure, but the tension remained.

She did not have time to question. A childish voice began screaming in excitement above, and the dog's howls and yips echoed wildly down the shaft. A small dirt and tear-begrimed face appeared at the grate above, and his garbled cries of delight obliterated any opportunity of coherent speech.

"Pippin!" Penelope gazed up at the boy in astonishment until she recognized the ugly hound sniffing the grate for more cheese. The hungry stray had some use, after all.

Adult voices sounded overhead and soon Pippin was replaced by the lined, anxious face of Guy. The shaft was deep and dark and he could not see into it clearly, but he could make out their shapes and recognized their voices. "Are you all right?"

"We'll be better when you get a confounded rope down to us. Look around up there. He's been using some kind of winch to get us down."

Reassured by the sensibility of Graham's words, Guy moved away. John's voice joined his as they searched the rocky ruin above. From a distance, the sound of horses and carriage echoed.

"I don't know how in hell your orphan brat found us, but I think I will send him to Oxford one day." Graham muttered this nonsense in Penelope's ear to calm her. She had started shivering with the sight of Guy and he could feel the gooseflesh rising on her bare arms.

"I sent Pippin and John to find Nell. They must have been together when they found me missing. And he's not my orphan. You found him first."

"I suppose I did. He never was one to stay put. He'd run away that time I met you. Where did he find the dog?"

"That's Mate." Penelope would have gone into further nervous explanation, but an eruption of excitement above distracted her.

"Here it is! Get that damned grate off. Pippin, get the blamed dog out of here before he falls down the hole!"

Guy's exasperation was apparent, and Penelope giggled. How had he ever led a company of soldiers when he could not deal with a small boy and a dog? Graham gave her a telling look, but made no comment on her giggles. Keeping her safely in his embrace as if fearful she would escape, he continued watching the rescue process above.

At last, the grate was removed and a thick rope began slithering down the wall. When it nearly reached shoulder level, Graham kissed Penelope gently and tilted her chin to look up at him. "Be strong, Penelope. Don't let me hurt you. I'm not worth it."

His words terrified her, as they were meant to do. She had not thought beyond getting out of this hole, but obviously he had. She didn't know what he meant to do, but she recognized the cold hardness of his expression. If she had needed any further proof that this was the man she had married, she could read it in the terrible scowl that Graham had perfected. Only the eye patch and maimed face were missing.

Before she could respond, Graham had released her to tug on the rope. He tested it with his full weight, then satisfied, gestured for Penelope to join him. Anxious faces peered down from above, but he ignored them.

"I'm going to need both hands to climb this. I want you to hang on to my neck. I'll wrap the extra length around us for protection, but don't let go, Penelope. It's much too dangerous. Just hang onto me and we will be out of here in a few short seconds."

It was a most unladylike position he asked of her, but Penelope nodded. Gazing upward, she could not imagine how he would haul both of them out of here, but she would not doubt his word. She allowed him to tie the rope around them, binding them together so he protected her in the shelter of his body. She wrapped her arms around his neck and clung to him for dear life as he reached up the rope.

She could not watch. She heard the quiet encouragement of those above as Graham pulled them up the rope, hand over hand, using his feet to half walk them up the rocks and to keep from bumping against the jagged edges. But she could not look down to their prison below.

Firm hands caught and pulled her to safety along with Graham. He crawled out of the hole beside her, his fingers rapidly working the knot between them. The sun still lingered up here, and Penelope opened her eyes to gaze up into his worried face. The knot slipped free, and Graham bent over to soothe her lips with a long, searing kiss.

"What the devil?" Guy's furious cry intruded as he grabbed the back of Graham's shirt and jerked him upward.

Graham instantly leapt to his feet and raised his fists, prepared to defend himself, but Guy backed away, bewilderment creasing his brow as he gazed from the handsome rake confronting him to Penelope, who was hastily righting her gown and scrambling to her feet.

Assured Penelope held no outrage for this assault, Guy turned his speculative gaze back to the dark curly hair and nearly perfect features of the man she had been trapped with. "Graham?" Incredulity laced his voice as he tried to put together the sound of his friend's voice with the appearance of this stranger.

But Graham did not have time for explanations. While Penelope hugged Pippin and fought off the excited kisses of his huge hound, Graham's gaze fell upon the man approaching from the carriage that had just stopped below the ruins. Scarred features tightened into harsh lines, and the fists already raised clenched in balls of fury.

Terrified, Penelope turned expecting to find the evil villain who had imprisoned them, but she saw only Arthur limping across the rocks in a hurry. Behind him and obviously disobeying orders, Dolly leapt from the carriage to run after him.

"By the devil, I cannot believe you'd be so dashed bottle-brained as to ever step in my presence again, but if you think that your infamy has gone unnoticed, you will pay for your conceit now." Graham strode forward before Arthur could make good his escape.

The screams of both women mingled with Guy's shouts, but neither man halted. Graham swung first and Arthur dodged the blow, but he had no such success with the second. His neatly frock-coated figure crumpled to the ground with Graham's left to his midsection, but gamely, he tried to scramble back up before the next one fell.

Guy grabbed Graham's shirtsleeved arm, holding him back with difficulty while Dolly ran to cover her fallen brother with her own body. Her tearful cries made no impression on Graham whose rigid jaw indicated he waited only for the opportunity to strike again.

"By gad, you cannot strike a lame man! Have you taken leave of your senses?" Guy positioned himself between the strange Graham and Dolly's brother.

Penelope rose and stepped hesitantly toward her husband, but he seemed neither to see nor care for her presence. Rage and hatred had drawn him into a rigid statue, rendering him immobile while the object of his disgust remained unobtainable. Was Arthur the man he had labeled the "troublemaker"? Surely he could not be the one who had betrayed him and left him to die? Five years ago Arthur would have been no more than a boy of twenty.

Arthur gained his feet and stared at the statue who so resembled the man he had looked up to all of his years. Leaning slightly on Dolly, he searched Graham's face without understanding. "How? How have you hidden yourself all these years? At least let us have some explanations before I call my seconds."

Graham glared at this delay, but scornfully, he moistened his finger and wiped at one corner of his dark eyebrow. The paint smeared, leaving a glimmer of gray in the thick hairs above his scarred eye. "Call your seconds, Reardon. I'm no invalid. The choice of weapons is yours, but with that leg, I'd recommend pistols. I think we can both see well enough to make it a fair fight."

"No!" Dolly screamed hysterically, clinging to her brother's coat. "Arthur, tell him! Tell him you have done nothing wrong!"

Guy continued standing between his two friends, eyeing Graham critically. Deliberately attempting to defuse the situation, he inquired, "How did you do the hair? It's been gray since we were boys."

Penelope ventured a step forward as she saw Graham's jaw twitch with fury, but John touched her arm, deferentially shaking his head as if to ward her away. Sick at her stomach, she didn't know which way to turn. These people were her friends. She had thought them Graham's friends. Why had he turned on them like this?

Silently Graham reached up and pried at the tight covering upon his forehead. The wig peeled off reluctantly, and he flung it to the ground. The wild mane of rough-cropped silver hair stood out against the darkness. To forestall further questions, he added, "And the scar was sticking plaster. Now get out of my way, Hamilton. That man is as responsible for Marilee's death as all the others, and this time, he's gone too far. Penelope could have died from that drug he gave her, or from a fall down that shaft. I'll not settle for his just leaving the country this time. I'm going to kill him."

Arthur blanched and began hasty protests, but Dolly's shrieks drowned anything he had to say. Guy looked too shocked to be of use as he looked to Penelope for confirmation, and determinedly, she shook off John's restraining hand and stepped forward.

"Graham, I cannot say that it was Arthur. I cannot remember anything. How would he carry me out of the house? He can barely stand alone."

The voice of reason made no more difference than Dolly's hysteria. Graham grimly ignored the pale hand resting against his shirtsleeve as he glared at the offender. "Ask Arthur how he did it. I daresay his good friend DeVere was very helpful, but the bastard really should have burned that note you wrote him, Reardon. He's grown too over confident, our friend has. He thinks I don't know of his involvement, that I won't come after him like all the others, but he's wrong. I'm saving him for last. You don't know much about the bastard you befriended, do you, Reardon? Well, the government is going to help me make his death one to remember. I understand they have rather unpleasant means of disposing of traitors."

The gasps this pronouncement produced brought no

satisfaction to Graham's demeanor. Penelope's face had grown as pale as Arthur's as she grasped the meaning of his words. Her hand dropped from his arm. When he glanced down at her, her violet eyes were still and wide.

"You pretended to be an invalid so you could spy on your friends? You deceived me so you could have your revenge for something that happened long ago? And now you would destroy the Reardons, your friends, me, and Alexandra by dueling over something that can be neither proven nor disproved? I do not think I know you at all, Graham. I can forgive you much, but I cannot forgive you if you do this thing."

For a brief moment, pain flickered behind Graham's eyes as he stared down at her. His hand raised to reach out to her, and then the moment was gone, his expression closed into that impenetrable mask she knew so well, and his hand fell back to his side.

"Arthur drove the carriage that night. He was the one who ordered the others to leave Marilee there, dying, with the rain pouring in her wounds. Would you have me forgive that?"

Dolly's shrieks had died to choking sobs. Guy turned questioningly to his young friend. Arthur offered no denial.

Still, Penelope searched her husband's face. "If you kill him, you will have to leave the country. Is it worth it for something that happened a long time ago, when he was no more than a boy?"

Graham's grim visage did not change. "I vowed to avenge Marilee's death. It is the only reason I survived that accident. I will not break that vow even for you, Penelope."

"I am sorry, Graham, I believe God would forgive you if you broke that vow, just as I believe He will forgive me if I break mine now. If you must do this, I will consider you not to be the man I married. The vows we said in the church would be meaningless."

The meadow and the fallen ruin they stood upon darkened with the shadows of twilight as they spoke. No sound other than Dolly's occasional sobs could be heard. Golden eyes stared expressionlessly to the disheveled creature who so bravely stood up to him now, as ever, then they looked away to the man waiting for the verdict.

"I will be expecting your seconds before sunrise, Reardon."

Without another word, Penelope lifted her skirt and started down the hill toward the carriage.

Chapter 36

PENELOPE was barely aware of how she arrived at the Hall and had even less notion of who accompanied her. She only knew that her bedchamber was dark and empty as she began deliberately choosing those few frocks she felt entitled to take with her.

She felt totally alone although the house was teeming with servants and eyes filled with curiosity. She saw none of them. Alexandra slept in the chamber above but she could not, would not think of her. She could not steal Graham's child away, no matter how great a beast he had become.

Her choices of clothing scarcely filled a small trunk. She left behind the jewels, the delicate slippers, the elegant gowns, and gossamer night wear. She would not need them any longer.

With equal deliberation she took the full sum of the last charitable allowance Graham had left for her the week before. Some good would come of this fiasco, whether he liked it or not.

Still aching in every dark corner of her mind and body, Penelope ordered the carriage brought around. She had only one place to go, and Graham knew it. There would be no point in hiding her destination. She gave the orders to be taken to Hampshire, and a footman obligingly helped her in. Graham had not yet returned to refuse her these services.

The carriage rattled along through the night. Penelope's head ached with weariness, but she could not sleep. There was so much left unexplained, so much she did not understand, but her brain still reeled from the effect of the last hours, and she was not capable of logical thought. She only knew she had to get away.

The dark cottage was not as welcoming as she had expected. Without Augusta, it became just another house, as the Hall was nothing without Graham. The loneliness of her plight brought tears to Penelope's eyes, but she would not give in to them. She had survived as much before. She would do so again. It would just take time to learn to do it on her own, without Augusta's sage advice or Graham's false security.

She let the footman light a fire for her, then sent him and the coach on to Stanhope Manor to rest. Adelaide and Brian would be over by day's end, but by then perhaps she would have perfected a reasonable story.

All she really wanted was to be left alone until she could reassemble the pieces of her broken life and patch them into some usable purpose again.

Graham knew she was gone by the time he returned to the Hall. He had known she would be, and he had given her time to do it. His only worry was Alexandra, and he hastened up the steps to the nursery.

He breathed a sigh of relief and frowned at the same time as he gazed down upon the innocent sleep of his daughter. Whatever became of him, he knew Penelope would always watch over Alexandra. Although it would have broken his heart, it would have been better if she had taken the child with her. They would both be safer away from here and they could have comforted each other. He certainly didn't deserve the gift Penelope had given him of Alexandra's love.

With that thought Graham silently closed the door and returned downstairs where the others awaited him.

Arthur sat wearily slumped in a tapestried wing chair of some antiquity that Penelope had rescued from the rubbish pile and ordered restored. Guy had sprawled across a sturdy leather sofa, his head bent over the arm and his boots crossed over the seat. Penelope had ordered that chair there for the use of his "uncivilized" friends who would have damaged a more delicate piece of furniture. Graham wrapped his fingers around the corner of a heavy library table for support as these memories of Penelope washed over him. He didn't think he would ever be free of them, even if he should die tomorrow.

Guy didn't even glance up to see the pain etched across his friend's brow. "You never deserved her, anyway. I hope she took Alexandra."

"She didn't. Penelope wouldn't." Graham lowered himself slowly to his desk chair as if he were the cripple he had pretended to be all these years. The crippling was on the inside now, but the effect was the same. He would never be whole again.

"Go after her, Graham. Leave this to Guy and myself. It's not your fight. It has never been your fight." Arthur's hoarse whisper of anguish barely reached their ears, so tired was the voice that uttered it.

Graham's scorn was all for himself. "I'll not have Penelope touched by any of this. She is innocent and will remain so. I started this long before you were of an age to understand, Arthur, and I will finish it. The worst has already befallen me. You two still have your lives ahead of you. Go on back to them and let me deal with the bastard. The wretch has cost me everyone I have ever loved, and I intend to make him pay."

"Oh, very well said, Othello," Guy mocked. "Or are we Hamlet tonight? I'm not much up on your heroes, but I'll wager there's some good swashbuckling to follow. I'll be deviled if I let you take the lead again, Trevelyan. Set one foot out of this house without me and I'll come after you first and DeVere later." These brave words were spoken tonelessly, without Guy moving a single muscle of his elegantly draped frame.

"Same here, Gray." Arthur twisted his cane between his hands and he gazed nervously at his childhood idol scowling in the far corner. "I cannot forgive myself for trusting the scoundrel. All these years of fighting and I still cannot prove to myself that it wasn't cowardice that sent me running to DeVere instead of for help that night. I've got to prove that I can stand up to him. You've already suffered enough for my blindness, Gray. Go after Penelope.''

''The bloodthirsty louts would probably have put a bullet through my head as well as the horse's that night if you hadn't come along. You did what you could. Let's not go over it again.'' Wearily Graham stared at the brandy decanter sitting on the corner of his desk. That bottle had been his only solace for too long. He didn't lift a hand to reach it now.

All these years he had thought Arthur a traitor, no better than the murderers who had sent the carriage over the bridge. How wrong had he been about the others he had hounded to death? Penelope had been right. Only God had the right to play God. But someone had to give Him a helping hand upon occasion.

He stared up to the dark face of his young friend. Arthur had tried to go for help that night. He had tried to prevent the ambush but arrived too late. Thinking Guy to be the victim, he had sent the others away and rushed to DeVere—Graham and Guy's old friend, DeVere—for help. To go to the authorities would have meant implicating his fellow club members. He had counted on DeVere to come to the rescue.

Foolish youth. Graham ground his teeth together and switched his gaze to the fire in the grate. He had known since they were boys that DeVere had some willful, sick streak in his character that enjoyed the pain of other living beings, but he had thought it a boy's viciousness and had not considered the effect when matured to adulthood. DeVere had fallen gleefully into the gambling, whoring ways of idle youth in London, but this, too, Graham had discounted. So many others of their age had succumbed to this pagan life that he could not condemn DeVere for it. He had simply ignored him and went on with his own life. Not once had he considered the older man's influence on others.

So, in a way, it was his own fault. Graham didn't doubt that DeVere had been the one to send his drunken playmates out to seek revenge against Guy. When the incident had got out of hand and Graham and his wife became the victims, it had probably not disturbed a particle of his warped soul. Graham had foiled his first attempt to silence Guy. In DeVere's mind, he had probably deserved his fate. Graham doubted that DeVere had lifted a finger or turned a hair at the news of the accident young Arthur had rushed to report to him.

If nothing else, the experience had completely disillusioned Arthur to his old friend's character or lack thereof, but it had destroyed the boy's confidence in himself, too. So what did the hands of God require him to do now? Save the lad's life by sending him home to his mother, or let him regain his self-esteem by allowing him to hunt DeVere down for the dog he was? Graham groaned and covered his eyes at the possibilities looming before them. He needed Penelope's wise judgment to guide him.

Patiently Graham tried to dissuade his friends. "DeVere is after me. He abducted Penelope and forged those notes just to lure me out where he can get at me. Penelope is better off away from here. I think he's finally realized that I know him for what he is and that I am coming after him as I did the others. You and Guy can't destroy him any longer, but I can. He will leave you and your families alone if you will just stay out of this."

Arthur started to speak, but Guy's harsh voice overrode him. "Balderdash! There ain't a soul safe while that bounder walks the streets. He'll be hitting Dolly over the head and carrying her off to one of his bordellos to get even with us. He'll decide we know too much and send one of his thugs out to throw us into the bowels of some ship as Navy deserters. The bloody monster has tried to assassinate public officials and has murdered women in the street to make you into a maniac. You want us to lie idly by and watch you get all the glory?"

This time Guy swung into a sitting position so he could glare at his obstinate companion. It would take some getting used to this new Graham with the best of his handsome features restored. The blasted man should be on stage.

Arthur had grown pale at the mention of Dolly's possible fate, and his face set as obstinately as Graham's. "He'll not suspect me just yet. I can't get about much, but I can be your eyes and ears. I'll say the physician has a new treatment for me and go up to London. Guy, you'll have to persuade Dolly and my mother to stay here and not accompany me. I want them kept out of this."

Guy studied the problem pensively. "Without you here, they have no reason to miss the Little Season. How am I to persuade two females from following their natural inclination?"

Graham gave up the battle. Glancing from one aggravating companion to the other, he gave the answer his wise Penelope would have. "By giving them a wedding to plan."

Both pairs of eyes turned to stare at him. Arthur's began to show a hint of laughter behind the weariness. Guy's stared in outright astonishment.

Graham shrugged at the question lingering there. "Since I am quite certain Penelope has no use for you, you might as well find a good woman and settle down. The sacrifice is worth it, don't you agree?"

Arthur began to chuckle as Guy struggled with the dimensions of the problem, and even Graham's lips began to twitch at the eligible bachelor's dismay. All the talking in the world could not compare to actually carrying out the deed. Guy might act with courage in battle, but one small female had him checkmated. Graham's grin grew wider as Guy gave up the fight without a protest.

"Tomorrow. I will ask her tomorrow," he muttered. At a look from both men, he amended, "Today. Let me get some rest and change my clothes. I'll ask her today."

Graham reached for the decanter and tray of glasses. "A little fortification is needed here, gentlemen. To tomorrow."

Chapter 37

PENELOPE glanced at the well-scripted letter of introduction in her hand to the very proper lady seated in the cottage's best parlor chair. Mid-thirties, she guessed, but with a youthfulness still about the mouth and eyes. The stiff traveling suit had been carefully brushed and pressed, but Penelope's experienced eyes found the traces of alterations made from some much larger woman's wardrobe. The letter of introduction simply confirmed what her eyes had already told her. Priscilla Greene came of impoverished gentility and supported herself by teaching the children of wealthy families. The letter also stated she was of good character and a hard worker, but Penelope had already developed that impression, too.

She smiled with genuine welcome. "Miss Greene, I think we will get on well together if you should accept the position. It is not the same as working in the comforts of an earl's estate, you realize."

A tiny bit of relief and excitement appeared behind that primly stoic face. "You gave me to understand that the girls' welfare will be in my management. To educate deserving young girls instead of pampered, bored youngsters without the interference of well-meaning but ignorant parents is worth every bit of discomfort I might suffer. I am a teacher, Lady Trevelyan. I enjoy teaching. Let me do what I know best and we will suit exactly."

Penelope stood and held out her hand. "Pack your trunk and prepare to move in as soon as possible, Miss Greene. We'll need to start looking for other teachers to help you. I know someone who is already preparing a list of girls deserving of our efforts. I hope you are prepared for the type of children you will be trying to teach.''

Priscilla Greene's chin set firmly. ''Were it not for a distant relative, I would have been one of them myself, Lady Trevelyan. I am more than eager to offer them the same chance I was given.''

And so the foundling home Penelope had dreamed of became a reality.

Graham didn't have the pleasure of that kind of immediate satisfaction. Once DeVere discovered his prisoners had escaped, he had gone into hiding. They had spent weeks tracking a cold trail. Graham glared at the ashes of emptied files in the cold grate of DeVere's small flat. They should have surrounded the prison cell in the old keep that first night and waited for the villain to return to the scene of his crimes instead of wasting time on arguments of duels and guilt. DeVere must have seen them and fled to the safety of the continent. Half of England seemed to be in Paris right now, gawking like tourists and engaging in sword play with the defeated French soldiers. Just the place for a blackguard like DeVere.

But they could find no trace of his having left England by any of the usual routes. He still carried the papers of his diplomatic office although his leave of absence from the department had long since expired. They had enlisted Fochs in their hunt, since he already suspected his employee of treachery, but his minions could find no record of DeVere's sailing.

Still suspicious of Graham and his dual roles, Fochs continued to conduct his own investigations in the matter of the assassination attempt and the street murders, but again, the clues were old. No new murders occurred, and there was nothing to say Lord Trevelyan hadn't murdered the diplomat as well as the soiled doves.

Graham slammed his fist against DeVere's desk. He couldn't let the rogue go just like that, not after what he had done to Penelope. He would grind the man's bones into dust for laying his filthy hands on Penelope. Unless he wished to believe Guy guilty of the crime, he knew DeVere to be the only other person capable of using the hidden passages of his home. That was the only way Penelope's abductor could have carried her out of the house without being seen.

They would have to lure him out of hiding. That was the only feasible solution. If DeVere had gone to the continent, it would not be easy, but Graham felt certain he was still here. He had come back to the flat, burned all his papers, packed his bags, and taken up residence elsewhere, presumably under a different name. There had to be a way of dragging him out.

When he finally came upon an idea, his companions were dubious but eager to try. Nell was understandably reluctant, but when shown the cape and eye patch hidden in DeVere's room, she wholeheartedly joined the plan. Pippin thought it a great lark. Now established in the household with a fancy uniform all his own and free meals for his ugly mastiff, he was willing to walk nails for his lordship. Tracking the villain who had hurt Lady Trevelyan sent his joy beyond bounds.

Guy continued to shake his head as Graham completed his plan. "I don't like it. It's too close to home. If he should have any suspicion of what we're about, he's apt to take off with Dolly or Alexandra as hostages. We can't risk it."

Graham tapped his pen thoughtfully against his desk. "It has to be some place he'll feel comfortable going to and that we know as well as he does. That eliminates everywhere else. Nell and Pippin know the East End, but we want to keep them out if we can, and city streets are just too easy to get lost in. It will have to be Surrey. Isn't there something that's been said about criminals returning to the scenes of their crime? I should think the old keep ideal."

Arthur leaned forward eagerly. "Guy can write an impassioned love letter begging Dolly to come to London to keep him company, and you can send Alexandra to Penelope. That should keep them both out of trouble."

Guy flushed a little at this suggestion. Still overcome by the shock of Dolly's acceptance of his proposal, he had not yet come to terms with the role of lovelorn bridegroom. He shifted uneasily in his chair and watched Graham do the same.

Graham had been looking for some excuse to talk to Penelope, any excuse at all, but this just seemed too casually opportune. After all these weeks, how could he just drop by the cottage with Alexandra in hand and say, "Oh, by the by, would you take my daughter? I might be killed any day now."

Graham shook his head in disagreement. Allowed to grow out, his hair had gradually begun to return to its natural state. He kept it trimmed, but paid little heed to where the curls fell, particularly when he ran his hands through it. The effect was a leonine mane that would startle the eye of a casual observer, particularly when he shook it as he did now.

"What would you have me tell Penelope that wouldn't frighten her to death? I'll just send for Alexandra and keep her here with the governess. I don't think DeVere brave enough to risk entering the house again, and if he should, he might be a little surprised at the changes made."

Guy and Arthur exchanged glances but made no objections to this plan. Through Dolly they had kept up with Penelope and her activities, but the estrangement between husband and wife appeared total. Neither mentioned the other unless the topic was broached by someone else. Both kept busy as if their lives remained unchanged from that of before their marriage. Yet they knew Graham fiercely protected Penelope from anything that might harm her and suspected the deeper reason for his actions. He could not bear to lose Penelope as he had Marilee, and he would suffer all the torments of hell before exposing her to any more danger than she had already undergone.

"Are you sure we can rely on this Nell of yours? It's dangerous business going in that sordid crib of DeVere's. Maybe we ought to send someone else."

Arthur broke the silence following Graham's declaration.

"Who else would you send? Nell knows the rules. If DeVere keeps any connection at all with the place, he'll get the message. Just her brashness in entering it ought to infuriate him into doing something stupid. We'll have to be certain she gets out of there, and I've promised her she can be there to watch us capture him, but she's a right one. She'll do."

They discussed the other details of their desperate plan to draw DeVere from his hiding place and departed after their separate tasks shortly later. Graham remained alone, still tapping his pen against the desk.

He tried not think of Penelope, for each thought made him all the more conscious of his pain in losing her. Yet nothing and no one would let him forget. Even Nell had pierced him with arrows of anguish when she told him how his clever lady wife had asked her to help locate girls deserving of a better home. Nell had been enthusiastic over the project, but Graham could scarcely listen for the pain twisting at his insides.

He could still see that wounded look on Penelope's proud face when he had refused to give up his revenge. He had been wrong, terribly wrong, but it was too late to go back and tell her now. It was better this way. She was safe and doing well without him. He had set up an account for her to draw on whenever she needed the money and ordered his banker to replenish it as necessary. He had no idea whether she had touched the funds or not. He just felt better having provided them. Now, if something happened to him, she wouldn't have to suffer and Alexandra would still have someone to love.

Thinking of Alexandra's anguished questions at Penelope's disappearance, Graham shook his head and turned it to other thoughts. Once he could be certain DeVere was behind bars, he would send Alexandra to Penelope for a while. He hated to be separated from both of them, but he knew Alexandra's agony. At least he could relieve hers, if not his own.

Never forgive. Those words haunted his dreams and

every waking hour. She had said she would never forgive him. Running his hand through his hair, Graham bent his head over the desk and groaned. All the deceits and deceptions she had forgiven unquestioningly, but he had refused the one thing she had asked. All these years of his own unforgiveness would be paid back in triplicate.

His cry of pain echoed through empty corridors.

The shadows in the wooded lane moved restlessly, arguing cautiously in the chilly October night. Three on horses and two smaller figures huddled together on the ground; they made little more noise than the night sounds around them, yet their argument was nonetheless vehement.

"You can't go out there, maggot-brain! One good shot and your spoon will be in the wall. It's light as day out there." Guy gestured toward the moonlit field and its rubble of stones.

"He's not going to come out where we can see him until he sees me. He won't shoot until he's certain I'm not Chadwell and can't give him the information he seeks. By then, if you value my life, you'll have moved in."

"He's bound to know you and Chadwell are the same! If he comes at all, it will be in anticipation of killing you. That's probably the only reason he has remained in London. Don't give us Spanish coin, Trev. The message said 'at the keep.' We'll just wait until he appears."

"He won't appear until I do," Graham explained patiently. "Pippin's animal should set up a howl when he scents him, so I'll know to protect myself. Just concentrate on catching the cad when I draw him out."

"By Jupiter, why don't I ever learn?" Guy groaned as Graham jerked his mount around and slowly walked him into the field. Graham's broad, straight shoulders made an ideal target as he rode away. The idiot wouldn't even lean over to disguise his bulk against the horse.

They sat in silence then, waiting for the prey to walk into the trap.

They should have known DeVere with his devious mind would be one step ahead of them. Keeping to the shadow of one of the toppled tower walls, he waited with pistol drawn as Graham approached. With the moon behind him, it was difficult to discern the horseman's face, but he knew by the size of the rider it had to be the viscount or his cousin.

Graham caught the brief flash of moonlight on metal and slowed. He had forgotten that wall would be sufficient to cover a man of DeVere's size. Knowing to run would be to risk a ball in the back, he swung down and approached the fallen stones carefully, keeping the horse between himself and his enemy.

The dog scented nothing unusual since the wind blew from behind, but the watchers in the trees stirred uneasily at Graham's sudden departure from his mount. They could see nothing, however, and dared not risk everything by riding out too soon.

Graham spoke first, in low undertones. His plan had not called for speaking at all, and he improvised quickly. "You wanted to see me, DeVere?"

The shadow waved the pistol menacingly. "Step out where I can see you. I'd like to know who has the audacity to label me a traitor and offer to save my neck in the same breath."

Graham gestured behind his back, hoping Guy and Arthur would have the sense to circle around behind the wall. That would take time, and he didn't have much of it. The normally cool DeVere sounded distinctly rattled tonight.

"More than your neck will be lost if you don't listen to me. Fochs has been searching for a connection between the monster maniac in the streets and the assassination attempt ever since you tried to implicate me. Thanks to a few of your girls, he's found it. They're moving in to close the brothel and gambling rooms tonight. Your neck will be all you have left shortly."

"That's ridiculous!" DeVere's voice rose nervously. "There is no connection. They can't possibly find one. The only ones who knew about it are dead. Even their damned women. People of that ilk talk too much. Give me a man of breeding anytime. That's you, Graham, ain't it? You always kept your lips sealed. So did Arthur. Guy was the only telltale. That religious mother of his, I suppose. Definite lack of breeding there. Come out from behind there, Trev. I've been waiting for you."

A scream came from the trees as the moonlight caught on the barrel of the raised gun at the same time Graham moved his horse out of range. DeVere's head jerked sideways at this unexpected female intrusion, and his gun wavered slightly.

Graham grabbed what small advantage offered. There wasn't time to move around the horse to grab his head. Instinctively he lashed out with his foot, kicking the wavering gun from DeVere's grip.

DeVere screamed in fury, but before he could dive for the weapon, he spied the other two dark figures emerging into the field. Betrayed, he spat on oath and leapt for his own horse, hidden in the shrubbery. Before Graham could remount, he was off across the field in the opposite direction.

With a cry much resembling a general's call to arms, Graham gained his seat and set off after the rapidly disappearing steed. Their horses were exhausted from the long journey from London. DeVere had obviously found a fresh horse before concealing himself in the field. Why hadn't they thought of hiding a horse behind the overgrown thicket near the wall?

Cursing his neglect of this simplest of stratagems, Graham raced across the stone-stubbled field. He sensed rather than saw the other two riders following close behind him. Arthur was already exhausted from the journey and risked his health in this madcap chase. Guy's roan was already too winded to keep up with Graham's stallion. It would be up to Graham to stay with the scoundrel. He had enough revenge in his heart to follow DeVere into hell.

DeVere negotiated the open field with safety, guided his horse in a flying jump over a hedgerow, and dashed into the cover of a stand of trees. Graham gestured for the others to circle around while he followed directly on their prey's heels. He'd not been on a hunt in years, but the emotions generated by the chase swarmed back with clarity as his horse sailed across the hedgerow after his quarry.

In the distance Graham could hear the dog's howl as Pippin ran down the lane to intercept their path. DeVere hadn't known of the boy and dog, but they would make small difference in a race like this one. There was little cover to hide a man and a horse. It was only a matter of time and the best animal.

Graham's blood pounded through his veins as he spied his target emerging from the trees. DeVere had cost him his wife and five years of his life and a love he could never hope to find again in this world. The insane bastard was going to pay if he had to strangle him with his bare hands. He pushed the stallion harder as it reached the flat expanse of a wheat field.

The field was only half threshed and DeVere drove his horse through the center, leaving a wake of crushed grain behind. This senseless destruction aroused Graham's temper to new levels. The man thrived on pain. Let him feel it for himself for a change. He spurred his animal faster.

He'd lost all sense of Guy and Arthur behind him and the dog's cries were faint in the distance. He thought he spied a light ahead and cursed as he realized another stand of trees lay in front of them. In the darkness it was difficult to tell, but he suspected the low lying limbs indicated an orchard. To ride upright through an orchard begged for a blow to the head and a topple from the horse.

DeVere took the orchard at a reckless pace, lying low against his horse's neck. He was not as skilled a rider as Graham, but his smaller size made him more maneuverable.

Vaguely Graham began to recognize his surroundings, but intent on keeping his seat as he dodged trees and branches, he didn't have time to put together his thoughts. Not until DeVere guided his horse over a turnstile and into the neatly turned earth of a dying vegetable garden did Graham begin to curse his ill luck.

Penelope's orphanage! How could he have forgotten? He had only been here once, but he recognized the brick edifice even from the rear. Not many farmhouses were so sturdily made.

The place had been empty of all but workmen when he had last been here well over a month ago, maybe two months. As his horse flew over the stile in swift pursuit, Graham had the sinking feeling that this was no longer true. Lanterns glowed in half the downstairs rooms, and he could see the occasional flicker of a candle above. Hell, surely DeVere didn't mean to seek shelter in a foundling home?

Even as he thought it, Graham caught sight of the villain leaping from his horse and running toward the house. Infamous! To take cover behind the skirts of women and babes was even lower than he had dared imagine the man could fall.

But he had to admit it was the only protection the isolated countryside offered. Negotiating the mangled cabbage patch, Graham dismounted less hurriedly than DeVere. This would take thought.

He heard the pounding hoofbeats of another horse and thought to wait for Guy. That was before the screams erupted from inside the house. He had no time left for thought. Leaping for the back step, Graham dashed through the kitchen doorway and into the house.

Guessing DeVere's destination before Graham, Guy cut across a corner of the field, avoiding the turnstile and cabbage patch and coming up short at the front porch Penelope had so carefully painted the summer before. The screams within nearly drowned the sounds of the howling dog running down the lane, but Guy grinned grimly at the sound. Their reinforcements: a boy and dog and cripple limping behind.

It had never occurred to him that DeVere would take a house full of orphans as hostage when they were making their plans, but it should have. Without another second's hesitation he threw open the front door and entered the uproar within.

It took a minute before Guy could grasp the whirl-wind of motion in the once sedate halls Penelope had envisioned. The waxed and gleaming floors leading from door to kitchen and stairway teemed with exotic life.

Women in mobcaps and wielding dusters screamed curses that would put a man to shame. Young tykes with golden hair streaming down their flannel night shifts screeched in upper registers from between the stair rails. Their words weren't exactly clear, but their murderous intent was obvious. Much larger girls filled the parlor doorways, their matching gray aprons not disguising their earthy bounty, and Guy nearly gaped as one voluptuous beauty turned in his direction with a broad wink before returning to the fray with a can-dlestick holder and a cry that would make a banshee quake.

Through this turmoil Guy finally discerned a se-verely flustered DeVere clutching a kitchen knife to the throat of a primly dressed lady of indeterminate age and amazed expression. She did not seem fright-ened so much as confused as her young charges turned to a horde of screaming demons in her defense. Her eyes had lifted to the only source of sanity in the midst of chaos. Following their direction, Guy spied Graham standing bemused in the kitchen doorway. His great size did not prevent a number of urchins from scam-pering in and out around him, arming the crowd with knives and iron skillets and rolling pins.

Even as they watched, one of the golden-haired tykes from above launched a pallet down the stairs while a trio of youngsters at the bottom took swift aim at DeVere's knees with their kitchen weapons. A rowdy miss with the arms of a wrestler smacked the villain's shoulder with a long-handled iron ladle, and the knife went flying into the air to the whoops and hollers of a tribe of wild Indians.

Guy couldn't help it. The look on DeVere's face as the prim lady broke loose and smacked him across the face while the screaming demons launched a full frontal assault doubled him up with laughter. Women had ever been DeVere's downfall.

Graham glanced across the room at the sound of laughter and struggled to keep his own face straight. By this time DeVere was on his knees covering his head with his arms, his cries beyond comprehension. The suave, polished diplomat disappeared beneath a flurry of dusters, pallets, and petticoats.

From behind Graham a small voice exclaimed with disgust, "Gor blimey, a gaggle of petticoats bummed the rat!"

Pippin's look of pure distaste broke Graham's last remaining hold on impassivity. His roars of laughter brought even the angelic twins from above to amazed attention.

The vengeance of the women DeVere had ruined or murdered was quite properly wreaked by the hands of little girls.

Chapter 38

GRAHAM gnawed pensively on the end of his pen as he stared out the window and not at the wide foolscap on the desk. He had never failed at words before, but his mind was completely silent of the pleas he would like to make.

He watched as the governess pushed Alexandra on the swing in the yard below. His daughter had grown pale and listless these last weeks in town while he worked with the authorities to bring DeVere to justice. By the time he had produced the evidence of the villain's involvement in the multiple murders and cleared his own name, Alexandra had even quit speaking Penelope's name. She looked at him as if he were a stranger. Returning to the Hall had not returned the roses to her cheeks. The only time he heard her laugh was over some antic of Pippin's, and now that the boy had been sent off to school, he never heard her laugh at all.

Perhaps he shouldn't have sent Pippin away. Penelope would have known the right thing to do. The boy was too clever to be left untaught, but Alexandra was lost without a companion to play with. Graham cursed and stood and began to pace the floor.

He should have written sooner. He should have told her he was wrong. He should have apologized, explained, pleaded, anything to make her understand. But he was terrified of her rejection. How could he say the words just right to make her understand and come back to him? She had said she would never forgive, and Penelope's pride was an unbreachable wall, much as his own had been.

Lost in tormented thought, Graham failed to notice the silent child slipping through the doorway. She perched on the edge of the leather chair and watched him through large, dark eyes. When he finally turned to discover her there, her eyes never left his changed face.

"Alexandra! I thought you were with Mrs. Henwood." Graham crouched before the chair, his big hand reaching out to stroke her lovely hair.

"Mrs. Henwood has a headache." Soberly Alexandra contemplated her father's countenance, golden eyes even with her own. Even without the patch and scar, his was a fierce visage. But the look on his face now was a tender one and she did not fear him.

Softly Graham asked what he had known all along he would have to ask. "Do you miss our Penelope?"

Dark eyes met his warily. "When will she come home?"

Graham sighed and stood, pacing back to the window. "I fear she will not." He turned to look at his daughter. "But if you would like, I could ask her if you could visit for a while. Would you like that?"

A small glimmer of hope leapt to the child's eyes. "I could tell her how much we miss her. Then she would come home. I know she would."

Graham shook his head sadly. "I don't think so, Alex. Do not get your hopes up. But I will write and ask her if you might visit a while. I'm sure she misses you."

Alexandra's wariness turned to defiance. "Penny said she didn't like to leave someone she loves. She must not love us. I don't want to see her never, no more."

Graham crossed the room and swept her up in his arms, crushing her in his embrace as he pressed her tearful sobs to his shoulder. "If Penny said that, then she meant it. She didn't want to leave, but I made her go. Please, Alex, don't cry. She loves you just as much as I do. I promise, poppet."

Alexandra lifted her head and sniffed back a tear. "Then make her come back! I'll help. I want her to come back more than anything in the whole world. She can even ride my pony. I'll tell her so. Penny said if we want something badly enough, we have to fight for it. And you gave me my pony when I asked. Maybe she will come home if I promise to be a good girl. Please, Papa, ask Penny to come home. Don't you love her any more?''

Graham had to turn his head away to keep the child from seeing the tears running down his cheeks. ''I'll write to her today, poppet. Then we'll see what happens''

Satisfied, Alexandra ran from his arms and out to tell her story to her pony. When the door closed behind her, Graham determinedly sat down at his desk and began to write. She might turn deaf ears on his pleas, but he would make her know why he had done what he had to do and beg her forgiveness. The words of love he longed to say would have to wait until he knew whether she would listen.

Penelope stood in the small dark room Priscilla Greene had made into a study, gazing out over the sunlit winter landscape. The bare trees looked as bleak as she felt, and for the thousandth time she repented her harsh sentence.

She tried to summon up all the arguments that had kept her anger fierce these last weeks. Graham had deceived her wickedly, cruelly. All the time he had whispered words of love, he was bent on revenging his first wife, his real love. For him to treat her like that, she could mean nothing to him. Nothing. Now that his disguise was revealed, he could return to the carefree society a young viscount of handsome visage and great wealth could enjoy. He certainly didn't need her any longer if the reports she had heard were true. With DeVere behind bars, he could seek the proper wife he needed, and he would no longer need a plain vicar's daughter to mother Alexandra.

Penelope's eyes remained dry as she contemplated these arguments impassively. She had used them so frequently, she had become immune to them. She only knew she needed to see Graham again, needed to hear from his lips that he no longer wanted her. His lack of letters should be convincing argument enough, but her heart wouldn't listen to reason.

Her worst problem now was that she knew herself too well. She knew that as soon as she saw Graham she would do anything conceivable to keep him, up to and including telling him of the child.

Her hand gently touched the slight rounding that was the only outward sign of her condition. He would have to know sooner or later, anyway. She knew the gossip flying between their houses would carry the news as soon as it was evident. She would have to speak to him before then.

As she stared out at the barren landscape, Penelope gripped her fingers tighter. If only he would take her back without knowing of the child, take her back because he wanted her and loved her as much as she did him . . . That would be too much to ask. She would have to be content with the love of the children and an occasional glimpse of the handsome husband who would endure her presence for the sake of them.

The tears slid down her cheeks then, but she hastily wiped them away as she heard the sound of footsteps outside the door and the laughter of girlish voices reminded her she was not in her lonely cottage.

Priscilla Greene took one look at her employer and closed the door. Now was not the time to talk of the new mathematics teacher or discuss the high cost of bed linens. She launched into a cheery explanation of her plans for the home's first Christmas celebration.

By the time Penelope left the orphanage, she had gathered the courage to do what she must do. It was late and there would not be time to return to Hampshire if Graham refused to see her, but she could always stop at the Reardons' to see how Dolly's wedding plans fared. Her letters had been joys to behold, but they would sound even better with Dolly's gleeful voice to speak them aloud. Perhaps Guy and Arthur would be there, too, and it would be almost like old times.

Not daring to believe Graham would even be at

home, no less willing to receive her, Penelope stepped
slowly from the carriage when it came to a stop before
the Hall doors. The house was as lovely as she remembered, and she stared up at it longingly, with all the
love she possessed and had ever been denied. She had
been a fool to throw it all away. Her punishment was
to discard her pride and admit her foolishness.

Graham came out of the upstairs study at the sound
of excited laughter in the front hall. In disbelief he
stared down the stairs at the lovely ladylike figure of
his thoughts gracing the entrance to his home. His feet
moved of their own accord, almost running until he
stayed himself, catching his eager hand on the stair
rail as he slowly descended, not daring to take his eyes
from the fantasy creature before him.

Penelope turned then and looked up at him. The
shadows of those violet eyes took his breath away, and
his hand lifted in silent entreaty. Penelope stepped forward, her eyes focused, bedazzled, upon his face, but
she said no word. Her heart pumped at a rapid rate at
the familiar yet strange sight of two long-lashed golden
eyes staring down at her from beneath a disheveled
mop of silvered hair. It took eternity for him to reach
her.

The servants melted from the hall, leaving Graham
to lead Penelope into the parlor. He closed the door
and leaned on it, his eyes feasting on the vision of
loveliness his painful thoughts had conjured into being. She seemed paler than he remembered, her cheeks
more hollowed and less pink, but if those full lips
would only turn up at the corners . . . His breath
caught in his throat as Penelope took off her bonnet
and twisted its ribbons between her fingers.

"I am sorry to disturb you, Graham." She couldn't
look at him any more. The sight of that pale scar across
his cheek disturbed memories so deep she could not
speak. She wanted to touch his face, to run her fingers
through his hair and ascertain his reality. She couldn't
believe that after all these weeks she was actually
standing in the same room with him. She felt faint,

and her hand went out to steady herself on the back of a chair.

Graham instantly came to his senses, offering his hand and gesturing toward a seat. "Sit, Penelope. My surprise . . . I wasn't thinking."

When he moved to take her pelisse, Penelope shook her head. She wrapped the protective folds around her and balanced gingerly on the chair indicated. Graham's proximity drove all thought from her mind and she did not know what to say next.

"Let me send for some tea. You must be cold." Nervously Graham started toward the door. He felt like a schoolboy again, helpless in the throes of first love. He didn't know what to say or how to act. He just knew he couldn't let her out of this room until she heard everything that needed to be said.

Penelope's lifted hand stopped his flight. "No, do not distract me. I must say what I have come to tell you before I lose my courage." She glanced apprehensively to where Graham had stopped halfway across the carpet. He turned to watch her with incredulous, doubting eyes, and her heart sank.

Before she could speak again, Graham imitated her gesture and held up his hand to stop the flow of words. "Perhaps I should be the one to speak first. I just don't know how to find the phrases. Help me, Penelope. Tell me what an ungrateful, unforgiving wretch I am. Curse me. Throw things at me. Just don't sit there with those wide accusing eyes and bring me to my knees, because I'll go down on them if it will help."

Penelope's lips parted in astonishment, and she rose hastily before he could do as threatened. Daringly she stepped closer, her eyes searching his for explanations. "Do you know then? Has your sister already guessed and told you? I would not have kept the truth from you, but I so much wanted to hear from you first, before you knew of the child. But you never wrote, and I knew I had said terrible things, and I didn't think I would ever hear from you again . . ."

Graham stared at her in disbelief, unable to comprehend the import of her words, only the tone. He didn't understand what she was saying, but it sounded as if she were apologizing. To him! Apologizing to the lying, deceiving, arrogant beast that he was. He could not let her, and Graham shook his head sternly, catching her shoulder and pushing her down in the chair again.

"Don't, Penelope. Let me speak my piece first. My behavior has been reprehensible to a degree beyond forgiveness, I realize that. But for Alexandra's sake, can we not find some common ground, some means of hiding the breach so we can be together again? I will do anything you like, explain everything I can, just don't turn your back on us until you've given us a chance."

Penelope's eyes clouded with tears and she shook her head. For Alexandra's sake, of course, she should have realized that. He would do anything for his daughter without even needing to know of the child she carried. He was offering her the opportunity to come back. Why, then, were the tears running down her cheeks and her heart disintegrating into painful shards of glass?

Graham took this response for denial and desperately, he grabbed her shoulders, forcing her to face him. Penelope refused, turning her head away, but he would not let her refuse him. With her slight frame enveloped in folds of wool, he could not so much as touch the fair skin of her throat, but he could feel the warmth of her burning his fingers, and he clutched her fiercely.

"Don't deny me, Penelope. You came here for a reason. Was it Alexandra that brought you here? Tell me, Penelope, so I can find the right words to keep you."

Penelope took a deep breath and met his gaze. "I came because I could not stay away. Pride cannot keep me company. It makes a very lonely bedfellow. Besides, I thought it would be best if you heard it from my lips first. I am going to have a child."

Graham's grip on her shoulders tightened reflexively. He still could not quite comprehend the words.

He continued staring at her, waiting for them to sink in. "A child?" Dumfounded, he staggered back a little, realizing his grip was causing her pain, overcome with solicitude but not knowing how to show it.

A pale trace of amusement appeared in Penelope's eyes at his stricken expression. "A child. I believe that tends to happen occasionally. Since you already have one, I rather thought you knew how it came about."

Even with that devastated expression on his face, Graham was so handsome it almost made her cry. He did not wear his frock coat, as usual, and the gold brocade waistcoat he favored hung unfastened over a snowy white cravat that did not quite tie neatly about his brown throat, but he could never be any less than the man she loved. She longed to touch his silver mane of hair, did not dare consider the effect of those firm, chiseled lips, but satisfied herself with waiting patiently for his recovery from her news. She had done it. Now, he could not turn her away.

Joy began to make its way across features she had once considered hard and impassive. The angular planes of his cheeks lifted, pulling with them the corners of his lips, until the breathtaking smile that resulted nearly destroyed Penelope's composure. Her heart galloped madly at the sight of the joy and delight shining in those remarkable eyes, and she could scarcely believe what she saw. She had expected resignation, politeness, perhaps some anticipation, but not this overwhelming, unrestricted, tremendous sense of joy.

Before she knew what he was about, Graham pulled her from her feet and swung her around the room in dizzying circles, his arms wrapped firmly about her waist until her toes scarcely touched the floor. A curl tumbled loose from her pins and her pelisse flew out around her like the wings of a great bird and her head spun giddily—not just at the wild dance but from Graham's intoxicating proximity. She did not want him to ever let go.

"Oh, my pretty Penny, I'll not make you sorry you married me this time. I'll make it all up to you, you will see. I will do everything right from now on and the child will make you happy and soon you will not regret having a fool for a husband.''

Laughing, crying, afraid to hear more in his words than was there, Penelope clung to his wide shoulders as if her life depended on it—as it did. He was her life, her soul, her happiness. She wrapped her arms around him and buried her face against the fresh scent of his linen-covered shoulder and gave into his mad ecstasy.

A moment later he was slowing down, apologizing again, his kisses trailing eagerly across her cheek and hair. "I did not think. You should be sitting still. Let me put you on the sofa. I'll have a maid bring a blanket to wrap around you. You shouldn't have been out in that cold. Let me get you some tea. I'll send someone to pack your things and close up the cottage.''

His rush of words stuttered to a halt as Penelope held a finger to his lips as he lay her gently against the cushions. Her smile was warm but did not quite reach her eyes as she tugged gently on his arm to pull him down beside her. Bracing his arm on the carved back of the couch, Graham looked down at her questioningly.

"I am glad that you are happy about the child. I feared you would consider it a nuisance now that you can safely return to your proper place in society. I just want you to know I will not hinder you in taking that place. Perhaps you would prefer it if I stayed in Hampshire. It's just . . . I would like to see Alexandra once in a while, if I might.''

Perplexed, Graham stared down at her flushed face. She was wearing one of her prim muslin gowns with the high-necked tucker, but it clung revealingly to the full curve of her breast in this position. His hand longed to stroke the fullness that would soon swell with milk for his child, but her words held him at a distance.

"I would not prefer you in Hampshire. I would prefer you right here, in my bed, where I can keep an eye on you. Somebody has to keep you from climbing ladders and gallivanting into slums. If you do not feel well enough to share my bed, I will understand, but you'll not get any farther than the next room, and then I would prefer you keep the door between us open.''

Laughing shakily, Penelope dared to lift a hand to his cheek as she had desired to do earlier. ''I am having a baby, not dying a lingering death. I am perfectly healthy and do not need a guardian angel. Just do not pretend with me for the sake of the child, Graham. I know we married for convenience. If I have gone a little over my head, it's my concern and not yours. I am quite independent. You need not think you must be beside me.''

Gradually the cause for her concern became clear, and Graham frowned, a horrifying frown that should have shook her to her toes. Penelope smiled, and he scowled worse.

''You are a greater fool than I if you think I intend to let you go your merry way again. To hell with convenience. You are my wife and you are carrying my child. I'll not let you out of my sight if it pleases me, and it does. Perhaps I have deceived you too long so you cannot trust me, but I am not pretending now, Penelope, nor will I in the future. I want you as well as the child.''

Penelope smiled sadly at the sincerity in his voice. How many times had he spoken words of love, cajoled her with soft caresses while pretending to be what he was not? He would not have let her go in the first place if he cared as much as he had promised.

''It would be better if we could start out honestly, Graham. I am grateful that you are taking me back. You need not pretend you are pleased to be saddled with a vicar's daughter.''

Graham growled irascibly and flung himself from her side, stalking up and down the floor as he spoke. ''I suppose this is what I deserve for having deceived you. What do I have to do to persuade you that I have never been less than honest in my feelings for you? You are the woman I want, the woman I wish to spend the rest of my days with. You have been from the very first moment I stepped across the portals of that damned cottage. I want the child, yes. I want many children! But I want *you* to be their mother.''

He was roaring by now, his deep voice vibrating the sounding board of the harpsichord and jarring a delicate bud vase to the edge of a table. With his back turned toward the door, he did not see it open, nor notice the small figure slipping through, crumpled paper in hand.

Penelope did, however, and her face lit with pleasure as Alexandra cautiously crept around her ranting father. At the look on Penelope's face, Graham swung around, and his frown was fierce as he noted the mangled foolscap in her hand.

"I want Penny to stay." Alexandra glared back at her father and stamped her foot. "And you do, too! It says so right here." She shook the paper under his nose, or more properly, his trouser band. "I just can't read all the words."

Swiftly before Graham could pounce on her, Alexandra darted around him and placed the precious letter in Penelope's hands. Penelope glanced down and recognized Graham's writing, then glanced questioningly back to him.

Graham managed to look embarrassed and annoyed at the same time, but he nodded curt permission for her to read. Penelope sat up and smoothed the paper lovingly, postponing the moment of revelation, wanting to savor the flavor of hope and not taste the bitterness of disappointment.

Carefully her gaze scanned the lines of explanations, his apology for not listening to her about Arthur, for deceiving her, his decision to protect her by leaving her in Hampshire out of DeVere's reach. She read this last carefully, not daring to believe, to let hope rise too high. She lifted her eyes to Graham, but he was staring into the fire he had made while she read. Alexandra was watching her expectantly, and she continued to read the long, sloping lines.

A tear formed in her eye as she read his words of love, the outpouring of a heart as proud as hers. He begged her forgiveness, if not for his sake, then for Alexandra's. He asked only that she see him again, allow Alexandra to visit, and no more. He had poured his heart into this letter and never posted it.

Penelope folded it carefully and glanced questioningly at her husband's back. "Graham? Why did you never post this?"

He swung around, searching her face for clues. "You came before I could finish. I could not find a line that would say how much I am sorry, how much I miss you, how much I love you, how much I want you back. I did not mind if you laughed in my face, but I could not bear it if you refused."

Tears rolled down her cheeks but the joy in her smile warmed her eyes to summer skies and she held out her hands to him. Dazed, Graham knelt beside the couch and pulled her into his arms where Penelope's tears mixed with her kisses as they scattered along his jaw.

"I think my beast may have turned into a handsome prince at last. I love you, Graham. Don't you know I could never refuse you?"

"Then know now, my sleeping beauty, you are mine forever after. That's the way the spell works."

As he bent to kiss her, a dainty black-haired fairy grinned hugely and crept out the slightly open door whispering, "And they lived happily ever after, just like the story says."

About the Author

Patricia Rice was born in Newburgh, New York, and attended the University of Kentucky. She now lives in Mayfield, Kentucky, with her husband and her two children, Corinna and Derek, in a rambling Tudor house. Ms. Rice has a degree in accounting and her hobbies include history, travel and antique collecting.